THE CRUELEST KIND OF HATE

CELESTE BRIARS

THE CRUELEST KIND OF HATE

BY CELESTE BRIARS
A Reapers novel

This is a work of fiction. Names, characters, organizations, places, events, and incidents are either products of the author's imagination or are used fictitiously.

Text copyright © 2024 Celeste Briars

Excerpt from *The Best Kind of Forever (Reapers #1)* copyright © 2023 by Celeste Briars

Excerpt from *The Worst Kind of Promise (Reapers #2)* copyright © 2023 by Celeste Briars

Excerpt from *The Flip Side of Fate (Reapers #4)* copyright © 2024 by Celeste Briars

All rights reserved.

No part of this book may be reproduced, or stored in a retrieval system, or transmitted in any form or by any means, electronic, mechanical, photocopying, recording, or otherwise, without express written permission of the author and copyright owner of this book.

ISBN: 9798878532747

Cover Design: Dar Albert, Wicked Smart Designs

Edited By: Deborah Dove

To any readers who feel like they're too broken to be loved. Someone will love you, broken pieces and all.

AUTHOR'S NOTE

Hello, dear readers!

For the best reading experience, I've listed below some potential triggers included in this book. While the story is mainly lighthearted, there are undertones of more serious issues that some readers may find upsetting. Please read at your own discretion.

Content Warnings:
Injury (on-page)
Self-harm
Chronically ill parent
Parental abuse/neglect
Death of a sibling
PTSD
Explicit sexual content
Emetophobia
Alcohol consumption

PLAYLIST

Theme Song: Greedy – Tate McRae

1. Kill V. Maim – Grimes
2. Chrome Hearted – Jaden Hossler
3. Shameless – Camila Cabello
4. Hypnotic – Zella Day
5. Sweat – Cash Cash (feat. Jenna Andrews)
6. Effortlessly – Madison Beer
7. Let You Down – NF
8. Skeleton Sam – LVCRFT
9. self sabotage – Maggie Lindemann
10. End of the World – bludnymph
11. Sand – Dove Cameron
12. Agora Hills – Doja Cat
13. Got Me Obsessed – Jade LeMac
14. cardigan – Taylor Swift
15. Save Myself – Ashe
16. Ghost – Justin Bieber
17. Siren – amelia milo
18. Don't Deserve You – Plumb

19. Dynasty – Miia
20. Out of the Woods – Taylor Swift
21. Better Off (Alone, Pt. III) – Alan Walker, Dash Berlin & Vikkstar
22. miss u – Josh Makazo

1
HOPE YOU HAVE INSURANCE
CALISTA

I'm late. This week's goal was to work on punctuality, but the universe is conspiring against me.

My dance class went over time, so I had to cram a twenty-minute drive into a measly eight minutes. I'm surprised my car even covered that much distance within such a small time span since it's on its last wheels.

I promised my little brother, Teague, that I'd be on time today. Another broken promise to a little kid who deserves so much more. With my father out of the picture and my mother bedridden, Teague is my responsibility. An eight-year-old, adorable, bad-mouthed ball of responsibility. But I wouldn't trade that responsibility for anything in the world.

When I pull into the massive parking lot, somehow every spot in the vicinity is occupied. Sure, Riverside is a big hockey city, and if you arrive at the arena after three o'clock, you're guaranteed to endure some traffic, but this is preposterous. And my brother is inside that teeming sardine can, where a simple "I'm here" text won't be enough to compel him out of the door.

If I'm going to get my brother home, cook him dinner, and get back to the studio for my final dance class of the night, I'll need to run in and get him. Right now, that's looking like the equivalent of voluntarily running into crossfire. But I have no choice.

Whipping my head around, I try to search for the nearest "parking space" that won't get me a ticket or my car towed. I can't park against the sidewalk because there *is* no fucking sidewalk, and I can't park in front of the rink with my hazards on because I'd be blocking the mouth of the parking lot entrance. I'm panicking. It's a mild panic, but panic, nonetheless.

And then, breaking through my figurative haze—and a literal foggy one—is a single spot calling to me from the hockey team's reserved parking spaces. Home to the Riverside Reapers. One of the best professional hockey teams in the league. And Riverside's pride and joy. We got close to the playoffs last season, and now everyone and their mother thinks we're going to win this season.

Look, I'm not blind, I know what the signage says— RESERVED PARKING. But I'll be out in less than five minutes. I highly doubt a team member is going to arrive in the next five minutes, find that I'm in *his* designated parking spot, and get me towed. Plus, this is the closest spot to the arena.

Kiss my ass, time management class I should probably be attending! I'm in control, and I've got this.

I pull haphazardly between the white-painted lines, kill the engine, and jump out of the car quicker than I think I've ever moved in my twenty-two years of life.

My threadbare shoes squelch in puddles of murky rainwater, and crushed autumn leaves disintegrate into muted hues of fiery crimson against the soaked pavement. The sky is the color of dragon's breath, with nebulous clouds shrouding the parking lot in a disquieting darkness—one that makes the rink look a lot more foreboding than usual. Cold licks up my spine, raising goose bumps on the exposed flesh of my arms as I try to circulate some warmth with my palms.

I push through the double, weatherproofed doors and into the arena. My eyes start to tear up, and my nose stings from the acreage of subzero ice in front of me. To say that the rink is packed would be an understatement. Hundreds of skates and little legs. A cacophony of shouts that ricochet off the tall, hollowed walls. Pucks zinging around like miniature missiles.

I bear the chill of the atmosphere, wishing I'd had a chance to slip on a jacket before entering the goddamn arctic. Dance attire wasn't made for a hockey rink. All I have on is a black bralette and booty shorts, and despite them covering all the necessary areas, I still feel like I'm going to contract hypothermia.

"Teague!" I shout from behind the plexiglass, waving my arms overhead like a lunatic.

My brother glances in my direction and says goodbye to his friends before skating over to me. The messily illustrated fire symbol on his helmet sticks out in a snowscape of white, and he steps off the ice with his hockey stick gripped tightly in his gloved hand.

"You're late," he says, jutting his lower lip out.

"I know. I'm sorry, Squirt." I sit him down on a nearby bench and start to untie the laces of his skates, all while he glowers at me with sharp eyes. "I ran over time. It won't happen again."

Teague sheds his gloves, then removes his helmet, unveiling a mess of sweat-slicked spikes on the top of his head. "You always say that. And it always happens."

My fingers falter in the polyester strings. I feel terrible. I do always say that, and nothing ever changes. I'm trying to juggle so much at one time. Teague is my main priority, but so is keeping a roof over his head and food on the table.

With some expert detangling and tugging, I manage to yank his skates off, mentally chastising myself for being the worst sister on the planet. With a feathery exhale, I rise to a stance, gripping a fistful of laces. "I know you're mad, T, but we really have to go," I tell him, unable to ignore the disappointment seeping into his expression.

He doesn't argue with me. He doesn't say much of anything, actually—which is unlike him. My brother's usually a bundle of untold stories waiting for an ear to listen. But I don't push him to talk to me, and the silence that follows is deafening.

I burst out of the rink, fumbling for my keys as he slogs behind me, when I'm accosted by the blinding sight of a bright red Jaguar sitting horizontally behind my car, boxing my little Honda in.

No, no, no.

A scream thunders from my throat, loud enough to garner shocked looks from families milling about the parking lot. "Fuck!"

Okay, think, Cali. Just...just go inside and ask the owner to move his car. And also pretend like you didn't drop the F-bomb in front of your eight-year-old brother.

I set Teague's skates down before grabbing him by the shoulders and forcing him to look at me. "I'm going to be right back, okay? Please, please stay here. This will only take a minute."

"Why can't I come with you?" he whines.

"It'll be less stressful for everyone if you stay here. And I mean it, Teague."

My brother opens his mouth, but no protest comes out.

My eyes flit over the obnoxious license plate as I scoff at the sheer idiocy of the personalized words emblazoned on the aluminum. Of course this person would be the biggest asshole out of Riverside's three hundred thousand population.

I turn on my heel, march back into that godforsaken rink, and *politely* ask the attendant at the front desk if he could be so kind as to call out the license plate to the red Jaguar parked illegally out front.

With a sigh, his monotonous voice bellows over the loudspeaker, "Will the owner of the red Jaguar please come to the front? I repeat, will the owner of the red Jaguar please come to the front? Uh, license plate: HUGE STICK."

Impatience cracks through me and sizzles along my ribs. I'm going to show this dipshit that he messed with the wrong woman. He couldn't wait a few seconds before boxing me in? Seriously? The world doesn't revolve around him.

A few minutes pass before there's any movement in the sea of hockey helmets, and then, sauntering over is a man nearly half a foot taller than me. He's dressed from head to toe in hockey gear, exuding a nonchalant air about him that triggers that fight response boiling inside me.

He has the *decency* to take off his helmet, and what I'm greeted with is a handsome face, much to my misfortune. Shaggy, brown hair parts down the middle, a few strands falling into green eyes. His long, dark lashes tickle his brow bone, his seemingly flawless face complete with a chiseled jawline, angular cheekbones, a set of pouty lips, and a nose too straight to belong to a hockey player. He has a face made to be seen, a face that could cure cancer, a face that could do some serious damage to me if I don't treat this situation with the utmost caution.

"This better be important. I'm in the middle of practice," he snaps, pinning his arms over his chest. A muscular-looking chest. Or maybe that's just his hockey padding.

Who does this guy think he is? He's acting like he's a goddamn gift from the gods and I should be blessed for simply existing in his presence.

The attendant immediately livens. "Oh, I didn't realize it was your car, Gage. You want me to deal with this lady?"

Excuse me?

Gage shakes his head, glaring down at me from his stupid, towering height. "I've got it, Ernie."

From the parking lot to the rink, I've had plenty of time to gather an arsenal of insults for the douche in front of me, and I'm ready to send those suckers flying like bullets from a machine gun. "You boxed me in, you fucking prick!" I shout, torrents of anger pouring through my veins as opposed to the usual trickle.

"Whoa, there. You're the one who parked in *my* parking space."

"I was only going to be a minute!"

"You can read, can't you? Those spots are reserved for team players. And last I checked, you're not on the team, sweetheart." Gage gives me a condescending head tilt that makes me want to pop said head off his spinal cord.

I'm fully aware of the audience we've amassed from the volume of our altercation, but I couldn't care less if someone gets my meltdown on camera. This dick needs to be knocked down a peg.

"I'm just asking you to move your car. I have somewhere to be, and none of *this* would be happening if you just waited for me to move."

His tone drips with sickly sweet sarcasm. "Oh, I'd love to stop what I'm doing right now for your benefit and move my car. In fact, I'll ask Coach to stop practice until we get this whole thing resolved. Do you want monetary compensation for your time too?"

A growl rumbles in my throat. "You think the world revolves around you just because you're a hotshot hockey player?" I hiss.

"You think the world revolves around you just because you're a stuck-up brat?"

That's it. I'm going to kill him and make everyone in the rink a witness to murder.

"Move. Your. Car. Before I shove it up your ass and gun it."

Gage steps closer to me, magnetizing grin and all—perfect,

blindingly toothy, with just the right amount of confidence to churn a storm of butterflies in my stomach.

He's so close to me that I can feel his breath plume over my face, can smell the intoxicating hint of pine in his cologne, can practically anticipate his touch on my skin if he moved slightly north.

"She has a bark," he drawls, impressed.

Our eyes clash for a moment—a world of arctic blues and forest greens meeting each other for the first time—but I smother the attraction cresting inside me. Any nonviolent feelings will be immediately terminated upon discovery.

Don't get too close, Cali. Long-term Gage exposure could result in radioactive poisoning.

My glare has enough venom in it to paralyze a single person, and it's reserved for Gage only.

"You couldn't handle my bite."

Something in him changes. It's fleeting. And thanks to being up close and personal with him, I can see how blown his pupils are, how the brown from his inner irises have somehow widened in diameter underneath the harsh, recessed lighting, drowning out the previous green.

"Wanna put that theory to the test? I love a girl who bites."

Something about the way he just said that makes the lower half of me tingle. That shouldn't be a normal bodily response, especially not with *him*. I tamp down whatever the hell is budding between my thighs and try to ignore that warm, oozing, honeyed lilt in his tone.

Ugh! He's so infuriating. Gage is the rudest, most arrogant, and most conceited person on this fucking planet. I'd rather have a Pap smear performed by Wolverine than be within a ten-foot radius of him.

My heart punches against my ribs, indignation streamlining to every part of my quivering body. "Fuck you!" I spit.

"That's all you got? Come on, I know a spitfire like you really wants to *give* it to me. Go ahead. Do your worst."

"If you don't move your car, I'll…"

You'll what, Cali?! What can you do that isn't illegal?

Everyone's staring at me. The whole rink has quieted. No scuffle of blades or clink of pucks on ice. There aren't even any whispered comments about how utterly embarrassing this whole interaction is for me.

The words die on my tongue, and my confidence goes with them.

Gage pastes on a too-wide smile that has pearly enamel twinkling underneath the fluorescents. "That's a shame. Looks like you'll be waiting to get your car back until after my practice is done. It should only be a few hours," he drawls. "It's not like you have anywhere else to be, right?"

Shock drives my precursory fury all the way to the state line. "I—"

But he's gone. He's turned around, gotten back on the ice, and resumed practice like he didn't just singlehandedly ruin my entire day. And everyone stood by to watch while it happened.

So, pushed to the brink of madness, I do what any reasonable person would do in this situation. I force myself to retain some semblance of calm, and I walk out the door with my head held high.

Teague perks up as soon as he sees me, anxiously shifting his weight from one foot to the other. "Is he going to move his car?"

I navigate my way around the crimson complication, opening my Honda's passenger door for my brother. "Nope."

"Then why are we getting in the car?"

"Because we're going to get out of here another way."

Gage doesn't think I have the balls to do anything, does he? I'm going to prove him wrong. I'm going to prove him so wrong that he'll regret ever speaking to me like that. In fact, if I *ever* see his smug face again, I'll make sure to rearrange it with my fist.

As I get myself situated—with that wicked plan of mine forming in my head—I stick my key in the ignition, make sure Teague's seatbelt is tightly secured, and then brace my hand over his chest before propelling backwards into Gage's expensive car.

2

NOT THE COMEBACK I HAD IN MIND
GAGE

Despite the chill from the rink frosting over me, my adrenaline is like oxygen to the uncontained fire smoldering in my chest. Every muscle in my body is swollen with an ache that only hockey gives me, and my fucking sinuses are on fire from the ice-cold atmosphere.

It's 5-5. There's only a minute left in the game. We need to win this. We're on a winning streak, and if we want to make it to playoffs this season, then we have to uphold it.

Sweat bleeds into my eyes, blurring the figures of my teammates, and hockey-padded silhouettes skirt along my peripheral, closing in on the goal. The screams from the stands meld with the shouts from the ice, and it's a sensory overload to every charred nerve ending. I have my legs in a half-split that hurts like hell, my grip on my stick is wavering with each passing second, and I'm not sure how many more beats my heart can take before it bursts from my chest.

The Denver Dingos are a few feet from the goal, and a giant number thirty is blared across the pixelated screen, signaling that if I don't save this next shot, the Reapers are gonna take home a loss.

You can do this, Gage. You've done this a million times before. Try and guess his next move—look at where his eyes dart, how his arm twitches. Cover as much of the goal as you can.

As a black-and-red player charges at me, swinging his stick completely backward before slapping the thick of the puck, I take a mental note of the arc of his arm, and the bulk of my body flies toward the upper righthand corner of the net.

Everything slows—time, my breath, my heart. My outstretched arm is the first to contact the edge of the disc, but as I continue to torque my spine, something in my hip strains, causing the rest of my body to crumple from the overextension. The puck continues its perfect trajectory into the nylon, and the eruption of the crowd drowns out the deafening pulse of blood in my ears, as well as the scream projecting from deep within my chest.

Fuck.

I can't move. I can feel every little needle pricking the lower half of me, preparing my body for the brunt of the pain, like a clear sky before a mosh pit of storm clouds. And then the needles transform into a legion of miniature knives, rendering me helpless in layers of suffocating gear. I can feel hot tears bubble up in my burning eyes.

Shit, shit, shit. What just happened?

I attempt to lift my leg to my chest, but I can't even test my mobility without a searing throb in my lower abdomen. I don't know how long I'm face-down on the ground. Puffs of heated breath slip through the metal bars covering my face, gusting against the pockmarked surface of the ice; that's the only indication I haven't passed out yet. The world's moving on without me, the raucous cheers from the winning team making my stomach sling sickness up my throat.

"Gage! Gage, are you okay?"

I think it's Fulton, my best friend, but I don't want to open my eyes to check. The last thing I need is a migraine to complicate the unbearable sting wrapping around my leg a goddamn spike strip.

"My hip," I grit out through my teeth, trying to siphon air into my heaving lungs. And as if my body's playing some sick trick on me, a violent spasm rips through my hip's muscle fibers, confirming that I did, in fact, fuck up my hip in a single, goalie-proof move.

"Okay. Don't worry. A medic is coming over right now. You're gonna be fine," he says, though I'm pretty sure it's more for his sake than mine.

Once other voices join the conversation, all wobbling with varying degrees of concern, everything becomes fuzzy. I don't remember getting escorted off the ice; I don't remember the state of the stands after our disappointing loss; I don't remember even seeing Coach or talking with my teammates. All I remember is feeling weak, like I could barely stand on my own two feet, and I hate that feeling. Powerless, helpless, vulnerable. I was all too familiar with that feeling after what happened to my little brother, and I swore to myself that I'd never feel that way ever again.

"Looks like you tore your hip flexor pretty badly. There's no need for surgery, and you will be able to walk again, but you'll need at least three months to recover until you can be back on the ice," our team's physical therapist discloses, offering me a consolatory smile. "I suggest keeping diligent about at-home treatment, but I'm also going to propose three physical therapy sessions a week until you hit that three-month mark, and then we can see how you're doing."

My stupid, injured hip taunts me, and my frustration at the situation shifts into utter hysterics as a clipped laugh shoots out of me. "Fucking great. That's great. I'm useless for three months."

"You'll still be able to go about your day. You may just need more help when it comes to walking."

So, useless.

I position my legs carefully over the edge of the table, grimacing from the pain moving my hip a mere two inches causes. I know this isn't a life-threatening injury, but how am I supposed to get around? Will the guys just give me a piss bag instead of wheeling me into the bathroom every time I need to go? Will they stock my mini fridge with food because I won't be able to get down the stairs? Or will they have to install one of those old-person stairlifts in the house? Oh, God. I need my legs.

And what about sex? Does that mean I'm going to have to enter a dry spell for three months? I don't think I'm strong enough for that. I think I'd rather just amputate the leg and get it over with.

"How do you expect me to stay off the ice for three months? I can't just sit around and do nothing," I grumble.

Hockey is something I enjoy. It's the epicenter of my life, and everything else I do is based around it. If you take that away, I don't know how to function. And if you throw in a handicap, then I seriously *can't* function.

Don, the physical therapist who's been with our team for twelve years, rubs the pronounced smile lines bracketing his lips. "I'm sorry, Gage. You'll have to get used to letting your body rest if you want to recover."

"Can't you just give me a bottle of painkillers and slap a Band-Aid on it?"

He chuckles softly. "If only healing was that simple."

I throw my head back, focusing on the ceiling tiles overhead, exhaling the weighted realization of my new life off my chest. I won't be able to help my teammates for at least thirty games. I may be at games physically, sure, but I won't be with my team spiritually. I won't be able to share in celebrations or feel like I'm making any difference. And I'm the reason we lost tonight. If I had blocked that shot, we would've tied. I let my team down.

I can't think of a worse hell to be trapped in. Not only that, but my car is still in the shop undergoing damage repairs after that crazy chick t-boned me. So even if I wanted to drive—which wouldn't be a good idea—I couldn't.

As my eyes travel over squares of white, I can't help but jump to the conclusion that staring at a boring-ass ceiling will be the highlight of my days while I hibernate in my king-sized bed. I'll go insane. I'll start scratching tally marks into the walls to keep track of how long I'm stuck in my room.

"Besides physical therapy, is there anything else I can do to speed up the recovery process?" I ask, pleading for a scrap of hope.

Don pushes his horn-rimmed glasses further up the bridge of his nose. "If you want to work on mobility and flexibility, taking a dance or yoga class could benefit you."

Uh. I've never taken either one of those. Yeah, I'm proud of my flexibility compared to my teammates, but I'm nowhere near putting my leg behind my head like dancers and yoga junkies do. Do they do that? I don't even know.

I tousle the front of my hair with my hand, the tangled strands falling back into place. "Is that my only option?"

"I'm afraid so, Gage."

Okay. Not great, but if that's what it'll take for me to get back on the ice, then you bet your fucking ass I'm squeezing myself into a child-sized tutu.

Before Don sends me on my merry way, he hands me a bag of ice packs, anti-inflammatory medication, a brace, and some handy-dandy crutches that make me look forty years older than I actually am.

When I hobble my way out of Don's office—navigating on my crutches like a newborn baby deer—Fulton's waiting for me by his car, pretending to look around nonchalantly. Then he spots me, composes himself, and would look fairly calm if it wasn't for the nervous twitch in his right eye.

Fulton and I are different in a lot of ways, but it's what makes our friendship work. He's the anxious wreck of a human being who faints at the sight of blood; I'm the unfazed one who probably wouldn't give a shit if I was bleeding out from a major stab wound. When shit happens to me, I know there's nothing I can really do to change it. So I just accept it and move on instead of worrying about what I can't control.

I wasn't always like that, though. One too many failures made me that way, and I'm not just talking about a missed goal.

Fulton, on the other hand, spends every waking second worrying about something. I'm pretty sure he has a perpetually high heart rate like one of those ancient chihuahuas that live for twenty years. I teach him how to chill out, and he teaches me to...be more empathetic, I guess. Fulton loves people. He never gets tired of them. I don't love people. I hate most people. There are about eight people that I tolerate, and the rest of the world could go up in a blazing ball of fire for all I care.

I'm extroverted when I need to be, but that's only reserved for party environments. If booze, babes, or bad decisions are involved, I'm pretty much there. But I guess I'll have to table that side of me too for a while. The only B I'm going to be getting is back aches.

Fulton fidgets with his hands, and then a bunch of words catapult from his mouth and steamroll over me. "How bad is it? Will you be able to play again?"

"In three months, sure."

His face is crestfallen. "Shit. I'm sorry, dude."

I brush him off with what I'm hoping is a convincing

enough shrug. "Nothing I can do now except hope it goes by quickly."

He nods and opens the passenger door for me, helping me into his car before throwing my crutches in the back seat. Fulton, despite making millions of dollars a year, still drives his beat-up Toyota Tercel, claiming it has sentimental value and refusing to fix the window crank because it'll "erase its character." I swear the side door almost flew off its hinges when we were on the highway the other day.

He sticks the key in the ignition but doesn't rev it, tapping his fingers against the steering wheel in a rhythmless drum. "Is there anything you can do to speed up the healing process?"

"Dance classes" is all I reveal, huffing out of my nostrils.

"You're going to take dance classes?" he exclaims.

"If I want to strengthen my flexibility, then I'll have to."

A smile sweeps over Fulton's lips like the first break of dawn over a never-ending night. "But you can't dance," he teases.

I brace my hand over my heart offendedly. "Oh, yeah? What do you call me memorizing every move to the Rasputin dance when Beer Comes Trouble was having karaoke that one night?"

"I call that deeply troubling and a result of way too much alcohol."

"First off, rude." I make a show of counting on my fingers. "And second off, just because I'm crippled doesn't mean I won't beat you with my crutches."

Fulton finally gets the car sputtering to life, and he looks over his shoulder as he begins backing out of his makeshift parking spot. "Still violent, I see."

"Still annoying, I see."

"At least I can walk."

"At least I don't throw up every time I talk to a girl."

He side-eyes me, pursing his lower lip out. "Touché."

We exit the parking lot and turn onto the main road, and I have to keep my knees from smacking into the glove compartment every time we go over a bump. Which is a lot more difficult when my hip has the mobility of a fossilized statue.

The outlines of vegetation and concrete buildings glide past the window, bathed in a post-afternoon haze, and shades of pomegranate pink hover on the horizon, waiting to be rolled out over shingled roofs and abandoned streets.

"Speaking of girls, whatever happened with that chick from the rink?" Fulton asks, waggling his eyebrows.

Suddenly, I get this surge of automatic hatred in my gut, and the thought of her is like a butane-covered match to a sky-high flame. I loathe that girl. More than humanly possible. Just thinking about the way she car-fucked poor old Natasha—my Jaguar I-Pace—drives me so fucking crazy that a court wouldn't deem me mentally competent enough to stand trial. Hell, I don't even know her name, but I'm determined to hold a life-long grudge against her until the day I wither away in my casket.

I play dumb because the alternative is getting the rage sweats. "What girl?"

"The girl you were having a huge yelling match with?"

"No idea what you're talking about," I mutter under my breath, picking at the hangnail on my thumb.

The car comes to a lurching halt at a red stoplight, and Fulton elbows me. "Am I sensing some sexual tension?"

Sexual? Ha. I wouldn't touch her pussy with a ten-foot pole, or if she was the last woman on Earth and I'd taken one of those chocolates that increase your sex drive. Yeah, I'd be a blind idiot not to notice the lack of clothing she was wearing when she confronted me, but no matter how much her large tits jiggled in that pathetic excuse for a bra, I'd never waste my breath being in the same room as her, much less using said breath to kiss her.

"There's tension, but none of it is sexual."

"Uh-huh." Fulton scratches at a tiny scuff on his windshield. "And are you going to press charges? You know, for her pretty much flattening the entire side of your car?"

I wanted to. I really did. That molten anger inside of me blisters with heat to make her pay (literally and figuratively), but the more reasonable, less kill-or-be-killed version of me still has a seat at the table, and he's telling me to take a Xanax before I ruin someone financially. Insurance covered the damages. I have enough money to buy a completely new car if I wanted, and it wouldn't make a dent in my bank account. There's really no reason for me to sue her aside from being a petty bastard.

As charged as I am with Olympian levels of fury, I just can't bring myself to put her in debt like that, even if I'm not her biggest fan. I saw the crap-show of the car she drove. Even if I did sue her, I probably wouldn't get much money from her. And what I could get would be more than likely financially devastating on her end. Therefore, I'm retracting my claws and doing the selfless deed by letting her off the hook.

"I don't want to sue," I tell Fulton, and the admission douses the last dregs of the fire running rampant inside of me, leaving nothing but coughs of smoke and hissing firewood.

The light turns green, and Fulton resumes his path through the intersection, shock nudging his brows to his hairline. "That's, uh, really responsible of you."

My belly does this weird flip, and I don't think it's from motion sickness. "Just another thing for me to deal with, honestly. And I don't have the time or patience for it."

"That's understandable. I mean, I've never been to court, but it feels like it would take a long time. And it would be super stressful." Fulton shudders. "Ordering food at a drive-thru is already stressful enough for me."

A chuckle catches on my lips, and the complementary squeeze in my chest makes me momentarily forget about the hip-related bad news I received today. Maybe this break will help me rethink my whole approach this season. Maybe I just need to step away for a moment and let my thoughts air out.

When we pull into the driveway of the house we share with four other guys, I'm in awe at how different it looks now from how it did in the summer. The gigantic, weathered mansion is now overrun with a medley of autumn leaves, covering the once-green yard in gilded golds and magnificent maroons. The gnarled trees that encircle the house are a testament to the changing seasons, a tale of transformation with their barren branches and the few handfuls of foliage that have yet to freckle the ground. And the air is ripe with a crispness that only precedes rain, suffusing the sky like ink on wet paper.

As we get out of the car, Fulton grabs my crutches and helps me find my footing. "You know, I overheard Aeris saying that she's been going to this dance class downtown. She says it's great. Maybe you could try there?" he proposes.

"That carves some time off looking, so thanks, man. If it's Aeris-approved, I'm pretty sure it'll be a piece of cake."

Aeris, one of my teammate's girlfriends, has been a great addition to the group. She's the only girl who's been able to tie down our team's biggest playboy, Hayes. Domesticated the poor guy. She's super sweet and can cook a mean chicken parmesan, but with all due respect, she has the worst coordination in the world. Like, born-with-two-left-feet bad. So if Aeris can do it, I'll be a pro at this whole dancing thing. Plus, how hard can it really be?

3

A ONE-WAY ROAD TO FAILURE
CALISTA

I've come to the conclusion that even with the help of time-telling devices, the world just loves to see me suffer. My hair is a rat's nest of tangles and grease, my patience is practically nonexistent, and I'm somehow juggling both Teague's hockey bag and my mother's medication.

My mother, Ingrid, was diagnosed with multiple sclerosis in her early forties, around the time I was seventeen. And now I'm her primary caretaker. She's pretty much bedridden, and the disease has resulted in muscle weakness, a lack of coordination, and chronic fatigue. My mother started to get bad around my junior year of high school, but her flare-ups spiked my sophomore year of college. After finding out how sick she'd gotten, I dropped out to take care of her. And due to her being indisposed, I became Teague's guardian when he was only in kindergarten.

It breaks my heart to see her wasting away in bed, constantly fighting pain, never knowing when she'll succumb to the sickness. There are days where I'm out of the house for extended periods of time, and I get this terrible feeling that I'll come home to find her dead. Or worse—Teague will find her before I do.

Not only do I feel responsible for my mother because she's, well, my mom, but she was *my* primary caretaker when we were struggling in an impoverished household. My father disappeared around my junior year of high school—when my mother's condition became too much for him to deal with—and I haven't seen him since. I don't know where he ran off to or if he's even still alive. Not that I care. He stopped being my dad the day he walked out on us.

My father was a good-for-nothing lowlife who leeched off this family and contributed nothing to our finances. So to remedy a single-income household, my mom sacrificed her entire life for me and Teague to have a somewhat normal upbringing. We lived in a two-bedroom apartment with an open-layout kitchen, a small bathroom, and barely enough square footage to constitute a living room.

Since my mother worked back-to-back shifts at the diner, she never had any time to clean the apartment. It was a mess: peeling carpet, roach carapaces melded to glue traps, traces of mold discoloring the walls of the bathroom, dirty dishes piled high in the sink, and toys and bills alike cluttered on every flat surface. My mother barely made enough money for weekly groceries, much less rent and utility bills. We were always behind on payments, and I began to realize how much money insecurity affected us when I got my first job my sophomore year of high school.

It was full-time at a local fast-food restaurant, which wasn't terrible for my first work experience but definitely interfered with the quality of my education. I went from an A student to a C student within a semester. But it's not like I could spend extra time studying and doing schoolwork when I had to assist my mother. So I traded school for the relief of carrying some of my mother's stress and providing for my family.

I forfeited my dreams of finishing college and becoming a professional dancer. I forfeited my social life and love life. I forfeited...*everything*. There are some days I wish my life hadn't turned out the way it did, but if I had to choose between my dreams and my family, my family would always come first—even at the expense of my happiness. It doesn't feel like much of a loss, though, when my life had barely begun. And maybe it's better this way: to kill something before it has the chance to grow.

Now I've become a permanent provider, leaving behind the typical twenty-something's world of carefree living.

"Teague, you better be ready in the next three minutes!" I shout, schlepping his bag by the door as I make a detour to the kitchen. As much as I wish it was for a quick bite, I don't have time.

I grab a glass from the cabinet, fill it with water, then bring my mother her beta interferons to help reduce inflammation. Thankfully, we don't live in that cursed two-bedroom apartment anymore. Teaching ten back-to-back dance classes a day, five days a week, I saved up enough money to help us afford a better apartment. It also helped that disability and social security covered a lot of my mother's medical expenses.

My mother's bedroom is the furthest down the hall, shadowed by darkness and a foreboding feeling that swathes the stale air like overcast clouds. There's this inexplicable cold that leeches to the nerves leading up my spine, and my heart always seems to hammer heavier at her door's threshold.

Cautiously, I creak the partition open, revealing the sight of her bed basking in a single square of moonlight, her hair strewn over her pillow and covering the sharp edges of her face. The musty smell of unwashed clothes assaults my nostrils, having festered in an air-sealed pocket for the majority of the day. It reminds me that I'll have to help her bathe when I get back from dance—if she's even awake.

"Mom, it's time to take your meds," I whisper softly, slowly inching across the unvarnished floorboards to the side of her bed.

She emerges from that cotton-fitted fortress, a thin spider-webbing of blood vessels in her eyes and her hair a mussed state of uncombed tresses. Her bony hand feels blindly across her mattress, skeletal fingers turning upward to catch the little white pills promising reprieve.

I let them plunk into her palm, and then I set her glass of water on the nightstand. It usually takes her muscles a few minutes to cooperate, but I have to make sure she's actually ingesting her medicine.

I love my mother, I do. But being in that freezing room with her, practically hearing the Grim Reaper's scythe knocking on her bedside window, rips my body apart and scatters every piece of my soul beyond rescue. I know she'd get better treatment in a hospital, but we don't have a quarter of the money it would cost for such an expensive bill. Plus, if she were to stay in a hospital, her time there would be indefinite.

"Thank you, Calista," she replies with a painful-sounding rasp, taking a sip from her drink before setting it back on the nightstand without so much as a scrap of evidence that it was even drunken from at all. I bend down to kiss the crown of her head, trying to latch on to any remaining remnants of her signature rose scent before she got sick, but that version of her is long gone.

"I love you," I tell her, though I'm not sure if it's intended for her ears or my guilty conscience.

"I love you too. Have a good class tonight." Her diluted smile is equal parts gracious and pained, and while I retreat toward the door, I watch as she hides herself away again, practically disappearing into her queen-sized bed.

Some days, my mother doesn't even show herself. Some days, she won't come out from under the covers or even look at me. As dismal as the situation is, I'm lucky she was feeling strong enough to take her medicine today. I don't know how to make any of this better for her. I don't know how to mitigate the years of pain that have built up—the years of pain that she'd be quick to carry herself if I was the one in her situation.

When I make my way back into the hallway, Teague is waiting for me by the door, geared up in tons of hockey padding and looking like the Michelin Man. A frown is plastered to his lips, an indecipherable expression souring his features.

Running late isn't a rare occurrence in this household. This pretty much happens every morning before school and before hockey practice. With how busy my schedule is, I'm surprised I'm even able to take him instead of our neighbors, who step in when I'm too caught up in work.

"Come on, Squirt. We have to hurry."

Keys jangling on my index finger, I swing my dance bag haphazardly onto my arm. But when I go to open the door, Teague doesn't move toward the exit. He doesn't bend down to pick up his hockey bag. He stares at me, the hard line of his brow and his matching pout both making his cherubic cheeks puff out.

A groan and a sigh merge in the tight cavity of my chest. "Teague, I don't have time for this. We have to go. Now."

"I don't want to go," he murmurs, bowing his head.

He doesn't want to go? Are you kidding me right now?

I drop my bag to the floor, close the door, and grind my teeth hard enough to loosen a filling. "What are you talking about?"

"I don't want to go to practice today."

"Since when?" I growl, digging the heel of my palm into my forehead like it'll magically cure the headache solidifying behind my eyes. We're ten minutes late. If I entertain this, it'll put my entire schedule thirty minutes behind.

Hey, God. It's me, Calista. I'm not sure what you're doing up there—if you're throwing your swanky Jesus sandals up on your cloud coffee table—but I really need you to listen. Please give me a break. I'm not asking for much. A small break. Something that'll keep my blood pressure in check. I'll literally do whatever you want. You want my unborn child? You got it. You want me to harvest the blood of virgins and sacrifice goats under the full moon? Sure thing, buddy.

"Cali, please," Teague whines, moisture pushing against the dam in his eyes, seconds away from breaking through the crack and rushing out in snot and sobs galore.

I tame my temper, suck in a breath, and then kneel down to his height. "What's going on, Squirt?"

Teague's never acted like this before. He loves going to hockey practice.

"I just...can I please stay home? Or can I go with you to dance class?"

The sad, puppy dog look on his face is currently beating my heart in with a spike-studded bat. I hate it when Teague's upset. And I hate it even more when I can't fix whatever's bothering him.

"You know I can't leave you alone, bud. And I can't bring you with me," I admit regretfully, tucking a wily curl of hair behind his ear. "Please just tell me what's going on."

His entire face turns a muted red, and he shrinks under his layers of gear, refusing to look me in the eye. "Some of the kids...they..."

I nod at him to continue, the pad of my finger soaking up a rogue tear that's made a great escape down his cheek. On the outside, I'm as cool as a cucumber. On the inside, tiny versions of me are running around in circles in my head and screaming as fire engulfs every inch of my brain.

"They what?"

His lower lip quivers, and that's enough warning before he collapses into a crying fit and flings his arms around my neck.

"They make fun of me," he bawls into my shoulder, scrunching my crop top up in his little fists.

Shock sparks my stomach, and then flammable barrels of rage light inside of me. "What?"

He's getting bullied at practice? Why didn't he tell me sooner? Why didn't I *realize* it sooner? I'm going to confront those eight-year-old pieces of shit and demand that they apologize to him. Can I punch a child? Is that legal? Or...ethical? Fuck it. I don't care.

He pulls away from me, his skin slathered in wetness, his eyes red and puffy, and his nose bubbling. "I'm...so b-bad at hockey...and they...p-pick on m-me!"

"Oh, Squirt," I console, bringing him back into an embrace, fully accepting that my shirt will be decorated in stains by the time I get to class. His small frame shakes as he wails, awakening that mama bear instinct within me as I stroke his hair and simultaneously plot total-world destruction.

"I'm so sorry that's happening, Teague. But you have to know that you're an amazing hockey player."

"You're just saying that!"

He's right. A part of me is just saying that. I've never really seen Teague play before. I've just been so busy—so absent.

"I..." My voice dies on a crack.

"Please don't make me go, Cali. I don't want to see them. Please, please, please," he begs, stomping his foot while more tears stream out of his eyes, splotching the ring of his jersey's neckline.

Guilt corkscrews deep into the flesh of my heart, and my apology doesn't need to be written out in big, bold letters for him to understand the tug-of-war position he has me in. "If I could bring you to my class with me, I would in a heartbeat. But it's not appropriate. I'm sorry, kiddo."

The shallow bursts of breath from his mouth descend into somewhat controlled sniffles. "I-I understand..."

I rub my hands up and down his arms. "Okay, here's what we're gonna do. All I ask is that you go for today's practice, and then we can talk about the next steps. Can you do that for me? Can you be brave today, Teague?" I ask.

"I think I can," he replies, and although uncertainty colors his tone, he puts on the bravest face he can muster.

His agreement dissolves my fleeting panic, but I know he can only keep the anxiety at bay for so long. "I promise I'll fix this."

I *will* fix this. I'll do right by my brother. I have to. I have to be better. A better sister, a better daughter, a better...everything.

So, now running the estimated thirty minutes behind, I get Teague buckled into the car, and I drive as fast as I can to the rink, glancing back every minute or so to see if the nervous twist of his face has straightened out.

I feel like I'm walking my brother to the goddamn gallows. Each intersection we fly through, each building we pass, each number that changes on the digital clock—they all contribute to the growing distress hatching marks on every inch of my body.

And when I pull up to the mouth of the rink, I watch helplessly as Teague straggles his way to practice, every atom of life drained from his once-happy spirit.

4

THE DEAL
GAGE

I must have the wrong address. There's no way I'm seriously standing in front of a dance studio called Sexy Stilettos. I got the address from Fulton, who got it from Aeris, but she did *not* disclose that it would have such an... interesting...name.

Please, God. Let this be a shoe store and the real dance studio is a few blocks down the street. The only dance studios within fifteen minutes from the house are this one and one called Xtreme Xplosions, and that one is a strictly competitive studio. The dancers there would probably eat my sad, pathetic corpse up like a family of crazed, bloodthirsty river otters.

With my new hip brace (which is surprisingly not as uncomfortable as I thought it would be), I hobble through the double doors, immediately stumbling across a giant wooden dance floor, which pretty much interrupts the choreography that's currently taking place.

Did I, uh, mention that I might've been like an hour late?

But none of that is even occupying the tiniest floorspace of my brain because what greets me isn't just a bunch of floundering beginners in workout gear—no. It's worse than that. So much worse.

Instead, about fifteen girls in scantily clad outfits are writhing around on the ground, complete with six-inch heels and a sultry soundtrack. It's like a strip club in the best way. Except I'm on the fucking stage with them.

I freeze. I freeze and full-on lose control over my brain and motor functions. I'm a guy. A red-blooded, simple-minded guy, and when in the midst of girls with their ass and tits out, I can guarantee that guys like me will almost always get a boner. A dance class is not an appropriate place to be parading your man pole around. And I'm not going back to jail—even though it was only for one night.

Every girl on the floor seems to stop and stare at me except for the instructor, who's giving it her all like she's performing at the Super Bowl Halftime Show. She sways her hips back and forth to the beat, her long, red hair whipping behind her, hands coming up to cup her overflowing tits. Then she slowly rolls her body halfway to the ground, all while arching her back and sticking her ass out. And it's the sexiest ass I've ever seen. Two giant globes hanging out of her nanoscopic shorts, recoiling with each jiggle.

Oh, God. I'm ogling this woman without her consent. I need to look away! Why can't I look away?

She makes it to the floor, sliding all the way into the splits in her heels, and then she finishes the routine by crawling on her hands and knees toward the wall-length mirror like some kind of irresistible succubus. Eyes smudged with kohl, plush lips that are the most breathtaking shade of red I never knew existed, and enough skin to fuel my fantasies for the rest of my life. She's stunning. So stunning that the whole "she takes my breath away" statement people throw around is actually fucking true.

She's the definition of gorgeous with curves in every

squeezable place, and she has toned lines of muscle running along her flat stomach.

My heart's struggling to pump in my chest, but maybe that's because all the goddamn blood is rushing on a one-way trip south. My stretchy gym shorts are suddenly two sizes too small. Oh, shit. I need to chill out.

She's just a girl, Gage. An attractive girl, but that's all. Nothing new, and definitely not wank-worthy. Get yourself under control. This is sad. Sadder than the time you were going down on your crush and let one rip in the middle of it.

I want to die from embarrassment. I'd take myself out if there was a revolver sitting on the table next to me, because the longer I stand here like an idiot, the faster my dick thickens in my pants. I'm not going to be known as the sad dude with the limp hip. I'm gonna be known as the creepy dude with the not-so-limp dick.

And to make matters worse, the moment the instructor turns around to face me, I'm consumed by the ocean-blue of her eyes—ones that I've not only met before, but stared down as I told her off in front of an entire hockey arena.

It's the girl from the rink.

NEEDLESS TO SAY, I didn't stay for the rest of class. I get that my shortcut to a quick recovery is royally screwed now, but I can't even focus on my disappointment over the red-hot embarrassment still swishing through my veins. I should've taken the loss when I had the chance and called for the nearest Uber to get me the hell out of Dodge. Instead, my Neanderthal brain has compelled me to wait by Rink Girl's car to talk to her after she finishes her class.

About what, you may ask? I have no idea. The truth is, I'm drawn to her in a way I can't explain. And maybe it's the lack of oxygen in my brain, but a part of me foolishly thinks she can help me.

I lean against the side of her Honda, trying to suppress the weird jolt of nerves in my stomach. Not normal nerves, either. I'm sweating more than usual despite the night air cloaking me in goose bumps, and it feels like my heart's about to croak and take me with it.

I don't even realize I've been muttering to myself like a complete lunatic until her icy voice penetrates my brain bubble and derails my train of deprecating thoughts.

"You here to serve me papers?"

She's taller than I remember—just a few inches below my eyeline—and her fire-toned hair has been thrown up into a high ponytail. With no coverage over her chest, my attention is painstakingly drawn to the plunging dip of her cleavage and the mist of sweat that accompanies it.

Jesus. It's...I...this is weird. When I talked to her at the rink, I wasn't this out of it. I was oozing charming machismo. Now, I'm oozing pathetic sadness. Maybe my fumes of anger were providing me with some kind of cock-blocking smokescreen that blurred my vision so I couldn't see how drop-dead gorgeous she was.

"What?" I ask fearfully, feeling pinned beneath her glower like a lifeless butterfly mounted in a glass picture frame.

"Are. You. Here. To. Sue. Me?" she reiterates.

Sue her? She thinks I'm here to sue her? Seriously? I mean, yeah, I was contemplating it, but I'm not anymore. I can't believe she thinks I'm a sad sack of shit who needs her money.

"I...um..." The words I want to say oscillate in my mouth, but I can't get any of them to cooperate and form full sentences.

Her lips are screwed into a thin line, her cat-like eyes narrowed in expectancy, and the cerulean hue of her irises are even starker against the canvas of night. She's got her arms crossed over her tits—thank God—and I'm pretty sure I can see steam hissing out of her ears under the gibbous moon.

I forgot how pissed she probably still is at me. That's...great.

"I'm not here to sue you," I finally get out, needing to table that very offended feeling curling through my chest.

"Then why the fuck are you here?"

Uh. Um. Fuck. I don't even have a good answer for her—or at least an answer that would keep all my fingers intact.

She juts her chin out and gives me a look that says, *Well?* Or maybe more like, *If you don't hurry the fuck up, I'll rip your throat out with my teeth and give you a real reason not to answer me.*

Apparently my body doesn't do well under stress—which is strange since I play a professional sport—because I blurt everything out in an attempt to rid myself of the shame plugging my throat. It's the equivalent of sea cucumbers vomiting up their insides when they're frightened as some kind of defense mechanism.

"I need your help," I stammer, instantly feeling my cheeks warm with a blatant blush.

She stares at me.

I stare back.

An undefined—yet long enough—period of time passes between us, pulsing with the delicateness of a live wire, and then everything combusts. The silent murmurs of the night, the guilty ache in my chest, they all crash in a head-on collision with the hyena laughter that breaches her lips.

"Oh my God," she cackles, the dimpled swells of her cheeks rising. "What?"

"I need your help," I repeat, losing the shy, shaky modulation in my voice and replacing it with a cut of indignation. My muscles tense as the air in my lungs decompresses like I've been punched in the diaphragm. That tiny ember that's been sitting in the pit of my belly has finally caught flame, and it has the destructive capacity of a Molotov cocktail.

I can't believe this. I should be the one with the upper hand, not the other way around. I was the one who was wronged here.

Her shoulders stop shaking with laughter. "And why do you think I'd ever help someone like you?" she muses, her tone laden with a bitterness that tastes sour in my own mouth.

"Do I have to remind you that you're the one who fucked up my car?" I spit, muscles roiling into a near-painful strain, my hands absentmindedly forming fists that have nothing to cushion their rage.

"I only did that because you couldn't wait two seconds for me to move!"

"Sweetheart, it took you a lot longer than two seconds."

She doesn't back down. Not that I expect her to. She inches closer to me, thrusting her finger into my chest, the unrestrained flicker in her eyes practically searing my very soul. "*You* had no right to box me in. *You* had no idea what kind of day I was having. *You* couldn't have any human decency even for a split second," she growls.

I push her hand aside. "And *you* had no idea what kind of day I was having. Your argument goes both ways. You do realize that, right?"

"Is that why you stalked me at my place of work? Then waited out here like a fucking psycho? Just so you could keep arguing with me over something that happened a week ago?"

"I didn't stalk you!" I exclaim, though I realize that to an outsider's eye, it definitely looks like I stalked her. She's seriously giving herself some credit if she thinks I'd be obsessed enough with her to resort to stalking.

"Whatever." She presses her key fob and her headlights flash.

"Wait!" I splay myself over her car, hoping that it'll give her enough incentive to hear me out.

Surprise settles over her face like an early-morning mist,

but it doesn't temper the irritation rolling off her in waves. "Move out of the way, or I'll break your foot when my car backs over it."

Dear God. This woman is probably the most terrifying person I've ever met. I admire that, though. I'd be lying if I said it doesn't somewhat turn me on. And I may be a lot of things, but a liar isn't one of them.

"Please don't."

"Then unstick your crusty body from my car."

She moves toward me, and panic jumbles the words in the back of my throat. "I need you to teach me how to dance!" I half-shriek, fully preparing myself for the bone-crushing treatment my left foot is about to get.

This time, she doesn't laugh. Dark shadows contour the sculpted edges of her face, carving the softness from her cheeks and the suppleness of her cupid's bow. Her eyes seem to muddy to a deeper shade of blue as she contemplates me. And once she deduces that I'm not joking, the hold of her shoulders loosens incrementally.

"You want me to *teach* you how to dance?" she echoes, a muscle in her jaw fluttering.

"No. Ah, I mean, I just need some dance lessons. Or...some flexibility lessons?" Every sensible word seems to dodge the runway of my tongue, so I point frantically at the brace on my hip. "I got into an accident, and my PT told me that dancing can help with my flexibility."

She nods slowly, condescendingly, like I'm a mush-brained toddler spewing out gibberish.

"Look, I know I'm in no position to ask you for your help, but your dance studio is the only one close to my house. You're pretty much my only hope at this point. I'm, uh, I'm a hockey goalie if you didn't know. And I *need* to be better to play again in three months."

She straightens, allowing me a glimpse at the tightened cords of her neck. "I know who you are," she deadpans.

"Right, uh..." The gravity of the situation—and her obvious lack of interest in helping me—batters my solar plexus, nearly swiping my balance on the rickety exterior of her car.

She quirks her head, and her bobbing ponytail follows suit. "You can't, I don't know, practice yoga instead? Preferably in the comfort of your own home? Preferably abstaining from hogging all the air in my presence and burning my retinas with your hobgoblin physique?"

Excuse me? Hobgoblin? Normally, I'd be quick to correct her because one, my body is a temple and my rock-hard abs can put Channing Tatum's to shame, and two, she's clearly a visually impaired woman with terrible taste.

But I digress.

"Yoga seems a lot more dangerous than dance. Plus, dancing is super easy. I'll get the hang of it in no time, and then I'll be out of your hair," I tell her confidently with a wave of my hand.

"Oh, you think dancing is easy?" A deadly dose of hostility leaks from her tone.

"Yuh-huh. All you have to do is move your feet in time with the music. It's nothing compared to hockey. Hockey requires discipline, strength, coordination."

"Seriously? You know dancers are just as disciplined, strong, and coordinated as hockey players, right?

I blow air out of my cheeks. "You can't compare dancers and hockey players. They're simply not on the same playing field."

"Wow. That's—you know what? I don't have time to tell you how fucking wrong you are, and I definitely don't have time to give you private dance lessons."

How have I gotten on her nerves *again*? I was just being honest. Jesus fuck. Pulling teeth would be easier than getting this chick to set down her pitchfork for one second.

"Now, if you'll excuse me, I have somewhere to be," she snaps, knotting the strap of her dance bag in her hand—probably in some valiant effort to keep from punching me in the face.

As indignant and stubborn as I want to be, I know that butting heads with her isn't going to get me anywhere. So I shed that strong-man guise of mine as desperation unfurls between the tight spaces in my ribs. I don't grab her wrist or her arm when she shoulders past me, but I don't need to, because what I say next carries enough ammunition to pique her interest.

"What if I offer you something in return?"

That reels her attention instantly, and for the first time during our entire conversation, she fails to rein in the curiosity cracking across her expression.

I'm going to admit that it never crossed my mind to just hire a personal trainer or dance instructor to help me with my hip. And now, standing in front of the one girl I know I won't be able to dislodge from my mind, I don't want to resort to those options. I want *her* to help me.

Call me a masochist, but I like that she's the first girl to ever challenge me—to call me out on my bullshit. I'm surrounded by yes men all the time. It's a breath of fresh air to meet someone uninfluenced by the media's portrayal of me.

I hold my hands up in surrender. "Just hear me out. I know I'm not your favorite person right now, but I think we can help each other. Let me plead my case. We can even do it over dinner if it makes you more comfortable. There's a burger joint just a few blocks from here."

"You're seriously asking me to dinner? After I rammed into your car?"

"Trust me, I'm just as surprised as you are," I mutter, mentally rifling through all the possibilities of what I could offer the girl who wants nothing to do with me. I'd probably be more cognizant if it weren't for the nerves jackhammering into my weakly beating heart.

Spitfire—since I *still* don't know her name—is looking at me like I just proposed we break into the Pentagon, her brows furrowed, and her crimson-tinted mouth gnarled into a frown.

So I continue, attempting to dredge up some of my good ol' bachelor charm that usually results in bras being thrown at my face. "It's half past eight. I'm gonna go out on a limb here and guess that you haven't had dinner yet."

As if on cue, her stomach lets loose an audible growl, but she doesn't say anything.

Fishing blindly into my short's pocket, I pull out my wallet and slide out my black card, waving it in front of her. Even though she keeps her lips sealed, her wide-eyed gawking betrays her.

"I'll pay."

Two words that usually make any girl's pussy leak like Niagara Falls. In fact, it's common courtesy for said girl to fling her arms around me and praise me with thanks. Though I'd be lucky to receive a grunt of acknowledgment from her.

Her pink-tipped tongue swipes along her bottom lip as if she can taste the possible residual of fast-food grease there, and it takes her a full minute to ponder my offer, eventually relenting with a—surprise, surprise—grunt of acknowledgement.

"Just because I'm going with you doesn't mean I forgive you," she grumbles, tightening her bag's strap on her shoulder, a fallen tress of sunset hair unraveling over her temple.

A strange sensation swoops in my gut, akin to what I think butterflies might feel like if I'd ever experienced them before. Or maybe it's my gut telling me that this is a bad idea. "Wouldn't dream of it, Spitfire."

5

MY MILKSHAKE BRINGS ALL THE BOYS TO THE YARD

CALISTA

I slurp on my well-earned vanilla milkshake, purposefully cranking up the noisiness as Gage stares at me from across the table. A double cheeseburger, two large fries, a twenty-piece box of chicken nuggets, and a stack of chocolate chip cookies all sit in front of me, which isn't my usual go-to dinner after class, but hey, the idiot was paying.

Even though I doubt I'd want anything Gage has to offer me, I couldn't say no to a free meal. I can't believe he found *my* studio and wants *my* help. None of this feels real. And no, not because he's some "world-famous" hockey player, but because I was expecting the next time I saw him to be from behind a glass partition in prison.

I'm surprised he didn't sue me—and even more surprised that now he's trying to be buddy-buddy with me.

I pluck a fry from my basket and swirl it around in the frothy layer of my shake before popping it in my mouth. "Why are you staring at me?"

He blinks as if he hadn't realized he was doing it, discreetly rubbing the redness smudging his cheeks. "Maybe it's because you're manhandling your food like some kind of he-man."

"Oh, I'm sorry. I didn't realize this was a *proper* dinner. Would you like me to eat my burger with a knife and a fork?"

"You can start by slowing down and closing your mouth when you chew."

I pointedly stuff a few more fries past my lips, chewing even louder. "If you'd stop interrupting my dinner, I wouldn't need to open my mouth and talk. Sue me for being hungry. I haven't eaten since breakfast."

For some big, bad hockey player, Gage looks particularly small in the booth, or maybe that's just because his stupidly big head has deflated since our spat in the rink. Realistically, he has to be between six one and six two, and yes, I may have called him a hobgoblin, but I'm not blind. I can acknowledge a man's attractiveness without being attracted to him. And in no universe would I ever consider swapping spit with Gage Arlington. I'm guessing it's a cesspool of STDs in there.

I hate that I know his last name. I hate that I hate-stalked him after our fight. I hate that he's shoved his way back into my life even though I've tried to squash his memory like the loathsome little cockroach he is.

It's a cruel kind of hate too. Maybe even the cruelest.

Annoyance looms over his features, though I'm not sure if it's because of my disagreeableness or my messed-up eating schedule. "Maybe you should take better care of your body."

I pick up the half-wedge of my burger as grease splashes onto the stained wrapper. "Didn't hear any complaints when you were staring at my tits earlier."

This endless tug-of-war seems to be awakening some malevolent side of me that I never realized I had. If dancing doesn't work out, maybe I should become a dominatrix so I can humiliate men for a living.

Gage rolls his eyes, but I don't miss the way he evades my laser beam stare. "Don't flatter yourself. I have a lazy eye."

To my utter horror, I laugh. Not in a derisive way. Like a... *joyful*...way. I don't like that reaction.

I scarf down the last bites of my burger, relishing the sharp tang of the cheddar and the charred edges of the perfectly cooked patty. Ugh, and the Thousand Island dressing is fucking orgasmic. I feel like I'm in heaven. Minus Gage. So maybe like... lukewarm hell?

"Do you have a contract or something?" Although these pleasantries have been oh so enlightening, I really don't need to spend extra time talking to him. This is an arrangement—if I even agree to it.

His gaze finally washes over me, and my heart does this weird thump in my chest. Not a heartburn thump, either.

He scoffs. "Why would we need a contract?"

"So you can't go back on your word."

"I'm the one who approached you. I'm the one who needs your help more than you need mine. And I don't go back on my word, though I'm not surprised you'd think that."

I'm not surprised you'd think that, my head voice mimics in an eerily accurate, shrill impression of Gage.

"What's your offer, Gage? What's the incredible offer that'll make me *tolerate* you for the next three months?" I hedge, waiting for him to bait me with money or a full-paid vacation or something else materialistic that he probably has an abundance of.

I know money could be useful in my situation. It'd let me cut back on my hours at the studio, and I'd be able to buy more than just the bare necessities every month. I wouldn't have to worry about making rent or the cost of my mother's medication. But I'm not going to be some girl indebted to Gage because he has a flashy car and waves his black card around.

He steals one of my fries and throws it down his gullet before I can slap his hand away. "I'm assuming a woman such as yourself couldn't *possibly* be paid for her services?"

A smile, purely curated from the instructions of the shriveled, black heart in my chest, contorts my lips. "Even if I could, you couldn't afford me."

Gage's chuckle isn't some regular *ha-ha*; it's this deep, guttural noise that rumbles through his chest and shakes his shoulders only slightly enough to convey merriment. So, in short, a cool guy laugh. A cool guy laugh that, for some reason, agitates a zoo full of butterflies in my belly.

Why the hell are those there? I don't remember those ever being there.

And to hammer the last nail into my coffin, he leans forward on his elbows—which makes his shirt sleeves ruck up over his bulging biceps—and stares me dead in the eyes with enough intensity to blot out the movement of the outside world. "I would never need money to get a girl to like me. And I certainly won't need it when it comes to you. You'll like me all on your own when we're finished."

I swallow the ball of nerves rooted in my esophagus. "Yeah, no. There's no chance in hell you'll ever get me to like you."

Although the table permits enough distance, Gage's inclining body allows me the briefest glimpse at the forelock that tumbles against his brow bone, the tiny pockmarks on his cheeks, the plumpness of his bottom lip, and the minuscule flecks of moss scattered throughout his irises. His whole face is strangely symmetrical, with angles and ridges that would put a Michelangelo sculpture to shame.

"It's already working," he whispers, drawing out the syllables to imitate a spooky, hushed tone.

I falter, shake off the Gage pheromones trying to invade my body, then fling a French fry at his forehead. "It's not," I assert, still wrestling with the weird flutters in my stomach.

It's not.

Exasperated, hot air puffs out my nostrils. "Can you just get to the proposal already?"

Thankfully, without having to endure whatever witchcraft entranced me in my moment of weakness, Gage acquiesces with an apathetic shrug. "You were at the rink for a reason that day, right? I'm guessing you have a sibling who plays hockey? Or skates?"

"Brother. Hockey."

"Does he want to go pro?" he inquires.

I wish I could answer him. But the truth is, I don't know. Teague's never told me. Or I haven't *asked* him. I'm so focused on getting him from point A to point B that I don't even spend the time in between talking to him. Everything else in my life consumes me so much that I don't remember the last time I hung out with him…just to hang out with him.

"Yeah, maybe," I lie.

Either I'm great at compartmentalizing or Gage does, in fact, only have one brain cell, because he doesn't pick up on my dejection. I scratch my fingernail against the chipped wood of the table as shame wiggles its way beneath my skin and burrows into my bone marrow.

"I don't know if you know this, Spitfire, but I'm a *professional* hockey player. Professional with a capital *P*. I could totally help your little scoundrel work on his hockey skills. Maybe take him under my wing if I'm feeling generous. Maybe even shape him into one of the greatest players the NHL has ever seen," he proposes, prodding the tip of his incisor with his tongue. "And then the crowd will be like, 'Ahh, Gage. You're my hero. You're so talented and insanely hot. And you're good with kids!' And I'll be like, 'No need to thank me, half-naked ladies. I'm just doing my job.'"

I throw up in my mouth a little. "Okay, first off, that's the most terrifying imagery to ever exist. Second off, why do you call me Spitfire?"

A half-cocked, arrogant grin winds his lips upward. "You didn't tell me your name," he points out.

"Maybe I didn't want you to know my name," I shoot back, resisting him with equal amounts of infuriating egotism. I can feel it sear the previous shame coursing through my veins, eating away at my last remnants of humility and reducing them to nothing but ash.

"You do know what Google is, right?"

Shit.

Just swallow your pride, Cali. Pray you don't choke on it.

"It's Cali."

Gage lowers his brows, studies me, and seems to do some kind of full-body scan with his eyes. "That makes sense," he eventually comments.

I chew on the tip of my straw to relieve what I can only assume is some feverish ailment that's attacked my vulnerable body. It's the only conceivable explanation as to why I'm not remotely feeling any violence toward Gage. "What makes sense?"

He tears a chocolate chunk off one of my cookies, and my gaze gravitates to the callouses on his large hands, the contrasting slenderness of his fingers, and the goddamn valley of veins snaking up his equally impressive forearms. For a split second, flashes overrun my mind—flashes of his hand bruising my throat, flashes of his hard body pressing me against a wall, flashes of him grinding his heavy cock into my thigh as he ushers my tongue into his mouth. And the worst part of it all is that the flashes or premonitions or whatever they are don't evoke feelings of disgust within me.

The opposite, in fact.

That sardonic tone of his bleeds into full-throttle flirtation. "A beautiful name for a beautiful girl," he says, staring at me through his long, thick lashes, all while his fingers bring the melted chocolate to his lips and his tongue flicks out to lick the pads.

Realistically, I know he just stuck his fingers in his mouth instead of wiping them with a napkin because he's disgusting. Imaginatively, he was tongue-fucking his fingers in slow motion as a breeze came out of nowhere and blew his luscious hair back.

My heart begins to thrash in my chest, the lower half of me swelling with a warmth that usually only presents itself in the presence of Henry Cavill films or a high-pressure shower head. I squeeze my legs together to dull the ache between my thighs, but now I'm self-consciously wondering if Gage can detect how flustered I am. Sweaty? Check. Darting eyes? Check. Might've just soiled my panties? AGH.

What is wrong with me? I hate him. I hate his cockiness and his entitlement. I hate his... his body! His totally ugly, not-at-all-fit body.

I can hear him talking, but I can't make out what he's saying. It's like I'm trapped in lusty limbo, and I'm about to get dragged into the underworld by the claws of my sex-starved subconscious.

"—a trade. Hockey lessons in return for dance lessons," he finishes.

Disjointed, I blink a few times to right my wobbling brain, my mouth filling with an influx of saliva. "But you don't really want me to *teach* you how to dance...right?"

"Right. Just...like...teach me some flexibility exercises. Help me strengthen my hip, and I'll help your brother hone his hockey skills. If you get me playing in three months, I'll make your brother the best player in the minor league."

It's obvious what I have to do. Yeah, three months is a bit of a long time, but I'd do anything for my brother, even if that means making a deal with the devil. And, I mean, Teague could definitely benefit from some hockey lessons. It's obvious he loves it so much. I saw how upset he was after those nose-picking nimrods teased him for not being good enough. I want him to be able to prove them wrong—to show them not to underestimate an underdog. I certainly can't help him, and commercial lessons will burn another hole in my already-scorched wallet.

As much as Gage's cockiness irks me, he has a right to be arrogant. He's a famous NHL player, which means he's a talented hockey player. And I bet Teague's teammates aren't getting one-on-one lessons with a Riverside Reaper.

Gage pauses before adding, "And I'm paying you. Three hundred an hour. If you try any of that holier-than-thou shit with me again, I'll just double it."

If I was eating anything, I would've choked. Kind of wish I was so I could hunk a glob of cheeseburger right in his face. "Are you insane? I'm not some cha—"

"Charity case," he finishes, making some kind of *offensive* hand yapping gesture. "It's not charity. I would've paid whoever got lucky enough to help me."

Lucky isn't the word I'd use, but there is three hundred plus an hour on the line, so I bite my tongue. If he's so adamant that I take his money, then who am I to turn him down? I didn't want to succumb to a monetary bribe, but if he's just throwing it in there to clear his conscience, then it's hardly a bribe.

A girl knows a good deal when she sees it, even if it's smothered in arrogance and stupid cologne.

Gage holds his hand out so we can shake on our agreement, and I inch my hand out before hesitantly jerking it back.

"That's all this is, though. A transaction," I vocalize, hoping that the permanence of the words will serve as a reminder for me to keep my distance.

I can't believe I'm even saying this—because I never imagined this would be a problem—but I can't fall for Gage. Whether that be an emotional fall or a physical fall...on his dick. Between taking care of my mom and my brother, there's no room for me to have a love life. I just have to remember my responsibilities, my priorities, and that none of those include me getting up close and personal with *any* hockey player's spare stick.

It might be a trick of the light, but I swear Gage's hand wavers.

"A transaction," he repeats, stone-faced, his voice harboring a frigidity unlike the feather-softness it usually possesses.

And as I snuff out the last of the Gage fantasies feeding on my clearly delirious mindscape, my fingers clasp his, sealing our deal for the next three months.

6

HOW TO GET AWAY WITH MURDER
GAGE

When I get home from the weirdest...*dinner*...I've ever had, all the guys are waiting for me in the living room, the vague, muffled noise of a video game rumbling through the house. I live in a two-story mansion with six of my hockey teammates, most of whom have a significant other that occupies a good portion of their time. Which brings me not only to the strangeness of them all sitting together, but to them all *staring* at me as I half-drag myself through the door.

I feel like I just walked in on some weird secret meeting they were having. "Uh, hey, guys," I greet warily.

"Hey, Gage. How was dance class?" Kit asks, and it would be convincing if not for the poorly stifled snicker tacked on at the end.

Dance class. Right.

A bead of sweat cascades down my temple as I look to Fulton for help, but judging by the sanguine blush warming his entire face, I'm looking at the fucking snitch who just cost me my now-tattered masculinity.

Bristol, our captain, is splitting his focus between the screen and my utter humiliation, while Hayes is stuffing his face with popcorn and Casen is very conspicuously whispering something into his ear.

I dig my thumb into the crease between my brows, massaging the oncoming headache threatening to skewer my brain. "You told them?"

Fulton's gaze hopscotches around the room, and a nervous tick pesters his jawline. "They forced it out of me!" he squawks.

"He told us willingly," Hayes corrects.

"I did tell them willingly," Fulton sighs.

Kit, who's currently manspreading, raises his hand lazily, a pleased smirk curling up one side of his lip. "I'm the one who did the research, which I'm surprised you *didn't* do before you went."

My teeth barely act as a barricade for the growl in my throat. "I was busy."

"Weren't you late?" Casen chimes in.

Have I mentioned how much I hate my teammates sometimes? Because I do. Hate them. Sometimes.

I can't believe I made that deal with Cali. I mean, I can believe it. I just can't believe I agreed to it being purely...*transactional*. I was seconds away from sprouting a half-chub just by sitting across from her in that scrap of fabric she called a shirt. Fuck. She's even more beautiful up close. Up close, I noticed that her hair isn't just red, but that it's highlighted with marmalade streaks, that she has eighteen freckles on the bridge of her nose and one hiding on the left side of her cheek, that she smells faintly of cinnamon, and that her eyes are such a deep blue that the ocean must've used her as inspiration.

But she barely looked at me. She was curt and weird and paler than usual. Did I just force a helpless girl into some negotiation with me? Does she feel indebted to me now that I promised to make her brother a champion? (I can, and I will, but maybe I was throwing promises around too carelessly.) I do need her help, but I also don't want to make her uncomfortable. I mean, it's clear she isn't interested. I'm surprised we got through the conversation without her throwing her milkshake in my face.

How am I supposed to abide by our agreement when she's touching me in all the right places? When she's gripping my leg and outturning it for a better stretch? When her breasts are hanging mere inches from my face? When I'm so enraptured by her scent that I accidentally get turned on in the middle of a session? I'm strong, but no man is *that* strong.

And aside from her witty remarks and fast quips—which I'm already dying to hear again, even though they're usually aimed at me—her body is fucking perfect. When she was threatening to run over my foot with her car, the only thing I could think about was turning her around and bending her over the side, raveling my fist through her hair, smacking her half-exposed ass in those cheeky bottoms, then taking my cock out and teasing her dripping slit.

I've never experienced hunger like that before—so primal, so painful. I think being that close to her actually made my brain malfunction and overheat. I couldn't think; I could barely speak. She occupied every cell, nerve ending, muscle, and stream of consciousness in my weak little body. The only reason I didn't eat with her was because all those...*feelings*... were using my stomach as a bouncy house.

That was a meal between two strangers. I'm losing my shit over a meal between two strangers in public. I can't imagine myself keeping my cool when we're stuck together, in a closed room, for a full hour, using our bodies as instruments or whatever the hell you do when you dance.

This is it. This is how I die. Not some freak accident where I'm driving behind a logging truck and one of the logs goes straight through my head. Not from old age or a murderer or some flesh-eating bacteria that I picked up from an impromptu vacation to Monaco. No, I die from Cali Whatsherlastname.

HERE LIES GAGE ARLINGTON: BELOVED TEAMMATE, TALENTED HOCKEY PLAYER, SELFLESS SON

SIMPED TOO CLOSE TO THE SUN AND WENT UP IN FLAMES LIKE ICARUS

A snapping sound halts my spiral of self-doom, and the guys are still looking at me when I come to, except their brow raises of judgment are replaced with brow raises of confusion.

"Hello? Where did you just go, dude? You disassociated for like a full minute," Hayes says.

I didn't realize it had been that obvious. "I...uh..."

Kit's raven-black eyes narrow, and the thin line of his mouth slowly transforms into a grin. "Wait a second, I know that look. Dazed, slightly sweaty, unable to speak. He was thinking about a girl," he announces to the whole room.

I'm going to kill him. And then kill myself.

"How do you know?" Fulton questions, his own forehead pursed in deep thought.

"The same look I had when I saw Faye's boobs for the first time," Kit explains.

Hayes immediately pauses his popcorn chewing, looks up from the bowl, then creepily turns his head eighty degrees to the side to stare at Kit. "What the fuck did you just say?"

Kit coughs into his fist. "I meant when I saw her b-beautiful face for the first time."

"Uh-huh."

Faye is Hayes' younger sister and is currently pregnant with Kit's child. Which was not planned. Happened when Kit visited her during UPenn's welcome back rager. When Hayes heard the news, he almost fainted. Hayes is a protective guy—to put it lightly. So they pretty much had to sneak around for a full summer behind his back, but *I* knew about them. Yeah, I have stellar detective skills.

And apparently Kit's getting back at me for all the shit I put him through, because now I'm the one whose ass is burning in the hot seat.

Fulton perks up, hope twinkling in his eyes. "Did you meet someone in class? Is she cute? Is she nice?"

"It's not that big of a deal," I lie, praying that downplaying my crush for this girl will prevent all my ooey-gooey feelings from pouring out.

"That usually means it's a big deal," Bristol intervenes, the periodic click of his controller's buttons underlying the amalgam of voices. There's an animated zombie shuffling over to his character with oozing pustules and flaps of bloodied skin, and then Bristol does some karate high kick to decapitate it.

"It's not," I retort, limping over to lean against the wall since I'm guessing this interrogation will exceed the cutoff of my leg standing capabilities.

Cali's more than just "cute." Her beauty can't be conceptualized; it can't be reduced to a single word, and definitely not when it's a word that impassionate. So breathtakingly beautiful and gorgeously stunning that it causes angels to weep? I'll accept that.

And nice? Yeah, no, Cali's the meanest person I've ever met. She'd probably get along great with my asshole friends, though.

"Come on, Gage. Tell us about her," Casen goads, swiping a kernel from Hayes' popcorn bowl.

I fold my arms over my chest, trying to approach this situation with the utmost caution, scrambling to maintain a level of calm that *won't* have my friends asking more questions or sticking their noses in places they shouldn't. I'm usually an oversharer—which I've been told to stop doing when I'm pissing in public restrooms—but this time, maybe I just hold back a little. I'm getting way ahead of myself. I only learned Cali's name tonight, and already, she's infected every corner of my mind.

I don't know why, but my heart tremors and my mouth dries. "Uh, it was actually the girl from the rink," I admit, causing every head in the vicinity to turn toward me.

Bristol drops his controller, and Hayes sets his popcorn down.

"Wait, the girl you got into a fight with at practice?" Kit asks, mouth half-agape in shock.

My tongue prods the inside of my cheek. "That's the one."

"Didn't she t-bone your car?" Hayes follows up.

I curb the laugh wanting to barrel up my throat, aware of the incessantly fast and entirely unrhythmic cavort of my heart. "Something like that."

Fulton's eyes have doubled in size. "Oh my God. So she's in your dance class with you?"

"Yep."

"Is there any way you can, like, go at a different time and not run into her?"

Aside from the blush I can feel tingeing my cheeks, my anxiety has made a return visit, drenching me in sweat and stirring bubbles of nausea in my belly. "Not...really," I say vaguely, swallowing down the profuse saliva in my mouth.

"Why not?" Casen inquires, speaking for the rest of the group.

"She's the instructor," I mumble under my breath.

"What?"

An exaggerated sigh. "She's the instructor."

"Oh my God..." Fulton covers his mouth with his hands.

I don't need to go around the room to take note of everyone's expression, because I can guarantee that shock takes the lead. Only someone as unlucky as me would seriously find himself in this situation and then *voluntarily* make it harder for himself by asking her to rehabilitate him.

Kit's quiet for a second, and then he keels over in obnoxious laughter. "That's...holy...I...that's incredible," he wheezes.

Fucker. Where's my crutch? I'm going to shove it up his ass and make him rotate.

"Yeah, yeah. We get it. Gage fucked up. Again."

"It's not like you have a thing for this chick, do you?" Kit manages between wiping the tears from his eyes and the breath-stealing guffaws rocking his chest.

"What? No! Of course not," I answer a little too quickly.

Hayes offers me a sympathetic grimace. "You can't just find another dance studio?"

I dial my focus on the frayed hem of my jacket sleeve, picking at the pigeon-gray strands with my bitten fingernails. "Not really. And, uh, we kind of made an arrangement with each other."

Why am I still talking? Gage, stop talking! This is embarrassing!

Bristol squints. "That sounds..."

"A SEX arrangement?" Fulton screeches, so pale that he looks like he'll be taken out by a light gust of wind.

As much as I present myself as a playboy, I'm not. I'm not fucking a girl every single night. I'm not flirting with the shortest skirts or highest heels. I'm not keeping tally marks on my wall of how many pussies I've "conquered." And because it's been a hot second since I've been with anyone, me and Fulton don't talk about our...extracurricular activities. Not to mention that Fulton has the sexual prowess of a scarecrow: stiff, unsettling, and should be posted up in a field far away from women. I'm pretty sure Hayes thought he was gay for the longest time because he never talks to girls.

The day my boy finally gets his cherry popped, I'm buying a cake from the store and writing YOU GOT FUCKED in red frosting on it.

"God, no. No. She's helping me with my hip, and I'm giving her brother hockey lessons," I divulge, finally mustering the courage to tip my head up and take in the unblinking faces surrounding me.

Casen scrubs a weary hand down his stubbled jaw. "I feel like I'm going to regret asking this, but helping your hip...how?"

I open my mouth to shut down *any* possible alternative explanations, but Kit beats me to it when he jumps up from the couch and humps the air, all while employing his best pornographic moans. "Oh, yes, Gage! Faster! Harder!"

Yep, that guy's gonna be a father in seven months.

Unfortunately, that scenario will never happen for as long as I live. There's a better chance of me breaking my other hip flexor than Cali ever wanting to have sex with me.

"Stretches," I grouse, not wanting to elaborate. I hate being indisposed. I would've resorted to violence way sooner if it wasn't for this brace hindering me.

Three months of stretches with the most beautiful girl that has ever graced this planet, touching me at every little convenience. I may be a competitive hockey player, but this is one game that I'm going to lose.

7

CHICKS BEFORE DICKS
CALISTA

"**T**his is him?" my best friend—and fellow dance instructor—Hadley asks, turning her phone around to show me a picture of Gage. And not just a professional headshot of him in his hockey jersey. No, she somehow managed to find the sexiest, most erotic picture of him posing without a shirt on as he seductively sucks frosting off his finger.

I don't know why that exists. I don't know how she found it. But it's currently singeing my optic nerves.

"Yes," I mumble as I lean over my outstretched leg, feeling the satisfactory burn in my right hamstring.

She's in a butterfly stretch to warm up for her pole dancing class, and she's staring a bit *too* intently at the pixelated screen. "Cal, he's hot as fuck. And that's coming from someone who isn't straight."

No! Argh. Why couldn't she say that he was a hideously deformed monster? Hadley's not one for sugarcoating, either. She's had plenty of opinions about my exes in the past, which is why they're *exes*.

I avert my gaze from the haunting picture, pasting on a rictus grin. "He's fine."

"He's better than fine. This guy could run me over and I'd thank him."

I'll run him over instead, free of charge.

"Uh-huh."

"And you said he was a hockey goalie?" she exclaims, bending all the way at the hip so that her folded legs are flush against the ground.

I switch to my other leg for a side stretch, warring with a muscle ache, and now, thanks to Gage's too-straight teeth and sexy grin, a stomachache. "So?"

She bumps me with her shoulder. "Sooo, goalies are really flexible."

I snort. "Not this one."

"They also have a lot of stamina," she adds, giving me one of her terribly coordinated winks.

Once I've stretched the life out of my thighs, I bring one leg behind me and fall into the splits, needing some real pain to distract me from this volatile pool of emotion welling in my chest. Another pro-Gage comment and it'll erode my bones like acid. "Why are you trying to pimp him out to me?"

Hadley gives me one of her famous *oh, sweetie* looks. "Maybe because you deserve to have fun for once? Let loose? Think about something other than work and your home life?"

"I can do that without getting in bed with someone," I insist, bouncing slightly against the wooden floorboards to test the give of my splits.

"True. But it's *sooo* much more fun if you do it in bed with someone," she sing-songs.

I'd give anything to have Hadley's carefree disposition. She's adventurous, spontaneous, open-minded. She always says yes, no matter how absurd the question is. She lives her life to the fullest with no regrets, and she has the best stories to tell me because of it. If she wasn't committed to three classes every week, she'd hop on the next flight to Barbados and live in a bungalow with whatever she could fit in one of those hobo sacks. She's also a big advocate for polyamory, which has helped with her mood in more ways than one.

"I just don't have time," I defend, although I don't miss the tiny seed of longing planting itself in the pit of my belly, trying to spread its roots in a restricted square of nutrient-deprived soil. That's what I am. A dying plant in a too-small pot. Never given the room to grow. Always destined to wither.

I'd love to have free time when worries didn't torment my mind. I'd love to feel confident in where I'm at, to feel stable in my career choice, to feel happy with the decisions I've made so far in my life. But that's a long way from ever happening. And although I may complain once in a while about my familial obligations, the structure of that routine and the relationships I've nurtured is what keeps me moored.

Hadley's optimism is like a shot of espresso at five in the morning. "Wouldn't you rather do the splits on *someone* rather than the floor of your studio?"

That's...that's preposterous. Hilarious, but preposterous.

"Please. If I wanted to bounce on a shrimp dick, I'd call my ex."

Hadley glances one last time at her phone before chuckling. "Oh, honey. Gage Arlington does *not* have a shrimp dick."

I give her what I hope is a deadpan look. I desperately need something—anything—else to occupy the topic of this morning's discussion. It's one thing to think about dicks while I'm bumping my goods against the floor in the splits. It's another thing to think about Gage Arlington's probably massive, veiny, girthy dick while my vagina is very much splayed out in a come-hither pose.

"How would you know? You secretly seeing him?" I jest, quickly tucking my legs back underneath me.

She fans herself. "No, but look at him, Cal. That man is a god. He has a six pack. His biceps are the size of my head. His quads are probably enormous. I bet he has a Jacob's ladder too."

Great. Now I'm imagining Gage splitting me open on his nine-inch-long, *pierced* dong. He seems dominant in the bedroom. The kind of dominant that would watch me come before he even touches himself. He'd make me work for his cock, make sure I'm stretched to accommodate his hulking size. I'd ride his abs until I made a mess of both of us—until I turned a strong-willed god into a whimpering mortal. I'd undulate my hips and rub my leaking pussy over each muscled ridge while my fingernails engraved bloody marks into his chest. His stomach would contract as I started to gush onto him, coating each curve and dip in a sheen of arousal. He'd throw his head back against the mattress and rough out praise, all while trying to keep his grip tightly secured on my hips. And then, after he massaged the flesh there, his touch would travel to my breast, torquing my nipple to a fully erect state with a twist of his long, nimble fingers. He'd buck his hips to seek any last promise of friction, his neglected cock prodding the slit of my ass, demanding relief after bearing too much pressure. And he'd beg me to help him, to take his dick in my cunt or my ass, to...

Hadley's voice continues to resonate in my head, and it dawns on me that I was just fantasizing about Gage. *Me.* I was the one fantasizing. About *him*. Do you know how fucked up that is? Oh my God. I'm a disgrace.

"You were totally just thinking about him." She does a little shimmy with her shoulders, and as much as I want to fake gag and brush her off, the ear-to-ear beam on her face is fucking contagious.

I suck in a deep, lung-expanding breath, already exhausted with all the mental gymnastics I've done before noon. I *was* thinking about him. And when I was, nothing else in the world mattered. Nothing else existed. I didn't feel this foreboding sense of distress; I didn't feel like I was biding time until the next chore had to be done. I was living in the moment, unfettered, and someone was taking care of *me* for a change. It was my own slice of golden-gated heaven. I don't remember the last time I ever felt so…at peace.

"Only because you haven't stopped talking about him," I counter.

Hadley mimics a zip over her peachy lips. "Just consider it. You guys will be working together for three months. You'd be amazed at what close proximity and sexual frustration can do to a person."

~

WHEN I ENTER THE REAPERS' rink, I make a mental note to myself to start packing a puffer jacket, because walking onto the ice in skimpy stripper attire is probably grounds for banishment or something. Or at most, total humiliation for younger brothers.

My class ended early today, so I'm surprisingly on time for once. And Teague will be surprised too, seeing how he hasn't looked anywhere in my direction in anticipation of my arrival.

I start to carefully shuffle my way toward the ice, waddling like a penguin while simultaneously being self-conscious about how much of my butt is showing, and that's when I feel a body displace the air beside me.

"You're going to freeze," Gage says, lumbering up to me with a lull in his gait and a hip brace over his pants. He's dressed in his warm-looking jersey and grey sweats, and I glance over at the practice happening a few feet away. He must've been watching it before he *unfortunately* caught my eye.

I *am* freezing, but I'll never let him know that.

"I'm perfectly fine, thank you." I turn my nose up defiantly.

"You have goose bumps."

"I do not—" I look down at my arms, which, in fact, flaunt a wealth of small bumps. "I just have naturally bumpy arms."

Gage shakes his crop of chestnut hair, cutting me off with a dart of his body and halting me in my tracks. His half-lidded eyes rake down the length of my figure before a mischievous simper splits his lips. "If you're not cold, then why are your nipples poking out like torpedoes?"

I gasp and cross my arms over my breasts, not bothering with confirming Gage's observation because it definitely feels like my nipples are going to chip off in this temperature.

"Fuck off. I'm just here to pick up my brother," I grit through my teeth, trying to make my way past him.

I can't. Dude has mile-wide shoulders and inhuman reflexes.

"You're not getting on the ice, Cali."

Excuse me?

I drop my arms to my sides, more than ready to shove my way past his mountain of a body. "I am."

"If you find some way to bypass me—which I doubt—then you need to cover up," he growls.

"Are you policing my body based on the fact that you, as a man, feel threatened by my lack of clothing?"

"What? No! I don't want you getting sick." The lines of his naturally hardened face soften upon his admission, highlighting the faintest crinkles bordering his eyes, and the concern in his tone starts to slowly whittle away at my reinforced walls.

His voice has a richness to it that's foreign to my ears, sometimes thick around certain syllables, sometimes grated into a gravelly drawl that continuously sparks my synapses. And right now, it's warm in all the right places. The kind of warm like the soft glow of the sun at midday as it casts buttery rays through a car window, lulling me into a soundless slumber.

"I'm not going to get sick," I argue, and if it wasn't for the shiver that just rolled through me, I probably would've gotten away with it too.

Gage grumbles out a string of curses before shucking his jersey off and unveiling the tight-fitted long-sleeve clinging to ropes of grabbable muscle. Hand extended, his jersey a peace offering, he shakes it in front of me. "Take it."

I push his arm away. "Yeah, no. I'm not putting on your smelly ass jersey."

He throws his head back—dramatically, mind you—and expels a long groan that has his breath misting into the frost-blanketed atmosphere. "This is me asking nicely," he threatens, something dark passing through his eyes.

Asking nicely? What is he, a mobster? We're in public. And Gage doesn't have the balls to do anything.

"O-kay. Sure, buddy."

Before I get the chance to move, Gage throws his jersey over my head like some kind of amateur kidnapping attempt, yanking it past my chin until it billows into place on my body. It dwarfs my arms and ends halfway at my thigh, covering every needed aspect, and surprisingly, it doesn't smell like the earring backs I was expecting it to. I'm not saying that it smells like Boy Scout wishes or anything. It smells like...*him*. A clean sort of musk with a masculine undertone that I want to inject into my veins or huff like whiteboard markers.

Finally, Teague glances over in my direction, lighting up as he waves at me.

Satisfied with my obedience, Gage turns around to wave back at Teague. "Cute kid."

Aside from the ever-present desire to choke Gage, contentment seems to settle over me at the thought of the two of them bonding over hockey. "Yeah, he is," I agree quietly.

Maybe Gage is the role model Teague needs. God knows I'm not. I may look like I have my shit together, but I don't. I can't believe I'm complimenting him, but Gage actually seems...levelheaded for a twenty-something. He's already dominating in his career, which is more than I can say for myself. It shows that he's committed, and that's something I wish I was better at being. I have one foot in and one foot out of Teague's life, when all Teague needs is for me to be a hundred percent in.

Teague skates over to us, that fire helmet of his sticking out like a sore thumb, a megawatt smile plumping up his cheeks. "Holy shit. You're Gage Arlington!" he squeals, hockey stick gripped in his little fist as he bobbles on his feet.

"T, don't say 'shit,'" I chastise.

Gage chuckles, squatting down as best as he can to be eye level with my brother. "Hey, Little Man. That's me. And you are?"

"I'm Teague!"

Look, I know the parameters of my Grinch heart don't allow for a lot of love room, but seeing Gage's big, burly body next to Teague's small one makes weird, tingling warmth blossom in my stomach. And the worst part is, no matter how hard I try to extinguish it, that fire remains lit like a trick candle.

"It's nice to meet you, Teague. Your sister has told me a lot about you," Gage says, the incandescent twinkle in his eye accompanied by a knee-weakening grin.

Teague's jaw practically hits the ground. "You know my sister?"

"I do. We met in this rink, actually."

I don't bother to cover my pig-snort of laughter. *Actually, Teague, this is the colossal dickwad who blocked us in. And the colossal dickwad whose car I destroyed on a justified rampage.*

"Really?! Cali, you didn't tell me you knew Gage!" My brother, bless his heart, is too young to be very observant of underlying tension.

Gage wobbles to a stance and slings his arm over my shoulder, pulling me into the side of his body before I have the chance to bat him away. "Your sister's just being humble. Knowing someone as famous as me must be exhausting."

My whole face puckers in revulsion despite my traitorous vagina yawning awake after a yearlong hibernation. He's so warm that I can feel the heat sizzling off his body like a desert-warped mirage, even with the layers of polyester swaddling his physique. And he's...hard. Not, like, his penis. His body. I could probably use him as a makeshift raft if I were ever stranded on an island in the middle of the ocean. That's if I didn't eat him beforehand to stay alive.

Teague's comically large eyes zigzag between the two of us, head angled innocently. "Are you my sister's boyfriend?" he asks, hope shining through his tone.

I choke on my own saliva, and it nearly results in me doubling over in a hacking fit. The audacity my brother has! *Is he my boyfriend?* What—what kind of question is that? I'm a ten, and Gage is at best a five point five. Maybe a six on good days. I clearly need to take my brother back to the eye doctor.

Thanks to Gage's stupid, fat mouth, he manages to answer at the same time I do.

"No!" I shriek a little too loudly.

"Not yet," Gage replies with a smirk, that pesky arm of his slowly skimming down my shoulder and nesting in the curve of my side. I don't miss the grip of his fingers on my skin, the urgency there, the promise of more when his roaming touch unlocks full access to every vulnerable crevice of my body.

Not yet? Is he serious?

I turn my head to face him, biting out through clenched teeth and a gum-showing smile, "Never happening."

He fully ignores me, pinching the fat of my hip in a nonverbal *yeah, right.*

I disengage myself from his grasp, choosing to change the subject before I projectile vomit all over the floor. "Teague, Gage is gonna help you work on your hockey skills. He's been so...*generous*...as to offer you free hockey lessons. Because he's *such* a good guy."

Please note the sarcasm.

My brother's vibrating with so much excitement that I expect him to rocket around the room like a deflating helium balloon. "Really???"

"That's right, kiddo. Coach Gage is at your service."

This is the happiest I've seen Teague in a long time. There's a lively spark glistening in his eyes—one that has been dimmed as a result of my unintentional neglect, and one that I was afraid I'd never see again. And Gage was the last person I ever expected to unearth it.

Teague bulldozes into Gage, wrapping his short arms around Gage's tree-trunk torso. "Thank you! Thank you! Thank you!" he chants, squeezing the air out of his new instructor as he simultaneously jumps up and down.

Wary of his hip, Gage returns my brother's embrace with equal enthusiasm, nearly swallowing his small frame.

I'm surprised at how...natural...Gage looks with my brother. Seeing as he isn't good with adults, I didn't think he'd be good with kids. But I was wrong.

A—dear God—compliment sits on my tongue, waiting to stroke Gage's already inflated ego, but I'm thankfully cut off when one of his teammates glides over to us, helmet gone and black hair curling down to his nape. He has a scruffy lumberjack look to him, with an impressively full beard for someone who I'm guessing is still in his early twenties.

"Gage, Coach says to get your ass back on the bench," he relays, leaning his chin on the butt of his hockey stick. He's got thickset shoulders just like Gage, and I'm beginning to think that Hulk-like muscle mass is a requirement for all hockey players.

"Yeah, yeah. Tell him I'm coming," Gage gripes.

And then, Mountain Man's dark eyes coast over me. "Shit.

I'm sorry. How rude of me. I'm D," he drawls, slipping his glove off to extend his giant bear paw of a hand.

Oh my God. He's tall, dark, and handsome. He's like a tortured, chiseled model pulled from the cover of some dark romance. And his name? I've never been one for mystery, but fuck, I think this guy's about to change my mind. He's one of the most attractive men I've ever seen, and my arm moves of its own accord when I go to shake his hand.

He brings my knuckles to his pillow-soft lips—the whiskers of his facial hair tickling my skin—and plants a kiss on the back of my hand. Lust prickles low in my belly at the way his mouth brands me, and I go brain-dead for a few seconds, trying to digest the fact that a man as perfect as him would be flirting with someone who's wearing two mismatched shoes and currently sweating through her deodorant.

"Calista," I reply, starry-eyed.

"*Un nom magnifique pour une fille aussi magnifique que le paradis lui-même*," he says in the most delicious French accent, calloused fingers still in acquaintance with my trembling hand.

HE'S FRENCH? Pinch me. I mean, I have no idea what he just said, but he could've called me a disgusting pig and I still would've swooned.

His dreamy eyes, the color of coffee grounds under the fluorescents, flick down to the jersey I forgot I was wearing. "Are you and Gage...?"

I look down in an effort to understand what he's insinuating, and I feel my cheeks boil with embarrassment. "No! No. God, no. We're—he's...just friends," I hurl out, instantly yanking my arm back so I can free myself from Gage's jersey. My arms flap about as they wiggle out of the sleeves, and my ears get caught on the neckline for a humiliating second, but I eventually pop my head out and throw it in Gage's general direction.

Remember when I said I had priorities? Consider those

priorities tabled for the time being. Hadley was right. I deserve to let loose and have fun, and if that means getting this handsome Sam Hartman lookalike's number, then so be it.

I'm pretty sure Gage mumbles something from behind the wad in his face, but my focus abandoned him a long time ago. In fact, I forgot he was even here.

"In that case, I hope I'm not overstepping if I ask you out to dinner tonight," D proposes, flashing me a smile with teeth so straight and white that they belong on a poster in a dentist's office.

Every inch of me suddenly grows unbearably hot, and my heart's roaring so loudly that I'm afraid he can hear it. "Overstepping? No, of course not. That sounds amazing. I'd love to," I ramble.

"Hey, hey, now," Gage interjects, inserting his stupid body into the one conversation that *doesn't* concern him. "Unfortunately, Dilbert, *Calista* here already has plans with me tonight."

I snap my head at him, growling under my breath, "No, I don't."

"Of course we do, Spitfire. First date, remember?"

I'm going to kill Gage. I'm going to buy four horses, have him drawn and quartered like back in the medieval days, then bury his dismembered limbs where nobody will ever find them.

Dilbert blinks owlishly, same with Teague, confusion marring both of their faces.

"Nope, definitely never agreed to that."

"Sure, you did. You must've forgotten." Gage does the wise thing and puts his jersey back on, but then he does the unwise thing and hangs his arm over my shoulder again like we're... we're...*dating*. "Sorry, Dil, but my girl is off the market. We just haven't gone public with it yet. You understand, don't you? Don't want the news taking away from the season."

"Uh, right..." Dilbert trails, sheepishly scratching the back of his neck. "Sorry, man. Didn't know she was your girl."

I'm about to protest, but Gage uses all his strength to pull me into the side of his body, making me squeak in surprise. My cheek squishes into his shoulder, and even though I'm resisting, his ironclad grip has me immobilized. Stupid Gage and the six inches he has over me. Stupid Gage and his buff arms. Stupid Gage and the annoying way his lips twist into a self-satisfied grin.

"No worries, dude."

Hackles rising, I harden my voice with a steel edge. "Gage..."

He pats me on my head, making my already mussed hair frizz up to new lengths. "Gonna take her out to her favorite Italian restaurant. You know...the one that has a live octopus tank. Heard the hosts check your bank account numbers before you can make a reservation since the food is so expensive. Authentic Italian and such."

He's talking to D like I'm not even here! And yes, I was doing the same thing, but this is—ugh!

Not only has Dilbert turned a flattering shade of scarlet, but he looks as uncomfortable as I feel.

Sweat stains his brow, and he shifts his weight between his skates. "Oh, that's..."

Gage cuts him off, doing that hand privacy thing where he's supposed to be *secretly* addressing him even though I can still hear every word he's saying. "She loves her lasagna. But we have to ask for the vegan ricotta. Cheese makes her gassy."

"Gage!" I smack his chest hard, making him wince.

"Anyways, tell Coach I'll be there in a second." Gage dismisses him with a flap of his hand, baring his teeth in a fake, patronizing smile.

Dilbert—poor, beautiful, stupid Dilbert—nods before skating away sullenly.

I finally manage to wrench myself from Gage's arm, shouting helplessly after Dilbert, mentally weeping when said shouts get masked by the idle chatter of the other rink inhabitants. "I'm not lactose intolerant! And we're *not* together!"

Gage fist-bumps my little brother in victory, and I'm pretty much a hair width away from throat chopping him in front of an entire horde of kids. He's so unbothered that his cocky grin stays intact, every muscle in his body so unbelievably relaxed that I can feel that one vein in my forehead bulge out.

"What the hell?" I snarl. "Why would you do that?"

He shrugs indifferently. "Need an emergency dance lesson. Tonight."

I bet you a million dollars that he doesn't. I can't believe this. He sabotaged me! Embarrassed me! Oh, he's going to pay. I'm going to make him pay. When will he get the hint that nothing will ever happen between us?

"Eight o'clock. Don't be late," he purrs as he starts walking backwards, aiming that hubris at me and finishing it off with an infuriating, blood-boiling wink.

8

THIS IS NOTHING LIKE FOOTLOOSE
GAGE

Fucking Dilbert. He better watch his back during practice. And games. And when he's home alone. Yes, I know Cali isn't mine, but jealousy kicked me in the stomach the moment I saw them talking. The way she was all googly eyes for him, the way he smiled at her. The two of them would've looked good together. Dilbert with his freakishly muscular physique, Cali with her gorgeous...*everything*. Jesus. I'm weak for her. Hopelessly gone.

I did what I had to, okay? I'm not proud of it. But it's better than breaking my fist across his face.

Considering I basically forced her into giving me a dance lesson, I don't know what to expect. She was definitely pissed earlier, and I doubt that she's calmed down in the span of a few hours. If I'm lucky, I'll still have my balls by the end of the night.

Since my request was an "emergency," the dance studio wasn't available for us to use on such short notice, so we've agreed that we'll be working in the privacy of her home. Which now seems like both a good and bad thing.

I stand outside of her Halloween-decorated door, taking in

the sight of the pumpkin string lights and the welcome mat that has an ornate Ouija board design on it. My fist hovers over the slightly worn partition, but my nerves halt me from announcing my presence. Sweat dampens the back of my neck, seeming to instruct the rest of the moisture in my body to coalesce on my tacky skin. I can feel it seeping through the loose-fitting shirt I threw on, and a quick glance at my armpits confirms that I'm already rocking some unsightly rings. My heartbeat's erratic, and my stomach's rolling so violently that the burrito bowl I had earlier might make a reappearance all over her doorstep. I've never been this nervous about anything in my life. Not playoffs, not live interviews, not my high school SATs, not that ten-minute oral presentation I had to give in Spanish.

I don't get nervous. I'm a go-with-the-flow kind of guy. In fact, any nerves trespassing on my turf will get choked out on sight. But an hour with Cali—the devil herself—bending my legs like a Barbie doll and probably yelling insults at me the entire way through has me rethinking this whole arrangement. Hockey be damned. Three months off the ice sucks, sure, but getting a "dance lesson" from the one girl who's preoccupied my mind is a new kind of torture. Not only has she been living in my brain rent-free, but she's moved in, furnished the place, and doesn't plan on leaving anytime soon.

I'm not sure if she has secret security cameras somewhere, but she opens the door a moment later despite me not knocking, narrowed eyes drifting languidly over my body.

"You look like shit," she says, tightening the beige belt around her hourglass figure.

She's wearing an oversized trench coat for some reason, and I may be stupid, but I'm not an idiot. Trench coats aren't dance appropriate. She's hiding something.

I cluck my tongue. "At least I'm not smuggling three raccoons."

I know I literally just saw her a few hours ago, but she's somehow gotten even more beautiful—if it's even possible. The darkness of the night brings out the vibrancy of her autumn hair, and the electric blue of her eyes pulls me in like an unforgiving tide, bringing my attention to the subtle brush of mascara on her lashes and the neighboring smatter of freckles.

"In case you hadn't noticed, it's fall. It's cold as balls, and people wear coats when it's cold out."

"Not inside their house."

Cali taps her bare foot impatiently against the hardwood floor, staring down at the imaginary watch on her wrist. "You've just wasted a full minute of our hour-long session. Want to make it two?"

"No," I hiss through my teeth.

She makes a little *hmph* sound—one that makes my dick twitch in my sweatpants—and then she begrudgingly angles her body to let me in.

When I stagger through the door, I see that she's transformed her living room into a makeshift dance space, with her coffee table, couch, and various potted plants pushed up against the wall. It looks like a Halloween bomb went off in her house.

Tones of orange and brown encompass the quaint area as patchwork pillows and a checkered quilt decorate her otherwise plain couch. Bat decals scale her wall, including the occasional glittery spiderweb strewn in the corner. Pumpkins varying in size and color border her ivory hearth, and old-fashioned candles stay propped up on the mantle, along with twine-wrapped bundles of artificial wheat stalks. And if I didn't think her cinnamon smell was addicting enough, it's everywhere. Walking into her house is the equivalent of voluntarily sticking my foot in a bear trap.

"Very festive," I observe, keeping my arms glued to my sides to disguise how painfully obvious my nerves are.

She hums to herself, picking a piece of candy corn from the metallic bowl on her coffee table and throwing it into her mouth. "Halloween's the best time of year. Scary movies, pumpkin patches, haunted houses, family-sized bags of candy."

I want to taste the residual sugar coating her lips when I kiss her, want to drag my tongue over hers as I fist her hair and pull it hard enough to subdue her, to finally force her to look me in the eyes and tell me that she doesn't feel the chemistry between us. I want her so fucking badly. Every part of her—the good, the bad, the messy. I don't care what hoops I have to jump through for her.

She slinks closer to me, runs her chrome fingernail over the ledge of my shoulder, then stuns me with a stare made from sin.

"Will I get a trick tonight, Gage? Just like that stunt you pulled at the rink earlier?" she purrs, dousing me in her spice-spiked aroma and batting her lashes. "Or will you be a good boy and let me give you a treat?"

I—dear God. I'm not going to last the full hour. I'm not going to last just being her friend. Fuck, I don't even think she considers us friends. We're more like business associates. My self-control is at an all-time low, and I'm positive that if she continues touching me, I'm going to blow a load in my pants. And that's *definitely* not dance appropriate.

My brain's currently undergoing a system failure. "You—I—"

Her index finger immediately smushes against my lips, shushing me. "Admit it, Gage. The only reason you called this 'emergency' dance lesson was because you didn't want me going on a date tonight."

Duh.

My cheeks thaw with a warm blush, and my eyes zero in on the most unsexy, yet somehow sexy, part of her body pressing into me. I mean, it's pretty obvious that I didn't want her going on that date. Am I man enough to admit it?

I wait a few beats, seeing what she might do, then I make the dumbest, most unsound decision and decide not to own up to the truth. I panicked, okay? And maybe I was too proud to admit that I was wrong—or more likely, that Cali was right. It would've given her more reason to resist the attraction between us.

I nip at her finger, and she pulls her arm back with a growl.

"My hip's been flaring up today. I cashed in on our arrangement. That's all," I insist, praying that she doesn't touch me again…or that she does. Or, fuck, I don't know! I have no idea what's going on with me. My belly's full of goddamn butterflies whenever she's around.

"Liar," she spits. "You pretended we were a couple."

"Because Dilbert's a creep!"

Not true. He's one of the nicest guys I've ever met, and therefore I hate him.

"Why do you care who I potentially date or not? It's none of your business."

My heart, now bruised from each punch of her words, plummets to the soles of my shoes. "Maybe because I'm trying to be a good friend and look out for you. Why do you feel the need to fight me every step of the way?"

An angry notch appears between her brows, and she ignores my question. "Fine. If you're not going to play fair, then neither will I."

I heave a sigh, irritation beginning to override the lust operating my senses. "What are you talking about?"

And in that moment, as ridiculous as it sounds, I see my life flash before my eyes. Real, cold, gripping fear engulfs me, pumping a tranquilizer through my bloodstream and holding my once-applauded arrogance hostage. I don't know how or why, but I think I just made the biggest mistake of my life.

"If we're such *good* friends, then you won't mind me getting into something more comfortable for our dance lesson today," she retaliates, her long, slender fingers settling over the strip of fabric around her waist.

Oh, please. Does she really think that showing me her bra and booty shorts is going to make me suddenly buckle under the pressure and admit my true feelings for her? It might've worked the first few times I saw her, but now I'm used to seeing that much of her skin. Consider my dick unbothered.

I fight off a smug smile. "Go ahead. Be as comfortable as you'd like."

Cali hits me back with a smile of her own, and then she unhurriedly unravels her coat, letting it hang open and slide off her shoulders like a river current rolling over mossy stone.

"Jesus Christ!" I half-scream, unsure as to why I feel the need to cover her with my body. There's nobody around…at least I hope not.

Because Cali isn't in her usual bra and shorts. No, she's in a bright red lingerie set that barely covers her breasts and pussy. A lace bra—bra being a generous term—hugs her large tits, and a flimsy triangle of fabric sheathes her cunt, a thin string riding high up on her hips. She also has matching thigh garters on, which squeeze the plushness of her legs and attach to a pair of see-through stockings. So, to sum it up, she's showing so much skin that she'd probably get arrested if she were to walk downtown right now.

"Are you fucking crazy?" I growl, averting my gaze to the best of my ability, yet the heat infusing every inch of my body is making it increasingly difficult to uphold my gentleman act. My dick's so not unbothered. In fact, it's seconds away from drooling pre-cum into my pants and affirming what Cali already knows to be true.

She blinks at me innocently. "What? This is what I always wear when I practice at home."

"You're telling me you practice in your lingerie when Teague's home?"

"Teague's at a friend's house right now. Plus, this gives my dancing a more...*authentic*...feel. You said it wouldn't be a problem."

"It's not," I croak, willing the tightness in my groin to subside, desperately trying to focus on anything other than the angry throbbing of my cock in my sweats. I can't run behind something to cover it. There's basically nothing I can do to make this situation less embarrassing than it already is.

Why can't I just tell her the truth? Because I'm afraid to lose her?

Okay, that's actually a very good reason.

But maybe I won't lose her. I mean, I've made it pretty obvious I like her, right? And she hasn't run for the hills yet.

Her lips twitch into a devilish grin. "Good. Then let's get started with your first warmup. On your back, Gage."

I laugh. "I'm flattered, Cali. But I'm a man who needs a little bit of foreplay before we get to the good stuff."

"If you don't get on your back, I'll just have to make you."

"Kinky. Is that a promise?" I step closer to her—bad idea, I know—and trace my finger along the hinge of her jaw, stopping at her chin and tipping it up. I don't have to lean down much to fan my breath over her champagne-pink lips, and thanks to the excessive Halloween LED lights everywhere, it's very obvious to discern when she blushes.

And what a fucking sight it is.

Her chest inflates with an unsure breath, and I watch as the column of her throat wavers with a swallow. Her gaze is weighted as it roves over my finger, lingering before she briefly glances at my mouth. This is the closest I've ever been to her, and she hasn't bitten my head off yet. This is unprecedented. An accomplishment like this should be memorialized in a museum.

Cali inches the tiniest bit closer to me, enveloping me in that cinnamon perfume or body wash that makes me absolutely feral, and I mistakenly think she's about to kiss me before she stops short and looks down.

It's then that I realize my, um, *uninvited guest*, hasn't gotten the memo to shrink into its sadder, less impressive state. My immodest dick budges against her stomach, straining the material of my sweats, and I'm crossing my fingers that I didn't saturate the front during her strip tease.

"I can explain," I rush out.

She lifts a perfectly plucked brow.

"I can't explain."

"Admit it, Gage," she orders. "You were jealous."

The gloating, all-knowing tone in her voice makes my gut sour. "Was not," I parry, adjusting the front of my pants and scraping together the leftover fragments of my dignity.

"You want to know what I think?" she whispers, dragging her manicured finger down the clothed center of my pecs, through the muscled divide of my abs, and stopping inches above my erection. "I think that you couldn't *stand* the idea of Dilbert treating me to a candlelit dinner...complimenting my dress...running his hand along the outside of my thigh in a disguised attempt to feel my skin. And I definitely think that you couldn't stand the idea of me bouncing on his *giant cock* in the back seat of his car while I moan his name when I come."

I lose it. Simple as that. There's no attempt to salvage any steadfastness. I lose my fucking mind.

Something possessive coils in the pit of my stomach, rearing its head back to strike, and I nearly take my hip out when I push Cali up against the wall, one hand encircling her wrist and the other holding the sides of her neck. Her breath hitches from the impact, tits rising and falling in a film of sweat, and her whole body shudders underneath my touch.

A low growl claws up my throat. "The only name you're ever going to moan is mine."

I can feel her pulse palpitating under my fingertips. The smallest, expertly placed pinch can make her heart thump like a kick drum. Her life in my hands for a change.

"And if he touched you, I would fucking kill him."

"Because you want me," she finishes, staring directly into my eyes, pools of sapphire melting the very legs I'm standing on.

"More than anything in this world, Spitfire," I finally confess.

9
A GLUTTON FOR PUNISHMENT
GAGE

My lips smash onto hers before my brain can leash me, and she takes only a second to return my eagerness, mauling me with the same desperation and urgency.

Something changes inside of me. I don't know what, but I can feel it.

With my dick nestled snugly against her belly, I release her wrist from my hand and opt to intertwine our fingers, using her to steady myself despite the wall supporting both our weights. As the kiss escalates from timid touches to a feverish flurry of tongues, I free the groan trapped in my chest and roll my pelvis over her sexy, red-clothed center. Her other hand comes up to enmesh in my hair, pulling the strands harshly enough to leave a buzz along my scalp.

I slowly unpeel my fingers from around her throat, slithering them down to her panties, where I take the string on her waist and snap it against her flesh.

"If I were to slip my hand beneath your underwear, how wet would you be?" I ask, rubbing the frilly lace between my pads, inching closer to that perfect pussy of hers.

"Drier than my grandmother's ashes," she says, hiking her leg up the side of my hip and draping it over my ass. I trade the thread of our fingers to support the underside of her thigh, scoring my nails into the fat there.

Our mouths are still close, so I take advantage of the space and rake her bottom lip between my teeth. When I let go, it snaps back with a *pop*.

"You're lying."

She furls her fist tighter in my hair. "You're overconfident."

"It's endearing," I quip breathlessly.

"It's annoying."

She's such a brat. And it's so fucking hot. She's enjoying this just as much as I am, but she'd never admit it. Her dilated pupils, the goose bumps riddling her skin, her pebbled nipples, the slight flush of her face.

There's a delicious stretch in my lower abdomen, intensified by the pressure mounting in my balls, and I spurt pre-cum into my boxers, needing to thrust my dick inside of her more than I need my next breath of air.

Even though her leg's strangling the life out of my hip, the pleasure outweighs the pain. "*Calista*," I whisper, tonguing the roof of my mouth to get that sensual *L*, testing how incredible her full name sounds when it's recited in the husky timbre of my voice.

She ruts her hips into the air, begging for me to tend to that unbearable ache between her legs—the spot I *know* is leaking for me. "Only my friends get to call me Calista," she hisses under her breath.

With her waist angled, the gusset of her thong nearly splits her clit in half, and I run my finger over her exposed, puffy lips, feeling her shiver under my touch. "That's right. We aren't friends, are we? You hate me."

A growl rattles in her ribs. "Yeah, I do."

"Fuck, that turns me on," I moan, throwing my head back.

"You know I can't stand you, right?"

"You don't need to stand at all, Spitfire. And you sure as shit won't be able to when I'm done with you. I just need you. Whatever you'll give me. Fucking burn me for all I care."

Cali lowers her leg that's hooked around me and spreads her thighs apart slightly, stretching her panties in the process. Her lust-clouded eyes stay on me as she takes two fingers and swipes them through her sopping clit, then she sucks her own arousal off with hollowed cheeks.

This girl's going to be the death of me, and I wouldn't have it any other way.

When she unsuctions her digits from her pouty lips, she places them against my mouth, letting the heady scent of her linger. She doesn't apply any pressure to push them between my lips. No, she doesn't give me the satisfaction. She exacts the control she knows she has over me.

"If you want to fuck me, Gage, you're going to have to beg," she drawls.

Look, I'm a man who loves getting on his knees for a woman, but I say when I get on my knees and for whom. Cali's already made it clear she's not going to give in so easily, and I'm on a mission to show her just how wrong she is.

I gently push her hand aside, that starving beast inside of me stalking closer to the surface, jangling the bars of its cage and upturning my restraint with a single, self-destructive body slam. My cock kicks against my sweatpants, a carnal kind of craving spooling in the depths of my belly.

"I'm not going to fuck you, Calista," I tell her, and maybe it's the sex high talking, but I swear she looks disappointed. "But I'll make you wish I had."

I crook my arms around Cali's legs, hoist her up onto me, and internally wince when my hip nearly caves from the additional weight. Though I'd take an eternity of hip pain for Cali to touch me like she is right now. The great thing about her apartment is that the kitchen and living room feed into one another, so there's only a small amount of distance I need to cross to get her on the dining table. I'd be a gentleman and carry her to her bedroom, but we both know I'm not a gentleman.

Pins and needles plague my leg every step of the way, but the moment I set her on that hardwood surface, I can't think about anything else but shoving my face between her thighs until she's screaming my name.

Her initial shock apparently hasn't worn off yet considering she hasn't opened her mouth once to insult me, and she gifts me with a bright blush skittering over her clavicle. She looks like a fucking goddess sitting before me, thighs bookending my hips and the soft swell of her belly filling with anxious inhales.

I place a kiss on her shoulder, sliding my index finger under her bra strap and slipping it down her arm. "How expensive is this?"

"Expensive," she gasps, pushing her voluptuous breasts out to me, those little pink buds sticking straight through the mesh covering.

"Good thing I have a lot of money," I say, and in one smooth motion, I tear her bra down the middle, the rip of the fabric ricocheting off the kitchen walls. Her tits spill out with a jiggle, and her expression instantly darkens, that habitual snarl of hers catching somewhere in the back of her throat.

"Gage..."

Fuck, I'm loving this too much.

I attach my mouth to her freed nipple, lapping at the sensitive area with a snap of my tongue, and I use one of my hands to massage the squeezable mound of her tit. She rests on her hands as her neck lolls back, and when the quietest of moans filter out of her, I'm so far gone that I've surpassed the ozone layer.

I suckle the small bud with vigor, indenting it with a gentle press of my teeth, all while Cali's hand weaves into my hair.

"Oh, God. I..." Whatever she was going to say gets broken by another mewl, and her cunt is flush with my aching balls, grinding into my hard cock with punishing rolls, searching for the one desire we have in common at this point—sweet, sweet release.

I nearly lose my balance, and it's not because of the flare in my hip. I pop off her breast, seeing her nipple glint with a layer of saliva. "You have no idea how perfect your tits are, Cali. They were made for my mouth. The minute I saw them in that black dance bra, I wanted to fondle them, fuck them with my tongue, bite them and leave my mark for you to see days later."

Her words brim with faux vexation. "If you give me a hickey, I'm punching you in the balls."

I skim my lips over hers, taunting her with a kiss, wanting to swallow the notes of sugar clinging to the inside of her mouth. "I'll make sure to leave it somewhere out of view."

Before she can protest, I grab a handful of her panties and rip them from her body, not even bothering with making a clean tear down the middle. The flimsy material snaps in my fist, and the straps of her garters slide down her calves, puddling at her ankles along with her stockings. She's completely bare before me except for the trimmed curls of hair smattering the hood of her drenched clit.

I can smell the intoxicating musk of her from here, and my mouth waters at the thought of the cloying taste of her juices pulsing over my tongue when she comes. Sweet and warm, like caramelized sugar popping on a scalding stovetop.

"Jesus, she's pretty. Such a pretty pussy," I whimper, staring at the wet, pink folds of her cunt, desire igniting in my chest and polluting my lungs with a thick, opaque smoke. Is this what it means to be pussy-whipped? Because I am. *I so fucking am.*

"I'll finish myself if you don't hurry the fuck up," she threatens.

For that to happen, I'd have to be buried six feet deep. Maybe seven.

I grab both of her wrists in a bruising hold, pin them to the table roughly, and relish in the way her body rocks forward from the force.

"Are you going to behave and shut that pretty mouth of yours, or do I need to do it for you?" I growl, challenging her with an unwavering stare.

Cali sloughs off her belligerence and shakes her head, not daring to defy me with a smart-ass comeback.

"If this is what it took for you to be quiet, I would've done it a lot sooner."

And then I bend down to her cunt, nestle my nose in her pubes, and rumble, "Now hold still. I didn't eat dinner before I came, and I'm fucking starving."

I don't bother with fingers because I know what my girl needs. She needs me buried so deep in her pussy that I don't come up to breathe until I've guzzled every last drop of cum.

I lash my tongue over her slit, circling it to spur an accumulation of pressure, and upon contact, her hips lift off the table.

"Fuck!" she screams, suffocating my head with her thighs since she's surrendered control of her arms.

I didn't realize she was that sensitive, but the way she's squirming confirms it. I want her to be a writhing mess at the mercy of my tongue, so overstimulated that it only takes a lick for her to shatter like a pipe bomb.

I drill into her swollen cunt, experimentally flittering at a fast pace, my own need to come growing exponentially more unbearable as I watch her unfold before me.

I prolong her orgasm, enjoying a sick satisfaction at the tense contortion of her face, how her brow crumples and she bites down on her lip so hard that it bubbles with blood. I continue to feast on the sweetest pussy I've ever tasted, switching from a stuttered sweep of my tongue to a continuous swirling motion.

She resists against my grip, her upper body convulsing, and the next expertly executed lap urges a string of curses into desperate moans. "Oh, God. Gage...I...don't stop," she pants, those muscled legs of her giving me a faint headache with the way they're crushing my skull.

"Wasn't planning on it, Spitfire. Wanna spend the rest of my life eating this gorgeous pussy. Need you to make a dripping mess all over my face."

The lewd squelches of my spit and her arousal reverberate in the small area. It's the hottest thing I've ever heard, and my dick agrees. It's exceeded an embarrassing dribble of pre-cum and fully flooded the front of my sweats. I swear I usually last longer, but when it comes to Cali, there's no chance I'll even last three minutes.

She's curving her spine off the lacquered wood, her giant tits recoiling, and I collect more of her juices into my mouth, swallowing the surplus. She's close; I can tell. Giving her a brief rest, I retract my tongue and ply her pussy with a kiss before trapping one of her lips between my teeth and biting lightly.

She practically slams her cunt into my face and almost breaks her wrists free, pleading for me to let her come and pelting me with the occasional threat if I don't.

"Come on. You can last longer than that," I croon, suckling at her pussy, feeling it clench from the anticipated intrusion of my skilled tongue. "Need you to last long enough to make my jaw lock, Spitfire."

"I hate you," she whimpers.

"Keep telling yourself that."

Before I dive back in, I gnaw on the delicate flesh of her thigh, puncturing blood vessels in a small mosaic of mauve shades. Seeing my mark on her—it gives me a sense of pride that I only thought was possible from hockey. Claiming her as mine makes every thought in my mind dissipate into a cloud of elation.

I continue with some more strokes, grinning as her thighs compress my temples. Her obedient cunt sucks me in with more sloppy noises, and I let both of her wrists go so I can press my palm down on her belly.

With my other hand, I stuff her with two fingers, targeting her G-spot, and crook them at just the right angle to open the floodgates inside of her. That, paired with the fast work of my tongue, reduces her to a trembling puddle stuck to the table. Her legs relax and shake by my ears, tears blooming at the corners of her eyes and streaking down her cheeks.

"Gage! I can't...oh, fuck. I'm going to...I don't..."

I'd encourage her if I could talk, but she doesn't even finish the rest of her sentence before her cum sloshes into my mouth, submerging my tastebuds in the salty tang of her. But she doesn't just gush onto my tongue, she squirts all over my face.

Crystalline liquid slathers my lips and drips from my chin, and the rest of her juices douse my nose, cheeks, and jaw. It's a miracle I didn't get any in my eye. I didn't even realize what was happening before it was too late. I've never been with a girl who's squirted before, but holy fuck, is it the hottest thing I've ever witnessed. I can smell her everywhere, can feel her arousal dribble in runnels down my neck and ooze onto the collar of my shirt.

My lower stomach cramps and my balls draw up, and then I spill into my sweats, a never-ending stream of warm, wet ropes that pour down my legs and paste the inside of my pants to my cum-drenched skin.

The minute I pull back from her clit, she instantly sits up, her hand covering her mouth in mortification. "Oh my God. I'm so sorry. I was trying to tell you to pull away, but—"

I don't mean to laugh, but I can't help it. This is the most flustered I've ever seen her. "Does it look like *I'm* sorry?" I ask, using my fingers to gather some of her cum off my face, then sucking the glaze off my digits.

She stares at me, shell-shocked, blushing up a storm.

If I could spend the rest of my life tasting her, I'd die a happy man. So much better than heaps of processed sugar—an addiction, a life source, a goddamn ambrosia. "You don't ever have to apologize for that, Cali. *Ever.*"

Cali averts her eyes, and my heart constricts when I pick up on the disbelief embedded in her features. "It's embarrassing," she whispers shamefully.

"Hey, hey." I tip her chin toward me, smoothing my thumb over the dried splotch of blood on her lower lip. "It's not. It's fucking incredible. Everything you do is fucking incredible."

Those big, blue eyes glance up at me, and shallow breaths broaden her chest. Her mouth quakes like she wants to say something, but nothing comes out.

"It's clear some fucker made you feel self-conscious about it in the past, but I need you to know that you don't need to feel that way around me, okay?"

She offloads a sigh, wiping the leftover moisture from her tear ducts. I hate the silence that greets me. I hate that I can't assuage her pain, that I can't turn back time and curb-stomp the head of whoever gave her shit over something she can't control.

"If it makes you feel any better, that was the hottest thing that's ever happened to me." I chuckle, feeling a bud of relief flourish inside me when she perks up.

"Seriously?"

"Seriously. It was like being baptized."

The tiniest of smiles creeps over her lips. I don't think I ever expected Cali to have such a vulnerable side to her, but now that I've gotten a glimpse of it, I can't wait to see it again.

10

INTERVENTION TIME
GAGE

"Dude, I'm so fucked," I groan, face-planting onto our table and rattling the silverware.

I feel Fulton pat me comfortingly on the head. "Aw, Gage. Everything's going to be okay," he tries, but his pity is practically tangible at this point, and it's almost as hard to swallow as the now-cold refried beans merging with the soggy tortilla chips on my plate.

"I had no idea the night was going to end like that. Like, yeah, I'm glad it ended like that, but now I'm headed straight for Caliville, and the brakes on the fucking car don't work, and I've never really fallen for a girl before, and it's all so scary and—"

"I'm gonna be honest with you. I heard, like, none of what you just said," Fulton tells me.

I lift my head up with an exasperated sigh, embarrassment slingshotting through my entire body and making it that much more difficult to sulk in peace. "I think I'm really falling for this girl," I rephrase, and I'm ninety-nine percent positive that all my admission has done is exacerbate the blush pooling in my cheeks.

This is a big change for someone like me. Someone who's never fallen for a girl before. Someone who prides himself on being a ladies' man, when in reality, I couldn't be further from it. I can't stop thinking about Cali. I can't stop thinking about the incredible night we had together, and how it ended on an even more incredible high note with her giving me a glimpse of the soft, vulnerable side I know is under that cold exterior. Getting physical with someone too early never bodes well in the, um, *emotional* development side of things. If I was already feeling drawn to Cali emotionally, eating her out—which I don't regret one bit, obviously—just made everything ten times more complicated.

I know I'm going to keep falling for Cali, and I also know she's probably not going to fall for me. It hurts, but there's nothing I can do about it. I can't just force myself to stop feeling things for her. And I can't force her to feel things for me.

Fulton scoops up a hearty mountain of cheese, beans, sour cream, and chopped tomatoes on a flimsy tortilla chip, shoving the whole thing into his mouth while my own meal sits untouched, wasting twenty expensive dollars for gas station-quality nachos. I couldn't eat if I wanted to. Nausea tears through my stomach, accented by those *wonderful* butterflies that have decided to take permanent residence in my gut for the foreseeable future.

Fulton's brows pitch upwards. "That doesn't sound like a bad thing."

"It is! It's a terrible thing, Ful. I don't think she feels the same way about me." I'm one unsteady breath away from hyperventilating.

"I'm sure that's not true—"

I lean over and yank Fulton by the collar of his shirt, shaking the table from the sudden hitch of movement, and I bring him so close that our foreheads are inches from touching. I want him to see the lunacy in my eyes. I want him to see the disastrous state of my appearance because Cali's been haunting me ever since that life-changing night. My hair hasn't seen a shower or comb in days, I'm riper than a jockstrap, and I'm wearing a jacket with so many mystery stains that it should be a goddamn health hazard.

"It is true. I've seen it with my own two eyes. And I really, really fucking like her. I don't know what to do. I don't know if I should keep investing time in this...*situationship*...if she'll never truly be interested."

Fulton's shaking in fear, and the volume of our not-so-private conversation has broken through the quiet calm of the restaurant, garnering some particularly hateful evil eyes from the people around us.

"Dude, you're scaring me," Fulton whispers, eyes so wide I can see my crazy, disproportionate reflection in them.

"You should be scared," I hiss.

He gulps and glances down at the death grip I have on his shirt, and I reluctantly release him, slumping back into the booth with another sigh that seems to echo off the brightly painted walls. I'm losing it, and the worst part is, Cali has no idea what she's doing to me. I'm suffering all by my lonesome. I'm the only person to blame for being in this mess. I just *had* to make a deal with her for the next three months.

I've always kept women at an arm's length to abstain from growing close to them, probably because of a harrowing loss I experienced in the past. I know firsthand how losing someone destroys a person. But I don't want to choose that route this time. Cali's different.

I always felt a surface-level attraction in my past relationships. They were great girls, but I never experienced any deeper emotion for them aside from a few skipped heartbeats here and there. With Cali, I can feel my heart *everywhere*. In my throat, in my stomach, in the soles of my feet. Anatomically speaking, I'm pretty sure that's not supposed to happen.

Fulton sweeps a hand through his hair. "Okay, okay. I can tell that this is really bothering you, so I might have a solution."

The last bit of my composure nearly boils over like a shrieking kettle on a too-hot stove. "What? Oh my God. I'll do whatever I have to."

I just need to...relax. I need to take it down a few hundred notches and realize that I'm blowing things out of proportion. What if Cali does like me, but she just shows it in a different way?

No, Gage. That's ridiculous. Cali doesn't look at me like anyone other than a fuck buddy. I mean, that's what we are, aren't we? We're not together. And she's made it clear that she doesn't want to *be* together. So the smart thing to do would be to nip this thing in the bud before I make our business relationship more complicated.

But I've never been very smart. At least, not in the ways it matters.

"Did you bring weed with you?" I ask in a conspiratorial whisper, my gaze darting to where a joint may or may not be hiding in his pocket right now.

"What? No!"

"Ohhh. The harder stuff?"

Fulton deadpans, "No, Gage. I brought—"

I feel the weight of an arm sling over my shoulder, and then my body gets cramped into the furthermost side of the booth when my fucking *teammates* squeeze in next to me. Three of them, with their stupid, hockey-built walls of muscle. Physiques that clearly overcrowd the capacity of this booth and squash me into the wall like a sad, little bug.

"Fulton sent us an SOS text," Kit explains, showing me his phone screen.

Fulton: Help. Gage is losing it in the middle of Taco Bout It.

Fulton: Update: I think he's going to shank me with a plastic spork.

My lips pinch together to make a *psh* sound, and I flap my hand. "I wasn't going to *shank* him. I was just having a strongly worded talk with him."

Bristol scoots in next to Fulton, and if you're wondering, no, he didn't barge into *Fulton's* personal space and flatten him against the wall. "It's alright, Gage. We're here to help."

Kit reaches for a laminated menu and begins poring over the afternoon specials. "Actually, I'm starving. I think I'll order a carne asada burrito. Ooh, how are the nachos here?"

A smile teases Fulton's lips, one of those blatantly clueless and slap-happy smiles that chubs out his cheeks. "Oh, they're great. You should get the beef-loaded nachos. Those are the best. Though I'd ask them to add their spicy guacamole for a good kick."

"Okay, but how spicy? Like on a scale of one to ten? I need a seven at best. Anything lower and I can barely taste it."

"Hmm. Maybe like a six? I know their hot sauce is really spicy. So like with the combination of the two it'll be a fifteen or something."

I slowly reach for my spork with murder on my mind, but Bristol just shakes his head and moves it out of my reach like a parent confiscating something pointy from a child.

"Look, I appreciate all of you coming down here, but I don't need an intervention," I growl, shoving Kit and his gigantic body over so I can breathe without my lungs being crushed.

Hayes frowns sympathetically. "No offense, man, but you've been a bit of a mess these past few days. Clearly something's up. I went into your room to get a load of your laundry earlier, and it smelled like an opossum died in there."

Kit nods in agreement. "I wasn't going to say anything, but you do smell—"

Rage rumbles through me so profoundly that it could've been a 7.5 earthquake on the Richter scale. "If you finish that sentence, so help me, God. I. Will. End. You." And I mean it.

Bristol may have confiscated my weapon of choice, but my fists are just as effective.

"Gage, the first step to overcoming a problem is admitting you have one," Casen says, completely ignoring my empty threat as he swipes a chip from my plate.

"This 'intervention' will never work," I counter, doing air quotes in lieu of the middle finger I *want* to give them.

"Just try it. Maybe you'll feel better talking about your problems rather than threatening us with the pointiest thing in the vicinity," Bristol offers, throwing me one of his *I'm-your-captain-and-I-know-what's-best* looks. He just has one of those inviting faces, you know? The face of a man you can tell your deepest, darkest secret to and he won't alert the authorities.

"Fine. I have a problem. A Cali-sized problem. A five-foot-seven problem that I'm going to be stuck with for three months."

One of the waitresses comes by to take the table's orders—which end up covering a page and a half of her notepad—and Kit busies himself with working on the appetizer that just so happens to be my abandoned pile of nachos.

"What makes her so different than the rest of the girls you've been with?" Fulton asks.

Just thinking about Cali has my blood pressure rising. I'm surprised my brain's even functioning enough to form a response to that. Usually it's a hit or miss situation. She gets in my head and ties all my wires together, right after she gets done sucker-punching me in the gut with *feelings*. "I don't really know. Everything? She's just...she isn't wooed by my status. She doesn't want to get with me for the fame or the money. She doesn't suck up to me either. She challenges me, and I guess a very twisted, masochistic part of me likes that," I confess darkly like a time-weathered alcoholic confessing his problems at an AA meeting.

"Damn, dude. You must have it bad," Kit mumbles through a disgusting mouthful of chips and cheese.

Thank you, Captain Obvious.

Hayes ponders me with a crinkled brow, then he holds his hand out. "Can I see a picture of her?"

"What?" I choke out.

"I'm just curious."

I fish my phone out of my pocket and go to the Sexy Stilettos website—which I was NOT stalking—and scroll down to Cali's professional headshot. I hand Hayes my phone, and he looks it over with concentrated focus. Everyone else at the table leans over to assess the rationality behind my minor breakdown, all murmuring in agreement with themselves.

"Mm-hm," Hayes concludes. "Just what I thought."

"What?" I ask, a low-level panic beginning to take the shape of a lead weight in my stomach.

Hayes pretends to shake his head like he's harboring bad news, and then a chuckle sneaks out of him. "She's way out of your league."

I groan and fold my arms over my eyes to block out the self-satisfied looks on my teammates' faces, slouching further into the booth to hide from the humiliation that never seems to give me a fucking break.

"Don't you think I know that? She's beautiful. That just makes it ten times worse." My words are muffled against my arms, but I'm not ready to face their annoying grins or pitiful stares. So far, Fulton's "solution" hasn't fixed anything. The only thing that's come out of this intervention has been a half-baked plan of revenge for those who've wronged me (i.e. my teammates) and the bruised state of my dignity.

If you're wondering, I'm going to glitter bomb their rooms. Glitter on the ceiling fan. Glitter in their beds. Glitter everywhere.

"They're being idiots," Bristol says to me, branching out

from the main conversation that all the other guys seem to be having.

"What's *really* going on, Gage?"

I slowly begin to move my arms off my face, feeling heat lick the back of my neck. I've walked this familiar path of shame before, and it's a dead end. Actually, it's a bluff that leads to a very jagged rock at the bottom. "I really like Cali, but she doesn't reciprocate my feelings...at least, not to the same degree. And I don't know whether I should see things through with her in hopes that maybe one day she'll feel the same way, or cut things off completely before she stomps on my heart with her perfect stilettos."

Would she actually stomp on my heart? Probably not, but what do I know?

"You're worried if the relationship is worth pursuing," Bristol summarizes.

"It's not even a relationship," I admit, swiping my finger through the condensation on my water glass.

I feel like this is an endless cycle. Me chasing after Cali—her giving me the "just friends" speech. Just because she was vulnerable with me for a single moment doesn't mean she's ready to be vulnerable with me in other areas. And of course I'd be willing to wait for her...but there's a part of me that feels like a giant idiot who can't take a simple hint. I don't want to get my heart broken, and I know she has the strength to do it if she chooses. Hell, she has enough strength in her pinky finger alone.

She's got me in the palm of her hand, and she doesn't even know it.

Bristol's lips nudge into a warm-hearted smile. "I don't know if this is what you want to hear, but if your girl is worth the heartbreak and the waiting and the sleepless nights of overthinking, then she'll also be worth the possible love. You don't know how she feels. Maybe she just needs time, or maybe she's feeling the exact same way you are."

My head perks up. "You really think so?"

"You talk about her all the time. It's clear you really like her. I know you're scared of wasting your effort and getting your heart broken, but you shouldn't keep those fears from pursuing a connection that may truly be there. Heartbreak and love go hand in hand with one another. It just depends on whether that heartbreak is permanent."

Bristol's right—like he always is. I can't predict the future. I can't feel other people's emotions. I'm only in control of myself. The heartbreak and the waiting and the sleepless nights of overthinking *are* worth it for Cali. Everything is worth it for Cali.

Even if she never felt the same way about me, that wouldn't stop me from being in her life. As much as it would pain me to know she doesn't reciprocate my feelings, it would pain me even more to stop being around her. She makes me sane. She makes me *happy*.

"Is she worth it?" Bristol asks, grabbing a chip from the nearly demolished plate on the table.

She is, my heart says. *I know she is.*

11

MURPHY'S LAW
CALISTA

"**H**arder!" I scream.
"Oh, fuuuck. I—I can't…"
"Don't be a wimp. HARDER!"
"You seriously want me to go harder?"
"YES!"

Gage is currently on the floor of my dance studio, on his back like a turtle, grunting in pain as I stretch out his hip. His leg is folded at a ninety-degree angle, with me pushing it back as gently as I can to apply pressure to his hip flexor. He's cussed at me about twenty different times—yes, I'm keeping track—and he's screamed about five. Whatever he did to sustain such an injury is seriously taking a toll on him. I don't know if I'll get him limbered up in three months.

After everything went down, or should I say, after *he* went down, the dynamic of our relationship has changed more than I expected. Like, yeah, I'm still mean to him, but I also don't mean everything I say anymore. For example, when he kept whining, I told him to swing a bat into his nut sack, but I didn't mean it.

I think he's making me soft, and I don't like it. I just don't like being vulnerable with anyone. Throughout my life, I only gave myself a small amount of time to be vulnerable. The rest of that time was dedicated to the responsibility I had to my family. It always felt like everyone else had it worse than I did—my mother, my brother. It made it that much easier to sweep my emotions underneath the rug.

And now Gage is the first person in forever to have truly seen me so...unguarded...and I'm scared. I don't like trusting people with my soul because it's already so fragile.

Though I will admit, the oral sex was great. It was the first time I didn't want to rip Gage's tongue out through his teeth.

"You're enjoying this, aren't you?" he mutters breathlessly.

"I really am," I say, situating my hands on his thigh to get a better grip.

Screw Gage for wearing a plain T-shirt during our session. It's distracting. *So distracting.* Especially being so close to him. I can see every ab muscle of his stomach contract through the material, and his corded biceps flex while he holds his leg in place, outlining every protruding vein and bundle of brawn. Sweaty strands of hair fall into his eyes, giving him this permanent bedhead look that shouldn't be as sexy as it is. It also doesn't help that he smells amazing.

With a labored breath, Gage extends his leg, making me withdraw my hands from the very intimate position they were in.

"I need a break," he wheezes.

I plop into a kneeling pose. "We've only been at this for twenty minutes."

"Yeah, and it hurts like a bitch."

"You're a hockey player. Isn't your pain tolerance supposed to be high?"

"I'm a goalie with about fifty pounds of padding on. Do you think I get hit that much?"

I shrug. "I've never seen you play. Maybe you're a terrible goalie."

He splays out all his limbs like a starfish, panting heavily and staring up at the sheetrock ceiling. "I'll have you know that I'm a *fantastic* goalie," he boasts.

"Oh, really? Then care to explain the injury I'm trying to help you stretch out right now?"

He lifts his head up only so he can narrow his eyes at me. "Touché."

I almost laugh at that. See! See what he's doing to me! I can't control my body's reaction to everything he does or says, and I've definitely tried to kill every mushy-gushy feeling fluttering around in my heart.

I clamber to a stance and help Gage up with an extended arm, our palms sweaty for two completely different reasons. He throws me one of his effortless, panty-dropping grins, and even with the shot lighting overhead, it's probably obvious I'm blushing. I don't blush. Ever. Especially not because of a man. I thought all these nerves would fizzle out by now, but I'm the same mess of hormones I was when we first made our deal.

Then, to rub salt in the wound, Gage lifts up the hem of his shirt and dabs the sweat caking his forehead, giving me an unobstructed view of his glistening, tanned abs. All six of them, each as defined as slates of stone, rippling with so much muscle that it physically shouldn't be possible to carry that much ammo around. Not to mention that he has the most delicious trail of semi-dark hair traveling from his navel to the unexplored depths below his waistband.

He catches me ogling him, and I only know that because our eyes make fucking contact while he's having his Zac Efron moment. All that's missing is a sprinkler soaking him in water.

He doles out one of his *look-at-me-I'm-so-hot* smirks. "Like what you see?"

I almost don't dignify his comment with a response. *Almost.* "I've seen better."

Ugh, I can't believe he has the gall to be this cocky. There's nothing worse in this world than an attractive man who knows just how attractive he is.

"Really? Because you've been staring at me for an awfully long time."

"Not my fault you don't know how to wear a shirt properly."

Stupid photoshopped-looking abs. Stupid smug smirk. This arrangement would've been so much easier if Gage was hideously unattractive. Yes, I'm staring at you, idiot. How can I not stare at you when you look like you're the lovechild of *Rolling Stone* and *GQ*?

"Cali, are you flirting with me?" he teases, and the lower half of me gives a shameful throb. "If you wanted me to take my shirt off, you could've just asked."

I sputter like an idiot because I can't put into words how much I hated every second of that, and then I resort to the one trusty response that always gets my message across—two middle fingers. But Gage must've grown some kind of impenetrable armor over the past few days because he isn't fazed by it. In fact, he blows me an air kiss.

I'll take that air kiss and jam it down his throat.

And then he has the audacity to ask me such a preposterous question that it dismantles my entire floating chunk of universe.

"Can I watch you dance?"

I choke on a spit glob in my mouth. "What?"

"I want to watch you dance, Cali," he elaborates.

He...wants to watch me dance? Nobody's ever watched me dance before. Well, except for my students and Hadley. In college, I was majoring in dance, and I became really close to one of my contemporary professors during a stressful semester. Contemporary was the first dance style I ever took, and it was then when I realized that contemporary in particular had a way of allowing me to be vulnerable without talking through my feelings. Dance was a way for me to escape from the stress of my other classes in college—from the state of the family I left behind, which continued to haunt me while I was hundreds of miles away from them.

After my semester with Ms. Katharine, she asked me if I'd ever be interested in being a teacher for a college-level contemporary class. Of course I said yes, so for the next semester, I was a dance teacher on the side. Teaching others to embrace dance and work through their emotions wasn't only rewarding, but it helped me understand my own emotions better.

So when my mother got sick my sophomore year of college, the first thing I allowed myself to feel was loss. Not just on account of my mother, but on account of the one outlet I'd grown to lean on—dance. I didn't want to return to my old life. When I went to college, I thought my mother would get better. I thought I'd be able to have a normal college experience and step into an actual career. But all of that was taken away in the blink of an eye.

My mother's condition had deteriorated so badly that she was no longer able to care for Teague, which necessitated my return home. And even if my father *had* stayed, there isn't a bone in my body that would trust him to adequately care for my mother. He always did things half-assed, even when it came to the well-being of this family—which makes sense as to why he never bothered looking for a steady job to help keep us afloat.

When I told Ms. Katharine that she'd have to find another teacher to take over, she said she ran a dance studio in Riverside that was looking for a new instructor.

She saw how important dance was to me, and she didn't want me to be without it. It was plain luck that a deal as good as that one fell into my lap—that I'd be able to help others, help myself (to some degree), and help my mother with expenses. The only catch was that the dance class they needed an instructor for wasn't a typical style of dance.

That's when I found heel dancing. It was sexy, different, and combined all the foundations of other genres of dance into one. The thing that appealed most to me, however, was running a class where women, no matter their backgrounds or personal lives, could come together and share in the strength of what it meant to be a woman. That safe space isn't always available in society, nor is it handed out all willy-nilly to those who want it. Safety shouldn't be a privilege; it should be a right. And I guess it felt like it was my duty to cultivate a safe space for others because Ms. Katharine's contemporary class had been a safe space for me.

If there's anything I want in life, it's to be someone else's Ms. Katharine.

And while heel dancing isn't something I'm ashamed of, I'm afraid to share it with other people. When I dance, all my emotions float to the surface, and everything's so easy to read from an outside perspective. Dancing lowers the façade I keep so firmly in place to hide my vulnerability. That's why I'm afraid to let people look under the surface—for them to see how broken I really am. And Gage wants under all my fucking surfaces.

"Yeah, not happening," I rebuke, folding my arms over my chest.

"Why not?"

Why not? *Why not?* Oh, maybe because I'm an absolute mess of a human being who channels all her emotional baggage into her dancing, and you'll be able to see just how messed up I am from a mile away. Then, upon seeing said mess, you'll bolt for the hills and think to yourself, *Phew, that was a close one.*

"I know you may be used to girls bending over backwards for your attention, but I'm not one of those girls."

Gage laughs heartily—which isn't the reaction I was expecting—and my stomach somersaults with a nauseating flutter. "Pretty sure *I* had *you* bent over backwards the last time we were together."

Oh my God. I can't believe he just said that!

"Plus, you don't need to vie for my attention when you already have it, Spitfire."

Curse Gage and his surprising wittiness that does make him more likable but is overall infuriating. I'm not ready to dance for Gage. I'm not sure if I ever will be.

So I rack my brain for a solution to stop the unstoppable—the unstoppable being Gage—and I take a second sifting through excuses and ideas before one presents itself to me. "How about we dance together?" I propose, adjusting the hem of my polyester tank top.

Gage's composure suffers a quick crack right down the middle, and his eyes enlarge to the size of discs, an unmissable blush scattering over his cheeks. "Dance? Together? Dance together?" he spews out.

"Yes, Gage. I mean, I'm going to give you the benefit of the doubt and assume you can kind of dance."

"I...it's just..." He's scrambling for an excuse just like I was until his darting eyes make a connection with the culprit of this entire lesson. "My hip! Yeah, my hip. I can't dance because of my hip, but you already know that." The strangest bird-squawk of a laugh ejects from his mouth.

Damn. He really doesn't like this idea. So I immediately *love* this idea.

Before he can feed me more pathetically unbelievable excuses, I divest myself of my tank top, throwing it to the side with a flirtatious wink in Gage's direction.

Gage's gone mannequin-still, his gaze now transfixed on my

tits like there's some kind of magnetic pull. A black mini romper gives my boobs a generous push, and the trim of it flares out in ruffled frills just below my butt.

I'm getting back at him for teasing me with all his stupid muscles this session.

How do you like the taste of your own medicine, Gage?

"Fuck," he croaks weakly, eyes skating over my body with such razor-edge intensity that it makes me shudder.

With a sensual strut, I trail a single finger up his stomach, over his pecs, and across his collarbone. I stalk around him, making sure to keep continuous contact. "Come on, Gage. Dance with me."

"I..."

I have no idea why he's so nervous. Gage doesn't strike me as the type to get nervous. He strikes me as the type of person to fight any nerve-type feelings like one of those hypermasculine guys who claim they can fight a grizzly bear.

"You're telling me you don't like the feel of dancing intimately with another person?"

His back is ramrod straight, every muscle tightening. Lungs hoovering in air, his chest rises in an erratic rhythm, and if I had to make an educated guess, I bet his heartbeat would break a heart monitor.

When he doesn't answer me, I come up from behind and nudge my lips against his ear, whispering, "The feel of their hands all over you? The feel of sweat rolling down both your bodies?"

Gage groans so loudly that the noise resounds in the studio, all efforts to resist me slowly dwindling when I lick the small patch of neck just below his earlobe. He's shivering just from a single touch, so wired with anticipation that I could do next to nothing and still have him begging on his knees—which, if we're talking about Gage, he'd probably do in a heartbeat.

Since my heels give me some much-needed leverage, I'm

tall enough to press my front up against his ass, smooth my hands down his washboard abs, and halt just above the groin of his pants, which is currently straining with his erection. "The feel of their breath on your skin? How about their body pressed up against yours, where the most erogenous zones rub against each other?"

"Cali..." he growls.

"Are you really going to stand here and tell me you don't want to dance with me?" I purr, my voice warmer than whiskey.

I can feel his stomach twitch underneath my fingers, and sadistic satisfaction funnels through my entire body in miniature, earth-shattering explosions. Wetness gathers in the gusset of my panties, triggering a needy pulse in my pussy which desperately craves some one-on-one attention with Gage's engorged cock. I grind the slightest bit into his ass to relieve some of the pressure, and the tiniest noise barges out of him while his ass cheeks clench in tandem.

He grabs my hands to keep them from moving, exerting levels of restraint that I didn't even know he was physically capable of. The guttural rumble in his throat nearly derails my whole seduction scheme. "If I get my hands on you, we won't be *doing* any dancing," he says lowly.

Promise?

"Show me. Show me where you'd touch me. Show me how I turn you on," I demand.

Gage turns around abruptly, his dick jutting against my belly, just inches from my slick cunt—just inches from ruining me right here in the middle of the studio. "Fuck, Spitfire. You can't ask me to do that."

I'll give him some credit. He actually looks torn.

"Why? Because you're a gentleman?" I scoff.

He pins me with an intimidating stare, running his eyes over the sinfully low dip of my cleavage, and his throat clicks with an audible gulp. "Because I'm *not*."

Welcome back, sexual tension. I've missed you.

The beginning notes of Lady Gaga's "Just Dance" comes blaring through the speakers, and I start to swish my hips from side to side in time with the beat, simultaneously running my fingers through my hair and letting the volume of it billow behind me.

Gage pulls me into him so there's no space between us at all, and I hang one arm over his shoulder as I roll my body against his, snagging his boner with my cunt. He pitches forward slightly as he throws his head back, growls of frustration slipping past clenched teeth and puttering out into hushed grunts. I'd turn around and grind on him if I didn't think he'd come in less than three seconds.

But where's the fun in playing it safe, right?

Before I get the chance to palm the bulge in his pants, Gage cups my pussy, grabbing the fabric of my romper and rucking it up in his fingers. I gasp loudly, the arm that was once slung lazily over his shoulder now steeling me in my moment of weakness. He pushes the offending material aside so that his fingers can inch their way over the seam of my panties, and my pussy reciprocates with an embarrassing leakage of arousal.

Gage leans into my neck, whispering, "You thought you could just torture me this entire session and get away with it?"

"Not hard when the man I'm dancing with has no self-restraint," I retort.

"Any man in his right mind would have zero self-restraint when it comes to you." He nips at my throat, teasing a bite that I know he's not going to give me, and any resolve I'd planned to weaponize against him dissipates into nothingness. "Now are you going to be a good girl, or are you going to be a cock tease all night?"

It's taking every muscle in my body not to moan right now. Gage is getting closer to his desired target, and all I want to do is feel his fingers inside me again, stuffing me full, making me gush down his knuckles and scream his name.

All my thoughts are frequent flyers on Arousal Airlines, and I fail to realize the weight of my next response before it materializes in the real world. "That depends. Are you going to man up and actually dance with me? Or should I find someone who will?"

I don't have time to contemplate the consequences of what I just said before Gage grabs my hips possessively and moves my waist in a figure eight, his freakishly hard dick still fighting to escape the flimsy containment of his pants. He then squats down halfway, his hands migrating from the curve of my sides to the dough of my ass. He smacks my left cheek before settling for a grab, and I emit a gasp at the force of it, nearly losing my balance and tripping over my own heels. I run my hands roughly through his hair to try and regain some control, but I should've known it wouldn't last long as he slowly begins to stand, dragging his nose all the way up my stomach and over the swell of my overspilling tits.

He's standing over me a second later, our foreheads pressed together, our mouths inching closer at a slow-moving pace, prolonging the tension that's snowballed within the last ten minutes.

Fuck, do I want to kiss him. So badly. And I don't want to stop.

But the second our lips brush each other's, the music cuts out in a staticky wail, and the ringing of my phone fills our ears instead. We're both huffing and panting, and I'm mopping as much sweat from my face as I can. That's when I notice Gage staring at me in a way I've never seen before. Not due to frustration or annoyance...it seems to be something stronger than all of that. Something that scares me as much as it tantalizes me.

"I'm sorry, I should get that." I break away from our intimate position with a guilty heart, unplug my phone, and answer the unknown caller.

"Are you Calista Cadwell, Ingrid Cadwell's daughter?" the speaker asks.

I freeze as my fingers grip the device tighter—as if squeezing it will somehow pacify the panic throwing me for a terrifying loop—and an oily sickness brews in my gut. "Yes, this is she."

"I'm sorry, Ms. Cadwell. Your mother has had a terrible accident."

12

THE BEGINNING OF THE END
GAGE

I never wanted our dancing to end. I'm not a dancer. I don't particularly like dancing if I'm not under the influence. But with Cali, I'll dance for the rest of my fucking life. *Sober.* I'm about to feel everything with this girl.

I know that I had my tongue in her cunt less than a week ago, but dancing somehow seems so much more intimate. She was inviting *me* into *her* world, and I didn't want to overstay my welcome. That's why I was so hesitant at first. And even though I might've claimed dancing was easy, it certainly isn't.

But all those first-time jitters seem so trivial now.

I hate hospitals. I have since I was a kid. The repugnant scent of ammonia, the harsh fluorescents, the eggshell-white walls, the continuous beeps and trills of machinery, the incomprehensible droning of hospital personnel as they deliver life-saving or life-ending news. And although the hallowed halls are bathed in buckets of bleach, it doesn't erase the noxious odor of decay that's seeped beyond vinyl and into the skeletal structure of the time-worn building.

But it wasn't just the atmosphere that made me sick to my stomach...it was the familiarity of it all. It's a part of my past that I don't like to revisit—a part of me that I keep in the dark for a reason.

My parents—using the word loosely here—were terrible fucking people. Two egotists who couldn't love each other without swallowing the other one whole. They were neglectful because they became so consumed by their own lives that they forgot about the life they brought into this world, and I'm not just talking about myself.

When I was a kid, I had a younger brother. We were four years apart, and when he was born, the doctors told my parents that he had a congenital heart defect. It was a chronic condition, but with treatment, he would be able to live a long, normal life. I didn't think much of it at the time since I was so young. I didn't treat him any differently, really.

Until he got weaker. And when he got weaker, I begged my parents to do something. But because they were going through their divorce at the time, fighting every second of every day and focusing all their attention and money on winning their child custody battle, they couldn't have cared less. All they wanted was to be the victor in their fucked-up relationship.

My brother needed a valve replacement, and since my mom and my dad were too wrapped up in their divorce to realize he was getting weaker, his heart stopped beating when he was only eight. The doctor told them that surgery could've saved him if they'd noticed his condition deteriorating, which is exactly what I tried to tell them. But it was like they never heard or saw me. It was like I wasn't even there.

My brother was promised a full life—one with obstacles, yes, but a full life nonetheless—and I misplaced my faith in the people I thought were going to help him. I couldn't do anything to save him. I was twelve. I didn't have the money or the jurisdiction or even the knowledge to ensure my brother got the surgery he needed.

I failed him. I lost him. And even though the blame sits

solely on my parents' shoulders, the guilt still chokes me. If I could've just...*done* something...maybe he would still be here. If I'd tried harder or somehow forced them to listen. If I'd gone to someone else for help instead of blindly relying on my parents, maybe things would've been different.

So as soon as Cali told me what happened to her mother, we took my car and raced over to the hospital as fast as we could. I wasn't about to let her go through the same pain I went through alone.

Since I'm not family, I wasn't allowed back with her. I sat for a devastatingly long time by myself, in an uncomfortable hospital chair, praying that Cali and her mother would be okay. Maybe I've lost my goddamn mind, but I feel this duty to protect Cali and her loved ones, as if it'll amend the mistake I made in not protecting my brother.

She came out of the room after about an hour and sat next to me. She'd barely gotten comfortable when the presiding doctor came over to talk to us about her mother's condition. Apparently, Cali's mom has multiple sclerosis, and she was admitted to the hospital during Cali's and my dance lesson. The doctor said she'd probably been suffering from a severe vertigo flare-up for the past few days. She was trying to open a window in her room for fresh air, and one of the neighbors saw her collapse from across the street. So they rushed over to the apartment and called an ambulance.

Cali never told me her mother was sick, or that she was her primary caretaker. And I took her away from her mother because I needed help stretching my stupid hip. If Cali had been home, none of this would've happened.

I wish she had told me what was going on. I wish I could've helped somehow, but all I did was make everything worse.

It feels like history's repeating itself.

I stopped keeping track of time after the sky darkened. Since the doctor broke the news, Cali and I have found refuge in the semi-busy waiting room, and I have a feeling that she won't want to leave until her mother gets discharged. The doctor said he wanted to keep her a few days to monitor her symptoms, assess the severity, and then form a plan of action to give her mother the best life possible with her chronic condition.

Cali and I haven't spoken for twenty minutes. She was, however, cooperative enough to let me give her my hoodie so she didn't freeze. Even though our chairs are right next to each other, I've never felt so far away from her. She's curled in on herself, hugging her knees to her chest, her face streaked with leftover tears and her sclera feathered with burst blood vessels. Her hair is a scraggly mess shielding her face, and even beneath the coverage of my hoodie, I can still see her body shake.

I don't know what to say to her. I don't know how to make any of this better. All I want to do is hold her and tell her that everything's going to be okay. But the worst part of it all is that I never knew how hard her life really was. She's had to take care of her sick mother and younger brother for years. No person should have to bear that much responsibility.

After my brother's death, my parents were so grief-stricken that they began to shower me with materialistic shit, as if that would somehow make up for the love I'd lost over the years. From there on out, they chose to stay together and give me everything I could've ever wanted. I flunked a test and wanted to go on an impromptu vacation? My mom would have a private jet ready for me within the hour. I needed a job over the summer but wasn't qualified for any? My dad would get me an internship at his business, or he'd pull strings with other business owners to hire me.

I haven't really spoken to my parents since I entered the NHL. I'm cordial with them, sure, but I don't rely on them for anything. I don't *want* to be around them. And when I'm older, I don't want my wife and kids to be around them either. Forgiveness is something I'm working toward, but it's hard when a person's sincerity is so weak it's questionable. And that's where my parents lie. They regretted their decision (or lack thereof) because the worst possible outcome came true. If the outcome had been a simple dip in my brother's health, they wouldn't have felt an ounce of guilt for not giving him the attention he needed. Now I wish they hadn't done shit for me—I wish I had grown a backbone and refused all their lavish gifts.

I didn't ever have to work for anything—aside from hockey. But Cali...Cali's had to work for *everything*. She's running a dance studio, looking after her mother and brother, and looking after herself (barely). It's no wonder she didn't like me at first. We're complete opposites. I was the self-conceited asshole with the flashy car who blocked her in because I was feeling petty. She was the struggling sister who needed an open spot to pick up her brother.

This girl teaches who knows how many dance classes a day, has to drop off and pick up Teague from hockey practice, then has to go home and take care of her mother. She doesn't get any time to herself. And that's just based on the information I know; she probably has so much more on her plate that she'll never tell me.

The waiting room is completely silent. Well, aside from the occasional hacking cough. We're crammed in a twenty square-foot area, and an endless line of hideous chairs wrap around the perimeter while the rest remains back-to-back in the center of the room. There're no TVs or magazines. Just a fuckton of chairs. Flimsy chairs with hard, wooden armrests, backrests with gaudy geometric patterns, and cushions that are the nastiest shade of shit brown. The only pop of color in this depressing landscape is a green snake plant in the corner, and even that dude doesn't look like he wants to be here. The accompanying glug of the water dispenser goes off every few minutes, as does the tick of the clock hanging directly above us. The waiting is excruciating. The distance, however, is going to kill me.

I gently rub Cali's arm, fearful of startling her but hoping that she'll give me a glimpse of her beautiful face. My hoodie is giant on her, turning her figure into a shapeless pile of cotton.

"It's not your fault, Calista," I whisper, working past a swallow in my shredded throat, my heart beating a slow, sluggish tune akin to the beeping of a vital signs monitor attached to a heavily sedated patient.

She bristles under my touch, but she doesn't say anything. She doesn't turn to face me. Her body remains in the same position it has for the last hour—half-fetal, so incredibly small that it's almost as if she's punishing herself for taking up too much space.

I hate seeing her like this—so helpless. I don't know how to help without overstepping boundaries. All I want to do is hold her, but I can tell that's the last thing she wants right now. Does she even want me here?

I know I'm going to regret it, but I try filling the empty space with words of consolation—to show her that I'm here if she needs me, and that I'm not going anywhere. "Your mom's going to be okay. I'll stay here with you for as long as you want."

Involuntarily, my hand reaches out to scrounge for skin-to-skin contact, but she's deprived me of that as well. I am lucky enough, however, to receive more than her usual grunt of acknowledgment. She turns the slightest bit toward me, only enough so I can catch a sliver of her face.

"I hate hospitals," she murmurs, displeasure crunching her brow and a frown fastened to her lips. "It feels like I've spent half my life in them."

Hospitals. I can work with that.

"I hate them too," I offer, notching my thumbnail into the woodgrain of the chair's armrest. "My brother was really sick when I was younger. He practically lived at the hospital. I knew every corridor by the back of my hand."

Cali's gaze crawls over to me, analyzing my face in search of grief. "Was?"

I press my bitten nail into the chipped wood, folding the keratin. "He's...not here anymore," I confess, unable to halt the grinding thoughts in my head about my late brother. About how sickly and malnourished he looked in the end. About how, despite frequenting the hospital, he never received the treatment he deserved.

"Oh, Gage. I'm so sorry."

"It's okay. I just...don't want to get into it right now."

Cali seems to sink further into her seat. "Right. Yeah. If you ever do, though, I'll be here to listen."

I want to say thank you, but the words turn to sludge in my mouth, and I don't have the energy to force them into the world. So, I carefully extricate myself from the conversation and focus on my own silence, on the air entering through my nose and the deep breaths exiting through my mouth. I focus on the acidic burn in my eyes from keeping them open for so long. I focus on the creaky discomfort of my hip from the subpar guest chairs. I focus on the faint gnaw of hunger in my belly since I skipped dinner.

Cali said that Teague was at a playdate when everything happened, and that he's being driven over to the hospital as we speak. Teague's just a fucking kid. A great kid who's dealing with the worst possible thing the world could have thrown at him. Cali and her family are the last people in the world that deserve this kind of heartache. If I could switch my life with hers, if I could bear the weight of her pain, I would do it in a heartbeat.

I don't know how to describe it, but it feels like there's this invisible thread connecting me and Cali. Everything she feels and projects into the world—I feel it too. Maybe not to the degree she does, but I feel it in aftershocks.

As exhausted as I am, I'm not going to sleep until Cali does. I need to watch over her, to make sure she's okay, and I can't do that if my head's dangling halfway off the armrest. I'm about to reach out and try my luck at starting another less morbid conversation when my stomach grabs my attention with a monstrous rumble.

The only thing worse than hospitals themselves? The food. And not just hospital cafeteria food, but vending machine food.

I don't want to leave Cali's side for too long, but I'm starving. And if I'm starving, then she has to be too. So, I internally debate with myself on what I should do, all while the continuous rumbling refuses to cease, and I eventually stand up for the first time in two straight hours.

My joints creak, and my knees pop. "I'm going to get some food for us, okay? I'll just be around the corner."

"Okay."

I shuffle into the hall with my useless hip, drag myself in front of the dilapidated vending machine, and stare into the clouded, tempered glass illuminated by spurts of blue light. The glass is covered in scratches and oily fingerprints, but the clarity of it doesn't seem to matter as there's barely any product inside. A few lone bags of chips, a single chocolate bar, and a package of corn nuts.

Great. Awesome.

I shove my hand into my pocket to fish out a few dollar bills —which are crinkled, of course—and quickly try to iron them out with my clammy fingers. Impatience cleaves through me while I stare dazedly at the cash validator. I take my (mostly) flattened bill and ease it into the slot, watching as it slips halfway in before the machine announces to the whole hallway with an ear-piecing screech that my money's been declined.

You've got to be fucking kidding me.

I smear both of my hands down my face, letting my fingers snag on my heavy eyelids.

Deep breaths, Gage. You need to stay calm for Cali.

With a determined grunt, I take the bill and straighten it on the edge of the wall, sawing it back and forth until...it pretty much looks the same as it originally did. I gently shove that fucker into the slot, wait for that infuriating screech to go off, but it never does. The bill slipped inside faster than a lubed-up cock.

I click one of the buttons for the last bag of Doritos and watch as the spiral pushes it forward comically slowly, the orange package of cheesy, heavily processed, triangular chips budging closer to the edge. And it tips forward enough that it could easily fall into the dispenser without additional help, but it doesn't. It doesn't move. The bag is stuck teetering on the ledge of its shelf.

This is some sick joke. It has to be. What did I do to you, God? I mean, I did do a lot of shit, but why do you have to punish me now? Couldn't it wait? Like, until I got home? Or three years from now?

I'm aware that the hospital is nearly silent aside from hushed voices and machinery. But I'm also aware that if I don't eat something soon, I'm going to turn into a fucking demon and start ransacking trashcans.

This might be controversial, but I start shaking the vending machine. Hard. My hip doesn't allow me to kick it, so shaking is all I have. The width is massive, but so is my arm span, so there's no strain in my arms when I manhandle it. The whole thing comes to life in a cacophony of metal and springs, which can definitely be heard all the way out in the waiting room. There's a point where the vending machine comes off the *ground*, but none of the items inside wiggle free from their spiral prisons.

"Motherfucker," I hiss under my breath, setting the

machine back on the ground and waving off the concerned stares of passersby.

I bang my forehead against the germ-ridden glass, watching as my breath fogs the scuffed surface. Screw this night. Seriously. Screw everything about it.

"Do you need help?" a small, polite voice asks from beside me. It's one of those kid voices that are bubbly sweet and basically ooze hope and sunshine and butterflies. It's annoying as hell.

"No, thanks," I grumble, peeling back my forehead and turning to face the ankle biter who decided to interrupt my sulking.

But upon recognition, my frustration ebbs, and my impatience swirls away along with it. It's Teague, and he's looking up at me with wide eyes, his puffy cheeks sprinkled in a red hue from the nightly chill.

It's a breath of fresh air to see the little guy.

"Sorry, Teague. I didn't see you there. How are you doing?" I ask, crouching down to his height, a consolatory grimace sliding onto my chapped lips. I ruffle his hair, but it doesn't seem to defuse the dark cloud lingering over his four-foot-seven body.

"I'm okay. Mom's been sick for a long time," he says in a disturbingly distant voice, no evidence of tears swimming in his eyes, and no tired bags under them alluding to sleep deprivation. He looks...normal. Maybe he's in shock.

I don't know what the mortality rate is for multiple sclerosis, but I know what it's like to see your loved ones suffer in pain for an extended period of time.

Unexpected moisture licks my eyes, and my heart weakly pulses with sympathy. "I'm so sorry, buddy. I can only imagine how hard that must be."

Teague ignores me. "Are you hungry?" he questions,

dividing his attentive eyes between me and the gloating vending machine.

"I'm fine, Little Man," I assure him.

He frowns—which makes him look just like Cali—and rummages around for something in his pocket, brandishing a fistful of multicolored, half-melted gummy worms. I have no idea where his hand has been…or what he's done with those things.

And suddenly, the riot in my gut is dead silent. "Let's go see if your sister wants one, yeah?"

I walk him over to the waiting room with the expectation of finding Cali burrowed even further into my hoodie, but to my surprise, she's standing and looking right at me. Her eyes are bloodshot, tears pearl on her lashes, and faint streaks have been left in her foundation from previous crying bouts. Her hair has the subtlety of a lion's mane, and I can see dark stains of tears and snot on my hoodie from when she probably used it as a tissue.

"I want to go home," she says quietly, hugging her arms around her midsection.

I cradle the side of her face, ghosting my thumb over the last remnants of water on her cheekbone, a smile emerging on my lips like a crocus shaking off powdered clumps of snow.

She came back to me. My girl came back to me.

I soften my voice, undoubtedly making Cali privy to the undercurrents of worry riding on my tongue. "Your home?"

"No. Yours."

13

WHO NEEDS THERAPY WHEN YOU HAVE CHEESY FRIES?

CALISTA

I shouldn't have asked to go home with Gage. I shouldn't have asked to be anywhere near him, but I couldn't be in that apartment—the one still fresh with the smell of my mother's sick body.

It's my fault that she's in the hospital. I should've been looking after her. I should've been *there* instead of playing pretend with some guy. This is what I was trying to avoid. I chose my social life over my mother's life, and now she's paying for my selfish decision. I deserve to be the one perishing in that hospital bed, not her. And Teague...God, *Teague*. He shouldn't have seen her like that. I had another duty aside from saving my mom—protecting my brother. And I failed both of them in the span of a single night.

Although I'm swallowed by Gage's hoodie, it doesn't provide me with solace. I'm a fucking disaster. Shattered shards of a wine glass glued together in an attempt to be whole, expected to still hold wine with a graveyard of cracks.

I don't bother turning on Gage's light. My flaming eyes have adjusted to the darkness, and my clamoring heart hides in the shadows of my ribs—hides from the pitiful and wounded look I know will greet me.

I sit with the afterburn of guilt; I sit with the slow-drying tears wetting my cheeks; I sit with the hollow pain of hunger clenching in my belly. I ram my fingernails into my palms until the surface breaks and colors my skin in rouge half-crescents. I deserve to hurt; I deserve to starve; I deserve to be punished.

There's a polite knock on the door, unneeded to enter one's own room, and an empty gesture all the same as the partition creaks open and lets a sliver of light in.

Gage, with his muscled body, irradiates in front of me in a soft, golden glow, startling the nest of nerves inside me. The sanctity of darkness has been stripped away, leaving me proverbially naked and bared to moral scrutiny.

"I left Teague with Fulton downstairs," Gage tells me, the evergreen of his eyes overcast with an unparalleled murkiness. "They're playing video games."

Even though I'm staring straight at him, I don't say anything. All I've ever wanted is to make my brother happy. And it always seems that I can only do so when I'm far away from him.

Fluxes of bated breath bury themselves in my lungs, words smudging their chalky graininess over my parched tongue. My whole body is hot despite the breeze from the open window, and unending moisture laves my eyes, searching for skin to chafe.

Gage looks just as bad as I feel. His face is bunched with worry and frown lines alike, there're purple shadows under his eyes, and tufts of hair stick out in an untamed mess. "Can we talk?" he whispers cautiously, as if he's afraid the weight of the question will clobber me.

I was planning to nod, but I'm shocked when my voice box gyrates. "There's nothing to talk about."

His large hand cards through the front of his hair, a hefty

sigh prying open his lips. "I know you don't want to talk to me right now, Cali. But you can't do this. You can't shut me out."

I don't want to. My *heart* doesn't want to. But closing myself off is the only defense mechanism I have. Keeping Gage in my life will only complicate it more, and I'm afraid that if I continue to get lost in him, I'll never find my way back to my mother, to my brother—to my normal life.

I turn away from Gage's gaze, feeling the tears return with a vengeance.

He strides over to me hastily, grabs my hands in his, no doubt prepares a heartrending speech that'll change my mind, then looks down at my palms. His thumb smears the tiny bubbles of blood from my self-inflicted cuts, and a cry gargles in his throat.

"Don't do that, Calista," he begs. "Please don't do that."

I pull my hands away from his, hiding the lacerations beneath his oversized hoodie sleeves, the self-pity in my gut flickering into an enraged fire. "Why? I deserve it."

"You don't. You didn't do anything wrong."

"It's my fault she's in the hospital. None of this would've happened if I'd been taking care of her like I was supposed to."

"She's been sick for a long time. You couldn't have known it would get this bad," he murmurs, abandoning his attempt to hold my hands and sitting beside me on the mattress. The woodsy scent of his cologne embraces me like I know he wants to, rousing my heart while my brain tries to corral every defiant, pesky emotion rising in its wake.

A growl rolls around in my chest. "I did know. I'm responsible for her now. When I got involved with you, I chose myself over her. After everything she's done to take care of me."

Hurt washes over his face, but he does his best to wipe the slate clean. "You shouldn't blame yourself for wanting to live your life. And you're doing the best you can as her sole source of income. You shouldn't have to choose between being free and being indebted to her," he says, fine-tuning the agony in his tone. "She wouldn't want you to live like this. You know that."

"You don't know anything, Gage," I sneer. "You don't know her. You don't know what my mother wants. I'm not indebted to her!"

Why is he trying to make me the good guy? I'm not the good guy. I didn't ask him to spew bullshit and make me feel better. Anger mangles my guts, scoops out viscera like the metal claw on an excavator. My chest begins to stutter with thin breaths, and my vision winks in and out of focus, bile soddening my throat.

"Shit, no. That's not what I meant. I'm sorry," he immediately apologizes, tipping his head back and showing me the tremble of his Adam's apple. "I just…I need you to know that you've done everything you can to give her the best life possible. She wouldn't still be alive if that wasn't the case."

"She's barely alive," I respond, staring at his bedroom floor.

Gage, with his stupid, inextinguishable determination, manages to capture my hands in an unyielding grip, forcing me to turn my attention to him. "Spitfire…"

"She'd be better off dead."

He slips his fingers around my nape, pulling my face close to his. Our foreheads touch, and our breaths mingle in an almost kiss. "Stop. Stop it. I know you don't mean that. She loves you so much. She's not ready to say goodbye yet, and neither are you."

Water inundates my blazing eyes, surging down my face in tributaries that convene at my jawline. Saliva swarms my mouth as snot blocks my nasal cavities, giving my already-strained voice a relentless hiccup.

I was determined to carry this pain by myself, to lock Gage out, but I'm not strong enough. The guilt is going to kill me. I've never had another person to lean on. I've never allowed someone else to help me carry my burdens, but he's right *here*, and my heart's unfurling like petals ready to blossom—ready to let the light in after months of darkness.

"Don't punish yourself, Cali. You're going to destroy me if you punish yourself. And I can't...I won't be able to heal if I lose you," he chokes, pain drenching his waterlines in fat droplets.

I've never seen Gage cry before. I never thought I ever would. I thought he was one of those guys who warded off emotions like a priest warding off demonic activity, but he's letting me see his vulnerability. He's imploring me to take his outstretched hand. He's offering me the support I've always searched for but never found.

I ball my fists into the back of his shirt, my heart racing so quickly that I'm afraid it'll burst from my chest and gallop off into the woods. "I don't think I c-can...do this...a-anymore," I sob, needing to ground myself on the firmness of his shoulders, needing to feel his heart beneath my hand to remind myself that he's real and he's here and he won't leave me.

Gage wraps his arms fully around me, bringing my shaking frame into his sturdy one, allowing my nose to nestle in the divot of his collarbone. "I know, Cali. Shh. I know. You can. I'm here, okay? You're not alone anymore."

Not alone anymore.

I've never known what it feels like not to be alone.

Everything hurts—my eyes, my heart, my throat. It feels like there's a tungsten needle piercing the membrane of my heart—slowly, *slowly* plunging into the barely pulsating muscle until everything in my body turns dark. "It h-hurts, Gage. I feel like I can't *breathe*. I just...I can't..."

He squeezes me tighter, as if he's afraid I'll float away if he lets go. "Give me your pain, Cali. Give me everything. I'm here, Spitfire. Right here," he croons into my neck, petting my hair.

Every emotion that I've compartmentalized since my mother's diagnosis ruptures inside me, and a bloodcurdling scream emanates from me, one so loud that it rings in my ears and drowns out the ambience of the night. Gage doesn't flinch. He doesn't let go. He inhales my pain, swallows every last ounce of it, and lets it detonate inside his body to spare me from the sharp, fragmented fallout.

Each wail robs me of oxygen, heating my cheeks and my forehead and the back of my neck. I don't open my eyes because I won't be able to see past the blurry, rippling caustics. I don't know how long I cry for, but it feels like forever. My throat's thoroughly abraded, and I know it'll hurt when I talk again.

"You're okay. You're gonna be okay. I'm not going anywhere," he hushes, rubbing circles on my upper back.

I need to move my face because I've saturated the spot of his shirt that I was previously occupying. "I...don't...w-want...to...t-trap...you," I gasp, finally looking up at him.

His thumb comes up to brush away a weltering tear, a small smile dimpling his cheeks. "You're not trapping me, Cali. Not even close."

"But—"

"No buts. Do you know that I'd give anything in this fucking world to be in your life? I don't care what that means—friend, lover, enemy, stranger that I occasionally run into at the rink. I need you in my life or I'll lose my goddamn mind."

I can't believe this. I mean, Gage hasn't tried to keep his feelings for me a secret, but I didn't realize they stemmed from more than just some hate attraction. He has to be delirious. This—this can't be how he really feels. "You barely know me, Gage."

"I know enough. I know that you're one of the most caring people I've ever met. I know that you put other people's happiness before your own. I know that you put a guard up so people don't see the vulnerable parts of you."

Shock shrieks through me. "How do you know all of that?"

"Because I notice the small things," he answers, catching

another runaway tear from disappearing beneath the neck of his hoodie.

His words have an unexpected cataclysmic effect on me, and more cries echo around his room, probably concerning the other inhabitants of the house. The dissonance of my whimpers and his string of coos whistle through my eardrums like wind through reeds of cattails.

I've never trusted anyone with my heart before because I was always so certain that it would only lie with my family, but Gage Arlington has somehow managed to shoehorn his way into the tiniest crack. "W-what if you leave?" I ask through a sniffle, hating how pathetic I sound.

Nobody's obligated to stay. Everyone eventually leaves. Just look at my dad.

Gage inclines his head, making his hair flop over. "Not a chance in hell. You'd have to get a restraining order against me before I ever decide to leave."

A half-formed chuckle barely scrapes out of me. "I doubt that I'd ever do that. Or that a slip of paper would keep you away."

"You're definitely right about the last part. But I don't know, I can be pretty annoying," he jokes, nudging me with his elbow.

I don't even realize that the tears have retreated for the time being, or that my lungs are bringing in fresh air again. "So you finally admit it?"

"Oh, I've known this whole time."

I wipe off the makeup-tinged massacre on my face. "Of course you did," I mutter.

He shoots me a grin like a well-thrown dagger. "It's my job to annoy you, Spitfire. Can't have you growing a big head like me."

"I should honestly thank you for saving me from Gage levels of stupidity," I tease.

"I live to please."

The lightheartedness from the conversation tapers, leaving a terrible taste in my mouth like cigarette ash on my palette. "What about my mom, Gage? I-I don't know what to do."

I don't feel any more wetness on my face, but Gage still brushes his knuckles over my cheekbone, warmth kindling in the sage pits of his eyes. "I'll help you both with whatever you need. If you need me to go down and visit her, I will. If you need me to take Teague to hockey practice so you can get to class on time, I will. If you need me to drive you down to visit her, I will. There's nothing you can ask of me that I won't do," he insists.

"That's...a big commitment," I whisper, staring down at the watery blemishes shimmering on Gage's sleeves.

"You're a big commitment," he reiterates as if it's the most obvious thing in the world.

"We're not together. You do know that, right?"

"Like I said, not *yet*."

That dreaded smirk of his haunts me in my dreams. And out of them. I roll my eyes, only to divert my attention from the unexplained pickup in my heart rate. "You sound just like you did when you embarrassed me in front of Dilbert."

Taking this next step with Gage not only means letting him help me with my mom, but it means spending more time with him than I already am, and time has a way of...stirring feelings up. Including sexual ones.

We can be friends who fuck. I appreciate all that he's done for me, but I don't think I'm ready for anything more serious. And I know Gage is. He was ready the moment I met him.

He releases a groan. "You really need to stop having another man's name in your mouth."

"Or what?" I egg him on.

In hindsight, I shouldn't have said anything. In hindsight, I also didn't realize how dirty my response sounded.

He yanks me by the collar close enough so we're nose to

nose, and I'm not sure if it's the moonlight or the strangely romantic setting, but his lips look softer than a snowbank. "Or I'll make sure to drag his face across the plexiglass the first game I'm back on the ice," he growls.

I blink. I flush. Or maybe I break out into hives. I don't know what I do, but as usual, my brain short-circuits, and my tongue ties itself into a cumbersome knot. Possessiveness isn't usually something that gets me so hot and bothered, but when Gage is the one outpouring with jealousy, my belly does all sorts of acrobatics.

I wish I'd ripped my foot out of my mouth before I spoke. "Psh. You wouldn't," I deflect nervously.

He wouldn't, right?

"Can goaltend just fine with a few bruised knuckles."

Oh, God. He would. Gage absolutely would.

Tight-lipped, I quickly change the subject when I notice his fingers still enwrapped in his hoodie, and then I realize I never gave it back to him. Uh, not that he'd want it now after I slobbered all over it.

I begin to lift it up over my head anyways, but Gage stops me.

"Don't," he commands in that stupidly gruff voice of his. "It looks better on you."

The hoodie slips back over my head, and I feel my cheeks toast at least twenty degrees hotter, undoubtedly ripening them into a bright pink blush.

A smile hangs from Gage's lips, and both of us dwell in the subsequent silence. None of it is awkward or uncomfortable—which I didn't know was possible—but I guess it just takes the right person. He's staring at me the entire time, and it feels like he's drowning himself in my eyes to get to the bottom of a pain-filled quarry.

"Can I kiss you right now?" he asks in a hushed whisper. "I know you're emotional, and I would never want to take advantage of you. I...fuck. I just really want to kiss you right now, Cali."

There's a surprising shamefulness to his tone, one that I've never heard before. "You want to kiss me?"

He leans in enough to make it apparent what he wants, but not enough to crowd me. "Every second of every day."

I melt, and my heart thunders with an unignorable yes. I nod, and he slowly descends on my lips, cradling my cheek to ease me into the kiss. It's soft and gooey and so unlike anything we've shared before. He's got me trapped in honey like an unsuspecting fly, and I need to taste him like an addict needs their next hit. He's gentle with me, but not in a way one would be when handling broken glass. He's gentle with me in a way that one exudes reverence for something delicate, yet not entirely fragile.

I'm caught up in him. I'm caught up in everything about him. The way he reassures me with comforting words, the way he showers me with affection, the way he looks at me like he'll forget me the second he tears himself away. I never want us to unentangle from each other. I never want this warm feeling to go away. But of course, it seems like there's always something standing between us. Without warning, my stomach makes this loud, drawn-out gurgling noise, and embarrassment practically swallows me alive.

Gage pulls back immediately. "Was that your stomach?"

I fold my lower lip over, wishing that a car would magically come careening into his second-story room and pin my lifeless body up against the wall. "You heard that?"

He shoots me a *really?* look. "I think the entirety of California heard that."

"Ass," I joke, but the humor seems to be lost on him.

"I'm sorry. I should've gotten you food at the hospital," he apologizes, and to my utter confusion, guilt seethes in his eyes.

Why is he apologizing? He didn't do anything wrong. "You don't have to apologize."

"But I do. The last thing on your mind right now is taking care of yourself, so I need to be the one taking care of you."

Tight-chested, I relinquish a breathy "Gage…"

"When was the last time you ate?"

Shit. I don't know. This morning? I've been running around all day. But judging by the already-pissed expression suffusing his face, I feel like telling the truth would do more harm than good. Though my silence is telling in itself.

"This morning," I admit.

Gage's mouth splits into a frown, and he runs his hand through his hair. "Fuck, Cali. It's ten at night. You're telling me you've barely eaten at all today?"

"I'm fine, Gage."

"You're not," he immediately chides, pinching the bridge of his nose in frustration. "Please tell me you had something nutritious. Protein, healthy fat, fiber."

I wish I could say yes, but I can't. I had a sugary blueberry muffin before I dropped Teague off at school. A sugary blueberry muffin that was a pathetic article of sustenance for the entire day.

Taking my silence as an answer, he stands up. "Jesus Christ, give me a second."

I don't know where he goes, but he leaves the room, and I'm left sitting in the figurative—and literal—darkness for a good five minutes. There's a lot of clanking going on downstairs, but I stay where I am, becoming increasingly aware of the empty state of my belly.

Finally, the aroma of slightly burnt cheese wafts through my nostrils, and Gage shoulders the partition open, carrying a plate piled mountain-high with cheddar cheese melted over oven-warmed fries.

"Please eat more frequently throughout the day," he implores, plopping the plate in my lap.

My mouth waters when I notice the tiny bits of bacon he's sprinkled throughout for some extra protein. "You really didn't have to make anything for me."

"I know this might be hard to believe, but I can't stand knowing that you're this hungry all the time."

"It's just my work schedule," I insist, trying my best to allay his concern. "Some days I forget to eat, but it's really no big deal."

The angry knit of his eyebrows tells me he's unconvinced. "That's a huge deal, Cali."

"It's not. I promise you I'm not even that hungry—" Of course, my traitorous stomach decides to chime in with a thunderous roar that lasts for several seconds, and I instantly slap a hand over my belly. My cheeks flare with heat as Gage's eyes drop to the source of the noise.

"You need to eat. And if you're not going to eat right now, then I'll just have to feed you. Is that what you want? Because we won't leave this room until you finish everything on that plate."

Gage is mad. Like, *really* mad. I've never seen this side of him before. It's concern disguised by anger, and it's somehow more terrifying than pure anger itself. I didn't realize my eating habits were such a big deal to him.

"I just don't want you to think I'm a burden," I mumble under my breath.

His entire face softens at the rather chaotic crash-landing of the truth, and a Gage-patented smile slings up the corner of his lips. "I don't. I could never, okay? When will you understand that I *like* taking care of you?"

Oh.

I can tell he's seriously contemplating force-feeding me the fries, so I quickly dig into the greasy dish before he gets the chance to baby me. And the minute the potato crunches between my teeth and the cheese slides down my throat, I groan.

"Thank you. This is amazing. Oh my God, I could kiss you."

"I would happily take that as payment," Gage chirps, pitching forward to slant his lips over mine in another world-spinning kiss.

I rear backward and immediately cover my mouth. "Not right now! My breath is all…cheesy."

"Cali, I couldn't care less." He moves my hand to prove it to me, kissing the rest of the night's pain away like he's always known his lips were made for mine.

14

WAVE THE WHITE FLAG NOW
GAGE

"Okay, remember what we talked about," I debrief Teague, looking down at him in his adorably oversized hockey gear.

"When my sister comes to pick me up, I make a goal and show her how good I've gotten," he recites back to me, readjusting the helmet that doesn't quite sit right on his head.

I twirl around the whistle hanging from my neck—yes, I bought it just for this occasion—and nod. "Because?"

"Because you're going to make a bet with her."

"About?"

Teague sighs, the smile on his face flatlining. "About me making the winning goal in my next game," he mumbles, his voice curling with dubiety.

My eyebrows draw together. "Hey, hey. No gloom and doom, okay? You can do it, buddy. I know you can."

"Coach Gage, I know you mean well, but we've only had a few lessons together. I don't think I'll be able to make the winning goal."

I feel for the little guy. Teague has heart, which is something a lot of hockey players lack. He's determined, but he refuses to forgive himself when it comes to his mistakes. He puts a lot of pressure on himself for someone who's only playing youth hockey. I want to help him feel confident in his skills, but I think it'll be hard for him to celebrate any improvement since he's lived so long punishing himself for not being "good enough."

I blame everything on the fucking snot-nosed twerps picking on him. When I was his age, I played hockey for fun. I wasn't focused on going pro. But I can tell Teague takes the game a lot more seriously than I did. I'm worried that he'll grow up and regret treating hockey like a job rather than a hobby.

I crouch down to Teague's height—with surprisingly little resistance since Cali's been helping me stretch—and lower my voice to a gentle register, pride humming in my heart louder than the resounding pucks in play around us. "You've improved so much, T. I know you don't see it, but I do. All I ask of you is that you try your best and have fun. There's no pressure to make any winning goal, even though your sister would shit her pants to see you do so."

I've never really liked kids. I mean, I don't hate them, but I never looked at one and thought to myself, *Wow. That kid is adorable. I want to have six for myself and make my own hockey team, then name them all different L names that sound eerily similar to one another.*

But Teague's brought out some weird paternal feeling inside of me that I never knew existed before. He reminds me a lot of my brother.

"Cali says you shouldn't say that word," Teague reprimands, trying his best to look all serious with a pouty frown.

"*Cali's* not here right now," I say, winking at him. "You can say it as much as you want around me. Shit doesn't even begin to scrape the tip of the iceberg, Little Man. My personal favorite cuss word is cunt."

Teague clutches his stick to his chest. "What's a cunt?" he asks innocently.

My favorite food.

I bite back a grin, but I lose when a chuckle climbs up my throat. "It's another word for butt face."

God, I love poisoning the minds of the youth.

"Ooh, there are a lot of butt faces on my hockey team."

"There are a lot on mine too," I agree, mentally picturing Dilbert and his punchable face, then picturing me punching said face. Then picturing Cali giving me a whopping kiss in front of everyone and chanting, "My hero!"

Teague looks down at his skates. "Can we...maybe go over the play one more time?" His voice is small, picked apart by a timidness that I wish he didn't feel around me.

"Of course we can. Remember what we discussed, yeah? Don't be afraid of the puck. I know it can be scary when you get that sucker in front of you, but indecisiveness will only slow you down. If you have a clear shot of the goal, don't give the puck up too soon. Try to follow through, even if you're scared. And when you are forced to give up the puck, make sure you look for options before blindly coughing it up."

Teague nods, but I'm not sure how much of that he retained. Or how much made sense. I've never coached anyone before—I don't know what the hell I'm doing. I want to make him proud. I want to show Cali that I take her and her brother seriously. So here's to hoping my advice holds some merit.

I position myself in front of the goal, tightening my hands around my stick and praying that my decision not to suffocate myself with goalie pads won't result in another injury. My hip's feeling better, but I'm not a hundred percent yet.

Teague slugs over to the center line, shuffling the puck inch by inch with his blade before bumbling to get it in front of him. As soon as I blow the whistle, Teague's whole body whisks into offense mode, and he treads across the ice as if it's an active war zone, closing in unbelievably slowly on the goal despite there being no outside opposition. If this is how slow he moves without being under pressure, I don't want to know what pace he moves at during a real game.

He's actually so far away that my muscles loosen from their defensive bind, and I stand up straight, guessing that he'll make it to me within two to three business days.

"Don't be afraid, T! Show that puck who's boss!" I shout.

His head snaps up at my encouragement. Something switches inside him, emboldening him to pick up his skates and charge the goal, and he gets closer to me before swinging his stick back and slapping the puck toward the net.

Granted, he did directly aim for the middle instead of the harder-to-defend corners, but I think that was the first time I saw him place any belief in his stick. I block his shot without having to strain my hip much, and Teague's shoulders slump in disappointment.

"I suck!" he exclaims, his tone nearing teary territory that I'm *definitely* not equipped to handle. He falls onto his butt as worked-up breaths sail out of his helmet's cage.

"No, you don't." I skate over to him and join him on the ground, clapping him on the back. "You're still learning. And the best advice I can give you is to be easy on yourself. I know how frustrating it can be when you don't get things on the first try, but you can't keep beating yourself up over common mistakes."

He sniffs. "You don't make mistakes."

HA. Oh, sweet, sweet Teague.

"All the time," I reply, a good-natured smile working its way onto my mouth. "In fact, I've probably made a thousand more mistakes than you have."

"Really?"

"Really. Sometimes I suck at tracking the puck, and I end up thinking I can block a shot just based on my peripheral vision. It's cost my team a lot of losses."

Teague throws his arms up. "But you're a professional hockey player!"

A tepid warmth like the tail end of summer consolidates in my chest, birthing different kinds of butterflies in my stomach. "Even professionals make mistakes."

I've never had someone look up to me before. It feels…weird. I'm barely responsible for myself, and now I feel this responsibility to make Teague proud. It freaks me out. I can't have Teague looking up at me with all this hero worship. That's how my brother used to look at me. And I failed him in the end. It's just a matter of time until I repeat the same process with Teague.

Thankfully, Cali steps onto the ice and saves me from my overactive thoughts, wearing her signature ponytail and a new zip-up hoodie to stave off the cold.

"Keep practicing your shooting," I tell him, hopping so quickly to my feet that a concerning stab lances up my hip, but the unmitigated yearning to inhale Cali's cinnamon scent and feel her pliable body in my arms makes me disregard my injury's outcry.

I teleport over to her, eliciting a gasp from her even though she saw me coming from miles away.

"Jesus. I really need to put a bell on you," she mutters.

"You can put whatever you want on me."

When she crosses her arms over her chest, her apricot ponytail flicks behind her. "You use that line on all the girls you schmooze?"

"No girls, Spitfire. Just you," I flirt, feeling warmth incinerate every inch of my body. Every time I think I have a handle on my nerves, they slip out of my grasp.

"What makes me so special?" There's a joking bite to her tone, and I wish she could see herself the way I see her.

It's like the stars handpicked her to carry on their legacy, to deem her worthy enough to be the bright light in my life, scaring away the darkness and desolation from the corners of my mind.

"How much time do you have?"

A blush assails the apples of her cheeks, turning her complexion my favorite shade of pink, and she rolls her eyes and tries to ease the spotlight off herself.

"How's he doing?" she asks, peering over my shoulder to watch Teague toy with the puck. The concern burnished in her gaze makes my belly somersault. Cali's a great big sister, and I'm going to help her see that.

"He's good. He's just working through some confidence issues," I disclose, matching her line of sight and tracking his small figure as he lands a shot in the net.

She doesn't say anything, which makes me briskly turn back to her. Her nose is scrunched in displeasure, and her bottom lip begins to wobble.

"Don't do that."

She throws me a look of utter confusion. "Do what?"

"Blame yourself for something you can't control."

Cali huffs in a knee-jerk response, carefully crafting her next set of words to exempt herself from a possible lecture. "I'm not...*blaming*...myself," she insists.

I lean my chin on the butt of my hockey stick, pulling my eyebrows together incredulously.

Approach with caution, Gage. You stick your hand in that enclosure, and she'll tear it right off your body.

"Cali, your lower lip trembles every time you get in your head." I sigh, wanting nothing more than to steady her mouth with my own—to alleviate her worries and swallow the self-deprecating comments that I know are waiting on the bed of her tongue.

Her fingers fling to her lips in betrayal, and her whole frame droops. "I just worry about him."

"I know you do, Spitfire. But you have to trust that he'll find his way on his own."

She perks her head back up to witness Teague sinking another goal, and she remedies her distress with a meek half-smile. "I guess he does look like he's getting better," she notes.

Uh, that's just because nobody is in the goal.

"He's improved a lot," I brag, lifting my head off my stick and puffing my chest out.

"Oh, really?"

"First off, your tone is hurtful. Second off, he has. He's gotten so good that I bet you he'll make the winning shot of his next game."

Was that a good bet to make? No. Do I have anything to lose? Just my dignity, and that's already been reduced to the size of a pea. I have full faith in Teague that he'll play better in his upcoming game than he ever has before. Goal-worthy better? That's...debatable. All very possible if he remembers what we've gone over—situational awareness, confidence, shooting, the good ol' *have fun out there, champ.*

Cali gives me a dick-wetting once-over, dragging her tongue over the front of her teeth. "What are we betting?"

I should back out now. A smart man would acknowledge when he's lost and save himself from further humiliation. I am not a smart man.

"If Teague makes the winning shot of his next game, you have to get my jersey number tattooed on you," I drawl, already scoping out the spots on her body that would be fucking *perfect* for my number.

None of that discreet tattoo shit. The side of her hip. Her upper back. The space between her breasts. God, her fucking *ass*. That's a million-dollar tattoo. Hell, I'd buy her a private island off Maui to breathe that image into existence.

She laughs in my face. Bends over, does the thing where the laugh turns silent, and then starts swatting the air. Thankfully, her theatrics don't alert the other hockey-goers, but my God, does this woman abuse my ego like a mail deliveryman throwing around a UPS package.

"I love my brother, but there's no way in *hell* that's happening," she says, and as much as I want to prove her wrong and shut her bratty mouth, I can't help but love the sound of her melodic laughter.

"It will. Just you watch."

"And if it doesn't?"

"Then I'll dress up in high heels and do a choreographed dance of your choosing during our last game of the season."

She ponders the two outcomes, and I'm not sure if she's been mind-wiped by aliens—or if the possibility of Teague not only making a shot, but making the *winning* shot is so unbelievable—but she sticks out her hand for us to shake on it.

"Deal."

I slap my hand against hers as a smirk tests the edges of my lips. "I hope you're not a sore los—"

"Guys, watch this!" Teague calls out to us, doing a little wiggle before kicking into high gear and speeding right toward the unoccupied goal.

The puck's in his possession, he has a clear shot, and I'm about to do a victory fist pump in the air for the obvious talent I've bestowed upon him...right before he trips over his dominant leg and goes crashing to the ice.

15

HORRIFYING CONCUSSIONS AND HEARTFELT CONFESSIONS
GAGE

Fear. I know it well.

Sometimes it presents itself to me in different forms: an icy grip on my neck, heart palpitations, the burn of bile on my tongue, a short-lived panic that suffuses heat to my head. Right now, I'm experiencing all the above.

Teague's helmet slams against the ice in a single freeze-frame, and then he goes absolutely still. My world goes even stiller.

My gaze quickly pivots to Cali, and there's a slash of fear on her face, ripping through her composure as if it's as flimsy as paper mâché. My throat protests the weight of a scream, but Cali's pained cry ends up defiling the ambience of the arena. A banshee wail—an omen of something far darker than just death.

"Teague!"

I throw my gloves off and take the lead in skating over to him as fast as I can, not even incapacitated by the anxiety sloshing around in my stomach. Cali's right on my heels, and I scramble over to Teague's lifeless body, trying to assess him without moving him.

Come on, Teague.

Multiple sets of unwelcome eyes drag over us, unwilling to lend a helping hand, only willing to exude sympathy.

No, no, no. This isn't happening. I'm not going to fail him like I did my brother. Realistically, somewhere deep in my subconscious, I know that the worst injury he could sustain is a gnarly concussion, but all I can think about is the possibility that he might not wake up, however irrational that thought may be. I underestimated my brother's illness, and his condition only deescalated. What if I underestimate this?

"Come on, buddy. Open those eyes for me," I whisper, waiting a few minutes to see if he comes to on his own, and I'm just about to scream for an ambulance when Teague groggily peels his eyes open with a groan.

"Did I make it?" he croaks.

I'm nearly to the point of tears, but not so far gone I forget to smile, and my lungs rattle with a bottled exhale, shooting out into the fifty-degree atmosphere like a gradually vanishing contrail. I know he's asking about the goal, but all I say is, "Yeah, buddy. You made it."

Cali's a hysterical mess, and maybe it's because my mind is in fix-it mode, but all I can focus on is alleviating her stress. I'm not granted a moment to lose it, even though that was single-handedly one of the scariest things I've ever witnessed.

Yeah, I'm a hockey player who's been injured a few times, but watching it happen to someone else you care about—someone who's just a kid—makes it all the more terrifying.

I squeeze Teague gingerly, then let Cali bear hug him, and I swear she squishes him so tightly his spine almost pops.

My head is still reeling, my adrenaline has yet to come down from its massive spike, and my heart is on its own goddamn warpath the way it's pounding against my ribs. I walk over to the edge of the rink—too riled up to skate that far of a distance safely—and I steady myself on the plexiglass.

Even though my body's not in any danger, it tenses in preparation for the nonexistent threat, all my senses being whaled on from every direction. My thoughts pinball around my skull, and I abandon my effort to go in search of a medic by simply just yelling for one, unsure if I'm stable enough to navigate the freezing corridors in the state I'm in. My vision wobbles and strains, and insuppressible nausea burbles deep in my gut.

I'm still terrified. I can't—I can't put into words what just happened. I thought I was about to relive the moment my brother passed away. Nobody in my life, except for Teague and Cali, has ever meant as much to me as my brother did. And when people mean something to you, the hurt and pain they experience affect you in the same way.

My brother's memory had been shoved down below the depths of my subconscious, never to buoy to the top for the rest of my existence. But in this moment, everything comes flooding back to the surface, drowning me in anger, guilt, sorrow, and regret. Drowning me in all those unresolved emotions I tried to quell beneath a storm-aggravated ocean.

A medic—who the arena keeps stationed here for Reapers practices—comes sprinting over to me with a first aid kit, and I walk him over to Teague and Cali, praying that Teague's injuries are minimal.

Cali gives the medic room to work, and she joins me a few feet away as I stare blankly at the little boy in front of me, who's putting on a brave face even after the horrifying experience he just had.

Fuck. Why wasn't I watching him more closely? I could've caught him before he fell. I could've prevented this from ever happening.

"Gage, you're shaking," Cali says quietly beside me, worry crumpling her features.

"What?" I look down at my pale hands, which are shaking

rabbit-fast, and I will them to stop, but it's like my control's been capsized.

She wastes no time enclosing them in her own hands, warming my frigid skin, and immediately, the tremors end. I blink a few times and pinpoint my glossy gaze on our layered fingers, still trying to wrap my head around how quickly Cali's touch calmed me, and now I'm mirroring her puzzled expression with one of my own.

"You freaked out as soon as Teague hit the ice."

"I..."

It hurts to breathe. Why does it hurt to breathe?

I'm trying to get my brain and tongue to cooperate with one another, but the words never budge from my mouth. Nothing's physically restricting me from saying anything, yet I'm struggling with a speechlessness that's foreign to me. My throat makes this pathetic gurgling noise in lieu of an actual response.

"Okay, let's sit down," she coaxes, guiding me to the side opening of the rink. I practically have to puppeteer my limbs to keep them from buckling underneath me.

We take a seat on the curb, and her concern has somehow grown tenfold over the minute it took for us to get here. Her face is veiled in shadows cast by the harsh lighting, and her teeth print impressions into her bottom lip. She hasn't let go of my hand since she grabbed it.

Her big, frisbee-sized eyes adhere to me. "Are you okay?"

Please say something. I'm fine. I'm good. Say anything, you idiot!

I moderate my voice as best as I can given my lack of breath. "I'm okay."

And like some weird fucking placebo effect, I force myself to believe it until my physical symptoms almost all wane, leaving me with the searing reminder of Teague's accident instead of the searing hole in my belly. Oxygen returns to my chest, the heat in my temples recedes, and control reaffirms its iron reign.

She doesn't stop examining my face, and her fingers only slip from mine so she can caress my cheek. "Gage, what happened out there?"

I'm done hiding my past from her. It's time to tell her everything. She deserves it. *I* deserve it.

"I haven't told you the full story about my brother," I admit, partially hating myself for not telling her my brother's story sooner, partially hating the way hurt dampens her eyes. She's patient with me while I choke down the rest of my qualms and free a long-hidden truth from a lockbox of trauma.

She slowly lowers her palm back onto my folded hands for moral support. If I thought mentioning him at the hospital was bad, this is going to be torture.

"His name was Trip, and he was my best friend. We used to do everything together as kids. We'd go on adventures down near the creek behind our house, we'd spend sleepless nights reading ghost stories to each other, we'd bake the most disgusting creations in the oven while my parents failed to supervise us." A laugh wrests itself from me—a laugh I didn't think I'd be capable of given the fucked-up trip down memory lane.

"He was, um, born with a heart defect. To be more specific, he had something called aortic stenosis, which basically meant that his aortic valve was too small. In order for his blood to flow properly, his heart had to work ten times harder to push blood out to the rest of his body. And over time, his heart grew weaker from the stress. The doctors told us he would be able to live a long, normal life as long as he received constant treatment, but my parents…"

I can't even say it. For a split second, I'm controlled by my fear again, watching helplessly as it tears at my insides and rips me asunder, letting me bleed out from pulled-apart muscle. The moisture in my eyes triples, but I don't blink, because I don't want to let a tear fall.

"I'm here, Gage. It's okay. I'm right here," she murmurs, salving my newly opened pain with her soft voice, sidling up against my body and keeping our laced hands close to her heart.

Aside from Fulton, I've never told anyone else about Trip. I never talked about him because I didn't want to share him with anyone. I didn't want people to know him because *I* barely knew him. I didn't get seventy-some-odd years to know him or see what kind of man he grew into.

I'm close to running away from this conversation, to hiding from that pitiful look in Cali's eyes. But the moment I feel the beat of her heart, it neutralizes that terror inside me. I know I should want to bury that memory, but this is the first time in forever that I don't punish it—or myself—for existing.

I square my shoulders and take a breath, comforted by the feel of our skin touching and by the lullaby her heart plays just for me. She gives me strength that I never would've found anywhere else. She gives me more support than my parents ever did.

"My parents are terrible, money-hungry fuckers who never gave a shit about me or my brother," I growl, feeling unchecked anger wring the last remnants of grief from my body. "They knew how sick my brother was, and they didn't do anything to help him. It wasn't a matter of money or resources or time. It was a matter of fucking *love*. And in the end, Trip suffered because of my parents' neglect."

"I'm so sorry, Gage."

"I could've saved him. If I'd just taken matters into my own hands, he still would be here today."

I've tried so hard to be okay. I've tried so hard to stop punishing myself, but the truth is, if I don't punish myself, I'll grow to accept what happened to Trip...and that's something I could never bring myself to do. The warning signs were all there. There was a sufficient amount of time for treatment to be done. This wasn't some out-of-the-blue illness that appeared overnight. I was a kid, yeah, but all I had to do was go to someone—*anyone*—and ask for help.

I can't believe I just thought he'd be okay. I was so fucking stupid. I was his big brother. I was supposed to look out for him, and I didn't. He relied on me to keep him safe. That was my *one* job. That was my purpose in life.

"Hey." Cali's cheeks tuck into a frown—a sight that I hate every time I bear witness to it—and she rubs circles over the back of my knuckles. Her touch isn't the electrifying firework show it usually is, though. It's so inexplicably cold that it doesn't even feel like she's there.

"None of it was your fault. None of it, okay? Please tell me you know that." A rare desperation rides on the heel of her words, and although her assurance is gentle in delivery, the weight of it bludgeons me.

"I was supposed to be his protector."

"You were a kid, Gage. *A kid.* You did everything you could to protect him."

I try to pull my hand away from her, but she doesn't let me. I don't care that I was just a kid. I could've done so much more to keep him here. When I remember my brother, I don't look back fondly on the moments we shared together. I don't celebrate his life. Instead, a forecast of depression and survivor's guilt threatens to drown me in the same way my brother's fate befell him.

"That doesn't mean shit, Cali. You were a kid taking care of your mother, and she's still here," I snap.

Cali flinches slightly, as if my words burned her. "That's different. You were so much younger—"

My lip curls back from my teeth in a snarl, and the volume of our private conversation seems to carry in the open-ended space. "How is it any different?"

My first mistake was assuming Cali would back down from

our altercation. Her irises dip into a darker shade of blue—one more reflective of a deep-water trench than of the ocean's glistening surface. "I get that you blame yourself, Gage. I get it, I do. But take it from someone who's punished themselves their whole life—it's not worth it. That self-destructive cycle will ruin you. You are the *last* person to blame in this situation. You were the *only* person who truly cared for your brother, and even though he's not here anymore, you filled his last moments with the love your parents were never willing to give him. You were there for him through it all. Do you know how lucky Trip was to have you as his best friend? He was so fucking lucky, and if he was here today, I bet you he'd say the exact same thing."

I don't…nobody's ever said anything like that to me before. I stare at her with beads of moisture smeared over my lower lashes, with my words stuck between my teeth like grade A chewing gum.

"Please don't live the rest of your life blaming yourself for something out of your control," she implores, sounding like a broken record that I've played many times before. And finally, the connection of our palms spark with heat, her once-frosted fingertips now leaving thermal prints over my skin.

I want to break down in her arms, want to uncork years of sadness and let it flood out of me until my body's nothing but a dehydrated husk. But I refrain, still unsure of where our relationship lies.

"When Teague fell out there, it took me back to the helplessness I felt when my brother died. If something happened to Teague and I failed to save him…it would break me," I explain, welcoming back the quiver in my voice, as well as the emotion no longer silenced by deafening indignation.

I never really understood why I was so drawn to Cali—aside from her being beautiful and terrible for my ego—but I feel like I understand now. The way Cali treats her brother is the way I wish my parents had treated Trip. She cares about the things Teague's passionate about, she cares about how he's feeling, she cares about how she can be a better sister. She's always there for him when he needs her. If my parents had even showed an *ounce* of what Cali practices in her heart, Trip would still be here today.

Both she and Teague fill the hole in my heart that was left by my brother. They're the first people to have ever made me even somewhat okay with revisiting Trip's memory. I hadn't realized how dark my life had been before they shared their light with me.

She wraps me in a hug that would've knocked me on my ass if I wasn't already sitting down, and she slots her nose into my neck. "Thank you for looking out for Teague," she whispers. "And thank you for telling me about your brother."

With the volume of her curls tied up, I settle for stroking her back, clamping my eyes shut, and finally letting a single tear sluice down my cheek.

Thank you for being the girl to heal me.

16

FRIENDS WITH A CAPITAL "FAKE"
CALISTA

It's been a week since Teague's accident on the ice, and thankfully, he made a full recovery. He only had a minor concussion that gave him a few bothersome headaches, but that was the extent of the pain. In fact, he's super pumped over sustaining his first hockey-related injury. Dear God. Hockey's a violent sport, right? I'm probably going to see so many more injuries in the future.

The whole week, I haven't been able to stop thinking about what Gage told me. I can't imagine going through that type of pain. That would be like if I lost Teague...like when I lose my mother. The more I uncover about him, the more he astounds me. He's so much more than the surface-level jerk I met at the rink.

I feel honored that he trusted me enough to tell me about his brother. And as much as I know that conversation needed to be had between us, I wasn't ready for the consequences it brought in its wake. We're closer. So much closer than we've ever been, and that terrifies me.

So I do what I always do when I face discomfort: I throw

myself into my work, hoping that all my problems will just disappear so I never have to confront them.

Both Gage and I have been busy this week with our own stuff, so it's given me some space to try and put a name to what I feel when I'm around him.

Spoiler alert: I haven't. In fact, I think I've made myself more confused.

"Incredible work today, guys," I praise, finishing off our lesson with a group clap like we always do at the end of class.

After only a few years of teaching, it still amazes me how powerful the human body is. How fluid and nimble our limbs can be, how our muscles strengthen under duress, how dancers are able to balance their entire body weight on the balls of their toes.

As the class disperses amongst animated chatter, one of my students jogs over to me, catching me mid-pack.

"Hey, Cali. Can I, uh, ask you for some help on one of the sequences we went over today?"

I glance up to lock eyes with Aeris, the brightest-eyed and most enthusiastic student I've ever had, and a shy smile is fleshed out on her face. She's really come into herself these past few weeks, growing more confident in her movements even when she doesn't get the steps completely right. And she's always willing to learn and improve, which is a gift that a lot of dancers don't always have.

"Of course." I rise up from my squat and shepherd her over to an unoccupied square of floor, a smile transferring onto my own lips. I've already taken off my heels, and I'm too exhausted to put them back on.

Aeris, still in her stilettos, starts the sequence from a wide stance with her fists on her hips. "Okay, I know that we do the hip stuff here." She demonstrates with two one-sided twists of her hips, flinging her arm across her body at the same time.

"Then we do the head roll," she recalls, coming back to the

middle. She rolls her head and pelvis in tandem with one another, whipping her messily secured ponytail around and tapping her hands against her waist to an invisible rhythm.

"And then we go to the floor."

With parallel feet, she keeps her thighs closed as she descends, finally dropping to the ground and opening her legs, bouncing a few times with the stability that her heels give her.

"But I get lost on how we do that spinny thing and end up with our leg over our head."

"Gotcha," I say, nodding. I mirror her position, falling easily into the stretch since my muscles are still lax and warm. "Once you're here, you're gonna turn clockwise onto your butt, making sure you use the outside of your thigh to cushion your landing."

I ease into the spinning motion she was talking about, using the momentum from the spin to turn me all the way back to the front. "Then you swing your weight to the right, letting your left hip come off the ground. When you swing your arm along with it, it'll help balance you."

I do as I say, keeping my right arm straight to balance my weight and jutting my pelvis out to get the desired outcome. "And the momentum from this pose will allow you to swing to the other side. You're gonna fold your left leg underneath you —still landing on the outside of your thigh—and then you're gonna bring your left side flush against the ground so you can extend your right leg over your head."

My leg flies up over my head as I point my toes, elongating the line. The top of my thigh brushes my head from years of flexibility training, putting me in a sort of single-legged half-splits.

"Ohhh, that makes a lot of sense," Aeris muses, observing me with an intent gaze, her brow pinched, and her fist placed against her mouth like the thinker statue.

I abandon the pose, giving my muscles a much-needed rest.

"Yep. It's a lot easier once you break everything down slowly and go step by step."

"Thank you. So much. For all your help and belief in me."

Heat swamps my cheeks, probably lifting a cardinal red to my skin. "You're an incredible dancer, Aeris. You dance with this authenticity that comes from raw emotion. You're so in tune with every little feeling, good and bad, that it comes across clearly in your movements. That's something you can't teach. I'd give anything for that kind of talent."

"You know, in the beginning, I didn't think I could do it." There's a genuineness that rings true in her tone, and poor Aeris looks like she actually might burst into sobs. "But with your guidance, I feel so much more empowered now. I feel the most confident I've ever felt in my body, and I never thought I'd get to that point in my life."

"That's what heel dancing is all about—finding your inner power. You did this all on your own, Aeris, and I couldn't be prouder of you," I reply, having to somehow suck the happy tears back in.

"Th-that's the nicest thing anyone's ever said to me," she hiccups, moisture glazing over her bourbon eyes. "Can I hug you? I'm going to hug you."

Even though she warned me beforehand, I don't have any time to brace myself before her arms maul me in a death-gripping hug, causing my voice to mutate into dog chew toy levels of squeakiness.

"No...problem," I wheeze. This girl's a pint-sized powerhouse. And wow, she gives some of the best hugs I've ever received. Minus the rib crushing part.

She gives me a last little squeeze, and I pat her back in response. I'm not used to someone outside of my inner circle showing me this much kindness.

"Um, I don't want to freak you out or anything, but I think

you have a Peeping Tom," she whispers, alerting every single mental siren in my brain and making them go off in a hair-raising screech.

Since my back is turned to her line of sight, I whip around and ready my hands in case I have to jab some pervert's balls, but the only *pervert* I see is Gage standing by the front desk with some kind of fluffy basket hanging from his hands.

We might've had a heart to heart, but that doesn't mean I'm going to treat him any differently. Banter is what makes our friendship...*friendly*. If it veers into other territories, I'm doomed.

"Oh, that's not a Peeping Tom. That's just the piece of trash I took out earlier that seems to have blown back in," I mutter, narrowing my eyes at him from across the dance floor. He's still grinning at me, so either he needs a new contact prescription, or he's just being his infuriating self.

Speaking of infuriating, that's exactly what I'll be when I'm picking out Gage's scandalous little costume for his end of the bet. I love my brother, but scoring the winning goal of a hockey game seems like something few players achieve during their career.

I'll *never* get Gage's number tattooed on me. Ever. But I will, however, enjoy a raunchy dance performed by the Reapers' goalie in stilettos and a disturbingly small crop top.

Aeris gets this terrifying *aww* expression on her face. "I didn't know you knew Gage."

"Unfortunately." I have no idea why he's just shown up at my studio looking all...*lovey dovey*...but this is the last place he needs to be. And that's the last look he needs to have! We're just two business partners who kiss sometimes. I have to stay focused on my other obligations right now—not skipping into the sunset and living out some fantasy life.

The animosity welting me like an oppressive ray of sun

fades to a curious buzz. "Wait a second, how do *you* know him?"

"He's my boyfriend's teammate," she admits with a bashful smile.

"So he's definitely not here for you then?"

She shakes her head. "He's never looked that happy to see me. And he's definitely never brought me a basket of candy."

He brought me a basket of candy? Is he clinically insane? Wait a second, of course he is. Why am I even asking myself that?

Aeris nudges me with her elbow. "Oh my God. Are you two...?"

"Nope! Definitely not. I honestly don't know why he's here. I'll just go and get him to leave. Yeah, he's probably here for another dancer," I prattle, speed-walking straight over to him without giving Aeris a chance to interrogate me further.

The nerve this man has!

Since there are still plenty of onlookers roaming around the studio, I sink my claws into his arm and yank him into a private section of the building—or I guess less of a private section and more of a glorified janitor's closet. Once the door snicks shut behind us, I tug on the pull chain of the lightbulb, dousing the small space in light.

"What are you doing here?" I hiss, keeping my voice low even with the added privacy of the closed door.

"Don't sound too happy to see me," he drawls with that irresistible, rumbling bass that makes me squeeze my legs together and my pussy flutter.

"You're just—you—you're out in the open!" I gesticulate with my arms wildly.

"This is a free country."

A warning growl ripples in my throat. "Gage..."

He holds his hands up in mock surrender. "Okay, okay. I should've called ahead of time, but I needed to come see you."

"Needed?"

"Wanted...badly. Wanted *very* badly."

It used to be so easy to stay mad at him, but now, with his big, verdant eyes staring at me like I'm sunshine in a fucking bottle, I can't. Gage is the least subtle person about his emotions, and if cartoon love hearts could bulge out of his sockets, they would.

A core-melting smile, a poorly hidden blush, body language that's not only exceedingly close to me but that's also more than ready to make up for lost time.

I'm not breaking the law by talking to him. I'm not going to be executed for fraternizing with the enemy. I'm just afraid that if someone sees us together, speculation about Gage's love life is going to happen—thank you, stupid superstar status of his. And if people start spreading rumors, it'll push him to want something real even more.

It's not just about focusing my efforts elsewhere, it's also about fearing the inevitable. When things get real, that's when loss does too. I've dealt with enough loss for a lifetime.

I don't want to break his heart. I don't want him to break *my* heart.

I don't mean to sigh so exasperatedly, but it kind of just trickles out of my mouth.

"Hey." He sweeps me into his big arms, dispelling the racing thoughts from my mind with each inhalation of his forest-thick cologne, and the warmth radiating off his body cocoons me tighter than any fleece blanket I own. "I'm sorry. I didn't mean to complicate things. I just...wanted to ask you something."

"You don't have to be sorry. I'm the one who overreacted," I explain, shivering when I feel him press his lips to the crown of my head. I want to bask in that feeling—and I can't let myself.

I pull away abruptly, masquerading my disappointment with a half-smile. "Gage, you know we're just friends, right? Friends with benefits. That's all."

There's a minuscule shift in his expression, but it's so well-modulated that I can't place the meaning behind it. "Right. No, I know," he says, turning his attention to the full basket still dangling from his arm. "I wanted to give you something. And ask you something."

He presents the basket in front of me, and maybe I'm the one who needs a better prescription, because it's not just candy that sits in the faux black fur. There's a box of ghost Peeps, a tube of candy corn, pumpkin Reese's Peanut Butter Cups, a cauldron-shaped mug, an autumn-scented candle, a plush bat, and fuzzy, skull-printed socks.

With a staggered breath, a strange feeling manifests in my gut. "Gage, what is all of this?"

"It's a boo basket," he answers matter-of-factly.

"A what?"

"You know, a boo basket. It's, uh, you put things in it and give it to...your friends."

I squint my eyes at him. "Uh-huh. Really?"

He hooks his finger in the collar of his shirt and pulls. "Yes, ma'am."

"So you're gonna give every one of your teammates one of these baskets?" I pry, standing up on my tiptoes to look him dead in the eyes and gain as much intimidating leverage as my five-foot-seven body can manage.

He snorts. "Everyone except for Dilbert."

"You know, I'm starting to think you and Dilbert have a love-hate relationship going on," I tease.

Gage grabs my jaw, forcing me to lower to my heels as his gaze broods with a darkness that frightens me as much as it turns me on. "What did I say about having another man's name in your mouth?"

I call his bluff. "What are you going to do, Gage? You gonna fuck it out of me in a disgusting janitor's closet?"

His fingers release my jaw, and although darkness still clouds his eyes, his voice has lost the envious compulsion it was under. "No, Cali. Because you deserve so much more than a quickie in a closet."

My mouth seems to fall open, which is funny because I have nothing to say. See? Just friends isn't a concept that exists in Gage's brain. You're telling me that he's this friendly with every person in his life?

He sets the basket on the ground, rubbing his hands together and preparing for what looks to be a big speech. I hope it's not the speech I think it is.

"What I *really* came over here to ask you is if you'd go to a Halloween party with me," he finally confesses.

Oh.

"That's it?" I ask.

"That's it."

"Wouldn't a text have sufficed?"

"Would you have answered?"

Good point, Gage.

I must not be concealing my skepticism well enough because Gage continues with his proposition, looking sweatier and more nervous as he goes on. "We're throwing a party at the house, and I'd really like for you to come. With me."

I contemplate my answer, weighing the very unbalanced scales of consequences in my head. Go to the party with Gage, get blackout drunk—or maybe just drunk—and have fun after a shitty and depressing week. Or stay at home with Teague while harrowing images of my hospitalized mother circulate in my mind. Seems like the answer should be obvious.

"Just as friends, though. Right?" I caution.

"Just as friends," he echoes rather convincingly.

He's acting…suspicious. I don't want to regret going, but I also don't want to regret *not* going. It's going to be an unsupervised party with an overflow of alcohol and maybe a handful of illegal substances. What's the worst that could go wrong?

I slide my hands a bit self-consciously down my dance attire. "I don't have a costume."

Gage slaps on an award-winning smirk, catalyzing that unshakable desire in my belly.

"Don't worry. I've already taken care of it."

17

ANNOYANCE AT ITS FINEST

October 15th, Tuesday, 3:47 p.m.
GAGE: I called you.
CALISTA: Yep. It rang.
GAGE: Why didn't you answer?
CALISTA: I'm busy.
GAGE: Doing what?
CALISTA: Ignoring you.
GAGE: Ha. You're talking to me now.
CALISTA: You're right, Gage. Let me put EVERYTHING I'm doing aside and focus my full attention on you.
GAGE: Thank you. I deserve it.
CALISTA: That's it? That's all you have to say? That's the reason you called me three times in a row?
GAGE: No. But you're being mean to me, and now I don't want to tell you.
CALISTA: If you're not going to tell me, I'll just put my phone on Do Not Disturb.
GAGE: I'll notify you anyway.
CALISTA: Ugh, you're so annoying!

GAGE: I think you secretly like it.

CALISTA: What did you have to tell me? And it better be life or fucking death.

GAGE: I miss you. *smiley face emoji*

OCTOBER 17, Thursday, 5:13 p.m.
GAGE: What size are your boobs?
CALISTA: Fucking excuse me?
GAGE: Like, how big are they?
CALISTA: Hi, Gage. I'm doing well, thanks. My day's been good. Woke up and put my shirt on inside out, so that was fun.
GAGE: Would you say like a size large?
CALISTA: Are you serious right now?
GAGE: This is important, Cali. I need your answer right now.
CALISTA: Why?
GAGE: It's for your Halloween costume.
CALISTA: First off, bra size isn't measured on a scale from small to large. It's based off band size and cup size, which use a number and letter system.
GAGE: Okay. So like a 57Z?
CALISTA: Jesus Christ, no. It doesn't go that fucking high. And shouldn't you be a better guesser? You've had them in your mouth.
GAGE: You're right. I'm gonna change my answer to a...45R.
CALISTA: *eye roll emoji*
GAGE: Maybe you can just send me a reference photo. Or you can compare them to household objects like a small potted vase or a large candle.
CALISTA: Ugh. They're a 34DD.
GAGE: That was going to be my next guess.
GAGE: Also, can you tell your tits I love them?

OCTOBER 18TH, **Friday, 9:41 a.m.**

CALISTA: Gage, since when did your contact have a heart by it?

GAGE: Aw, Cali. I'm flattered.

CALISTA: No, dickwad. I obviously didn't put it there.

GAGE: Ohhh. Did you put an eggplant instead? For my giant penis?

CALISTA: I actually put a shrimp.

GAGE: That's hurtful. And very untrue.

CALISTA: Did you somehow unlock my phone with your gremlin fingers?

GAGE: I have no idea what you're talking about, and frankly, I don't appreciate being accused.

CALISTA: You're a second away from being blocked.

GAGE: And? I know where you live. I know exactly what apartment number is yours.

CALISTA: Is that a threat?

GAGE: Do you want it to be?

CALISTA: I'm changing your contact name to STUPID WHORE.

GAGE: I love how you have little nicknames for me. *kissy face emoji*

CALISTA: Every day I pray that murder will be legal.

GAGE: It would be an honor to die by your hands.

CALISTA: Don't think you'll like it that much when I'm choking the life out of you.

GAGE: On the contrary, I'll fucking love it.

OCTOBER 20TH, Friday, 8:11 p.m.
    GAGE: Come outside. I have something for you.
    CALISTA: I'm not home right now.
    GAGE: I know. You're at the studio.
    CALISTA: Ugh, you're such a creeper.
    CALISTA: How do you even know that?
    GAGE: It's actually this really cool thing called the internet. Invented in 1983 by some crazy computer scientist dude.
    CALISTA: Hardy fucking har.
    GAGE: God, woman. Will you just come outside? You're ruining the surprise.
    CALISTA: If this is a quickie in the back of your car, I'm not interested.
    GAGE: Who do you take me for?
    CALISTA: Do you really want me to answer that question?
    GAGE: *expressionless face emoji* Fine then. I guess you don't want the California roll I brought you.
    CALISTA: You brought me dinner?
    GAGE: Yes, Calista, because unlike you, I actually care about your well-being.
    CALISTA: Gage, you didn't have to bring me dinner.
    GAGE: I did because you probably would've forgotten to eat otherwise. Am I wrong?
    CALISTA: ...
    GAGE: Exactly.
    CALISTA: I can take care of myself.
    GAGE: I know you can, but that doesn't mean you have to all the time.
    CALISTA: Thank you. Ugh, I don't like it when you're all... *nice*.
    GAGE: Oh, so you mean all the time?
    CALISTA: HA. I think that's the first funny joke you've made since I met you.

GAGE: Wooow. You know what? I think the rabid squirrels down at the park will enjoy some fifty-dollar sushi.

CALISTA: FIFTY DOLLARS? You spent fifty dollars on a single roll?

GAGE: I would've bought the hundred-dollar one with the gold flakes if they weren't out of it.

CALISTA: Now you're just showing off.

GAGE: No, Spitfire. You're worth the most expensive sushi in the world.

CALISTA: Ugh! Stop being so...so...

GAGE: Charming? Sexy? Hilariously endearing? *winky face*

CALISTA: ...

GAGE: I'm just going to pretend that you're so overcome with gratitude that you can't think of a sufficient enough adjective to describe me.

CALISTA: Sure. Let's go with that.

GAGE: Now come out here. I'm lacking some Vitamin You right now and need my next dose before I die.

CALISTA: That's the worst pickup line I've ever heard. And you have some serious issues.

GAGE: Nope. Just separation anxiety.

CALISTA: Print my face out on a piece of paper and stick it to your body pillow.

GAGE: You act like I haven't already done that.

18

EVE WAS BIBLICALLY A...
CALISTA

Remember when Gage said he took care of my Halloween costume? He did NOT take care of it.

I don't know what I was expecting—since Gage has the creativity of a hand turkey—but I was at least expecting something wearable. A plain black T-shirt and cat ears to match. One of those blow-up animal costumes. I would've even settled for a bald cap and a mustache.

But this...this is so much worse than being a hairless dude in his mid-fifties.

My bikini top and bottoms are smothered in fake ivy leaves, but despite their abundance, they don't begin to cover up the amount of skin I'm showing. Thin vines coil up my arms, sparsely speckled with more synthetic material, and a wreath of foliage rests in my heat-curled hair, matching the green, glittery eye shadow dappling my eyelids.

"Gage, I can't wear this," I say, looking down at the small, revealing bra and the even smaller thong pulled low on my hips.

Gage's costume matches mine, except his underwear covers *everything*, including the massive baguette he's packing down there. It's huge. Like, yeah, his muscle mass kind of hints at him being well-endowed, but he's not even erect, and there's this mouthwatering bulge just begging me to take it to the back of my throat.

I can't tell if him opting to wear next to nothing is a good or bad thing. On the plus side, I can see every oiled-up and stone-carved ab of his, the chiseled contour of his pecs, the protruding biceps barely contained within his own bracelet of vines, the naturally unattainable musculature of his thighs—which has to be a hockey thing—and the broad sculpt of his shoulders that could probably block an entire doorway.

On the downside, my hormones are whipping into action faster than a Bugatti's turnaround speed. Bad, salacious thoughts are marinating in my sex-deprived brain, urging me to rip his poor man's loincloth off and have him fuck the living daylights out of me. With each not-so-subtle glance at his physique, desire lubricates the gusset of my panties.

"Sure you can," he chirps happily, rubbing his hands down my arms.

I look down at my pillowing boobs, which do *not* fit into the too-small bra Gage got for me. "I'm going to flash someone tonight."

"That was the last size they had in stock," he replies, though he doesn't look the least bit regretful about it.

"And were you planning for this to be a couple's costume?" I probe, placing my hands on my hips. "We said just friends. Not friends who occasionally wear coordinating outfits."

"I—this—it's—this isn't a *couple's* costume," he stammers, running his knuckles along his clean-shaven jaw. "It's a group costume. My best friend, Fulton, is the apple! Yep. He's the apple."

That's right. We're Adam and Eve. The rated R version.

"He's the apple?" I repeat, hoping he can hear just how ridiculous he sounds. There's no way in hell Fulton agreed to a threesome costume with his best friend and his situationship.

"It was his idea. He's very...religious. Loves God and all that. Yeah. But he also loves, um, feminism. And the freedom to wear provocative clothing."

"Uh-huh."

I don't need to be some human lie detector when it comes to Gage. I've pretty much memorized every tell he has.

I rub two fingers into my temples, trying to vaporize the headache that's drilling into the backs of my eyes like an out-of-control nail gun. "I can't believe you got us a couple's costume," I groan.

"If it makes you uncomfortable, you can always just put my jersey on," he offers.

I gag. Like I actually feel bile scald my esophagus. "You know what? The costume is fine."

Gage's eyes are as big as globes when he plants them back on me, but their beguiling twinkle is masked by a sadness that was never there before—or one that was well-hidden under sarcasm and sharpshooter wit.

"I'm just asking for one night, Cali. One night where I can pretend that maybe there's more to us than just being friends with benefits."

This is tearing me up inside. It probably doesn't look like it, but it is. My heart wants the same thing, I know it does. It doesn't fucking shut up when Gage is around. It pounds a million times per minute. My stomach gets all queasy, my knees turn to gelatin, and it feels like the heat in my body is frying me from the inside out.

It's just one night, right? Nothing bad can happen in one night. And how bad could it really be if I want to play pretend too?

If I had to play pretend with anyone, it would be Gage.

I only realize my hands are shaking when Gage silences my

nerves with his touch, rubbing his thumb over the back of my knuckles. "It's okay if you don't—"

"One night," I agree, nodding.

His previously sapped energy has backtracked and blasted into him, livening those sulking features and returning the glimmer of hope I was afraid I'd never see again to his emerald eyes. He immediately hugs me, nuzzling his nose into the crook of my collarbone, arms sandwiching me in a squeeze that tells me he isn't planning on letting go any time soon.

Please don't let this be a mistake.

THE NIGHT BEFORE HALLOWEEN, and all through the house, not a creature was stirring...except about three hundred bodies.

I spent the entire day at Gage's place, but I wasn't expecting the party to already be in full swing by the time we got downstairs. The mansion is fully decked out in tacky Halloween decorations, red cups infiltrate everywhere I turn, and half-naked bodies rave to the energized tempo of house music. Multiple foldable tables have been constructed for drinking games, and a few familiar faces mill about in hockey-related costumes, greeting newcomers with a raucous howl and more booze to shove down their gullets.

I lose Gage when he gets stopped by three different people, and I have to maneuver past a tipsy throng of girls all belting out the wrong lyrics to a Shakira song. It's like crossing a goddamn battlefield to make it to the keg in the kitchen, and with this amount of people, I'm going to need to catch up on a few drinks before my social battery's at a cool yellow. Grasping my drink, I take a hefty swig and wince when the lukewarm beer tumbles into my gut. It's grainy and tastes like piss, but I'm not going to search for anything harder.

I nearly get trampled exiting the kitchen. This place is

dangerous. And definitely breaking fire code laws. The lack of oxygen in this place seems to finally be getting to me because I walk straight into someone and clench the ever-living life out of my cup to keep it from spilling.

A girl dolled up in a green bodycon dress turns toward me, and I heave out a string of apologies after steeling myself.

"Oh, God. I'm so sorry. I—"

But my mind buffers when my gaze absentmindedly slides to her slightly engorged belly—which is accentuated by the tightest dress I've ever seen—and the hand she has placed over it.

"Are you okay?" I blurt out, glancing at the protective way she cradles her midsection, like maybe I inadvertently knocked into her stomach somehow.

"Oh, I'm fine. Are you okay?" she replies, a smile adorning her lips instead of the judgmental frown I was expecting.

"Yeah. Sorry. I should've been watching where I was going."

I didn't think my gawking was that obvious, but she follows my line of sight to the hand still resting over her belly, and she chuffs out a laugh once she connects the dots. "Don't worry. You didn't elbow me in the gut. I know my baby's just the size of a raspberry, but I guess I'm already a little overprotective."

Baby? She's pregnant? What's a pregnant woman doing at a party? Her baby bump is almost nonexistent. If I wouldn't have known any better, I would've thought it was just a bit of alcohol bloat. And she looks young, like around my age. Her costume also starts to make more sense, as her stomach's covered in this brown fabric to signify what I think is supposed to be an avocado pit.

"You're pregnant?" I comment in shock.

She rubs the area on her lower belly, crinkling the skin-tight fabric of her dress. "Two months now."

I blink a few times. "That's—wow. Congratulations."

She waves her hand nonchalantly. "It was an accident."

Great. Now I'm speechless too. My brain's the consistency of pulp, and my throat's dry despite the beer I've been nursing. It's also like a hundred degrees in this Easy Bake Oven, the stench of body odor and marijuana undercoating the precious air.

After what feels like a full minute of us just staring at each other, I force myself to open my cotton mouth. "I'm sorry if this is forward, but, uh, should you be at a party right now?" I ask, perusing the sea of bobbing heads for the person I'm hoping accompanied her.

"I'd honestly love to be in bed right now, but I'm here visiting my boyfriend," she tells me, sounding far more enthusiastic than I would be if I were two months pregnant and yanked to the equivalent of a frat party.

"Your boyfriend?"

As if on cue, the tallest man I've ever seen saunters over to us, bending down to peck a chaste kiss to her belly. His tan, light-brown skin complements the inked lacework of tattoos spiraling up his arm, and his beefy chest stretches the T-shirt he's wearing, which includes a cartoon image of a piece of toast right in the middle.

"I brought you some ginger ale for the nausea," he says, handing her a small metal can, his lips giving way to a smile that so obviously proclaims the love he has for her. The crinkles under his eyes are a dead giveaway, same with the fact that he stares at her longingly like she's the most beautiful girl in the entire world.

I feel like I've seen that stare before.

"Ugh, thank you," she whispers, taking it from his hands and sipping it in graduated increments.

Suddenly feeling like a third wheel, every awkward molecule in my body seems to seize the lapse in conversation and respond with a verbal word vomit. "You know, my aunt was pregnant once. Said it almost tore her vagina when she pushed out her eight-pound baby. Her husband was significantly shorter than, uh, than your boyfriend, though, so maybe you'll have like a nine-pound baby? Is that physically possible? I mean, I'm sure your vagina won't rip in half or anything. Ha... that would be, that would be bad. But they can stitch you up! You just don't really have control over your bowels anymore."

Oh my God! Stop talking, Cali! You're embarrassing yourself.

I snap my lips shut several moments too late as they both stare at me, as still as obelisks.

With a rough-sounding throat clear, I drown myself in a generous pull of beer, downing the rest of it to avoid having to look them in the eyes. I can't believe I just commented on the future state of this woman's genitalia.

Where's Gage? Why did he leave me alone? I'm blaming this on him. I blame everything on him.

When I resurface, praying that the buzz mellows me as soon as possible, the pregnant girl explodes into goose-like honks of laughter, her shoulders shaking endlessly. "Knowing my luck, the baby probably will be a mammoth," she chuckles.

And then she turns to the panicked man beside her and deadpans, "And it's all *your* fault."

He grimaces. "I'm sorry for impregnating you with my monster spawn."

"Thank you." She beams, giving him back her drink.

I definitely don't want to get pregnant any time soon, but it makes me fantasize about what my life might be like in ten or twenty years—who I'll settle down with, where I'll be, what I'll be doing, how Teague will be off in college and on his own, how my mother might finally be at peace. I've never allowed myself to look into the future. I've always lived in the present, with the occasional steps into the past. I know these people are just strangers, but seeing the way they act around each other...it reminds me that I'll still have a purpose even when the people currently in my life don't need me anymore.

I'll have a purpose to live for *myself* rather than for others.

And when I think about living for myself and what my heart wants, I think about—

Gage suddenly bowls into my side, the amber liquid in his cup sloshing over the rim just a little from the impact, an impish grin lifting the corners of his beer-slicked lips. "Cali, you found Faye and Kit!"

His eyes are blacked out and glassy, there's a canopy of blush on his lean cheekbones, and he lolls his head onto my shoulder.

"Hi," I greet quietly, waving.

"Wait a second. Cali. As in Gage's Cali?" Kit asks, and the implication of Gage and I being together has my heart conducting a discordant beat.

"She's...we're not...together," Gage hiccups.

I gently pry the cup from his fingers, using our close proximity to whisper while maintaining a polite smile, "How much have you had to drink?"

I have no idea how much time has passed, but I guess it was more than I thought.

He twines his finger around a strand of my hair. "Not that much. A drink or two. A lot of shots, though," he answers groggily, the rumbling vibrations of his voice nurturing the ache between my legs.

"But I'm kind of buzzed. I think."

Kit chortles, which means that our conversation wasn't anywhere near quiet. "You have to watch out for him. He's a lightweight."

Oh, great.

"I'm sure he'll be fine." I jab my elbow hard into Gage's side, causing him to bounce straight back up.

Gage sticks his finger in the air and wiggles it. "For your information, *Kit*, I'm not a lightweight. I just get drunk very easily."

"That's the definition of a lightweight," Kit says.

"You're just jealous because I can outdrink you," Gage slurs.

"Outdrink me, my ass. The last time we had a chugging contest I beat you by a full minute and you yacked in the bushes. Or do we need to have a redo to jog your memory?"

"Faye, tell your boyfriend he's a dick."

"Cali, tell your non-boyfriend he's a bitch."

"O-kay." Faye claps her hands together, defusing the testosterone bomb about to consume everyone in a ten-foot radius. "I think the rest of the team is getting a drinking game ready in the living room. We'll meet you guys over there, yeah?"

I nod as I watch her shove Kit in the general direction of the living room, and Kit gives Gage the universal *I'm watching you* sign, forming a V with his fingers and pointing at his own eyes before whipping them around.

Gage, however, is too focused on caging me with his gaze like some lovesick fool. "You're really beautiful, Cali. Not just right now. Like, all the time. Every day I'm in awe of you. You deserve someone who'll always tell you how beautiful you are, and I feel like I don't tell you enough. I'm thinking it, though," he murmurs, tapping his head. "Up here."

Oh, Gage.

I set Gage's cup down on the nearest flat surface I can find. The truth is, even though Gage does have an affinity for getting on my nerves, he's always made me feel wanted, seen. He tells me I'm beautiful in every breath he can, so if that's any indication of what he's thinking, it must be a recurring thought.

"You don't need to say anything, Gage—"

He shushes me by jamming his finger into my lips. "I do. You're literally"—hiccup—"the most gorgeous girl"—hiccup—"in this entire universe."

"And you smell sooo good," he adds drunkenly. "Like a Cinnabon store."

My mouth opens to stop him, but he just keeps going, and

the tingling sensation his touch imprints on my lips leaves me comatose.

"I love your hair. It's the prettiest color I've ever seen. I didn't know this shade of orange even existed before you. It's like a sorbet orange crossed with a sunset orange. It's my favorite color. It wasn't always my favorite color, but after you came along, it *became* my favorite color," he blathers, tangling his fingers in my hair like a newborn. "Fuck. Sometimes it hurts to look at you and remember that you aren't mine."

He's drunk. He doesn't mean this stuff...right?

My stomach sinks. "Gage..."

"I have to tell you something, Spitfire. And it's important."

Uh, uh, uh. What do I do? WHAT DO I DO? That sounds super serious, and I know we said one night of pretend, but once you say something serious, it never really goes away. And the worst part is he probably won't remember any of this after tonight, so I'll be left with the agonizing truth for as long as I live, and it'll weigh me down until I implode from the pressure.

"Gage, please don't say—"

"Come closer," he whispers, beckoning me like he's on his goddamn death bed.

Run away, Cali. That's a perfectly appropriate response. Or maybe don't leave him alone because he's inebriated and bound to do something reckless.

I shamble an inch closer.

"Closer."

Another inch.

"Closerrr."

With a suspended breath, I finally get as close to him as I can, trepidation setting up camp in my chest and pistoling through every part of my body with dead set determination. I think I stop breathing for a full minute. I think my sweat is deteriorating the copious amounts of hot glue on my costume.

Here it goes: the sentence that'll change everything. The

farewell to our friendship. The death to our dynamic. The bon voyage to our banter.

And when Gage leans in slightly, he belches loudly and blows it in my face.

"Gage! Oh my God!" I instantly cover my nose before all my nose hairs get singed off, and I flap my hand to air out his sulfuric breath cloud. "That's so fucking disgusting. It smells like something died in there."

He laughs like a maniac. "Hey! You have to be nice to me tonight. Thems the rules."

"Um, no. That was never a part of the agreement."

"Yuh-huh."

"The day I stop being mean to you is the day I've kicked the bucket," I growl, pinching his earlobe between my fingers and dragging him toward the living room.

I need a drink. Or like twenty.

19

NEVER HAVE I EVER
CALISTA

I can't believe I actually thought Gage was gonna drop the L-bomb on me. God, I'm stupid. We've only known each other for two months. I should be relieved, right? So why does it feel like my heart's tied into a fisherman's knot?

The game hasn't even started and I'm on my second drink. I want to forget about tonight. I want to forget about the disappointment that Gage and I will never be anything more than friends. Not when my family still depends on me, and not when my self-preservation instincts are programmed to protect me from further heartbreak.

I've wanted to be just friends for so long—no strings attached, no memories to be reminisced. But now, I'm beginning to think that maybe I was wrong. Now, I'm beginning to wonder how different my life could be if I stopped fighting love.

Gage's housemates and their significant others have gathered around a large coffee table, and I guess it's apparently tradition for them to play some big drinking game every once in a while. Faye and Kit are snuggled on the adjacent couch together, with his hand draped protectively over her belly. I recognize Aeris from class, and the blonde she's been glued to at the hip must be the boyfriend she was talking about. But aside from them, I'm an outsider to the group. An outsider who just so happens to be matching with their beloved goalie.

"Everyone, this is Cali. Cali, this is everyone," Gage introduces, to which I wave a meek hand.

It takes about a good five minutes for me to place names to faces, but I know that Hayes is Aeris' vampire-bitten boyfriend, Josie and Casen are the matching skeletons, Bristol is the football player, Fulton is the nerd, and Faye and Kit are the avocado toast combo.

Gage has his arm dangling over my shoulder in a very couple-y manner, and I'm so close to him that whenever he laughs—which is a lot, considering he's as drunk as a skunk—the breadth of his chest shakes my entire body. Not only is he my own personal heater, but the proximity allows me a preview of those taut abs and the path of hair disappearing below the band of his ivy undergarment.

There's something very wrong with me tonight. I'm horny as hell. Whenever Gage looks at me, I practically purr like a cat in heat. The whole half-naked thing really does it for me, and I know Eve should not sin, but would it be acceptable if Adam was looking like a five-course meal?

I want to slip away from the group and take him into the bathroom. I want to get on my knees on the cold tiles of the floor and take his gigantic dick in my mouth, sucking him down only halfway because he'll definitely be too long for me to swallow. His meaty girth will stuff the pouches of my cheeks, and he'll thrust into my throat while he braids his hand into my hair and guides me. I want to feel my scalp sting when he underestimates his strength; I want to watch as his half-mast eyes struggle to stay open. I won't stop until I'm a drooling mess on his throbbing shaft—until there are tears in my eyes and they shower my face. My nose will be squashed against his trimmed thatch of pubes, inhaling the masculine scent of his sweat and musk, and when he unloads in my mouth, I'll gulp everything he gives me—

"Cali, it's your turn," a voice interjects, and I slowly come back down to earth to find a horde of eyes waiting for me to speak.

"Sorry, I zoned out," I apologize, an inferno of heat amassing in my cheeks. "What are we playing?"

"Never Have I Ever," Gage whispers, squeezing the cap of my shoulder and unknowingly delivering a series of pleasured pulses to my cunt.

"Right, uh…" The swallow I take chafes my throat, but the penetrating stares disallow me an interval of time to drink from my cup. "Never have I ever…gone skinny dipping."

A few of the people around the circle drink, as well as Gage, and I get this jealous twinge in the bottom of my belly—one that I definitely did *not* invite to the party.

Of course Gage has gone skinny dipping. If you have the goods, show them off. Did he go skinny dipping with a girl? Did they fuck in a lake? Did she get to feel him bare as he slid into her? Was he in love with her?

Oh my God. I sound like a crazy person. Why do I care so much? Gage and I aren't together. Gage is a handsome, talented, young NHL player who probably has boatloads of women throwing themselves at his feet.

He's not mine.

Aeris goes next, her plastic vampire fangs glinting underneath the low light, and the messy patches of glitter on her skin occasionally catch the ochre refractions splicing across the floorboards. "Never have I ever…been arrested!"

Surprisingly, nobody drinks. Except for Gage.

His throat undulates with each swallow, his hair a storm of umber locks that spill down his temples.

"You've been arrested?" I ask in shock.

He wipes the back of his hand across his mouth. "Yep. I stole a llama from a petting zoo once when I was really drunk."

"We're not going to have a repeat of that tonight, are we?"

Gage showcases a double-dimpled smile as he bops me on the nose with his finger. "Nope, because you're gonna look out for me."

And I thought sober Gage was annoying.

"Ugh, get a room!" Kit shouts, a bunch of laughter rioting from the group. The boisterous noise of overlapping voices seems to drown out the rest of the party, and everyone's too distracted to eavesdrop on the barefaced filth that exits Gage's agape lips.

"I wouldn't mind getting a room," he says, nose running the length of my neck, his mouth just barely grazing my sweaty skin.

Oh, no. Stay strong, Cali. My thighs wham together like magnets, hoping to redirect the pressure in my pussy, and I feel a hint of moisture seep through the bikini bottom of my costume, a preface for the waterfall that's just waiting to flood the dam. The worst part is that Gage is so drunk I don't think he even realizes what he's doing to me.

Fulton pipes up beside us. "Never have I ever...cheated on a test!" he announces enthusiastically.

"Really, Fulton? You've never cheated on a test?" Bristol inquires, languorously swishing his drink around in his hands.

Did I mention that Fulton is definitely *not* dressed like an apple? He's dressed in a pressed button-up, suspenders, and square-framed glasses.

"And jeopardize my chance of getting into a good college? God no." He shudders, committing to the nerd bit by pushing his glasses up higher on the bridge of his nose.

Every single person drinks, including me. When I was spending sleepless nights working shifts at the restaurant, I didn't have time to study for tests. This will probably be the only time I drink during the entire game. I'm just realizing now how... abnormal...my adolescent years have been. I didn't get to live like a regular teenager and make the occasional reckless decision.

Gage chuckles at his friend's ridiculousness, having switched from periodically squeezing my shoulder to tracing patterns on my arm with his fingers. There's nothing inherently sexual about touching someone's arm, but I nearly moan.

Bristol—who's rocking eye black and a football jersey—goes next, cataloguing the bored state of the players and obviously cooking up something troublesome in his head. "Never have I ever...had sex in public," he declares, holding his solo cup up to cheers with our side of the room. "That includes oral."

Multiple groans peal throughout the space, and I watch as Faye drinks her ginger ale, Kit drinks, Aeris and Hayes drink, and of course, Gage drinks.

I glare at him, a growl rumbling in my chest. I thought this game was supposed to be fun. In fact, this is so unfun that I'd rather take my chances in the very unsafe mosh pit that's formed over by the sound system.

Gage's dilated pupils bore into me, and the stupidest smirk ticks up his lips. "Spitfire, are you jealous?"

"Of course not!" I huff, crossing my arms over my chest and pouting like a petulant child. Nobody's focused on us, thank God, as they continue on with the game I've lost interest in.

"Are you sure?" he drawls, nipping playfully at my earlobe. "I wouldn't blame you. I know I'm irresistible."

"You're irritating."

"You're fucking hot when you're mad, you know that?" The lushness of Gage's lips suddenly hardens into a bite, and he pulls on my lobe slightly with his teeth. "Even hotter when you're jealous."

I want to shove him away and give him a complementary

slap, but I love the feel of his mouth on my ear. My back arches against the sofa, and I have to remind myself that we're in public, and that my resolve is stronger than this.

Faye's airy voice saves me from my own destructive tendencies. "Never have I ever...played hockey."

The entire team drinks, and Faye and Aeris share a smile with each other. I think Fulton drinks for the first time tonight, and I'm glad I'm not the only sheltered person here.

I need to drink. I'm not drunk enough to be here right now, to pretend like Gage isn't singlehandedly ripping out the nails of the boarded-up enclosure keeping my sex-hungry beast at bay.

Josie takes her turn, wearing the same skeletal makeup as Casen, except she's in a miniature black dress as opposed to his full leather outfit. "Never have I ever...given someone a lap dance."

Fucking finally.

Surprisingly, Kit downs his drink. I almost don't want to know.

I have over half of my beer still left, and the minute the rim touches my lips, I chug the entire thing. I begin to regret it when the alcohol plops into my stomach like expired milk, but I soldier through until there's nothing left.

Gage stares at me. Everyone stares at me.

"You gave someone a lap dance?" he exclaims, jealousy blatantly lining his tone, a muscle in his jaw bunching with enough strain to crack enamel.

Correction: I gave *Hadley* a lap dance, but he doesn't need to know that.

"I guess we're both full of surprises," I mutter, standing up and making my way to the kitchen to refill my cup.

Gage tails after me, grabbing me by the elbow and spinning me around to face him, the full extent of his rage unleashed in the fiery depths of his eyes.

"Who did you give a lap dance to, Cali?"

Anger spars for dominance over my features. "Who did you have sex with in public, Gage?"

He expels a guttural growl, not bothering to hide how infuriated he is with me, the hockey-hardened muscles in his biceps flexing as his abs tighten. "I'm not going to ask you again."

"Maybe it's none of your business," I snarl, turning on my heel so my hair goes flying in his face.

I try to lose him in the crowd, but he's on my trail like a fucking bloodhound. I'm mad, but I think this is a first when I say that Gage is even madder. If he was a cartoon, he'd have smoke coming out of his ears and nostrils. His face is already as bright red as a fire engine.

"It is my fucking business." He drags me into a vacant hallway and pushes me up against the wall, his arms bracketing me on both sides. His shoulders are hunched, his neck strains only slightly to look down at me, and the hard planes of his stomach are just inches from my body.

I don't cower. I don't shrink. I push my chest out and match his iron glare. "No, it's not. We're not together."

"Yeah, you keep reminding me, and it kills me each time you say it."

"I wouldn't have to keep saying it if you'd just get it through your thick skull!"

There's a glitch in his expression, revealing the hurt lingering just below his tough-guy surface. "You're so hot and cold with me, Cali. One second everything is good between us, and the next you want to pick a fight with me. What the fuck is going on?" he snaps, the smallest grain of desperation lodged in his voice.

"Nothing's going on!" I yell, fruitlessly trying to squirm past his boulder-sized body.

"Then why did you get jealous back there?"

"I didn't! You were the one who got jealous!"

Gage closes the remaining distance between us, the warmth from his figure and the dizzying scent of his cologne making my belly woozy.

"Yeah, I did. You're *mine*, Calista. Do you understand that? The thought of sharing you with anyone, even when I wasn't in your life, drives me fucking crazy. The thought of you touching another man—the thought of *him* touching you makes me so angry that I can't think straight. It makes me want to track that fucker to the ends of the earth and shove my hockey stick down his throat."

If it wasn't for the confusion skyrocketing inside me, I would've been immobilized by Gage's confession. Even though he's been drinking, his frustration must've sobered him up. He doesn't have that dazed, faraway look in his eyes anymore; his irises are portals created to devour me whole.

I soften and reach out to touch his arm, unsure if I'll be met with resistance. "Gage..."

"What are you so afraid of, Cali?" he whispers in a defeated breath, gently guiding my outstretched hand to rest on his bicep.

So much. I'm afraid of so much.

I try to quash the overflow of tears in my eyes, try to clear the way my vision tunnels, but none of my efforts seem to be working. Everything I've suppressed for these past weeks is done being condemned to the darkest depths of my soul. My emotions are crawling up the dungeon walls in strides, determined to regain their freedom, but I'm not about to let them escape and wreak havoc in the world.

"I'm not afraid of anything. I just need to focus on my family. There's no room for love in my life right now."

"You mean there's no room for *me* in your life right now," Gage corrects.

That's not true! my heart wants to yell, but it's my head that makes the ultimate decision.

"Friends with benefits is all we'll ever be. I can't keep living in this fantasy world with you when my real world needs me—when my family needs me."

"You said that we could pretend tonight. That we could pretend to be something more. I'm not asking for a lot, Cali. I'm just asking for you to imagine a life where you could have everything you want. A life where you didn't have to choose between your happiness and the happiness of others."

That *was* what Gage asked for—something deliverable and doable—and I failed to keep my end of the promise. Even if I wanted to come clean with the truth about me falling for him, I don't think I could bring myself to do it. Am I scared of consolidating all my efforts on a relationship that might not even last? Of course I am. Am I scared that this relationship could completely knock my family out of the picture? Fuck yes.

And no amount of play pretend will bury those fears.

When silence is all I can offer, Gage is quick to amend it.

"Please, Cali. You may have stopped fighting, but I haven't."

How long are you going to keep this up, Cali? How long are you going to push him away until he never wants to come back? It's either my family or him, and the scales are so close in weight that the right choice isn't clear anymore.

Moisture sticks to my lower lashes like dewdrops, and I self-consciously bite my bottom lip to stop it from its habitual tremble. I don't know what to say. This is killing me inside, and Gage probably doesn't even realize it. Guilt tangles around my limbs in black tendrils, curved thorns scarring flesh and tissue and tendon, severing the picture-perfect front I've been trying to upkeep.

"I..."

I want to run away from this night. I want to run out of the door right now and never look back. But even if I did, I know that Gage would be right behind me.

Gage suddenly registers the hurt on my face, and he caresses my cheek, softly brushing his thumbnail over the dark shadows under my eyes. "Cali, I'm sorry. I'm just...I'm *selfish*. I don't want this to end. I don't want to return to a life where I don't know you. I've foolishly been thinking that if you let me in, I can have you all to myself. But it's destroying you, and that's the last thing I'd *ever* want to do to you."

I keep my head lowered, using my hair to curtain my face. "I just need a moment to breathe."

I don't lean into his hand. I don't look at Gage. I'm falling apart like a poorly built sandcastle crumbling under its own weight.

Even though Gage is great at giving me what I want, this time he doesn't. He says *fuck it* and brings me into his body, encasing my frame in his arms and soaking up the chill of my skin with the heat of his own.

"Breathe, baby. Please breathe," he coos, rubbing the back of my head. "I'm sorry I pushed you to make a decision. I'm sorry that I set up this fucked-up ultimatum of me over your family. That was never my intention. I know you have a responsibility to your family. I just...I wanted to show you that you can have it all. You can balance that responsibility and balance your own life. You can live for others while still living for yourself."

My fingernails gouge into his bare back like I never want to let go. "How am I supposed to do that?" I muffle into his shoulder.

"I don't know, but I'm willing to help you figure it out. I'm willing to do whatever it takes."

20

SHE LOVES ME, SHE LOVES ME NOT
GAGE

This wasn't how the night was supposed to go, but like always, I have a tendency to fuck up all the good things in my life. And right in front of me is the best thing that's ever happened to me.

I have to remind myself that this girl isn't just some figment of my imagination—that she's the greatest blessing I could've ever received on this planet. That no human could've been conceived to be this perfect. That she must be some higher deity who's given her hair color to California's sunsets; that the constellations must've borrowed the formation of her freckles for their beauty; and that the ocean could never possibly rival the blue of her eyes.

Cali murmurs something unintelligible, still stamping marks into my skin, a new layer of wetness signaling that her tears must have finally fallen and found purchase on my upper back. With our lack of clothing, I can feel the pummeling of her heart. I can hear it in the vacuum-seal of space we're in, and it's cathartic.

"My head and my heart want two different things," Cali

burbles, the clarity of her words obstructed by thickening saliva and sporadic sniffles.

We disentangle from each other, and the moment I see my girl's gorgeous face, my heart sings for her attention, her touch, her love. Goops of mascara streak down her cheeks, and her red eyes suffer from burst capillaries. But despite the struggle on her face, I've never seen her look more beautiful. Raw.

"Which one is more important to you?" I dab at the leftover tears blemishing her pale complexion.

"I think…I think it's my heart."

To see Cali so numb, so drained—it cracks a fissure deep in my sternum, one close to splitting my heart at the seam. I want to be there for her, to prove to her that I'm not going anywhere, but I fear that her self-preservation will keep me far away.

What are you supposed to do when you want to take care of someone who's too afraid to let you?

"Then maybe you should listen to your heart."

"But my heart's selfish."

"Humans are selfish by nature. That's just a part of life, Spitfire. And I know you probably won't believe me, but you're the least selfish person I know," I tell her, unable to tear my palm from the curve of her tear-softened cheek, anguish curdling in my stomach.

She bears desolation in the hard lines of her face, and it's like I'm standing idly by as her inner light begins to dim, eclipsing her in perpetual darkness. Everything seems duller—her hair, her eyes, her posture.

She doesn't say anything. She doesn't look up at me. Her eyes are downcast, finding interest in the smears of dirt that begrime the hallway floor, courtesy of numerous soles of shoes.

"Calista." I use a knuckle to tip her chin up so she finally looks at me, and immediately, affection twins with something deeper in my heart, leaving it in a state of disarray. "It's okay to put yourself first. It's okay to dream and want. It's okay to *be* selfish if you've been selfless for so long. But if you never go after what you want, you'll never allow yourself the chance at a better life. The chance at a *happier* life."

"I don't want to let anyone down," she wails.

"At this point, I think the only person you're letting down is yourself. You play one of the most important roles in this whole equation. If you're not taking care of yourself, then everything else falls to chaos. You're the glue that holds your family together."

Cali wraps her arms around her midsection, salty water refilling her eyes, distorting the darker blue rings of her irises. "I'm so tired of being the glue. I don't want to be the glue for the rest of my life."

"I know, baby. And you won't be. Your mom's going to be alright; you've done everything you can for her. And Teague will find his footing as he grows older," I tell her, catching those sickle-shaped droplets as they begin to drip down. "And as for us, even though there isn't really an 'us,' I'm not going anywhere. I'm here to show you that none of this works without you prioritizing your own happiness."

Saying all these things to Cali—things that sound a lot wiser than I would've ever assumed myself capable of being—makes me realize that hockey isn't my only purpose. After Trip, I was certain it was. Hell, I was so determined to get back on the ice after my injury that I went out of my way to take dance lessons *and* do physical therapy.

My purpose might've been hockey, but that all changed the moment I saw Cali. The moment she cussed me out and threatened me in front of half the local hockey community. The moment I realized that this girl has a hold on me unlike any other, and that even if she decides to let me go, I'll run right back to her.

Everything is second when it comes to Cali.

"Thank you, Gage. I just...I think I need some more time before I'm ready to invest in a relationship. I'm sorry."

She's considering it.

And even though it's not the answer I would've liked, I'm more than happy to wait. "You don't need to be sorry, Cali. I'm a patient man."

"I really don't deserve you," she cries, flinging herself into my body and knocking me backward with the force, her small arms latched around my thick torso.

I bark out a chuckle. "*I'm* the one who doesn't deserve *you.*"

She rears back in confusion. "What?"

My heart begins to hiccup, everything else coming to a standstill except for *her*. She's a lightning strike in a chasm of deep onyx, beautiful to look at but dangerous to touch up close. Dangerous yet alluring. A once-in-a-lifetime kind of phenomenon.

"After all this time, you still don't understand what you mean to me, do you?"

Cali blinks at me with those doe eyes of hers.

I take her hand and rest it over my heart, feeling it speed up drastically. I'm convinced my heart could distinguish her touch even if I lost my eyesight.

"My heart's always this fucked up when you're around. You make me so goddamn crazy that I can never think straight when it comes to you. You're just...you're perfect. So insanely perfect that you should come with a warning label."

I want to say those three words. I want to say them so badly. I know she's not ready to hear them, but the feelings I have for her will never change. Maybe it's too early. Maybe this is all infatuation. Maybe I'm just a young idiot who's fallen completely head over heels. I don't care what it is. All I care about is clinging to this emotion for as long as I can.

She spares me a smile just bordering on toothy benevolence, and slowly, the light begins to rekindle inside her. "You can be really sweet when you aren't being an ass," she admits humorously.

Her hand drops from my chest, giving my poor heart a reprieve, and I bring her body closer to mine, my hands roving over the curve of her spine and the small dimples resting just above her butt. "See? I'm a changed man because of you."

"I wouldn't be so sure about that."

"Oh, really?"

Cali lowers my hands until I grasp the bottom of her ass—which is more than bare and cheeky thanks to her scrap of a thong. "You're still a dog, Gage Arlington," she drawls in an erotic whisper, her breath mangling when I knead the plentiful fat there.

"Then fucking chain me up, Spitfire."

For the first time, she's the one who initiates the kiss, servicing every Cali-starved crevice of my body, her tongue rolling over mine in a slow, deliberate stroke. My fingers squeeze her ass cheeks so tightly that plumpness spills through the slats of my digits, and I'm a hundred percent certain I'm going to leave a red handprint behind. I groan into her mouth, feeling my erection harden like granite, and I'm gonna give myself two minutes before I tear through this flimsy costume and flash everyone in the nearby vicinity.

When she takes my bottom lip between her teeth, a cocktail of desire and oxytocin mixes with the unwise decision of a few too many drinks in my stomach.

"Cali, we can't do this here."

"You're right," she purrs. "We haven't even danced yet."

I freeze as the aridity in my mouth grows. "Wha—"

I don't even have time to construct a robust response before the lyric-less EDM music over the speakers changes into a pop anthem. The tempo has sped up, and thanks to numerous car rides with Fulton torturing me with hits from the 2000s, I immediately recognize the beginning notes of Britney Spears'

"I'm a Slave 4 U." A giddy grin seizes Cali's face, and before I can protest, she pulls me onto the dance floor.

The blood in my ears, however, overpowers my sensibility to evacuate the scene as quickly as possible. Remember when I said dancing was easy? I was wrong. *So wrong.* It's harder than anything I've ever done before.

With lips full of innuendo and an arresting sway of her hips, she's dancing in front of me, her plunging cleavage mashing against my chest thanks to the leverage of her heels. My hands settle on her butt as my fingers brush against the thin strip of fabric getting swallowed by her ass cheeks. It'd be so easy to slide these off her right now without anyone noticing, and the access makes heat swelter in my fattening cock.

I've never met a girl who can move like Cali, and I'm cherishing every fucking second of this dance. And then, as if she can sense just how insanely hungry my erection is for the slightest attention, she spins around so her back is flush with my chest.

Holy fuck.

She guides my arms to her waist, rolling her body in time to the music. Her hips move back and forth in a sultry way that makes me grip her curves even harder, and her butt jiggles each time it grinds against my dick.

This was a bad idea, Gage. A terrible idea! But also a really good one.

She's throwing her hair all over the place, placing my clammy hands on her sweaty tits, dancing with the skill and sensuality of a stripper. My cock is doing everything in its power to refrain from slamming inside her.

Three's a crowd, dude.

Pleasure sparks like tinder in the bottom of my stomach, making it hard to concentrate. Cali is still jiggling her butt carelessly, her silhouette backlit by a pulse of strobe lights. She's touching me in all the right places, notching her crack with my boner, undulating her hips to build a friction so delicious that it stings.

She seems blissfully unaware of what she's doing to me, and that makes it hurt even more. I've never felt anything like this before—this craving to taste every inch of her until I overdose. I want to fuck her. No, I *need* to fuck her.

My fingers grip Cali's hips harshly, enough to leave raised scratches on the squishable meat there. I lean into her ear breathlessly, my voice dropping an octave from the pain currently shackling me. "*Calista.*"

"*Gage.*"

"You're playing with me."

Instead of letting me rest peacefully in the bed I've made, she moves one of my hands to her ivy-hidden center, arching just slightly against my crotch. "I thought you liked it when I played with you," she purrs.

Shit, shit, shit! Keep it together, man!

The only reason I'm okay with what's happening right now is because the dance floor is pretty congested, and it's way too noisy for anyone to overhear our conversation.

My chest bloats with a low, animalistic growl, and my desire metamorphosizes into a bloodlust that's far from human. "Baby, I fucking love it when you play with me. But if you keep moving like that, you're going to be the first girl I bend over in the middle of a party. Is that what you want?"

I keep my hand over her pussy, feeling the heat seep into my palm. My other hand is on a mission to fondle her overspilling boob, and if I wasn't already fighting off a full-body fever, the warmth of pre-cum wetting the material of my costume makes my life that much harder.

I'm not going to last the rest of the night if she keeps teasing me like this.

"You want to fuck my pretty pussy, Gage?" she taunts quietly, inching my hand just a little farther south, where my fingers catch on the hood of her clit. I'm so close I can practically feel the wetness secreting from her swollen lips.

A nasally whine hisses out through my nostrils, and my dick's in so much pain that it hurts to move, let alone imagine the tireless trek upstairs while I clench to prevent from coming everywhere. "Want it so bad, Spitfire. Want to impale you on my giant cock and milk that sweet cunt until there's nothing left in you."

She continues to gyrate against me effortlessly, and I have to pretend like I'm not desperately sucking in air just to keep up with her. Her hand then intertwines with mine, and she extends her arm up, letting me spin her around—and also letting the cramped bodies nearby get a look at my glaringly obvious boner.

And when she stops right in front of me, she licks her lips. "*Then fucking do it.*"

21

FORGIVE ME, FATHER, FOR I HAVE SINNED

GAGE

The minute those words left Cali's mouth, I had her upstairs and in my bedroom in record time. Thank you, hip, for not giving out during such a monumental moment.

"Gage, I know you're drunk," she says, keeping me at arm's length like I'm some rabid dog trying to hump her leg.

I kind of am, but still. If she thinks I won't chew through my leash to get to her, then she's dead wrong.

"Are you sure this is what you really want?"

"Cali, that little dance number you pulled out there was like a bucket of ice water on my head. Whatever buzz I had going is long gone," I assure her, ignoring the distance between us and stepping into her so she's forced to confront me.

Her long lashes tap the ruby apples of her cheeks. "I just don't want you to make a mistake."

I thumb her chin, getting her to look up at me. "That word doesn't fucking exist when it comes to you. You know that, right? In no universe could you ever be a mistake."

My hands survey her body, getting the feel of where she's the most responsive, lingering on the places that make my dick jerk in my costume. "You know there's no going back after this, right?"

A canyon of silence stretches between us before she utters, "I know."

I'm expecting resistance from her—like I always get—but her next move consists of her stripping off her heels and tossing them aside. I'm struck dumb as usual by anything she does, unsure how thin the ice I'm standing on is, but then she wastes no time in mauling me, littering sloppy kisses all over my neck.

When she tongues the outline of my pulse point, I smack her on the ass, the sound reverberating in the confines of my bedroom, her skin recoiling under my fingers from the force. She mewls and roughs up my hair with her hand, fisting the roots to steady herself before biting the thin skin just above my collarbone.

A slew of keening moans hurtles out of me, and the pressure she's exacting on my throat makes me grind my hips against her pussy, letting her feel the weight of my desire while it presses against her inner thigh.

"You gonna leave a mark, Spitfire? You want everyone to know I'm yours?" I taunt, my voice jumping when she begins to suckle and form a tender bruise.

"Don't need to leave a mark," she pants, licking a long, thick stripe up the side of my neck. "You'll be screaming my name loud enough for the whole party to hear."

My cock fucking shudders from that idea alone, spitting pre-cum into the inside of my undergarment, which is thankfully hidden by so many leaves that nothing will be visible. I get a sharp lance up my abdomen—one colluding with my ever-growing erection—and I'm afraid I'm going to lose my load before I even get inside her. She's not going to make this easy for me, I already know it. And I'm going to fold. Every. Fucking. Time.

She continues to perfect the hickey, sucking and nibbling, even moving to another area to stipple a motley mulberry over my naked skin. And as she tortures me, her giant breasts flatten against my torso, dangerously close to my face.

"Bra. Off. Now," I growl.

She unlatches her lips from my throat, a fine layer of spit coating them. "You're a big boy. Do it yourself," she hisses.

Look, I don't have Herculean strength or anything, okay? Cali's just conveniently happened to wear a lot of poorly made clothing whenever we've done anything. My hands demolish the bra that's been teasing me all night, a tornado of plastic leaves flying all over the place, and her tits bounce free, swaying from their heavy weight. They're perfect. Everything about her is perfect.

Haloed in moonlight, my attention homes in on the beaded points of her nipples, my mouth watering to taste her flesh again. It's been too long.

"Need those gorgeous breasts in my mouth, Spitfire. Better yet, need to slide my dick in between them and watch them bounce as I tit-fuck you."

"If you get cum in my hair, I'm going to castrate you with a pair of scissors."

"I'll take that chance," I say with a smirk, lowering my head to suck one of her nipples into my mouth, flicking my tongue back and forth over the erogenous zone until I pull my first moan from her.

She pushes her chest into my face, allowing me deeper access, and crude slurping noises muffle around the rosy bud. Her hand entangles in my disheveled hair, tugging until my scalp burns, and I'm pretty sure she rips a few strands out. It doesn't falter my pace, though. I lightly indent her areola with my teeth, dragging them until I get to that delicious pucker, then popping off before she gives me a goddamn bald spot.

"I need you, Gage," she begs, pain dancing across her

screwed-up expression. "I need your tongue in my cunt. I just... oh, God. I need you. Right now."

Ladies and gents, I present to you something that I never thought would happen in my lifetime: Calista Cadwell begging.

And fuck, does it turn me on more than her insulting me does. Which I didn't know was even possible.

If I wasn't loving this so much, I would be the one begging her. My dick is so hard that it hurts like a bitch. And my balls ache to the point where I can feel the pressure escalate in my lower abdomen.

"You gonna admit you're drenched for me? How I'm the only person who makes your pussy throb and gush like that?" I slap the hood of her clothed clit, watching as pleasure crosses her face, liquifying every muscle in her upper body.

"No..." she starts unconvincingly.

I slip my finger past the gusset of her bikini bottom, contacting the flooded state of her slit and softly brushing over her liquid desire with the pad of my digit.

Her hips cant to take me deeper, and she claws into my back, denting my shoulder blades with her sharp nails. "God, fuck, yes! Yes, Gage!" she cries out, quivering against my chest, nearly coming undone from a single touch. There's a spent lull in her voice, raspy as all hell, pleading with me to whet her lust.

So sensitive.

"We're not in heaven. There is no God here. You understand that, Cali? I'm taking you to fucking hell tonight," I whisper, squelching the length of my finger inside her, all the way down to my knuckle.

I don't have to move much to get her to squirm, and when I begin to make good on my promise with a precise twittering motion, she moans loudly, her cunt squeezing in response. That smart mouth of hers is planets away, slackening with the intrusion of my digit. She's a whimpering mess while I plunge another finger in, swirling both fingers around, hitting the destruct button that makes her gush even more onto my hand.

"This is nothing," I warn her, juxtaposing my rough abuse of her cunt with a soft kiss to her cheek. "You keep moaning like that, and I'll have no choice but to give you my cock."

Trapped in the throes of absolute rapture, she keeps her watery gaze on me, a litany of whimpers fighting their way up her throat. The more I tend to her pussy, the more frequent her squeezes become, her pelvis thrashing and the swell of her belly drawing in with anticipation.

She goes to open her mouth—probably to damn me—but I cover it with my free hand, scissoring my digits until a ring of sticky liquid lathers around the base of them. "You don't get to talk. Listen. Listen to how wet you are."

She mewls against my palm, but it's muted beneath the loud squelching of her cunt.

"Fuck, that's such a pretty sound. You hear that, Spitfire? That's what I do to you. I own your pussy. All this lying to me about being dry isn't going to fly anymore. Do I make myself clear?"

All she can do is nod, still bucking fruitlessly into the air, unsatisfied by the thickness of the two fingers already jammed in her.

"Such a greedy girl," I tut, teasing her with the addition of a third finger, then feeling her walls dilate hollowly around the girth. She continues to let loose all kinds of sounds behind my hand, so I slowly remove the blockage from her lips.

"Need your dick," she demands, her impatience offsetting the bliss still splayed on her features.

"I'm not hearing a 'please.'"

She suddenly glares at me and growls. "If you don't take it out, I'll do it for you."

Okay, noted. Nice Cali only lasts a few minutes.

"I haven't even made you c—"

"If you think you're getting two orgasms out of me tonight, you're wrong. You're only getting one."

I withdraw my wet fingers, bringing them to my mouth and sucking every last drop of her arousal off of them. "Oh, I can get two," I quip confidently.

She grabs me by the shoulders, spins my back toward the bed, and throws my body onto it. Granted, it's more like a shove, and I don't know how she manhandled all one hundred and ninety pounds of me, but she did, and it was hot as fuck.

When I situate myself at the headboard, she crawls on top of me, breasts hanging and ass up in the air, bridged by the sexiest arch of her spine. Our lips mesh together, and my hands snake into her hair to grab a fistful, wrenching her neck slightly.

Kissing her never gets old. It's a rebirth every time. It's the equivalent of a cold glass of lemonade on a sun-scorched day; it's the feel of silk sheets on a freshly washed body; it's the satisfying remembrance of something you've forgotten; it's the smell of petrichor in a lush green forest on a morning walk. It's every human emotion rolled into one.

I keep my lips puckered like a fool before realizing she's moved to my stomach, marching her lips downwards in open-mouthed kisses, and when she gets to my navel, she licks it. I moan embarrassingly loudly, and thanks to the very thin walls in this house, if anyone's on the second floor they can probably hear what's going on in here. My abs flex as my swollen dick weeps for a single touch, sacrificing my manhood for a morsel of mercy.

And then I feel her fingers finally reach my costume, and I'm expecting a sudden wave of release when—

"Holy shit. No way. I'm not putting that thing inside me," she says, immediately sitting up.

I look down at my distended cock resting against my stomach, seeing nothing but nine inches of an angry, red-hued, vein-riddled appendage. Oh, and the metal barbells piercing the underside of my shaft.

"You didn't tell me you were pierced!" she exclaims.

"You didn't ask!"

"Why would I—why the fuck would I ask you that?"

"I don't know! Why are you freaking out?"

She gestures to my offending penis. "Because that *thing* is going to shred my vagina like a small, medieval torture device!"

My eyebrows climb up. "Small?"

She groans, throwing her arms up in exasperation. "Decently sized."

"Big," I counter, propping myself on my elbows, staring her down until I get her to agree.

"Slightly above average."

"*Big.*"

Dear God. Arguing with her doesn't make the pain go away. It's somehow inflating my cock even more, and the bulbous tip leaks more pearlescent pre-cum into my belly button. I'm *this* close to just giving myself a few pumps.

Her face is wrought with horror. "Fine! It's big. It's disturbingly big. And not only will it rip me in half, but it'll tear me up with those miniature metal stabbers!"

"I can take them out," I reply quickly.

When girls see that I'm pierced, they're either all for it or all against it. Each sexual experience differs from person to person. For some, the piercings enhance everything. For others, it's uncomfortable.

She drinks in a centering breath, closing her eyes for a brief second, then opening them again. "No, you don't need to do that, Gage."

"I want you to be as comfortable as possible, Cali. We don't have to do this."

She shakes her wavy locks, which have lost some of their volume from me combing my fingers through them like a cracked-out raccoon. "It's not that, it's..." She trails off, chewing on her lower lip self-consciously.

Her voice becomes small. "Will it hurt?"

"It, uh, it depends on the person. I've been told it feels uncomfortable before, but I've also been told it feels great," I answer.

She deadlocks with my dick, just mindlessly staring at it while God knows what spins around in that pretty head of hers. I stare back at her, suddenly feeling very naked under her analytic gaze, and all those nerves begin dogpiling inside me.

Why didn't this possibility cross my mind? If anything was to go wrong tonight, it would be my fucking dick jewelry. Is she disgusted by it? Did I just ruin the mood? Will she call me Pinhead for the rest of my life?

After a beat of silence, her brow sets into a determined line. "Okay. Let's do this."

"Are you sure?"

She runs her finger over a dominant vein tracking all the way to the head, and even though she isn't applying any pressure, my cock twitches for the relief only she can offer. Grinding my teeth together seems to be the only preventive measure I have from humiliating myself in front of her. I'm as sensitive as a fucking tripwire.

"I'm sure."

I open my mouth in search of reassurance, wanting to make sure she really means it, but she's stripped her thong off before any words can take flight. That perfect, gorgeous pussy is waiting for me, drenched in pent-up arousal, and I want her to disgorge all over my length until I'm dripping onto the sheets.

"Let me get a condom." I reach for my nightstand, praying that they haven't expired since it's been eighty thousand years since I've had any action, but Cali stops my hand.

"I want to feel them—you," she murmurs almost shamefully. "I have an IUD."

Am I about to die? Is that why so many good things have been happening lately? Feeling Cali raw...fuck. It's something that hasn't even crossed my mind. I always wrap it before I tap it. I've never *not* wrapped it. I also don't know shit about IUDs. Is that the little metal thingy that goes in the arm? Is it even an effective contraceptive?

"Yeah?" I ask.

"Yeah," she assures wantonly.

With the mobility my hip allows me, I swiftly switch our positions so she's beneath me, letting my cockhead snag over her damp clit, just giving her a taste so she can brace accordingly. When her eyes widen, I realize the top of my piercings must have grazed her folds, and a small gasp traps itself in her throat.

"Are you sure you're okay with this?" I ask softly, arms stationed by her head, making sure to keep the majority of my weight suspended so I don't crush her. Putting this amount of pressure on my knees definitely isn't good for my hip, but if sex with Cali means I'm set back three months in recovery, then it's fucking worth it.

My stomach clenches in a combination of both anticipation and arousal, though I'm not sure which is more potent. "At any point you want me to stop, you just tell me."

She looks like the sexiest centerfold sprawled out underneath me, breasts heaving in a thin finish of sweat, swatches of pink dusting her cheeks, and her flaming mane fanned out on the pillow. She nods, but worry stilts her next set of words. "If you think that'll fit inside me, you're insane."

"You can take it. I was made for you, Spitfire. Only you."

When Cali consents and spreads her legs wider, I slowly slide myself in, calculating the pace based on the contortion of her features—how her nose scrunches and a phantom grimace wrings her lips. The minute her cunt greets me with a welcoming slurp, I'm shock-stricken by how perfect she feels around me, and my brain has to hotwire itself back to its regularly scheduled programming.

I'm only halfway in, but my piercings have been swallowed up inside her, kissing her inner walls with every adjustment of her hips. I don't move until I get some kind of confirmation from her.

"Oh, God," she gasps, heeding the breach of her pussy, still tentative to move around or suck me any deeper.

I start to panic. "Is that a good 'Oh, God' or a bad 'Oh, God?'"

"It's—I—" She throws her head back, reveling in the sensation, her mouth forming a stunted *It's good* before she wiggles around some more.

I don't think she realizes how excruciating all her flailing around is. She's involuntarily playing with the most sensitive part of me, and grunting through the pain doesn't seem to be working.

"Spitfire, you need to stop..." I smash my molars together as my biceps shake. "Moving so much."

She stills, so timid that it's endearing. "Oh, sorry. A-are you in all the way?"

"Does it *feel* like I'm in all the way?"

Her hands anchor themselves in my sheets, and her belly flattens when she inhales sharply. "What the hell are you waiting for? Just do it!"

"Oh, I'm sorry for trying to be gentle," I scoff.

"Does it look like I'm a woman who wants gentle? I swear, Gage, if you don't—"

I slot myself between the juncture of her thighs before she can finish that sentence, pushing, pushing, and *pushing* until I'm buried to the hilt, my blunt tip bullying her cervix. Her throat works with a pained whimper, but she parts around my girth, stretching to adapt to my size like the good girl she is.

"Fuck, you're tight," I hiss, balls tapping gently against her ass, my own ass clenched like my fucking life depends on it.

"I'm not..." she huffs, gnashing her teeth. "You're...huge!"

"You don't need to flatter me. I'm already inside you."

"I hate you."

I bend down to whisper in her ear, already starting a measured pace as I snap my hips, plowing the furthest I can go and letting her natural lubrication help with the consistency of my thrusts. "Then fuck me like you mean it."

When I probe a sensitive spot, her hands feast on my back, nails raking down in smarting stings and scarlet scratches. I nearly lose my balance, but with the earnest way she's milking me, I'm kept in place. I can feel the obtrusion of my piercings catch on her inner walls, but she doesn't resist.

Cali moans, practically shaking the walls with the volume, pulsing around my dick and lifting her hips for me to find a better angle. I take advantage of her willingness, lining my waist up with hers to drive in askew to my previous position. I almost regret losing momentum until her back arches, and it feels like her fingers draw blood. Her eyes shutter closed, as if minimizing her vision will somehow dull the pressure in her lower belly.

"Look at me, Cali. Look at how well you're taking me," I demand in a husky whisper, easing myself out enough so she can watch as I slide back in.

Her eyes nearly pop out of her head as she watches, and she continues to cling to me, rolling her hips against mine. Her words are a blend of pleasured garbles and mewls, her tits bouncing when I take the liberty of speeding up. "So...good. Gage, it feels..."

"I know."

It feels better than good. It feels fucking *fantastic*. Everything is heightened with Cali—the feel of her soft skin, the taste of malt on her tongue, the sight of her unraveling as her orgasm closes in, the little noises she makes that stroke both my ego and my cock, the intensifying smell of her arousal as more of it seeps into the suction we've made.

"Such a good girl with the way you're squeezing me—letting me abuse this perfect cunt of yours. The best girl," I praise, feeling my dick spasm as the coil in my abdomen begins to stretch. "Take what you need from me, Spitfire. Take whatever the fuck you need."

I'm not going to last long. Jesus, it doesn't even feel like we're fucking. I'm gonna sound like a sappy shit, but it feels like we're making love. A little rough in unpolished places, but soft overall, words of affirmation traded for our usual clash of tongues.

"Need you filling me up, Gage. Need to feel your cum dripping out of me," she coos, wrapping her legs around my torso and giving me an all-access pass to that holy paradise between her thighs.

"Fuck," I groan, punctuating my eager agreement with a body-rocking pump, feeling her grasp me even tighter, nails following the irritated marks she made prior. "You have no idea how much I want that, baby. Want to paint your walls until you're leaking onto my sheets. Gonna worship this incredible pussy so you'll remember this moment long after it's over."

"Trust me, I'll remember," she whispers.

I press my forehead to hers. "I will too."

I double down on the roughness of my strokes, going as hard as I possibly can without hurting her. My orgasm is scaling an impossibly tall mountain, just inches from reaching the summit, and I can see the golden glow of release just beyond the snow-capped peak. Her legs tremble and her feet lose momentary hold on my lower back, her tits recoiling from each now-sloppy rut. Our moans harmonize, rising above the party's commotion, and my knuckles are bleached from digging into the mattress.

I have no idea how my stamina or my hip have lasted so long, but I'm not complaining. I spear my cock into her, balls slapping against her asshole, and I flex myself to make sure she can feel my piercings stimulate every nerve in her cunt.

"Mmm, Gage! Oh. Oh, God. I think I'm gonna…"

I can tell she's getting closer with the strain of her eyes, the uneven hitch of her breath, the viselike clench of her cunt. She isn't self-conscious about what's going to happen next like she was the first time we were physical, and getting to see her fully let go is better than saving the winning shot of any hockey game.

My dick prods her G-spot, giving her the first taste of her long-awaited orgasm, and it only takes a few more shunts until she falls apart in my arms with a guttural cry, squirting all over my dick in concentrated pulses. Her cum leaks around the plug of my cock, dripping onto the sheets and splattering the lower half of my body.

Feeling her bathe my cock, seeing her all over my navy sheets, is enough for me to sputter inside her, spraying long, thick ropes of cum that intermingle with the overflow from hers. Everything is warm and wet, coddling my happily softening dick, and I don't rush to pull out of her.

My milky spend travels down her legs, accentuating the sticky slap of her thighs, and the combined scent of our desire steeps the space around us. This is a goddamn dream—seeing her spent beneath me with my cum trickling out of her.

The breath Cali's not wasting on insulting me is flowing out of her in quick pants, face flushed and a dazed look in her eyes. "That was…"

Still hovering over her, I grin. "The best Halloween you've ever had?"

She looks up at me through her lashes. "Second best."

"Good thing I'm not done with you yet."

Cali props herself up on her elbows, tits rising and falling with overtaxed breaths, her thoroughly fucked expression a lick of fire to the flickering wick still burning strong in the bottom of my stomach. "We're going to miss the party," she says.

Even though her glorious cunt is keeping my cock warm, I pull out of her, letting a viscous string of arousal stretch between us before it soils the sheets below. "I promised you another orgasm."

She goes uncharacteristically quiet, her cheeks prickling with embarrassment and her eyes looking everywhere but where I yearn for them the most. "I don't think I can have another..."

She doesn't even finish her sentence. I can tell she's still hungry for me, though, with the way her body tenses in lustful anticipation, how her tongue wets the cushion of her bottom lip, priming it for the slight indentation of her teeth.

"Guess we'll just have to find out, won't we?"

Before her self-conscious thoughts become cobwebbed in her head, I spread her legs apart, slapped in the face by her pretty, puffy pussy lodged full of my load. I know something about eating my own jizz should turn me off, but when it's undercut by that sweet escape between her thighs, it doesn't even bother me. All gentlemanly sweet talk—or ungentlemanly dirty talk—is abandoned when my tongue finds her soaked clit, and I press the flat of it to her still-sensitive entrance, feeling her writhe slightly and shake the bed.

She's still on her elbows, except her back is arched this time, her legs are wrought by tremors, and the tiniest of moans previews the chorus of obscene noises just waiting to penetrate the stillness of the bedroom.

I lick over her outer lips, tasting the first dregs of salt on my tongue, and then I breach the opening of her cunt, immediately doused in the overwhelming scent of sweat and cum. A ribbon of possessiveness weaves through me, cementing the unbelievable fact that I get to taste the two of us out of what might as well be a golden chalice, and my dick's quick to react with an appropriate rush of blood.

I swirl inside her, lapping at her tender walls, simultaneously swallowing the heady abundance now steadily dripping out of her. All my senses are going off like a security alarm, too slow to register one before the next happens, so overstimulated that every thought in my head poofs out of existence.

I chance a glance at Cali, more than satisfied with her mouth cutting into a tight-lipped grimace, her head tilted back, the soft curve of her stomach quivering. When I brush over a supposed receptive spot, her pussy begins to strangle my tongue, hips lifting higher into the air, mewls so loud they practically break the sound barrier.

"Ohhh, fuck. Oh, Gage."

I could spend hours down here, but she'll probably only last a few more minutes. I speed up my pace with fast flicks, exploring areas that her exes doubtfully ever ventured, using my hands to clamp onto her thighs and prevent myself from melting into a pathetic puddle of goo. She's fully thrashing now, riding my tongue greedily, clenching fistfuls of sheets between her hands as a multitude of moans make my now-hardening dick pulse.

Devouring her like this—witnessing her as vulnerable as an exposed nerve—causes pods of butterflies to hatch in my belly, salaciousness slithering serpentine through the very structure of my DNA. I never want this to end. I never want to spend a moment *not* pleasuring Cali. She deserves to have me buried between her thighs twenty-four-seven, and that's a job I don't take lightly.

Her orgasm is fast-approaching, courtesy of every lash of my tongue, and I give her an added incentive when I suckle on her slick folds. Her legs, surprisingly, aren't choking me out like they were the last time. She's so exhausted from the pleasure pendulum ride I've subjected her to that she doesn't even bother with saying anything—everything's either a soft gasp or an animalistic moan that doesn't bode well for the state of my dick.

Just a little longer, Spitfire.

I retract my tongue the slightest bit from her cunt, looking up at her through her shaking legs, walking on razor-thin wire with the teasing she's about to make me regret. "You like stars, baby?"

There's an impatient inflection in her tone. "What?"

"Stars. Do you like them?"

Her hand darts out to grip some of my hair, and she pulls harshly, a nonverbal message telling me that I need to put my tongue to better use. But she humors me anyways, a desperate attempt to ensure she finishes quickly. "Ugh, yes. Yes, I like them," she groans.

"Good, because you're about to see a fuckton of them," I growl, delving my tongue right back inside her, not stopping for a breath of air until I've swung her all the way to the highest point of her climax.

And finally, after a continuous succession of slurps, she cries out my name, and the sound clatters against my eardrums. A ripe wave of cum slathers my mouth, rushing down into my belly like pressurized water on a waterslide. Her arousal leaks down my chin, but I'm diligent enough this time to guzzle the majority of the excess up, so drunk on the taste of her that I neglect my painfully throbbing erection.

After her orgasm razes her, every tight hold of her muscles liquefies, and she's a sweaty pile of bones above me, starving for air with urgent gasps that never seem to end. Her legs flatten against the bed, and I drag myself up a few inches, resting my chin on her belly.

"Wow" is all she manages, bringing her hand to her forehead.

"See? Told you I could get two."

22

TRICK-OR-TRAUMA
GAGE

"Boo!" Cali shrieks from behind me, jostling my shoulders and relishing in horrifying eldritch laughter when I clutch my imaginary pearls.

Frozen, I'm like a deer trapped in the line of a hunter's bow, and it takes a few seconds for my brain to reboot and assure me that the only plausible threat in the vicinity is a threat to my manhood.

"Jesus," I breathe, feeling my poor heart spasm underneath my fingertips. "You can't keep doing that, Cali."

"I wouldn't if you weren't so easily scared," she says, reaching for the lollipop she stowed behind her ear and slowly peeling off the red, cellophane wrapper. She nabbed it at the first house we visited, and she's been secretly plucking a few unsuspecting candies from the bottom of Teague's pumpkin pail.

I fiddle with the tube on my proton pack, which matches the *Ghostbusters* group costume Teague has orchestrated for all of us to participate in. I never really partook in trick-or-treating when I was little, partly because the Halloween decorations scared the crap out of me, and partly because my parents never volunteered to take me and my brother. But I'm glad to be here now, with Teague and Cali, facing my irrational fears of kid-friendly jump scares and house-sized animatronics.

Teague's a fucking trooper. He's way less afraid than I was when I was a kid. In fact, he's gone up to every doorstep all on his own and broke out that pageant-winning smile of his. His pail's so full that there's barely any room left for more candy, and we still have a few more blocks to go until we've cleared the neighborhood.

Teague's walking by my side and slowly making a dent in his king-size Hershey's bar, while Cali's taking up the front and inadvertently torturing me with the way her ass moves in her tight-fitting uniform.

The streets are overrun with tiny, colorful bodies, and every house is so backed up that we have to maneuver through flocks of first-time parents and disinterested older siblings, all being pulled by children who've reached max sugar capacity. A tapestry of darkness swallows the night sky, save for the full moon that hangs above us and casts ribbons of light over sprawling asphalt. Houses are lined with glowing jack-o'-lanterns, seven-foot skeletons and blow-up black cats occupy every lawn in sight, and fog machines exhale a sinister mist over fake gravestones. The skeletal limbs of molting trees sway with the last of autumn's leaves, causing a few runts to fall to the ground in a flurry of crimson and canary yellow. It's chilly out tonight, and I'm glad for the coverage of my costume to keep my balls from shriveling into raisins.

When Teague stops at an impressively decorated house—complete with a walk-through scientist's lab—we stand in a fifteen-minute line full of overstimulated kids and the occasional fussy baby. Teague, however, bounces up and down with unrestrained excitement, which is probably a byproduct of the copious amounts of sugar he's already ingested.

The line's stopped moving, allowing my aching feet a rest,

and Cali leans against my side, having found a new method of torturing me while she sucks on her lollipop, hollowing her cheeks and flicking her tongue over her semitranslucent candy.

"You know you didn't have to come with us, right?" Her carmine-stained lips glisten underneath the moonlight, and my saliva glands go into overdrive when I imagine myself cleaning the cherry flavor from her mouth—getting drunk on the aftertaste of a bad decision.

"I wanted to," I respond, and to corroborate my statement, I ruck my lips up into a smile, mirroring the inflation of my heart. "There's really nowhere else I'd rather be."

I didn't think I'd ever be trick-or-treating with Cali and her little brother. This feels so...serious. We're not just *hanging* out. This could be a core memory for Teague. After his concussion, Cali's family has been weighing heavier on me. The more I hang out with Teague, the more I want to be in his life. And tonight isn't an exception.

Each time he faces his fears and goes up to a house all on his own, pride crystallizes in my veins, and I want nothing more than to pick him up in my arms and tell him how proud I am. There's always a split second before the door opens that he looks back at me for reassurance, and a supportive thumbs-up galvanizes his confidence.

Don't get me wrong: a part of me also wants to keep my distance. A part of me doesn't want Teague to look up at me like I can do no wrong—because I can, and I have. I've convinced myself that I don't deserve love after the mistake I made with my brother. And would Teague really look at me the same way if he knew his hero wasn't so perfect?

Cali shoves her lollipop to one side of her cheek, puffing it out like a chipmunk's. "He's really happy you're here, you know," she whispers to me.

"I'm surprised he hasn't gotten sick of me," I joke, but

there's an inkling of truth in there somewhere, and it makes my stomach writhe with the intensity of a washing machine.

"Are you kidding? He's obsessed with you. Never stops talking about you. It's always 'I wonder what Gage is doing today.' 'Can we please hang out with Gage?' 'Cali, did you know that Gage is the coolest person ever?'"

I smirk. "He's right. I *am* the coolest person ever."

The line shuffles forward the slightest bit, and every so often, I catch a glimpse of the two gigantic tarps over the multi-purpose garage pulsing with a plethora of neon-colored lights.

"It amazes me how big your ego is," she grumbles.

While Teague's bucket-deep in search of his next treat, I take the stick of Cali's lollipop between my index and middle finger, slowly easing it out from between her lips. She doesn't say much apart from a gasp, and I push the lollipop into my own mouth, hyperaware of the excess saliva on it. "If I remember yesterday correctly, you were a fan of *something* that was big."

I can tell she wants to retaliate, but since there are little ears present, she settles for an exasperated, "Ugh."

Chuckles dwindle into the ambience of the night, and I tip my head up to the map of stars, watching as my breath coalesces into thin, gossamer strands, eventually evaporating into the fifty-degree atmosphere. It's just dawned on me that I'll never be able to take Trip trick-or-treating now. And the worst part is, I'll experience so many things with Teague, and they'll all remind me of the experiences that were taken from my brother.

Cali must've descried my uneasiness because she comes to join me at our quick rest stop, leaning against the fence. "You okay?"

I clear my throat in an attempt to reinstate my conviction. "Huh? Oh, yeah. I'm all good."

She eyes me like a hawk, and she leans in just slightly,

concern seasoning her tone. "Gage, there's obviously something that's bothering you."

The lollipop lodged in my mouth suddenly couldn't be less appetizing. "I was just thinking about…"

I can't even say the words. My guilt's giving me away like a large, conspicuous, flashing neon sign.

"About?"

"I was worried about coming out tonight," I admit, somehow feeling claustrophobic in my own skin—feeling like no matter where or how far I run, my past always catches up to me. "I was worried that I'd think about…"

And immediately, Cali catches on to my unspoken truth. "Oh, Gage. I'm so sorry. I didn't even think about how tonight would affect you after your brother."

"No. It's okay. I'm glad I get to be here with you and Teague. It, uh, it doesn't hurt as much as I thought it would. You guys make it a lot less painful."

"Are you sure?"

I angle my chin so I can kiss the crown of her head, smiling when her curls tickle my nose and I get a whiff of that heavenly cinnamon scent. "Yeah, I'm sure. Seeing how excited Teague is…it just reminds me of how excited Trip used to be when Halloween came around."

She looks up at me through her lashes, and I transfer the lollipop from my mouth into hers. She jumbles it around so she can speak. "I take it he loved Halloween?"

"Big fan. Our parents never took us trick-or-treating, but Trip would always dress up," I tell her.

"You do know your parents are on my shit list, right?"

"Oh, mine too."

Laughter boomerangs between us, rich and rumbling like a faraway motor engine, and I feel Cali's hands hug my arm as she lists closer to me.

"What did Trip like to dress up as?" she asks, nuzzling into me.

My hand comes up to rest over hers, which are freezing to the touch. "He loved dinosaurs. His favorite movie was *The Land Before Time*."

"So one of those blow-up dinosaur costumes?"

"Yeah. One of those ridiculous, blow-up dinosaur costumes."

It feels really good to talk about Trip without also talking about his death. It feels good to acknowledge him without grieving him. I don't remember the last time I was able to talk about who he was, truly—the things he was interested in, the memories we made together. And talking about him with Cali gives me a sense of closure I've never found anywhere else.

Cali chews the rest of her lollipop before discarding the stick in Teague's pail.

"I, um, I hope I'm not upsetting you by saying this, but..." The last of her words are swallowed by a rocky breath, and the way she looks up at me has my heart clenching around a bullet-sized hole of fear.

"But?"

Her fingers absentmindedly squeeze my bicep. "How are you so happy all the time? I mean, I know you aren't, but you seem so put together."

I was expecting her comment to floor me, but all it does is produce a small smile on my lips and generate a newfound warmth between our hands—one that travels all the way to my cheeks and scorches a presumable blush. "It's not always easy," I admit with a hollow chuckle. "When Trip died, I had a choice: either I could let his death drown me and take me under, or I could let his death strengthen me. It was then that I realized I didn't want to live the rest of my life in sorrow. I wanted to find a reason to be happy again, and the more I presented myself that way, the more it tricked my brain into believing I *was* truly happy."

"You don't always have to put on a happy face," Cali says quietly. "It's okay to break down every once in a while."

"I know that now, thanks to you. One reason I've always been so happy-go-lucky is because I'd suppressed Trip's memory. I refused to revisit it or even *think* about it. It was easier to be blissfully ignorant than confront my past. But ever since I met Teague, he's helped me come to the conclusion that my brother's memory is always going to be there, no matter how hard I try to ignore it. And it would be a shame for Trip's memory to disappear all because I was too cowardly to share it."

Cali doesn't say anything before she rises to her tiptoes and presses a kiss to my cheek, the stickiness of her lip gloss gluing down the faint stubble starting to crop up. "I'm so proud of you, Gage. I know you don't talk about your brother with anyone."

"You're not just anyone, Cali," I whisper.

Suddenly, I feel a tug on my sleeve, and Teague's looking up at me with huge, glossy eyes, his lower lip trembling like a leaf in the wind. "Gage, I'm scared," he says quietly, to the point where I nearly don't hear him over the background chatter.

His gaze cuts briefly to the ominous-sounding garage, and I follow his line of sight to find that only a few people stand between us and the haunted house. The exaggerated, eardrum-blasting noise of evil scientist laughter can be heard from our spot, and there's a pre-recorded mess of clanking machinery that acts as white noise beneath well-rehearsed dialogue.

And all my worries disappear to make room for his. I hunker down to a squat so I'm level with him, and I give his shoulder a comforting rub. "Hey, Little Man. It's alright. We can turn around right now."

Teague shakes his mop of ginger hair, mouth set in a thin,

hard line. "I don't want to turn around. I want to go in. But I'm... scared."

"You know, I'm kind of scared too. Maybe if we hold hands, it'll be less scary, yeah?"

I can tell he's skeptical as he glances between me and the foreboding garage, but he eventually nods his head in agreement, clinging to my hand so tightly that he cracks my knuckles. Am I scared? Hell yes, I am. I don't know what the fuck lies behind those sketchy-ass tarps. Will I punch one of the scare actors if they jump out at me? I'll try not to.

Teague hands his bucket off to Cali to hold through the haunted house, since she's the least likely out of all of us to feel any terror walking through it. She's a horror junkie—which makes sense as to why she's so scary sometimes.

The tour starts relatively calmly, with our guide dressed in a blood-splattered lab coat and his hair an electrified mess of spikes on top of his head. He leads us through the first room, which consists of a man being bound to an operating table by leather restraints, squirming and thrashing while he screams bloody murder. Another scientist hovers over him with a drill to his head, complete with fake blood squirting from the realistic-looking wound on the man's temple. If that wasn't gross enough, there are tons of glass vials and bottles filled with unidentifiable body parts and murky liquids. Blinding lights flare in my eyes, and a particularly gruesome jump scare thieves my breath and makes Teague grip my clammy hand harder.

I keep him hugged to my leg as we creep through a pitch-black corridor, only illuminated in spurts, timed with the screams from both actors and traumatized kids. I have no idea where I'm going, and I can hear Cali squealing and falling into easy laughter behind me. The fear in my body is palpable now, my heart juddering at an alarming rate, and my stomach relocating to my goddamn esophagus. When we round the corner, a new, disturbing scene is laid out before us: a woman strapped down on a table, but this time, her body has been severed in half, and the scientist is digging through a gory spillover of entrails with his bare hands.

Dear God, this is terrifying. This is definitely not suited for children. Teague has his face buried against my hip, and I feel for the little guy. Cali's having a blast behind us, totally unfazed, and I'm beginning to question how unmanly it would be if I grab onto her arm for support. The last room is a sensory nightmare, with the prominent stench of rotten, spoiled food perfuming the musty air. It takes everything in me not to gag. I don't even want to know how these people *replicated* that smell.

The final victim is a man who's getting all these dismembered body parts sewn onto his new body like some twisted Frankenstein retelling—the brain from the first man and the lower body from the second woman. There's less blood on the actual actor, but there's more carnage in the background, discarded limbs piled high and soaking in a mess of bodily juices and syrup-thick ichor. We get ushered out quickly to accommodate for the conveyer belt of incoming bodies, and I'm thankful, because the stench was overbearing.

When we stumble back into the real world, my chest swells with a much-needed fresh breath of air, and the horrified shrieks of other children detonate like a nuclear blast in that surprisingly large garage.

"Wow, that was incredible!" Cali gushes, already rummaging around for another piece of candy like she didn't just witness someone's intestines slopping onto the floor.

"Uh-huh" is all I have the energy to say, trying to shake those creatively morbid images from my brain—which will probably come back to haunt me when I'm sleeping tonight.

Poor Teague is quivering against me, and I don't think he's opened his eyes yet to notice that we're safely outside. I rub mollifying circles on his back, trying to coax him to look up at me. "Hey, T. We're outside. You can look now."

He hesitates for a moment, as if he's trying to decide whether or not the coast is clear, and then he glances around, all while keeping his unrelenting grasp on me. "That was scary," he mumbles under his breath.

"I know. I was terrified," I agree.

His mouth forms an O shape. "You were?"

"Oh, yeah. But you were being so brave in there that I knew I had to be brave too. I don't think I would've made it without you by my side, Little Man."

Tears dollop on Teague's lashes, and I'm not trained enough in kid etiquette to know if they're good or bad tears. So, I'm about to console him when he charges into me with a lineman-tackle hug, squeezing my legs with his arms. I can hear Cali *awwing* in the background, and love nestles deep in my heart at how close I've grown to Teague in the past month. All the pessimistic thoughts working a full-time shift in my brain—the ones claiming that I'm not good enough to be a role model for him, that he shouldn't look up at me with hero worship—they're instantly silenced by the way he smushes his cheek into my thigh.

I was scared of Teague putting me on a pedestal—unaware of the mistakes I made in the past with my brother—but seeing him lean on me for support through such a scary event…it feels like maybe I was put on this earth for that exact reason. Put on earth to be someone's hero. Put on earth to hold shaky hands and calm the tremors.

I want to be in his and Cali's lives. I want to be a role model who he can look up to. I want to be a father figure to him, especially because he doesn't have one—and neither did I.

I just…I want to do right by him. By my brother. By Cali.

Careful not to startle him, I scoop him up under his armpits and haul him onto my shoulders, keeping a secure hold on his legs. It hurts my hip a little, but the look on his face is worth every twinge of pain. He's giggling uncontrollably, and the three of us start walking back to the Reapers' mansion to turn in for the night.

"Can we have a sleepover at Gage's house?" Teague asks Cali from above me.

Cali chews off the end of a Twizzler, humming thoughtfully. "That's up to Gage, kiddo."

Teague thumps his little legs against my chest. "Pleeeaaaseee, Gage. Please can we sleep over at your house?" he whines, inspiring laughter to ripple up from my belly and fill the slowly growing silence as we distance ourselves from the main road.

"As long as it's okay with your sister."

"Cali, can—"

"Yes, Teague. It's okay with me," she chuckles.

"Yay!" Teague squeals with enthusiasm, and I keep his shins clamped in a stranglehold before racing down the street as fast as my hip will allow, leaving behind the encroaching fear and misguided self-blame from my past.

23

THE NO-ENTRY ZONE
CALISTA

It's day three, and I've been trapped in the bathroom for the past three hours. I don't know if I'll survive this time. I don't remember what the sun feels like on my face or what it feels like to breathe fresh air. Death is a privilege ungranted, condemning me to a weeklong trial run of my own personal hell.

I canceled every dance class I had this week because I've barely been able to make it out the door. I haven't made contact with the outside world at all. I'm beginning to lose my sanity, and soon, I'll lose all concept of time. The only thing keeping my mind intact is the life-altering sex I had with Gage at the Halloween party. My soul practically ascended over the way he rubbed his ribbed cock inside me, making sure I could feel each and every one of his piercings as he fucked me hard and slow. I'd never admit it to him, but that was the best sex I ever had. And now my body craves him every second of every day, throwing a tantrum whenever I can't mount him like a bonobo monkey.

God, and if he wasn't already irresistible enough, the way he was with Teague on Halloween made my heart soar. He acted like he was meant to be a role model...a father figure. It was like he was meant to be in our lives, if that even makes any sense. Am I making sense? I don't know.

Everything hurts. This isn't some painkiller-fix type of hurt, either. It's the kind of hurt that has you sweating like a pig, on the verge of passing out every few minutes, praying to whatever higher power there is for relief, and making your body so feeble that you can barely unscrew the cap of a pill bottle.

I slump on the floor of my bathroom, resting my head against the cool porcelain of the toilet, waiting for the nausea to run its course. Teague's knocked a few times to ask if he can help me with anything, but I've barely had the energy to answer him. My mother's still recovering in the hospital, so in a sick turn of events, I guess Teague's technically my caretaker now.

The fluorescents burn my eyes, but if I turn off the lights, it might put me in some weird pain-sleep coma. So my retinas suffer through the blinding laser treatment as my equilibrium attempts to right itself from the constant dizzy spells jumbling my brain.

Exhaustion pulls at my limbs like strings on a marionette, and my lower stomach cramps and twists, as if there's barbed wire shredding my womb into bloodied ribbons. Not to mention that the overpowering stench of copper is everywhere, only worsening the headache in my skull.

Every single month it's the same old torture—bleeding, cramps, sometimes puke, crying, and damning my female anatomy for having to shed my stupid uterine lining. Granted, the alternative is being pregnant, so it's a lose-lose situation.

I'm so dehydrated that my eyes are beginning to droop shut, despite tap water being just out of reach. I'm too afraid to move in fear of passing out. Thankfully, that possibility doesn't look like it'll be happening any time soon. My pain receptors are working overtime, alerting me to the pins and needles in my legs, to the staccato beat of my heart, to the heat sprawling throughout my body like a gradual forest fire, and to the periodic contractions in my belly.

But I don't get a second of peace before there's an incessant knock on the door that seems forceful enough to bust the entire partition down.

"Teague, go away," I groan, curling into a fetal position in the delusional hope that it'll allow me some magical reprieve.

A low and growly baritone rumbles from the other side, far too mature to belong to Teague, and far too angry to successfully fit in my baby brother's four-foot-seven body. "Calista, open the door."

Shit. Shit. Shit. It's Gage. Why is Gage here? How did he get in? How did he know I was even here?

Conjuring the tiniest scrap of energy, I unfold from my pathetic position, scrambling and pressing my back against the thick stump of the toilet. I stare down at my bloated belly protruding over the jeans I failed to button, and I nearly fall victim to another snot-filled crying session. Gage can't see me like this.

"Don't come in here!" I scream, staring at the little piece of metal keeping me from feeling Gage's full wrath. I need to make him leave. I need to think of the most disgusting excuse in the world so that he'll never be turned on by me ever again.

"I have…uh…explosive diarrhea. Yeah. It's terrible!"

"I don't care if it's coming out of both ends, open the fucking door, or I'll force it open myself."

I don't doubt that Gage is more than capable, given his mountain of man muscles. He'll rip that door right off its hinges or pull a Jack Torrance and axe it down.

I'm too weak to get up and barricade the door. I'm too weak to keep arguing with him. All I want to do is fall asleep on this cold bathroom floor—probably teeming with germs and the possibility of pink eye—and drift into a weeklong hibernation until The Crimson Wave has receded back into the depths of hell from which it came.

Knock.

Knock.

Knock-knock-knock-knock.

BUT I CAN'T. Because Gage is determined to play a goddamn drum solo on the door until I let him in.

"Gage, please go away," I whimper, feeling the beginnings of a fever start to work its way through me like a slow-acting poison. And now the rhythm of Gage's knocking has somehow translated into my own head, bolstering my run-of-the-mill headache into a fully powered migraine.

I expect another curse to fall on my ears, but to my surprise, Gage's shadow moves from under the door and his footfalls shallow down the hallway.

Did he just *listen* to me? I can't tell if this is a good or bad thing. For any regular person, when someone does what you say, it's a good thing. But for me, when Gage does what I say (usually stubbornly), it means that hell's waiting to break loose. Is he going to the store to get a battering ram? I don't think stores sell battering rams. Where does one even acquire a battering ram?

With this newfound silence, I try to focus on the cold of the ceramic tile as it scares away the heat nesting deep inside me, reverting it to nothing but an infant flame.

And when peace is just a grab away, levitating outside of my arm's reach, a strange, tinny noise sideswipes my attention. It's like this grating, scratchy sound, as if someone's trying to insert something into a hole.

This bitch.

My eyes cut toward the commotion to confirm my suspicions, and of course, the doorknob is jiggling all over the place. Gage is picking the lock.

I probably have approximately fifteen seconds before he

gets the door open, so I'm pretty much helpless at this point. Fifteen seconds is nowhere near enough time to make myself look presentable. This is it. He's going to see me in a sweaty puddle on the floor, get disgusted by me, then probably never want to speak to me again. I mean, I'm bleeding out of my pussy. My pussy! That's the furthest thing from sexy.

When the lock makes this little *plink* sound, I hear the doorknob turn, and then I come to a staring impasse with Gage, who's huffing and panting and looking a tad bit homicidal.

"Why"—wheeze—"didn't"—wheeze—"you"—wheeze—"open"—wheeze—"the door?"

"Um, maybe because I didn't want you to come in here!" I snip, doing my best to cover the bulge of my belly with my arms. Embarrassment paints my face in shades of pink, and all I want to do is sink into the floor, have it absorb my pathetic body, and die a peaceful death underneath the crawl space of my apartment.

It takes me a few seconds to register the heaping pile of plastic bags next to Gage's feet.

"Gage, what are—"

"Do you know how worried I was, Cali? I was fucking sick to my stomach after not hearing from you for three days. I had to ask Aeris if she knew what was going on with you, and when she told me you hadn't been in class, I lost my goddamn mind."

I worry my bottom lip, swallowing around the thickness in my throat. I feel like an even bigger bitch for not telling him I was sick. I just didn't want him to, well, do what he's doing right now. I didn't want him to drop everything to come take care of me. And hearing myself say that in my head reminds me of how good of a guy Gage is. How he's been there for me like no one else has in my life. How he'll always be there.

"I'm sorry," I blubber, face-planting into my palms. "I should've told you. I'm not sick, Gage. I'm..."

He's somehow materialized right next to me, crouching

down to my level and brushing snarled strands of hair out of my face. "I just want to take care of you, Spitfire. I need to know I'm taking care of you," he says softly.

"I'm on my...meriod." I whisper the last part under my breath, retracting my hands from my face so I can stare at the off-white bottoms of Gage's shoes.

"What?"

"My...shmeriod."

A growl sits precariously in the pit of his chest, rumbling outwards though his body. "Cali..."

"I'm on my period!" I exclaim a little too loudly, still evading his eyes as a drop of shame rolls down the bumps of my spine.

The concern on Gage's face seems to retreat, sated by the news of me not contracting a fatal disease, and it's replaced with a snort of laughter. "That's all?"

"What do you mean 'that's all?'"

Gage gently rests his hand on my arm, and my pulse flutters like that of a bird trapped between the maws of a hungry predator. "It's a period, Cali."

"It's disgusting! *I* look disgusting."

"Stop," he snarls. "You do not look disgusting. You've never looked disgusting a day in your life. You're the most beautiful girl in this entire world, and I'll keep telling you until you get tired of hearing it."

Normally, I'd have a barb perched on the tip of my tongue for him, but right now, the only response I have for him is...a fountain of tears.

They begin to pour out of me with the complementary hiccups here and there, and sobs break through the seal of my throat, bursting to the scene with enough volume to probably reach the neighboring apartments. Everything intermingles on my face—tears, snot, sweat—and they form a sticky resin that'll need a good wiping afterwards.

"Oh, baby," Gage sympathizes, doing his best to wrangle some of my tears with the soft pads of his fingers.

"I'm s-sorry I'm s-so emotional," I wail, desperately trying to maintain some picture of calm while my hair looks like it's been electrocuted, and my face is a teary, acne-ridden mess. My chest racks from the turbulent sobs, and my vision has been indefinitely fogged by my stupid hormones, reducing Gage to a shapeless blob in front of me.

He caresses my cheek. "It's oka—"

"I'm breaking out, I smell terrible, and I'm on the toilet for hours!"

"Okay, I didn't need that much informat—"

My lungs empty a breath, only so I can launch into another tangent. "And my stomach! Oh my God, I look like I'm pregnant," I whine, grabbing the dome of my rock-hard belly. "I don't want to look pregnant."

"Calista," Gage commands in that hauntingly low voice of his, picking my attention up by the goddamn scruff and forcing it to behave. His eyes are a slate-colored tone, every chiseled line on his face making an appearance, and I've never seen him look so serious before—so darkened by the frivolity of my self-deprecating comments.

Calista. My full name. I never liked it growing up as a kid—because a lot of people didn't know how to pronounce it—but when Gage says it, it's a sweet-sounding melody designed just for me.

"I don't care what you look like. I've seen you at your lowest when you were bawling your eyes out, I've seen you at your highest when you were nonstop smiling. I've seen you in a stained hoodie and sweatpants, I've seen you in that black romper that drives me crazy, I've seen you in my goddamn jersey. The bottom line is—each time, you were nothing less than stunning. And that doesn't change now," he tells me, soaking up the rest of my tears with the built-in tissue he calls his hand.

A sigh exits me, and I blink the last of the moisture from my bleary eyes, now feeling the full extent of the burning taking place there. My whole body feels drained—not that it was bursting with energy to begin with. The only good thing to come out of my therapeutic crying fit is my precursory humiliation dwindling to a much more manageable size.

A warm smile favors the right corner of Gage's lips, summoning some of that lopsided charm he has flying out the wazoo. "Plus, you'd look sexy as hell if you were pregnant."

I glare at him. "Do *not* get any ideas."

"Trust me, I want you all to myself before I have to share you with a little demon spawn."

He rises to a stance, reaching out to help me off the floor. I swipe the snot from under my nose with my forearm before accepting his outstretched hand, and he lifts me effortlessly to my feet.

I forgot how amazing his hand feels in mine. The warmth from his palm, the callouses over still-tanned skin from however he spent his summer, the more than adequate acreage for my hand to feel fully protected in the cradle of his fingers.

"Thanks," I murmur, nearly forgetting that we're still holding each other's hands.

But I think Gage remembers.

That smile of his has evolved into a full beam, the crepuscule shadows in his eyes lifting to reveal the first glimmer of sun encroaching on the horizon. He's staring at me like I've bewitched him.

"I'm always going to be here for you, Cali. Even when you don't want me to be."

My eyebrows shoot up. "How did you even get in the house?"

"Teague let me in, and I didn't even have to threaten him.

He's such a nice kid. I have no idea how you two are related," Gage ribs, a chuckle of amusement building at the base of his throat.

I honestly don't, either.

I prepare my elbow for a Gage-directed jab, but then a stabbing pain flares up in my stomach, forcing me to keel over at my midsection and clutch the source of the unabating cramping. I hiss through my teeth as another tidal wave of heat crashes over me, and I mentally plead for this to be a normal cramp and not one calling for the assistance of the porcelain throne right in front of me.

"Shit, Cali. Is it cramps?" Gage's disembodied voice asks from somewhere beside me.

"It hurts," I whimper pitifully, apparently not having said farewell to my tears because they're rallying in my bloodshot eyes.

"I know, baby. We're gonna get you in bed and get you some painkillers. I'm gonna be right here. It's okay. You're gonna be okay."

With a weak nod on my part, Gage scoops me up in his arms and carries me bridal-style to my room, choosing me over his injured hip. I close my eyes to placate the blistering sting in my corneas, and the unevenness of his gait bumps me against the hard planes of his chest. I loop my arms around his neck, burrowing my face into the clean linen of his shirt as I simultaneously breathe in his unadulterated musk. I don't know when we make it to my bed, but I never let go of him.

24

LOVE THY DANCE TEACHER
GAGE

I'll never know what cramps feel like, but I'm guessing they're the equivalent of having someone wring out your intestines like a wet sponge. Consistently. Over a seven-day period.

Pretty soon after I got Cali to bed, she passed out, which is probably a good thing considering she was crushing the bones in my neck when she was holding on to me.

When Aeris told me that Cali was sick, she didn't really go into specifics. She said it could be one of two things. One: it could be a common cold that comes with the changing weather, but none of the students in her class were sick, so she thought that seemed unlikely. Or two: she was on her period. And then Aeris, as usual, overshared some very traumatizing memories about her period which I definitely didn't need to know.

So I did the wise thing and stocked up for both with the usual soup, tissues, cough medicine, cough drops, thermometer, and Gatorade. And the usual pads, tampons, tissues (again), chocolates, heating blanket, bath bomb, herbal tea, and candle. Oh, and a vanilla milkshake from Been There, Bun That.

I know next to nothing about periods. The only walking pamphlet of information I was afforded was the random middle-aged woman at the store staring at me while I was in the feminine product aisle.

I wanted to do something for Cali to make her feel better, so I enlisted Teague to help me spruce up her room for when she wakes. And he so generously offered to lend me some of Cali's favorite movies, which—a surprise to no one—are all very graphic horror movies. Not a chick flick or Disney movie in sight. There's even one in black-and-white because the color version had been banned in several countries.

Even though the rest of Cali's apartment is decorated for Halloween, there were no decorations in her own room. So I took the liberty of finding a few twinkle lights and hanging them around. I then laid out everything I got her at the foot of her bed, ready to sprint to the bathroom in case she needs me to draw her a relaxing bubble bath. I heard heat helps with cramps. I also have trusty dusty Tylenol in case none of my efforts seem to work, but here's to hoping they do. I have a tendency to fuck shit up a lot of times—mostly from carelessness, sometimes from overconfidence. I don't want this to be one of those times. I don't want there to be a time at all when it comes to Cali.

I know I should be watching practice right now, but there's no way in hell I'm leaving her in the state she's in. And honestly? There's nowhere else I'd rather be.

While she's curled on her side, snoring quietly, I relegate myself to the other side of her bed and keep a respectable distance between us. I don't want to overstep any boundaries here. Like she said, we're not...*we're not together.* Just friends. But sometimes it feels like we're more. It's all really confusing, but she's not ready yet. And I'll be ready for when she is.

I know the future isn't set in stone, but I think about it all the time. Specifically with Cali. I wonder if she'll still be teaching when she's in her fifties. I imagine myself swinging by Been There, Bun That and getting a milkshake to bring her after class. I'll stand by the front desk and watch her dance, all as the condensation from her milkshake drips into my now-freezing hand, and she'll keep dancing like nobody's watching. But I'll always watch her. Until my old heart stops beating.

I'm tearing up just thinking about it. Thinking about if we decide to have children. Thinking about us bantering like the old married couple we'll eventually be. (Preferably) not thinking about having old person sex as our bones clank together like plastic skeleton Halloween decorations. Thinking about how grown-up Teague will be, and how he'll probably be the one to put us in a retirement home after he gets fed up with our shit. Thinking about—

"Are you crying?"

I get whiplash when I spin my head around, staring bug-eyed at a very sleepy Cali sitting up next to me, her curls even more fluffed up from her short-lived nap.

"What? No," I grumble, wiping my (only slightly) watery eyes with the back of my hand. "I have allergies."

She reaches out to touch my arm, like one would comfort a crying child. "Men are allowed to cry, Gage. It's okay."

My heart begins to rev at an off-road kind of speed, and that cinnamon scent synonymous with her embraces me, as fresh as the aroma of oven-baked cinnamon rolls. Like I've said a million times before—she's perfect. From her head of fire to her black-painted toes. She insists she looks unattractive right now, but I don't see it. Not one bit.

"You know, I'm regretting saving you from the bathroom," I mutter.

"If you regret it so much, then why does it look like a cloud threw up in my room?" she asks, gesturing to the white string of lights and the very girly products strewn over her quilted bedspread.

"It's my charity for the day."

She makes this little huffing noise that's still scratchy with sleep, and I know this is the last thing I should be thinking about, but it sends a direct line of arousal straight to my dick.

Dude, read the room.

"Considering I almost died today, I think you should be a lot nicer to me," she declares, turning her nose up with a fake—yet entirely irresistible—pout.

Since I'd self-exiled myself to my own side of the bed, I scoot a little closer, still very much aware of the invisible delineation that exists between us. "Actually, since *I* saved *your* life, you should be a lot nicer to *me*."

When she glowers at me, butterflies tight-fist my gut, and a smile blusters over my face. But it's not a deliberate smile—I mean, it is. It's involuntary. As natural to me as breathing. Maybe I'm just permanently smiling whenever I'm with Cali.

"This *is* me being nice to you," she snaps in her "nice" voice, rearing her arm back to hit me somewhere on my body—it's a surprise every time—but she winces and groans before she can do any real damage. She leans her head back against the headboard, gripping her lower belly and performing some weird breathing technique to get through the pain.

I hate seeing her in pain. I'd do anything in the world to make her pain go away.

I quickly lean over and grab the Tylenol on her nightstand, along with a glass of cold water I brought in for her while she was sleeping. "Please take some Tylenol for me. You'll feel better once you do."

I pop off the lid of the pill bottle and dump three small tablets into my palm, then hand them off to her. She throws them into her mouth without any protest—which I'm thankful for—chasing the dry capsules down with a hearty gulp of ice water.

She mumbles out a quiet thanks, seeming the slightest bit

relieved that the healing process has begun, and her fingers continue to rub the crux of the pain just below her navel.

Since I'm not putting all my trust in the Tylenol, I grab the rolled-up heating pad and hand it to her. "I know you probably already have one, but I got this for you."

She takes it and looks up at me, and I can't tell if the tears in her eyes are from the gift or the cramps. "You got me a heating pad?" she exclaims in disbelief.

"Of course I did."

Cali's eyes scan all the gifts on her bed. When her gaze connects with the half-melted milkshake sitting in a bowl I scavenged from the cupboard, a gasp rises in her chest, stuck somewhere between her throat and her mouth. "You remembered."

I remember everything about you.

"Vanilla's an easy flavor to remember," I say casually, brushing it off as I tuck my arms behind my head and lean back against the headboard.

"Thank you," she whispers, and I don't know what it is about this particular smile, but this is the one that knocks the breath out of my lungs. It's not big enough to show teeth, but it does make her nose scrunch up, and there's no gloss or ostentatious color to tarnish the natural beauty of her lips.

I want her to smile at me like that all the time.

The blood rushing in my ears sounds like the ocean, there's sweat breaking out on my hairline, and my stomach keeps doing nauseating handsprings whenever she glances my way.

All I have the brain power to say is "Mm-hm." Definitely not calm, cool, or collected anymore. More like panicking, panicking, PANICKING.

Cali opens her mouth to say something, but she's interrupted when she crunches over again in pain, this time clenching her teeth together and emitting a tiny whimper.

My back snaps straight, and I immediately reach for the

heating pad in her hand. "You need to turn it on," I say, but as I go to grab it from her, she swats my hand away.

"I'm fine. It's not that bad," she lies.

"It's not fine. You were on the fucking bathroom floor when I found you."

"Gage, I don't nee—"

I reposition myself on the bed, plastering my back to her headboard and spreading my legs apart so that there's room in front of me. "Come here," I demand, brooking no room for argument as I pat the comforter.

I can tell Cali wants to protest with the way she glares at the spot like it's been contaminated with some kind of biowarfare poison.

"I think I'm okay over here."

"Cali, get your sweet little ass over here," I growl, whacking the mattress again for good measure, though I'm not above grabbing her and planting her right between my thighs. Which, in hindsight, probably won't turn out well for me.

She gives up the heating pad like a dog stubbornly relinquishing a chew toy. Rolling her eyes, she crawls over to me—which shouldn't look as sexy as it does—and then squeezes herself between my legs, moving her butt around until it's perfectly snug against my cock.

She turns to look over her shoulder, her eyes like spearpoints aimed directly at me. "Why am I sitting here?"

"If you'd just *relax*, I'm going to massage the cramps out."

"Pfft, there's no way that's going to work."

"It is going to work, and you're not going to fight me on this because I picked your lifeless body off the floor less than thirty minutes ago."

Cali grumbles to herself but slowly melts into my chest, sheathing her claws and fangs enough for me to wrap my arms around her torso, placing my hands over her bare, rounded belly. The hard fly of her pants digs into my forearms, but it doesn't bother me.

She flinches. "Your hands..."

My hands flinch alongside her. "What?"

"They're warm," she observes, eventually settling into the mold of my palms and letting me feel her stomach balloon with a deep breath.

She's gone boneless against me, resting her head against my chest, and I begin to knead her lower abdomen, exerting pressure as my fingers rub meticulous circles into her flesh. The steadiness of her voice dips into a raspy moan, dialing my hunger for her to a ravenous ten, and the fact that her ass is swallowing my dick doesn't do much to satiate my soaring libido.

I locate a tight muscle and coax the tension out, determined to fend the cramps off for as long as possible. Is massaging the best preventive measure? Probably not, but I'll give anything to be skin to skin with her for even a second.

"Oh, God..." She lurches forward as far as our position allows, too slow to quiet her cry before it pierces the air, just bordering on being loud enough to warrant a visit from a curious eight-year-old.

"Quiet, Spitfire. Teague's still in the house, remember?" I nip at the stretch of neck below her earlobe, feeling her pounding pulse bash against my lips, tasting the salt from the traces of sweat still lingering on her skin.

"But it feels so good," she whines.

You have no idea.

I continue to massage the swell of her belly, listening to the concoction of heated breaths and muffled whimpers in the otherwise silent space. I wish I could see how lax her face is—the dopey smile sewn onto her mouth, the struggle to keep her eyes open.

Sexual bodily desires aside, I focus on just being here with her in the present, committing to memory the feel of her body in my arms. I don't allow myself to mourn her absence yet, even if I fear the self-imposed distance that follows. Whenever I'm away from her, all I can think about is running straight back to her. Running *home*.

"Are you feeling any better?" I ask, allowing my fingers to rest below her navel.

I'm not expecting much aside from a "yes," but Cali turns around to face me, looking a thousand times more relaxed than she did a few minutes ago. No tight cinching of her brow, no concerning flush on her face, no misty eyes rife with fever.

A big, blush-inducing smile rewards me for my efforts, something strange and foreign swirling around in those stormy eyes. "Thank you, Gage."

"You don't have to thank me. If you got your period every day, I'd give you a massage every day until you felt better." I'm probably as red as a beet, but I don't feel the need to hide it anymore. If my body wants to make a fool out of me and broadcast my emotions for her to see, then so be it.

"Of course you would say something like that," she chuckles.

"Because it's true."

Cali grabs my hand—which is still buzzing with the warmth from her skin—and interlocks our fingers together, not caring that my palms are a little clammy or that my blush deepens and slopes down my collarbone. "Because you're *you*," she corrects.

Maybe I'm love-drunk or dehydrated or extremely sleep-deprived, but I swear that the anomaly forming in her now-gray irises resembles something close to...*love*.

I squeeze her hand as my gaze carves a languid path from the striking beauty of her eyes to the ample tenderness of her lips. Two things in great contrast to one another that somehow work on the same canvas—two things that would never work on anyone else except *her*. "I'll always be me, but I'm yours above it all."

There is no preparatory cheek-holding or prolonged eye contact. It's a rush of her mouth on mine with a breakneck urgency that I've never known possible, and she kisses me like she'll die if she doesn't.

I'll die, too, if she ever stops.

But eventually she does, and I whine to have her lips back on mine.

"I have to apologize," Cali says embarrassedly, ears red-tipped and fingers playing with the forefront curl of my hair.

Maybe it's because her hands feel so good tugging at my scalp, but I have no idea what she's talking about. "What?" I ask dumbly, coming down from a post-kiss high that's rendered me slightly speechless and a whole lot brainless.

"I have to apologize. About hitting your car the first time we met," she elaborates. "I was in the wrong from the beginning, but I was too proud to admit it. I'm sorry. I shouldn't have taken your parking spot in the first place. And I definitely shouldn't have damaged your car."

The lights turn back on in my head, and laughter fizzes up in my chest like carbonation in a sugary drink. My hand comes up to gently caress hers—which is still laboriously curling my hair—and I calm her aimless fidgeting. "You don't need to apologize, Cali. I'm the one who's sorry. I shouldn't have boxed you in. And I was a ginormous dick for not moving my car when you asked me."

"No, Gage. I still—"

"Hey. It's okay. The damages barely cost anything. Money was never an issue," I assure her, moving my hand to cup her cheek instead, and she's generous enough to lean into my touch. "Plus, it was about time someone knocked me on my ass."

25

THERE'S BEAUTY IN THE BROKEN
GAGE

"Are you sure you're okay with watching a horror movie?" Cali asks in a small voice, snuggling into my side when I open my arm up to her. Her cramps seem to have subsided for the time being, which is good, because I don't know how long I'd be able to sit here while she's squirming in pain.

"Of course I am. Why wouldn't I be?" Though I'm nowhere near prepared for whatever proverbial roller coaster I'm about to be strapped in, I'm determined to give Cali the day she deserves, and if that includes three painstakingly long hours of over-the-top gore, then so be it.

"I just know you aren't the biggest fan of horror."

I make a sputtering noise, bracing my hand against my chest in faux offense. "I'm not *not* a fan of horror. Plus, I want to watch whatever you want to watch."

Cali grazes her teeth over her bottom lip before chewing on the middle, glancing unsurely between me and the television that projects the title card—*My Ex-Therapist Is a Hatchet-Wielding Psycho*—complete with a half-naked woman drenched in a fountain of blood, aforementioned hatchet raised above her head and cherry-red lips frozen in a scream.

"If you get scared, we can turn it off," she promises.

"Cali, I don't get *scared*," I scoff. Ironically, at the same time, apprehension begins to soak into my bones like rot, and a sinkhole opens in my stomach where regret—and only regret—dares to wade across a sea of popping acid.

I'm going to have nightmares. It's not an assumption. I *will* have nightmares. If I thought a few store-bought, plastic organs on Halloween were terrifying, the realistic-looking ones are going to make me weep like a goddamn baby. I don't do well with horror, much like the majority of the levelheaded and rational population. And I especially don't do well with gore. It's not normal for a person's insides to be outside, okay?

But I know Cali loves horror movies, so I'm going to force myself to love them too, even at the expense of a good night's sleep. I'd do anything to spend time with Cali.

So as the movie begins, with her head resting soundly on my chest, the opening scene hardly acts as a soft, predictable gateway into the spine-chilling terror I'm about to endure for the rest of the night. I try to keep my focus divided between the screen and the excitement flitting across my girl's face, and I'm pretty sure that if the volume wasn't so deafeningly loud, she'd be able to hear every cry for help from my poor, overstimulated heart.

I jump. I flinch. I twitch. I shut one eye and try to keep the other open. My blood pressure shoots through the roof like Superman on speed. Meanwhile, Cali's smiling and chuckling like the last victim's stomach didn't get hacked all the way open.

I thought I'd soldiered through the worst of it when the antihero ends up curb-stomping a dude's head in with her stiletto heel, and I bury my head in Cali's shoulder while I swallow down a gag that sounds seconds away from being productive.

She pauses the movie—thank God—and sighs sympathetically, stroking the back of my head with her hand. "You really are a big baby when it comes to horror, aren't you?"

"'M not," I muffle against her shoulder, disregarding the fact that I'm barnacled to her side and clinging to her like I'm weathering a California-grown earthquake. I can feel sweat seep past the waistband of my pants, I bet my complexion is sickeningly white, and I can't get the hyperrealistic squelching noises out of my head. Not to mention that fear's been diffusing through my stomach at an alarming rate, solely responsible for the bile backwash searing my throat's lining.

"Oh, really?" Cali muses.

I lift my head up slightly, hand still curled in the fabric of her shirt. "Uh-huh. I just wanted to...snuggle."

Not fully a lie, alright? Cali smells nice, her body is soft, and she gives hugs so good they blow old people hugs out of the water.

"Gage Arlington, golden boy of one of the scariest hockey teams in the league, wanted to snuggle?"

"Why is that so hard to believe?"

Cali snorts a few times until her laughter devolves into giggles, and she fails to hide the larger-than-life smile overtaking her face—one that shoves all my blood to my cheeks and gives me a permanent just-fucked look.

I was fucked. Figuratively. This girl plays with my emotions like a cat plays with its food. Never in a million years would I picture me voluntarily scaring the living shit out of myself to impress a girl.

"You're just...I don't know. You're not the same guy I met at the rink months ago," she admits demurely, brushing the back of her knuckles over my shameless blush, all while adoration shimmers on the ocean-blue surface of her eyes.

I'm not, I think to myself. *You've made me a better person.*

"Are you going to make me beg for a snuggle?" I groan,

dramatically splaying myself over Cali's body and pretending like I'll see death's doorstep unless she showers me in affection. "Because I will. I'll even admit it, Spitfire. I'm scared. I'm scared, and the only solution is for us to snuggle...for the foreseeable future."

Cali rolls her eyes. "The foreseeable future?"

"I think I'm already getting flashbacks."

"Ugh. Fine. Shut up and come here."

Considering I'm already all over her, I plunk my head right over her heart, wrapping my arms around her midsection and nuzzling my nose into the dip of her sweet-smelling neck. She's like a cinnamon scratch-and-sniff sticker.

Cali doesn't turn the movie back on, which is probably for the best. Instead, we lie together for what feels like forever, basking in the slight stirring of each other's breaths, her fingers composing a soundless tune on my forearm. I'd planned to fall asleep on her, and I probably would have if it wasn't for the grating sensation of her palms on my skin. But even in my sleepy state, I've never noticed her hands to be rough with callouses.

I gently guide her hand palm-up to reveal the scarred crescents stamped into her flesh, and the comfort that once coddled me slips through my fingers before I can grab it.

I know Cali hurts herself. I've known ever since the night her mother was hospitalized, but I didn't want to upset her more by talking about it. But fuck, seeing the state her hands are still in, I wish I had.

The blood has congealed and darkened, contrasting starkly against the paleness of her palms. Eight deep wounds span the width of her hand, structured in a line that looks like a botched stitch job. And I don't need to press into the half-moons to know the skin surrounding them is delicate.

"Why do you do this, Cali?" I ask quietly, abstaining from explicitly commenting on her self-harm and choosing instead to ever-so-gently brush the pads of my fingers over her lacerations.

She looks at me in confusion at first, but then her gaze drops to the conjoined caress of our hands, and a frown ghosts over her lips. She almost refuses to answer me. She strangles her words, shuffles the truth around like a deck of playing cards.

"I..."

My stomach turns—a repercussion of treading on unspoken territory. Her eyes are beginning to gloss over, and her teeth tug at her cracked bottom lip.

"Calista..." Heartache cowers in my tone, and I feel like I'm breathing through shot lungs. This is killing me to see the evidence of a lifetime of self-blame and self-loathing etched into the life lines of her palms.

Her voice is reedy, on the verge of breaking into unintelligible cries and spit-obstructed garbles. "I do it to punish myself," she confesses shamefully, focusing her gaze on the skin-deep marks, almost as if she's remembering each time she mutilated herself.

Tears swell over my lower eyelids, and it takes twice the amount of power to rid my response of throat-clogging emotion. "Oh, baby."

"I didn't use to do it. It started when my mom got really sick. And each time I saw her suffer, I'd dig my nails into my palms. It was a way of punishing myself—a way to remind myself that I need to do better by her. A way to remind myself that I wasn't doing enough."

I wish Cali could see herself the way I see her. She's made so many sacrifices for the well-being of her family. And she's harbored just as many emotionally scarring consequences. People like Cali are rare. She has this selflessness about her that some people only have less than one percent of.

"I wish you didn't do it," I whisper pathetically.

"It doesn't hurt," she responds quickly, backed by a numbness that tells me, at one point, it did. It hurt, but it wasn't strong enough to counteract the guilt.

"It hurts *me*."

Cali freezes in shock, right before her whole frame collapses, and I can tell she's trying to evade my eyes. She even tries to pull her hand away, but I don't let her.

She swallows thickly. "I never wanted you to see them. God, they're so ugly."

I tip her a half-smile, shaking the corkscrews of hair that dangle against my temples. "They're not ugly. They're beautiful. They're a part of you—even if it's a part you're adamant about hiding from me. I adore you. Scars and all."

Clocking the obvious disbelief rippling off her, I look around for something to show her just how truthful I'm being, and that's when I catch sight of a purple, felt-tip marker sitting on her nightstand.

I grab the marker and uncap it with my teeth, then rest her hand against my belly. She squeaks in surprise, but she doesn't dare say anything when I begin to trace over her scars with lavender ink. I connect the fractured puncture wounds with one continuous line, adding angles and miniature stars to make a constellation.

She watches raptly as I elongate each line, and when I finish my masterpiece, her lesions have transformed into a breathtaking work of art. Her fingers twitch while she admires the hastily scribbled stars and inaccurately portrayed constellations, but she smiles all the same, and a barrage of moisture hinders her eyesight.

"See?" I say. "Beautiful."

She titters. "That's because you covered up the ugliness."

For someone who's a self-proclaimed baby when it comes to blood and gore, I don't see any of that when I look at Cali's hands.

"No, Cali. You're a survivor, and I see the beauty in that. All I've done is accentuate it."

"Gage—"

"I don't want to see you hurt yourself anymore. But I know that's easier said than done, so I'll be here to help you heal. I'll be here to hold your hand when you feel like you want to harm yourself. I'll be here to love you and your scars on the days that you can't."

Cali, surprisingly, doesn't fight me. She doesn't tell me how wrong I am. Instead, with gratitude woven in her eyes, she leans in to kiss me, wrapping me up in the heat of her lips. Our hands connect, palms flat against each other, and the still-wet ink from my hand-drawn constellations smear onto my own skin.

A transference of pain.

26

THE DARKEST BEFORE THE DAWN
CALISTA

Hospitals never used to bother me when I was younger, seeing as I was in and out of them a lot with my mother. I got desensitized to the aching groans of dying patients and the sobs of families now harboring terrible news. I got desensitized to the miasma of death and the stench of hydrogen peroxide. I got desensitized to the blinding fluorescents and the shitty food and the uncomfortable waiting chairs. There was even a point when I accepted that my mother's life was tethered to a countdown clock, and there was nothing anyone could do to stop it.

But now, sitting in this dark and cold doctor's office, with the outside cavalry of heart monitor beeps and the hushed exchange of doctor jargon closing in on me, I hate hospitals. I hate them with everything I have.

I promised myself that I wouldn't cry. Not because I was afraid to embarrass myself in front of whoever was saddled with giving me the bad news, but because I didn't think I'd be able to stop once I started. Unremitting anxiety kick-starts inside me, baking my skin in a suffocating heat that didn't exist before I stepped through those stainless steel doors. And that anxious feeling only trickles down to my gut, where it churns the ham sandwich I had earlier, threatening to trigger that delicate reflex at the back of my throat.

It feels like I'm back in my mother's old room—one hundred forty-four square feet of death camouflaged in peeling wallpaper and fossilized possessions. There's a darkness here that weighs heavy on my chest, sharpening the jagged edges of my nerves.

The doctor's face is trimmed to smooth perfection, a cruel kind of cold that only exists within sociopaths or serial killers. There's no hair out of place, no speck of dust on his pristine jacket, no wrinkles on his skin that could allude to how old he is. Everything is carefully constructed, a façade, an inhuman mask that he mistakenly believes makes him human. I could look past everything else, but it's his eyes that haunt me. Soulless, unfathomably deep, the color of obsidian, yet even with no life to be found within them, they still follow my every movement.

"Ms. Cadwell, thank you for joining me on such short notice," he says, and even in his tone lies an aloofness, as if getting too close to someone like me repulses him.

Doctor Grandfield—according to his name tag—folds his hands into a steeple on his desk, lowering his eyes disdainfully at the unprofessional appearance of my stained jacket and sweatpants.

"Uh, thank you for seeing me," I stammer.

"I'm sure you're aware that your mother has end-stage multiple sclerosis, correct?" There's no soft landing for his unsympathetic words. It's a harsh shove against the hard ground, one that scrapes the skin off my bloodstained face and imbues my tongue with the taste of rust.

I swallow back bile. "I'm aware."

"I've consulted with other doctors, and we believe it's in her best interest to move her into a nursing facility while her body continues to deteriorate."

Nursing facility. Deteriorate.

A peaceful place for her to gradually die, is what he's saying.

I nearly vomit on the spot, chunks of half-digested bread and lunch meat all over his desk and his classified papers, all over that stupid suit of his.

We won't be living under the same roof anymore. I'll have to drive to see her; I'll have to sign in and get a visitor's pass just to *see* her. I don't want my mom to go. I want her to hold me in her arms again and tell me that everything's going to be okay.

"I see" is all I have the energy to say. Stagnant. Void of emotion. A hollow acceptance. I'm so numb right now that the tears don't even exist. They're not banging on the backs of my eyes begging to be freed.

"I'm sure this is a big change for your family, but I assure you that Sunrise Pointe is a perfectly adequate facility to tend to your mother's needs," he tells me.

I know that admitting my mother to a nursing home should quell the worries blizzarding inside me, but it doesn't. What if the one day I don't visit her is the day she passes? What if she dies all alone, without me or Teague by her bedside?

My leg shakes underneath his desk, slamming against the surface of my hard, plastic chair. It feels like a bucket of ice water has been thrown on me, soaking me all the way to the bone. This will be her new life now. This will be Teague's and my new life now. Fuck.

Will Teague hate me forever? Will Teague blame *me* for letting her go? I already blame myself, but that's a responsibility I can bear. Having Teague blame me is something I won't survive.

Doctor Grandfield slides a pamphlet across his desk to me, and even his nails are perfectly filed. "Here's a pamphlet with more information. It includes a lot of the benefits, services provided, frequently asked questions, and most importantly, the cost of it all," he recites like he's giving a presentation.

The cost. Oh my God. I haven't even thought about the cost.

I robotically flip through the pamphlet, quickly passing the exaggerated smiles and the outrageously grandiose architecture until I make it to the small cost section at the very end... that boasts an unattainable four thousand dollars per month. While my mother does have Medi-Cal, the nursing facilities that take that type of insurance aren't the best in their treatment. The only way I'd feel comfortable moving my mom into a nursing facility is if it's a good one.

I can't afford this, even with the extra cash from Gage's and my arrangement. How am I going to make enough money in a short amount of time to give my mother the care she deserves? And that's per *month*. My salary is only enough to keep me and Teague afloat, and it just barely helps with my mom's medication.

I don't know what to say. All I do is stare down at that intimidating number, each fume of breath harder to expel than the last one. If I can't afford it, I'll fail my mother. I refuse to do that. I'll work back-to-back classes. I'll get two more jobs. I'll sell whatever I can to make money. But that can only help me so much in the beginning, and then the tiring cycle continues each month.

And what about Teague? If I throw myself back into my work (more than I already do), I'll become even more absent in his life. I made a promise to myself that I would start being there for him more. The only way for this to work is for me to... destroy myself.

My belly grumbles nervously, and a hunk of acid and food jet up my throat, filling my mouth until I'm forced to swallow it down. I'm going to be sick.

"Can I...can I think about it?" I lie, trying to conceal the urgency in my tone, needing to get the hell out of here before my day becomes even worse—and before I make *his* day a lot worse. I'm already up and out of my chair, the chair legs screeching against the uncarpeted floors as I scramble for the pamphlet on the table.

The minute I tuck it under my arm, I sprint out of that windowless enclosure, not caring to listen to whatever advice he's throwing over my shoulder, taking a secluded set of stairs all the way down to the first floor. And once I'm spit out through the swinging front doors, I find the nearest trashcan and lose the contents of my lunch inside it.

I'm not sure how much time passes as everything gushes out of me in one thick torrent, but it's long enough for me to listen to a lovely soundtrack of thirty dollars-worth of groceries splattering over already-rotten food.

Maybe I'm too drained to freak out, or maybe it's because I'd recognize the feel of those hands anywhere, but someone starts to rub circles over my back. The air shifts, giving way to a warmth unparalleled by the sun itself, and I know for a fact that Gage is the person right behind me. I feel my hair get swept back from my face as my loud and definitely indiscreet retching continues, having to sit with the vile taste of liquidized food on my tongue while my body rejects everything I ate in the last twenty-four hours.

"You're okay, Cali. I'm right here. Get it all out."

When the nausea passes, I'm forced to overcome my embarrassment. I lift my head up, wipe my sleeve over my vomit-slicked lips, and try to keep some distance between me and Gage because my breath undoubtedly reeks.

We speak at the same time, in two *very* different tones.

"Did you follow me here?" I ask.

"Are you okay?" he asks.

Gage, surprisingly, looks just as embarrassed as I do, and he rubs the back of his neck. "Um, Teague told me you were speaking with your mother's doctor today. I just...I know you didn't invite me, but I wanted to come in case you needed the support."

In any other universe, I'd be mad at him for following me to something so personal. But I'm not. I mean, he was there in the hospital with me while we waited for my mother's results. I don't know why I didn't invite Gage. I guess I just felt like this wasn't his problem. Not to mention that I'm used to doing things on my own.

Even with the beating sun out, gales of wind slip through greasy strands of my hair, whipping them across my pale and sweaty face. Maybe it's because I don't have any saliva in my mouth anymore, but I don't say anything.

Gage takes a step toward me. "I'm going to ask you again, Cali. Are you okay?"

I take a step backward, resting one hand over my belly to try and calm the inner turmoil. "I'm fine." My burning eyes simmer with post-puke tears, and even though my arms are protected by my flimsy jacket, goose bumps race up and down them.

I can tell he wants to say, *No, you're not*, but he doesn't.

"Can we go talk somewhere?" he proposes, stuffing his hands in the pocket of his hoodie, respecting the distance I've set between us.

Talking is the last thing I want to do right now, but what other option do I have?

"Okay," I concede, still clinging to the now-crumpled pamphlet in my other hand and wishing that I had brought my purse with me—or at least a pack of gum.

∽

I KNOW I already look like shit, so I choose a very shaded bench for me and Gage to sit on, hoping he doesn't look too closely at me.

News flash: he does.

His body is completely turned toward me, his gaze focused on my face like he's trying to search for answers in a twitch or a micro expression. The breeze doesn't cease its onslaught on his hair, blowing back those front curls and turning the tip of his nose scarlet. "What happened in there?" he inquires, nearly losing his voice to the raging wind.

I'm sitting with my back to the current, but he chose to sit with his face to it and endure the worst of it, all so I don't have to. I make my first sound decision of the day and hand him the crinkled pamphlet, because there's no way he'll be able to hear me.

He takes it from me with a curious look, and I watch in silence as he flips through the pages, his eyes examining the material diligently, searching for the reason why I upchucked in front of, like, twenty people.

When he finishes skimming the pamphlet, he tilts his head. "I don't understand. This...this seems like a good thing, right?"

I turtle into my jacket, staring down at my sleeve-covered hands, using my thumbnail to pick at the blue, fraying hems. "I can't afford it, Gage," I whisper, too ashamed to bring this reality into existence, too frustrated that I don't even have four thousand dollars to spare on my dying mother. No money saved up. No nothing. There's a part of me that wishes he didn't hear, but he did. Over the howling winds, over the quietness of my voice, over the bustling chatter of the people around us.

His face drops. "Cali..."

"I don't know what to do. I don't know how to help my mom; I don't know how to help Teague. I'm his legal guardian, sure, but I hardly act like it. I've failed both of them. I'm not... I'm not strong enough to hold this family together," I confess, every terrible reminder of the ways I've let them down hijacking my brain, spitting derision and scorn like shrapnel against my bleeding heart.

I want to cry. Fuck, I want to *feel* something. Anything. But my body's been feeling for so long that there's nothing left for me to feel.

"Please tell me you know that's not true," Gage says, tearing down the invisible wall I've erected between us and enveloping me in his warm arms. "It's not true."

I don't embrace him back. I'm stiff and cold and so goddamn empty that I can't feel my own heart beating anymore. "It is true."

"No, it's not."

I push him away from me. "It is, Gage."

Gage doesn't snap back at me. He doesn't yell. He doesn't even move, really. I have no idea what his next move is, and the sight of his composure isn't an accelerant to my rage—it's the complete opposite.

I'm so tired. I'm so tired of everything. I'm so tired of carrying all this weight by myself. I'm so tired of trying to do everything on my own. And the more I hang on to this self-loathing and rage...the more I begin to question if it's even worth it anymore. I don't want to live my entire life punishing myself. I don't know how to save myself.

The final moisture I've been waiting for—the preemptive droplets of rain before a torrential storm—wells in my eyes, and the rest of the world stills around me, freezing this exact moment in time where the only medium is the broken cradle song of my heart. I look down at my hands, right where my nails continue puncturing old wounds.

I forget that Gage is right beside me, and I'm only reminded when his voice breaks through the dense fog.

"I want to pay for everything," he says quietly.

I level him with an incredulous look. "What?"

"I want to pay for your mother's care," he repeats, scooting closer to me, refusing to sever our eye contact even for a second. He's laying his heart out on his sleeve, offering it to the least deserving person in the world, and ignoring the very real possibility that I may be the one to crush it between my hands.

My body screams *no* in imaginary, violent thrashes, practically pleading with him not to make such a huge mistake, and this blindsided pit in my now-empty gut pulses with a mind of its own. It's formidable as it grows before my very eyes, latching onto my stomach lining like a parasite.

"Stop. I can't take any more of your money, Gage. You've already given me too much."

"I want to, Calista. I want to help you and Teague and your moth—"

"*Stop*," I hiss, picking myself up off the bench and attempting to storm as far away from this conversation as humanly possible.

But I was stupid to think I'd get very far before Gage grabs my wrist and forces me to look at him.

"Why are you fighting me on this?" he growls, that dangerously low bravado of his flirting along a wrathful edge.

Something visceral snaps inside me, like the inexorable rip of a rubber band, and anger power-blasts me from all sides, tensing every muscle and gearing my brain into hyperdrive. "You're always fixing my problems for me. You're always going out of your way to make my life easier, and I'm constantly taking advantage of your generosity."

"You're not."

A frown clips my lips. "I am."

Gage's brazenly indignant attitude vanishes, and the inflation in his tone softens to a melody akin to svelte fingers plucking at a harp's string. "Hey," he croons. "You can't take advantage of something I offer willingly. Plus, it's my money. I can do whatever

I want with it. And I'm *choosing* to do this for you." He's annoyingly calm as he always is in high-stress situations, still looking at me like I've hung the fucking moon and stars for him when in reality, I've showered his world in nothing but eternal darkness.

"You're making a mistake." I don't try to rip my arm away, because there's nowhere in this world that I could possibly go without Gage finding me.

His eyes take on the color of the impending storm clouds above. "I'm not. There's nothing you can say that'll make me change my mind. I wasn't able to save my brother, but I'm able to save your family."

"I can't let you do this, Gage."

"Are you going to stand here and tell me that you don't want it? Are you going to stand here and lie to my face?"

This is about your mom, Cali. It's not about you. It's not about your bruised dignity. It's not about your fucked-up self-punishment agenda. He's offering you an escape. He's offering you freedom. He's offering you a chance at peace. And most of all, he's offering your mom a chance to live out the last of her days in the best environment for her condition. Why aren't you taking it?

There's a small voice screaming with the same desperation in the back of my head, a little voice that once belonged to a girl who was forced to grow up too quickly.

Help me! Please, help me! I can't do this by myself!

Gage brings me into his solid chest, and my half-exerted flailing is no match for the unbeatable strength of the two arms that pin me into submission. He holds me to that life force slamming against his ribs, so hard and fast that I can feel it shock my own lifeless heart like a defibrillator.

"I know you're used to doing everything by yourself, but you don't have to anymore. You can give me all that pain, Spitfire. You can give me all that weight, and I'll carry it for the rest of fucking time if it means that you'll finally be able to breathe easy again," he whispers into the alcove of my neck, petting my hair like he's done countless other times.

"Why do you care so much?" I hiccup.

And then, as if Gage has been preparing for this moment his entire life, he says, "You're my everything, Calista Cadwell. My morning, afternoon, and night. My beginning, middle, and end. My life doesn't make sense without you in it. I wake up for *you*, Spitfire. I breathe for *you*. My heart beats for *you*. It's always going to be you, no matter where we are in time. It's always going to be you, even if we're oceans apart. It's always going to be you in whatever universe we find ourselves in."

The beat of Gage's heart and his confession are the only things that tear me from the nightmarish landscape of my mind, reminding me that I'm here, in the present, and that my story isn't over yet. I don't even know if I've digested everything he just unloaded on me. But I got the gist of it, and the gist is enough to make me cry like a baby.

The tears surpass streams and rush out in a flood, drenching every inch of my skin in their unfortunate path, and I cling to the back of Gage's hoodie like he's a porous rock keeping me above water in the writhing waves of a merciless hurricane.

"Help me," I beg. "Please help me."

27

A LETTER TO MY MOM
CALISTA

The minute I saw my mother's lifeless body lying in that hospital bed, I wanted to leave. Not because I don't love her, but because I love her so fucking much that it physically pains me to be in the same room as her while she's suffering right before my eyes. I honestly shouldn't have left her side, but I wouldn't have survived alone with her—alone with my *thoughts*.

I've visited her on and off while she's been in the hospital, bringing Teague with me on occasion, but this is the first time I've really come in to sit down and be with her. I've been too much of a coward to face her.

No matter what I do, nothing will magically cure her. I have to live the rest of my life as she struggles to keep her head above water, and I'd give anything in the world to be able to switch places with her.

After the talk with Gage regarding my mother's expenses, I knew I needed to come see her before she was moved.

I clutch the potted geraniums—my mother's favorite flower—to my chest, hypnotized by the clacking of my heeled boots against the tiles. I make my way to her room on autopilot, having already memorized the tearstained path from when she was admitted. As soon as I enter that cold, sterile chamber, anxiety strikes a chord within me while nausea tears through my restless stomach. It's enough to bog me down, demanding more exertion from my noodle-like muscles just to simply put her get-well gift on her nightstand. The sky is completely dark outside, shunning the moon's rays from coruscating over the spotless floor.

I slowly drag a chair over to my mother's bedside, perching on its mint-green edge like I'm waiting to eject myself from it at any given moment. Even though it has enough cushion to support my back—maybe even invite me for a much-needed nap—I don't let myself indulge in the comfort it offers. My mother sleeps soundlessly in her bed, arms folded over her midsection, her breath so quiet that I'm not even sure she's really breathing.

I follow the slight movement of her chest, admiring how peaceful she looks with her hair moved away from her face. Even though I want to reach for her hand, I don't want to wake her. The surprising steadiness of my breath belies the emotional turmoil rampaging through my body, starting with the deafening soundtrack of my hummingbird heart and ending with the abysmal thoughts trying to weasel into my brain tissue.

My jaw cracks to accommodate a swallow, one that barely soothes my sandpaper throat. "Hi, Mom," I finally say after a three-minute silence, feeling the tears I promised myself I wouldn't shed start to fester in my eyes.

"I know you're sleeping and won't be able to hear any of this, but I just wanted to...I just wanted to tell you how sorry I am that I couldn't save you."

Saying all these words into an empty space, for no one to hear, somehow makes them more painful, and that false steadiness I came into this one-sided conversation with has taken two point three seconds to slip from my fingers. I don't know why I thought doing this would be a good idea. I don't know why I thought I'd be able to recite any words of substance without breaking down into tears.

I press the heels of my hands into my eyes, hoping to wring out the tears that flee down my cheeks, and I'm not fast enough to stifle the cries that desecrate the tranquility of the hospital room. They're louder than the slight percussion of rain that's plinking against the fogged window.

Everything hurts. I feel like I'm made of glass, on the cusp of shattering. I feel like a little girl again crying for my mother to make things better, running into her arms for safety and comfort.

"I miss you, Mom. I miss when you would hold me and tell me everything's okay. I feel like I can't do any of this without you. I don't know how to be a good big sister. I don't know how to give Teague the childhood he deserves. I'm so lost..." My words peter off, desperately searching for a home that's been prematurely taken from them.

I rest my head against the powder-blue blanket draped over her body, no longer trying to oppress the tears that soak into the fabric, leaving behind physical marks of my heart breaking in half. Anguish laps at my heels like that of a starving, mangy wolf, gradually closing in on me.

"I'm sorry that my best wasn't good enough. That my best couldn't save our family. I sh-should've been there by your side. I sh-should've done more to save you. And now it feels like I'm slowly losing you, no matter what I do," I wail, no longer caring if I rouse her from her sleep as I cling to her arm, trying to pull her back to me, trying to bargain with fate to make her stay here on earth with me, where I need her.

She's everything I have. Please don't take her from me.

My chest racks violently as I whisper *sorry's* like a mantra, foolish to think that enough groveling will fix this mess. Her arm is bony in my irresolute grip, chilled to the touch, yet it's the only anchor I know. Like a newborn animal snuggling against the cold corpse of its mother, not fully understanding she's gone but knowing something's wrong.

"I'd give anything for you to be okay again. *Anything*. Take me. Please. Whoever's listening, take me instead."

I thought I was strong enough to come here by myself and face my demons, but I'm not. Not with Gage's help, not with anyone's help. I'm weak. I'll always be weak, and my brother deserves more. *Better.*

Everything I want to say is impeded by hiccups, left to curdle on my tongue. I feel my throat weld itself shut, feel my lungs begin to shrivel, feel my heart give some pathetic stutters before it maybe stops completely. With watered-down vision and heat stewing in my head, I lose control of my body, just like I've lost control of my life. I'm a prisoner to the bawls that don't seem to stop, that can probably be heard all the way down this hospital wing, that broadcast to other families that there's always someone out there doing so much worse.

And just when the lightheadedness starts to settle into my bones, I feel my mother's fingers rejoice with mine, and I immediately lift my head up. Even in the darkness, her smile shines through, and it's the sign I've been waiting for—a sign no longer as frequent as it used to be, but one that I welcome all the same.

"Calista," she says on a sigh, squeezing my hand as hard as she can. "My beautiful girl."

I nearly break down into another crying fit. I don't know what to say. There's truly nothing I could say to encompass how much my mother's changed my life. My love for her goes beyond simple sentiments and words of affirmation. It's almost something I can't conceive of.

So I freeze, trying to memorize her face even in the lack of light, trying to memorize the crow's feet that show themselves at the corners of her eyes whenever she smiles. She seems...different. Almost more renewed with life, if that's possible.

Instead of easing into the conversation, I dive headfirst, panickily slapping together a nonsensical apology that would be hard for anyone to follow. "I'm so sorry that you're here. It's all my fault. I should've tried harder. Oh my God. I'm so sorry, Mom. I'll never d—"

"Cali," she interrupts, and I can almost envision the way she used to shake her head at me. "It's okay. I'm okay."

My voice is the quietest it's ever been, yet it ricochets around the room like a gunshot. "I'm afraid of losing you."

I can hear her breath falter, a telltale sign that the pain is starting to worsen, and she takes a full minute before answering. "I'm still here."

The tears revolt as moisture reenters my vision, and I spear my teeth into my bottom lip to keep another obnoxiously loud cry from upsetting the calmness of the late evening. *I'm still here.* Three words that have never held so much weight until now. She's fighting every day to be here with me and Teague—to watch Teague grow up.

There are so many things I want to say to her, but I know that holding this conversation is incredibly hard for her, so all I plan to say is how much I love her.

But that's not what comes out.

"I'm scared, Mom," I confess in a shaky tone, feeling the strength that my mother's passed down to me start to trickle out of my body, searching for another host that would be more deserving of my mom's mountain-moving vigor and resilience. "Everything's about to change."

I'm careful not to put too much pressure on her chest, but I hug her for the first time in what feels like years, and instantly, all the panic and the voices and the self-doubt are quiet. She quiets them all, just like Gage does. It's a silence I've been chasing after for so long, believing I'd never achieve it. But it's real. It's possible. And it's so fucking peaceful.

My mother still smells of the rose scent I'd feared she lost, and I fit into the cradle of her arms just like I always have, even if they're not as strong as they used to be. It temporarily transports me back to the past, when my worries were nowhere near as prominent. It transports me back to a time when my mother was the real hero, sacrificing her soul and body to keep the lights on, sacrificing her social life and love life so we could eat, sacrificing everything to give her children the best life possible.

"I know," she whispers against my hair, holding me, rocking me, absorbing the pain of my shameful admittance. "You're going to be okay."

Everything I didn't fully cry out of my system with Gage, I cry out now, and as much as I love the feel of her arms wrapped around me, there's a part of me that imagines Gage's arms instead.

"You're my strong girl, and I'm so proud of you," my mother says. "You've kept this family together. You've looked out for your brother, just like I always knew you would. You've looked out for me, even though I never asked you to. You've sacrificed so much for this family. If I had to leave today, Calista, I would go happily, knowing that the best part of me is still here on Earth—that the best part of me is you."

Surprisingly—and maybe it's because I've wasted all my energy on tears—I don't resist her compliment. I don't provide a counterargument. Her words exorcise the fearmongering demon right out of my own body—the one who's been haunting me this whole time; the one who looks like me.

Is that really how she sees me? She doesn't blame me? She doesn't think I'm a failure? She doesn't think I'm *broken*? After all this time, I thought she was disappointed in me. I thought I'd let her down. But the only person who was disappointed in me was myself. The only person I let down was...myself.

I didn't know how badly I needed to hear that until now. And just like that, after years of self-deprecation and self-punishment, it only takes a minute for my heart to feel so much lighter. The last time I remember my heart feeling this light was when I was a kid. But the feeling is back, it's real, and it's somehow even more therapeutic than before.

Slowly, I un-koala from my mother, brushing the invisible dust motes off her blanket and the not-so-invisible tears. I'm not in a hurry to leave her, but I do want to change the subject and give her voice a rest. So, I start by telling her how Teague's been doing lately, and how good he's getting at hockey. I tell her about my dance classes and how wonderful my students are. I tell her about the new friends I've made. And then I tell her about the one person who I haven't been able to get out of my head.

My talk with Gage lingers in the back of my mind—how I'm his morning, afternoon, and night. His beginning, middle, and end. How I'm his number one priority, and how it'll always be me. How he's promised not to go anywhere.

I didn't want to accept his money at first because I felt like he was making a mistake, but he's proven to me just how wrong I am. Being strong isn't just about doing everything yourself, it's about knowing when you need to ask for help.

I feel the echo of a smile pull over my lips, and my heart's no longer getting by on barely there thumps. It's beating steadily, healthily. No part of my body is stuck in permanent panic mode. Everything's, well, *peaceful*. And when Gage isn't driving me crazy, he does seem to have that peaceful effect on me.

"I met a boy," I tell her like some giddy schoolgirl with a crush. "I met a boy, and he's perfect, Mom. He's kind and caring, and he's great with Teague. He's there when I need him, but he doesn't always just fix things for me. He *helps* me fix things. He supports me; he believes in me. He just...he means a lot to me."

I'm not expecting my mother to weigh in at all, but she does, and it's like a bellows blowing on the burning coals of my admiration, feeding the fire that Gage has reignited within me. She caresses my cheek, and now that my eyes have adjusted to the darkness, I can clearly see the wide, toothy smile that uplifts her cheeks.

"That's all I've ever wanted for you."

Maybe it's because I'm an emotional wreck, but I swear I feel the tears regroup and scheme to plan another attack. "I like him. So much."

Gage is the only person I see in my future. There's nobody else. I don't know what will happen with us, but he's one of those rare people that comes along and just changes everything. He's the kind of person who makes you fall back in love with life—the kind of person who alters your brain chemistry forever.

"Remember this feeling," my mother replies softly. "Hold on to this happiness, Calista."

And I do. I hold on to it more tightly than I've ever held on to anything in my entire life.

28

GO, TEAM, GO!
GAGE

The rink is alive tonight.

Okay, it's more like half-awake, and it's the afternoon, but still. I forgot how much I love being in the throes of a gnarly game—the hiss of skates slicing through ice, the mini snowstorm of loose shavings whirling in the atmosphere, the overlap of voices all competing for attention over the blood pulsing in your eardrums.

With all the stretching and flexibility Cali's helped me with, I talked to my physical therapist about possibly getting back on the ice for the Reapers' next game. I honestly wasn't expecting him to even consider it, but my hip flexor's healed surprisingly quickly, and he actually cleared me to play this upcoming Saturday.

Maybe it's the time away or Cali's anxiety rubbing off on me, but I'm pretty sure this is the first time I've ever really been nervous about playing. Well, aside from my NHL debut.

I just...I failed my teammates when I couldn't block that last shot. And I've failed them every game since by not being there. This is my one chance at a comeback. This is my one chance to show the fans that I'm better than ever, and that I'm still a good fucking goalie. This is what I've been working toward for almost three months.

But today, it's Teague's turn.

Pods of tiny bodies skate across the ice, all shouting and attempting to chirp at one another with the cutest, most PG-13 insults. None of them could look intimidating if they tried—it's like staring down a bunch of animated clouds. Their chunky, gear-swaddled figures bump into each other clumsily, shoving to claim the coveted title of star player. I'm impressed by some of the quick puck handling skills and well-executed defense strategies, but I'm equally as entertained to watch the more clueless players chase after the puck like lost puppies.

I don't know if this pseudo parenting shit is getting to me, but me and Cali are the only ones repping any kind of spirit. The rest of the exhausted parents here settle for the occasional holler and cheer.

My parents never disapproved of my interest in hockey—or the fact that I wanted to pursue a career in it—but they never showed up to games or offered me any kind of support aside from money for gear, equipment, private lessons, and travel expenses. So I understand how important it is for kids to have a support system that goes deeper than half-assed promises and monetary compensation. If I successfully embarrass Teague with my overenthusiasm and large-ass poster, then I've killed this whole non-parenting parenting thing. A plus, baby. Read it and weep.

I pull out the gigantic poster I spent all night creating—to which I lost a few fingerprints in the process of making because of whatever dumb fuck created hot glue—and I'm pretty sure I still have glitter in places glitter shouldn't be.

Cali's entirely captivated by the game unfolding in front of us, and she's so focused that her face is practically smushed against the plexiglass. It isn't until my very loud poster scooches into her personal space that she rears back and glares at me before said glare melts into a look of comical shock.

"Oh my God. What did you do?"

I suck my teeth. "Why do you always have to sound so judgmental?"

"That's going to distract him!" she whisper-hisses.

"Psh, he won't even notice this thing is here," I insist, keeping the twenty-inch cardstock monstrosity firmly plastered where everyone can see it, pride puffing out my chest.

Cali gives me her famous—and usual—unamused scowl. "A pilot from thirty thousand feet up in the air could see that thing and mistake it for an SOS signal."

"You're being dramatic."

When I see Teague's number flash past me, I whistle and point at the sign that says, GO, TEAGUE! HE'S THE MAN. IF HE CAN'T DO IT, NO ONE CAN! with a bunch of glittery hearts and poorly drawn hockey memorabilia.

Little Man's head perks up, and a full-fledged smile sprouts on his lips...right before he's bodychecked into the boards by someone twice his size.

Everyone in the front row winces, and a collective *ooh* eddies out on warm breaths. Cali's on her feet within a second, nervously chewing on her nails while her eyes zip from player to player, following the slippery puck like a lioness hunting her prey. Her leg's been shaking this entire time, subjecting my ass to a miniature earthquake, and her concentration face looks a lot like an I'm-going-to-shit-myself face.

I slowly drop the poster (probably for Teague's best benefit) and rub my hand over the outside of her leg, encouraging her to look at me.

"Relax, Spitfire. He's doing great," I say, nodding my head as he chases after the puck.

Cali sits down with a sigh, anxiety sparkling like a half-lit fuse in those deep blue eyes of hers, and her leg has taken a brief pause from its ongoing quaking. "I'm just...he hasn't made a goal yet, and the game's over in three minutes."

"I know. It takes a while for players to gain enough confidence to score goals, especially if they take on new coaches during the season. Your brother's never had any coaching before."

I give her thigh a squeeze, and the tension in her worked-up shoulders loosens just a bit. "I know. I don't expect him to score a goal. I just don't want him to be disappointed, you know? He's been working so hard, and what if the other kids are still picking on him and—"

Never in my twenty-two years of life have I ever met someone with a heart as big as Cali's—a heart made to hold an infinite amount of love despite the small physicality of it. Her compassion is so great that it could set off an avalanche in the stillest parts of winter, that it could be felt across snow-drenched mountain gorges and in the most hard-to-reach crevices.

"As long as you're proud of him, he'll be proud of himself," I reassure her, draping my arm around her frame and pulling her gently into my side, where she rests her head on my shoulder.

A flyaway hair of hers tickles my cheek, and if we weren't in public, I'd stick my face in her curls and inhale until cinnamon flows through my bloodstream. I want to stay like this forever. My first home and my second home, meeting each other for the first time. Hockey—once the greatest love of my life—passing the baton to the one person who trumps it completely, and who's rebuilt my entire way of living by tilting my world on its axis.

Just three months ago, I was getting my ass ripped by this five-foot-seven spitfire in front of my entire hockey team, and I was determined to hunt her down, find some random dog shit and bag it, then light it on fire and throw it on her porch. But everything's changed. No fecal warfare or pyro projectiles for me.

She's my whole world, and whenever I look at her, I wonder how a single person could mean so much to me—how she unknowingly has the power to destroy me completely.

She instantly raises her head to glance at me. "I am proud! I'm so proud of him! Oh, God. Does he not think I'm proud of him?"

A deep laugh gathers in my chest like a rumbling thunderstorm. "He does. I'm pretty sure you're the proudest sister in this entire universe."

"Oh..."

While she's still facing me, I gently hook my thumb under her jaw, my eyes falling to her lips and lingering there, a grin stretching over my own. I don't kiss her right away. I internally freak out that I even have the privilege of kissing this girl, and I revel in the proximity she grants me, the one that only ratchets my growing, inexplicable need for her.

She stares down at my mouth, then she nudges her nose against mine, and our foreheads gently knock together. Her minty breath is warm as it hits my face, and if I hadn't lost all branches of thought, I would've made the first move. But she kisses me this time—a slow, indulgent kiss that triggers butterflies in my belly and strikes me with enough brute force to render me speechless.

There're no aggressive tongues or grabby hands. It's something chaste yet everlasting in memory.

We both pull away at the same time, and if her cheeks are the slightest shade of pink, then mine must be as subtle as a flashing traffic message board.

The game continues to roar around us, and I keep an eye out for Teague's jersey in the cyclone of red-and-white bodies, all of whom are still screaming at the tops of their lungs and ping-ponging around like out-of-control fireworks.

"How are you feeling? About your mother?" I ask, interlacing our fingers together. Cali's freezing from the rink, and I squeeze her palm a little to try and circulate some warmth. Her scars have begun to thicken, which means she hasn't felt the need to harm herself. And that's a good sign.

I know her mother is a sensitive topic, but we're moving her into the facility tomorrow. I need to know that Cali's going to be okay.

I'm surprised (and relieved) that she's allowed me to help with her mother's expenses. I don't think I would've been able to sleep or eat or drink if I continued to stand idly by as she dealt with everything by herself. It's my unofficial duty to protect Cali and her family. It's the only thing in this world that matters to me.

Her chest rises with a steady breath, and the tip of her tongue plays peek-a-boo against her lips. "I'm actually doing okay," she says quietly.

"Cali, that's great."

She glances out at the rink. "And Teague...I think he's doing okay too. I don't think he fully understands what's going to happen, though."

"I think it's better if he doesn't understand. He'll look to you for security because he's so uncertain, you know? Instead of spiraling," I admit, rubbing my thumb over the ridge of her knuckles.

"I never really thought about it like that."

It feels like my aching heart grows twice the size. "You're his whole world. However you react, he'll react."

That worried, tightly pulled expression of hers morphs into a rare calm that I wish I saw more of, and realization settles like rapid-hardening cement in her arctic irises. "I have to be strong for him," she concludes.

"You have to be strong for yourself," I correct.

She tosses me a glance—one transient in nature but lasting

in effect, living as a core memory in the hub of my brain despite being so mundane.

"When did you get so wise?" she quips.

I stretch my arms over my head. "Oh, I've always been wise, baby. It's just taken you this long to realize it."

"Oh, please. The only wise thing you've done is taken your PT's advice and stumble into my dance studio."

"Best decision of my life," I concur, my lips lifting into a lovestruck smile—one that never existed before I met Cali. One that I didn't even know I was capable of. And now one that I can't seem to stop wearing.

Her cheeks steam with an infectious blush, and even though Cali's confidence is tangible, she always grows shy whenever she receives any type of compliment. It's like she knows what I'm saying deep down about her is true, but she isn't used to hearing it. And I'm determined to be the only man in her life to hail her with compliments until the day I die.

"Thank you for making that poster for him," she says, changing the subject.

I shrug. "It just felt right. This is a win for all of us. I know I'm not, like, his dad or anything. I just wanted to make sure he knows I support him. And that I'm here for him. And that I'm proud of him."

Cali reaches up to subdue an unruly curl of my hair, fingering it before tucking it back behind my ear. "He knows, Gage. He adores you, and you don't have to be related to us for him to look at you like a father figure. You've done more for him than our dad ever has. And I never even asked you to."

"Every second of it has been worth it. You guys are…"

My family? My world? My everything? Three months ago, I was a sad, self-pitying loser who thought he was going to die if he didn't get playing time. I was a loser who always joked about having a multitude of women knocking down my door, when in reality, I was beginning to believe that my person wasn't out there.

If I hadn't been late for practice that day, if I hadn't been a complete asshole and boxed Cali in, I never would've found the woman I want to spend the rest of my life with. The world gave me an angel when I was least deserving of it. Okay, possibly an angel *disguised* as a demon, but still. I know this is long overdue, but I want her to be my girlfriend. Officially. I want the entire world to know she's mine, and I want the entire world to know what an incredible human being she is.

I don't like sharing Cali, but maybe this is one exception I can make. Hiding her is like trying to hide the moon—impossible, fucking idiotic, and a disservice to those who'll never witness her inner and outer beauty.

She's staring at me with those big, Bambi eyes, her brow slightly wrinkled with nervous expectancy, but before I can man up and come clean, the ambience of the rink changes on a dime. A few parents in my peripheral clamber to their feet, peppering the air with rowdy shouts of encouragement, and the ground beneath me begins to shake with the renewed liveliness of the crowd.

My attention barrels to the rink, where a tiny player has the puck and is moving at immeasurable speeds. It's only a second later when I realize that it's Teague.

"Holy shit. He has the puck!" I yell, shaking Cali by the shoulders while simultaneously keeping my eyes on his swerving figure.

Cali's head whips around upon my observation, and she springs to her feet, hauling me up with her as we both watch Teague narrowly dodge an incoming opponent.

"Come on, Teague! You can do it!" she screams, fear and pride grappling for ultimate traction over her face.

I force myself to glance at the clock. There's exactly thirty seconds left.

He's going to do it. He's going to score the winning shot.

My stomach roils with anxiety, and my legs feel like pillars about to crumble, the gravity of the situation laying heavy on my voice box and restricting words from taking shape. He's doing everything I taught him. He's staying by the puck, keeping his eye on it, and remaining confident.

He's a few feet from the goal, and the low defensive position the goalie's in tells me he's not expecting a high slap shot. It doesn't even really look like he's expecting Teague to get a shot past him at all. And that's a fatal mistake to make. Never underestimate your opponents.

Cali grabs onto my arm like she's determined to rip it from its socket, and Teague swings back just in time to make a shot before he's swallowed up by the wave of offense riding his tail.

His stick arcs slightly off the ground, he smacks the puck with the surface of his blade in a full-force slap shot, and the disc heads directly for the upper corner of the net. The frenzied arena stills. Everything silences around me, like the distant garble of sounds when you're underwater. My heart stops beating. My breath stops flowing.

And then, even before I hear the audience erupt into ear-bleeding chaos, I see the net billow back from Teague's winning goal, and the goal lights flash that perfect fucking red color, just as the buzzer signals the end of the game with a ringing drone.

I can't believe he did it. Oh my God. He fucking did it! I knew he could do it, but a shot like that is—it's insane. I know world-renowned players who haven't even accomplished something like that. Do you know how much confidence it takes to carry the responsibility of the last shot of the game? How if you miss it, even if your teammates don't say it to your face, they probably blame you for the loss? And Teague never faltered once when he was up against those intimidating, post-growth-spurt opponents.

"He did it! He did it!" Cali cries, bouncing on the balls of her feet and clapping her hands.

Teague stands in shock, as if he can't believe it himself, and the rest of his team swarms him, chanting his name and pumping their sticks into the air. Their war cries and victory screeches harpoon the glacial atmosphere, intermixing with the applause of proud parents and the protesting groans from sore ones.

"He did it," I whisper under my breath, pride and admiration re-energizing the organ in my chest to resume its pounding rhythm.

Cali hugs me, still jittery with that rush of adrenaline, squeezing me in her arms as a silent gratitude for helping Teague.

But he did this all on his own.

I squeeze her back with the same undiminishable excitement, lifting her off her feet and twirling her around as she squeals and clings to me even tighter. I never want this feeling to end. I never want to know what it feels like not to hold her in my arms.

The world stops again, but for a different reason this time. The world stops and allows me to immortalize this memory, to lose myself in her smell and her laughter and the way she holds on to me as if she's afraid of being forgotten. Or maybe she's afraid that someday she'll be swept away by the tide and washed out to sea, to live as a faceless character in a hazy story that I keep locked away deep inside, so nobody knows the true extent of the pain I'd live with if I ever lost her.

But I could never forget Cali. Never in a million years.

When I set her back down, she wields a high-voltage smile despite being slightly breathless, and her hair is tousled around her blanched face.

I pull her so she's flush with my chest, brushing my lips over hers without fully caving into a kiss—because once I start, there's no way in hell I'll be able to stop. "You know what this means, right?"

She gasps into my mouth, steadying her hands over my hastening heart. "What?"

"I'm booking you a tattoo session."

29

VICTORY'S SWEET, BUT REVENGE IS SWEETER
CALISTA

"**T**wo scoops of fudge! No, three! No, maybe two," Teague debates with himself, standing on his tiptoes to peek over the counter.

He looks to me for permission, popping his lower lip out in that cute kid pout, and I ruffle his helmet hair. "You can get as many scoops as you want, Squirt," I tell him.

Gage squats down—which seems to be less strenuous for him after all the sessions we've done together—and nearly explodes my ovaries with one of his famous, dimple-popping smiles. "Little Man, if you want an ice cream cake, I'll buy you an ice cream cake," he says to Teague.

Teague's eyes turn into saucers. "Really??? Cali, can I pleeeaaaseee have an ice cream cake! Please, please, please."

I frown. "Let's just stick to one cup, okay? That's a lot of sugar for someone as little as you."

"I'm not little! I'm five feet tall!" he counters, huffing and turning his nose up.

"You're four feet and seven inches."

"Oh, yeah? Well, you're a big poopy face!"

This little shit's going to send me to an early grave, I swear. I lunge forward and dive my hands into his ticklish sides, scratching my fingers over his ribs as he collapses into a fit of screams and giggles.

"He'll have three scoops!" I yell over the commotion, dodging an incoming elbow while he flails his limbs like he's being kidnapped in broad daylight.

I'm so proud of how hard Teague's worked over these past few months. He scored the winning shot! Granted, it'll cost me a stupid tattoo—*which I'm definitely not getting*—but if that empty promise tricked Gage into bargaining with him to score the last goal, then it was a sacrifice well made.

Gage rises to a stance and leans against the counter. "And two scoops of vanilla and two of rocky road," he orders, fishing his wallet out from his pocket.

Teague squirms under my hands, trying to retaliate with a tickle strategy of his own, but his adorable, stubby little arms can't reach me. I eventually grant him mercy and haul him up by his underarms, plopping him back on his feet.

"We don't call others poopy faces in public," I mock-chastise.

Nobody else is in the shop since it's a little past five on a weekday, which gives us some much-needed quiet after the maelstrom of hockey that's been ravaging the household this past week. Teague needed me to read him an extra story every night because he was so worried for the game today. And in the end, there was nothing for him to worry about. Gage has been telling me that scoring a winning shot is a *very* hard thing to do. I still don't understand hockey. I don't know if I ever will, but I'm pretty sure I can count on Gage to give me the CliffsNotes version of it.

The server deposits three cups onto the counter, all overflowing with miniature mountains of sugary decadence, and her ponytail bobs as she waits for Gage's payment to go through.

"Fine. But can I call them cunts instead? That's what Gage said I can call them!" Teague exclaims in his outdoor voice.

Oh my God.

My hand slaps instantly over Teague's mouth as Gage chokes on his own spit, all under the unamused eye of the girl slowly pushing buttons on the cash register.

"On second thought, poopy face is fine," I rush out, still muzzling him in case a plethora of new curse words find their way out.

Gage quickly apologizes to the server before scooping our ice creams up in his arms and making a brisk walk toward the exit. Teague, like the little devil he is, runs ahead of us to a small knoll just outside of the quaint ice cream shop, plodding through fallen autumn leaves that cover the once-green grass.

"I can't believe you said that in front of him!" I reprimand, and not in a mocking tone this time.

"I didn't think he actually listened to me!" Gage defends, albeit poorly.

"You better hope he doesn't say that out on the ice."

"Don't worry, I've heard far worse insults out there."

I stubbornly take my ice cream from him, but I've gotten far worse at hiding my smile whenever he does something remotely stupid. I used to be so good about it too. He's finally achieved his tireless venture in making me soft. Now I'm like, goo-puddle soft.

As we climb up the knoll, I bump my shoulder with his. "Thank you. For the ice cream."

"My dad was never around to buy me ice cream after games. I don't want Teague growing up thinking his accomplishments aren't acknowledged."

It tears me up inside that Gage's parents will never realize how amazing he's turned out, despite their obvious lack of parenting. That's every parent's dream—for them to roll out a decent kid. I'd never tell Gage to his face, but I hope Teague grows up to be just like him one day. Caring, ambitious, courageous. Maybe minus the annoying part. But I'm pretty sure that's just some deformed gene specific to Gage himself that won't be passed down to anyone other than his offspring.

Ugh. Imagine having miniature Gages running around. Hold on a second. Why *am* I imagining that? And why, in my imagination, am I dressed in an apron and setting the dinner table like some kind of domestic housewife? Oh, God. I don't want kids. Not even when I'm pushing fifty. Get me out of here, brain!

"He appreciates it, even if he doesn't say it," I assure Gage. "You're spoiling him, you know."

Gage sits down on the desiccating land, brushing away some of the crisp leaves and making a poke-free seat for me. He hands Teague his tower of fudge ice cream, but he keeps his eyes firmly set on me.

"I like spoiling the people I care about."

My entire body heats up, undoubtedly saturating my cheeks in a bold blush. The sun sags just beneath the shingled roof of the ice cream shop, pouring shades of orange and pink over the tinted sky. I can see glimpses of it through the sparse, flaxen-colored foliage hanging above us, attached to a grand oak that sways in the autumn breeze, lending its rustling susurrations to the background of our conversation. The weather is still warm, not yet warranting the need for a sweater or a cardigan, and I let myself bask in it like a heated, golden-painted caress.

Teague digs into his treat right away, somehow getting chocolate all over his face within the first few bites. Gage volunteers to run back to grab some napkins, and I attempt to rub some of the filth off my brother's face with a wet thumb.

"You know we're helping Mom move into her new house tomorrow, right?" I remind him, surprised at how steady my voice sounds.

Teague continues to make a dent in his ice cream, unfazed like his usual self. "Yep! I hope she likes it. I heard they have a pool. That's so cool! I wish we had a pool."

I brush my hand down his head and chuckle. "You know, if you're nice enough, I'll put in a good word for you. Ask the nurses if you can go for a swim."

"Really?"

"Of course, Squirt. But you have to promise to come visit Mom with me *every* Sunday, got it?" I stick my pinky out for a Cadwell pinky promise, wiggling it like that'll entice him more.

I think I've been looking at this new chapter in our lives all wrong. This is a new beginning for my mother—a beginning that I could never offer her on my own. This is another chance at who knows how many years this place will gift her, giving her a life full of laughter and love and less pain. This is a good thing. It's scary and different, but it's good.

My brother eagerly hooks our pinkies together. "Deal!"

Teague's suddenly wrangled into Gage's arms as Gage fruitlessly starts to wipe the fudge from my brother's sticky skin with a napkin. "Hold still, bud."

Teague kicks and squeals, moving his head around so that Gage's efforts to clean him are useless, and he darts out of his grasp and chooses to barrel-roll down the small hill. His shirt and pants are covered in fragmented chunks of leaves, and he stays close by us as he runs aimlessly around and does whatever weird ritual eight-year-olds do when they experience a giant sugar high.

"If he pukes, I'm blaming you," I growl, wiping my chocolate-stained fingers on the napkin.

Gage snorts. "He'll be fine. Look at him! Kid's on cloud nine."

My brother does like to run around in circles when he's happy. He even has his tongue lolling out of his mouth like a dog.

I take my ice cream cup in my hands and start to prod at the ice cream with my spoon before realizing that it's completely white, save for a single, red gummy bear sitting in the drooping middle. Vanilla. Of course.

Gage pops a loaded spoonful of chocolate and marshmallow into his mouth. "The gummy bear's me, obviously. And you're the vanilla."

"Boring, bland, white?"

"Reliable, well-liked, comforting, sweet, revolutionary, timeless. Need I go on?"

A smile turns up my lips, my blush probably still in full force. I abandon my spoon and begin to lick a groove through the slowly liquifying mound, immediately relaxing when the sugar clings to my tongue.

Gage and I eat for maybe a minute of uninterrupted silence, but then he clears his throat and takes a break from his demolished ice cream. "I wanted to ask you—"

I turn to give him my full attention, but instead of focusing on whatever it is that he's saying—which I'm sure is important—I'm distracted by the drips of chocolate sliding down his knuckles.

Either my brain cells have deteriorated after my sugar consumption or my judgment has been heavily impaired by the freakishly good-looking man sitting next to me, but I don't grab him a napkin. I don't even remember that there's an unused stack in arm's reach.

"Gage, you're dripping." I grab his hand—which is still wrapped around his now-drenched cup—and lick the melted ice cream off his knuckles, cleaning his skin like some unspayed house cat.

It's not until I've gotten every last drop that I fully realize what I've just done, and we both stare at each other, waiting silently for the other to say something.

Hey, Cali. Why did you do that? Why couldn't you, I don't know, just give him a napkin? Or better yet, don't mention it at all! It clearly wasn't bothering him. He would've cleaned it eventually.

I pick up the corner of a napkin and drape it over his knee, which is barely blocking the...um...*situation* taking place in his pants, and I avert my eyes out of...respect? My sincerest condolences?

"Sorry. That was...weird," I apologize, my nerves sticking like a burr to the inside of my throat.

Gage blinks, the gravel in his voice splintering into glass. "I, uh, it's fine. You're fine."

He sets down his cup, but he doesn't cross his legs or bring his knees into his chest. Nope, his giant erection just kinda sits there, and I've never been more grateful for Teague's situational unawareness.

My mouth waters, and it's not some aftereffect of the ice cream. Fuck, I would give anything—and I mean *anything*—for him to take me right here, in public, while he splits me on his fat cock doggy-style, sliding so deep I can feel him in my guts. The first time we fucked, it was everything I'd ever fantasized about. It was sweet and gentle with just the right number of rough touches in between. But I need him. Again. Uncensored and unrestrained. Mounting me on that pierced monster between his legs until I'm crying and screaming and clawing at him for release.

I open my mouth—maybe to defuse the awkward tension with some out-of-pocket comment—but Gage beats me to it.

He fully struggles to get it out, neck thickly corded, eyes darkening in a lust-filled haze. "Calista, if Teague wasn't with us, I'd bend your pretty little ass over my lap and slide my fingers down your pants until I get to that delicious fucking cunt." He leans into me, whispering under his breath, "And if I ask you again like I did that night at your apartment, how wet would you be?"

He runs his nose along my jawline, and my breath snags in

my throat. I don't have some witty remark poised on the tip of my tongue. All that exists inside me is pure hunger, and it responds to every touch and every tease that Gage dangles in front of my helpless body.

"Dripping," I admit quietly, feeling arousal leak into the gusset of my panties.

Jesus Christ. I need him. Right now. Need every inch of him filling me up, pounding into me until I'm so sore I can't walk for days. I don't want to make passionate love. I want to fuck like primal animals, taste his flesh between my teeth, selfishly chase after that all-consuming satisfaction. I crave him like flowers long for sunlight, like deserts yearn for rainfall.

"Good girl," he rumbles, sliding his hand over my thigh, just skirting along the denim seam that borders my wet center, and my pussy clenches at the phantom fullness of his fingers lodged inside me.

It's been too long. God, I'm going to come in my underwear if he keeps touching me, be forced to sit in my sticky filth the whole ride home until I can make a beeline to the bathroom and wash the embarrassing residue from my legs. This son of a bitch knows how sensitive I am.

In my head, I'm a badass who makes men beg on their knees for the tiniest scrap of attention. In reality—at least right now—I'm the one begging for his attention, whimpering for Gage to punish me for my smart mouth, to stuff it shut with his leaking cock.

"Not so hard to admit, was it?"

I shake my head, desire clawing at the depths of my stomach, urging me to align my hips with his fingers, to feel him cup my cunt through my jeans.

"Gage..." I whine, using superwoman levels of power to refrain from bucking against the air.

I'm ashamed. Trust me.

"When we get home, I'm going to fuck your throat, Spitfire.

Gonna make you choke on my dick until there are tears in your eyes, and then I'm going to watch as you swallow down every last drop of my cum. We're not stopping until you've milked me dry and I've bruised that jaw of yours."

I'm shivering and shaking and seconds away from unraveling like a spool of thread when Teague bounds into my peripheral, sweaty faced with the faintest hint of brown still smudged over his lips.

"Cali, I'm tired," he says, yawning and stretching his arms.

Gage scoots away from me immediately, ineffectively blocking his boner with his inadequately sized ice cream cup.

"Okay, Squirt. We'll head home soon. Just...give Gage a minute."

I glance at Gage, my confidence reappearing in the form of a coy grin. "Or more like five."

30

ALL'S FAIR IN LOVE AND GOOD HEAD

CALISTA

Getting Teague to bed was surprisingly quick and seamless. Thanks to the heaping amounts of sugar we gave him, he crashed pretty hard. He probably —*hopefully*—won't wake up in the middle of the night. If he walks in on something he's not supposed to see, I'll personally pay for his therapy bills.

And now I have Gage all to myself. After a long, painful ride home, I sobered up enough to regain my bearings and form a plan of action. I'm not going to give in so easily. At least, not if I can help it. That sadistic side of me demands the wheel this time, and I'm going to have him on his knees so I can see how pretty he is when he begs.

Gage peers around the dark corner to make sure the coast is clear, forfeiting a sigh of relief. "God, that was close. I don't think Teague would ever recover if he saw us playing tonsil hockey. I mean, I saw my parents groping each other once and it was truly scarring—"

I cut Gage off by pushing him up against the adjoining wall of the kitchen, drawing out an unmanly squeak in the process.

"Gage, shut up," I growl, my palm pressed against the rapid

thudding of his heart—which only quickens under my prolonged touch.

He's staring at me with a measure of fear in his eyes, and blood floods to the surface of his cheeks, lightening his skin in a hue of pink. I take my index finger and drag it down his torso to the hard cut of his muscled stomach, then hook it into the loop of his pants and pull him closer to me. I can already feel him filling out his pants with his erection, and his turgid length obtrudes against my belly, the weight of him incurring more liquid desire to saturate my already-damp panties.

I palm his generous bulge, making him hiss between gritted teeth. "You had your fun earlier, but that's not how this night is going to go. I'm going to be the one in control, and you're going to be the one begging *me* to touch *you*. Do I make myself clear?"

Gage nods wordlessly, the tendons in his neck quivering, the sturdiness of the wall the only thing keeping him upright. A rare nervousness rules his expression, but it's combated with gut-wrenching anticipation.

I lightly pinch his cock through the material of his pants, and a shudder shimmies through his body as he throws his head back against the wall.

"It hurts, doesn't it? All that pressure building inside, that painful strain in your cock, that insatiable ache in your balls. All you can think about is coming so hard you can't see straight, right?"

"Fuck, yes," he groans, a drop of briny sweat rolling down his temple, teeth scuffing his bottom lip until blood beads and congeals on cracked skin.

I slowly unzip his fly, but not far enough to let his dick spring out. Even swathed and safely contained, that *thing* is still intimidating. "You want me to make you feel better? You want me to take your cock out, rub it until you can't take any more, and then shove it down my throat?" I drawl, all feminine wiles and "innocent" bats of lashes.

"Would give anything to fuck that gorgeous throat of yours, Spitfire. I'll beg on my knees if I have to."

"That's a start." I pull Gage's pants down to his thighs, smacked with the droolworthy sight of that carved Adonis belt and the sexy strip of hair underneath his navel. His cock's practically bursting at the seams, a sizeable spot of pre-cum seeping through the front of his boxers.

"Take your dick out," I command, tracing my fingernail along that plunging V-line, savoring the way his stomach jumps —the way I hold the power of his orgasm in an expertly placed touch.

I'm expecting a slow buildup of obedience, a measured acceptance of defeat because of his God-like ego, but he fumbles with his underwear, hooking his fingers in the elastic band and pulling them down to blunt the pressure.

His long, forearm-thick cock stands at attention before me, a red, angry hue from this roulette game of teasing, curved just slightly to the right and drooping a little low from the heaviness of its own weight. His piercings glisten underneath the naked bulb in the kitchen, same with the milky dribble of pre-cum pearling at the tip, and little rivers of blue-grey veins feed into one larger one stemming along the underside of his shaft. The perfect detonation point.

I take an exploratory finger and follow the dominant vein, keeping the pressure featherlight, and Gage's legs collapse for a second. A loud whimper gets caught somewhere in the back of his throat, as if he's too proud to vocalize it but too weak to keep it confined to his chest.

"Sensitive?" I ask, ending my torturous trek at his sodden slit, where I swirl my digit around his arousal and electrify every nerve ending in the bulging head like a touch-activated sensor.

"You have no idea." His voice is hoarse, his dick twitching and oozing more pre-cum onto the pads of my fingers, his thighs still shaking of their own volition. I can smell the ripeness of his musk, even the tinge of sweat underlying it, and my mouth waters to taste the saltiness of his cum, to drink it down until he's filled my belly and I've drained every drop from him.

With saliva clotting my mouth, I purse my cheeks and gather a wad of it on my tongue, parting my lips to allow a string of drool to lower to the ruddy tip, where it hits its target with an obscene splat.

"Rub my spit in, Gage. Rub it in with your cum like the good boy you are, then start stroking yourself."

Another little whine. Another little wordless concession.

He takes his thumb and begins to mix my saliva with his spend, priming the head with a thin gloss of lubrication. There's not enough spit to coat much of his length, but there's enough to wet his palm so he can gain some traction.

"Calista," he groans, struggling to keep his eyes open, just starting to stimulate himself with some half-hearted pumps, a *slick* noise pervading the kitchen. He performs every rub slowly, as if going too fast will augment the flowering pain.

"I know," I purr. "You're doing so well."

His hand speeds up at my praise, and he bares his throat to me with a toss of his head, his Adam's apple bobbing under tight skin. The muscles in his arms pull impossibly tight, highlighting each protruding vein, and his chest rises and falls in uncontrollable heaves.

Something ferments in my belly, something I *thought* would be arousal but turns out to be a modicum of purebred jealousy. I'm jealous. Of his hand. Of the fact that I'm not the one making his eyes roll back.

I give him a few minutes of shallow breaths and grunts, his hand now falling into a steady rhythm as he rubs up and down, seeming to apply the most pressure at the base before wringing it up his length and letting it disperse at the top.

I fight the gush in my panties, fight the frisson of excitement swan diving to my toes, fight the way my thoughts cut in and out like the static of a radio. As much as I want to touch myself, I'm focused on pleasuring him, knowing that he'll return the favor the minute he comes. But fuck, does everything burn. My pussy doesn't cease its palpitating even when I force the reins from his hands, replacing his controlled strokes with my faster, rougher ones.

His hands slap loudly against the wall, and he cants his hips forward, his body purging a pornographic moan that practically rumbles through the foundation of the house. My fingers fail to close entirely around the circumference of his girth, but I squeeze lightly on a half-stroke anyways, distributing delicious pressure throughout his length, feeling the skin crease under my fingertips. When I get to his head, I smooth over the tip with my thumb, picking up the sticky excretion there, and I rip another noise of contentment from him.

"You want my mouth on your cock, Gage?" I ask in a patronizing tone. "You want me to suck you dry while I gag on your giant dick? You want to fuck my throat until my jaw locks?"

Gage forces himself to look at me, all heavy-lidded and glassy-eyed, and he manages to find an ounce of control, that dominant side of him tearing through his soft and submissive underbelly. "Gonna look so pretty when you're choking on my cock, Spitfire. Gonna fuck your tonsils until you can't take it anymore, and then you're gonna take every last drop from me because it's all yours—my dick, my cum, everything."

I slowly drop to my knees, facing his dick head-on, which is a lot scarier than I initially thought it would be. How is that thing supposed to fit in my mouth when it barely fit in my vagina? Have people actually died from choking on dick? That's literally the worst possible way anyone can go.

I table the little voice of caution in the back of my head and scrub the nervousness from my face. "You're right. It is all mine. *You* belong to *me*."

"Damn right I do. And I want everyone in the fucking world to know it."

With one hand on the root to anchor myself, I part my lips and make way for the nine-inch intrusion, having to unhinge my jaw after I pass his head. His cold piercings tickle the walls of my mouth, and I swallow him down, inch by inch, my incisors brushing the thickness of him until his tip is finally settled at the back of my throat. And then I begin to milk him, hollowing my cheeks with a tight suction and bobbing my head back and forth. My hands work the base while my lips ascend his shaft, gripping around his cock in wet slurps, the overproduction of saliva slipping down my chin.

Gage begins to spear his dick against my tonsils, and he taps my gag reflex momentarily, the brunt of him causing the corners of my mouth to crackle a bit from the agape angle. I choke him down as tears pool in my eyes, adding to the already-slick mess on my face. The smell of him is overwhelming, and I'm stuffed to the point where all I can do is breathe through my nostrils. Once I adjust to his size, I slip up and down at a languid pace, taking my time to experiment with where he's the most sensitive. I pop off him for a second to lick the throbbing head, and Gage's hand flies out to nestle in a chunk of my hair, yanking so hard that it makes my neck crick.

"Cali," he growls, but unlike his usual brassy warnings, this one holds no power.

I delicately skim my teeth over one of the metal knobs of his piercings, causing his hips to convulse and his expression to lose its set-in-steel control to irrepressible euphoria. His muscles can't decide between being relaxed or strained, so I make the decision for him when I suckle only on the tip, doting on that slit with titillating laps.

"Good boys beg," I say, sitting back on my haunches, waiting patiently for him to obey me.

"Please…"

I press a kiss to a vein traveling up his length. "I know you can do better than that."

"Please, Cali. Fuck. I—please keep sucking. Need to come down your throat. Need to show you how much I appreciate you. I'll be a good boy, I promise. I'll do anything to have your incredible mouth on me," he begs, a mess of a man with his pants down and cock out in my kitchen, six feet and one inch of honed muscle surrendering to a seductress in a five-foot-seven body.

I slowly—achingly slowly—reacquaint myself with his dick, switching between hand-curated pumps and earnest sucks, watching as his abdomen contracts and his thighs tauten, forewarning me of the last few stretches he has left in him before tipping over that precipice. And then I take him the farthest I can, deep-throating him, deriving a drawn-out groan that zaps straight to my pussy. He slams himself against the tight walls of my throat, rendering my tongue useless, and keeps a hand on the back of my head while he abuses my esophagus with thrust after agonizing thrust.

It's a lot. The most intense sensation I've ever felt aside from him fucking me raw. Gage is in control now, deciding how rough to push, using the stutter of my gags to gauge when it's too much. My nose is buried in his trimmed pubes, and my bottom lip skims the skin of his hair-matted balls.

"God, you feel fucking amazing," he says, continuing to snap his hips against my face, this time repositioning his hand over my windpipe, fingers settled over the slight bulge of him stretching in my skin. "I love feeling myself inside you."

He keeps his hand there, losing comprehensibility when he gets out the rest of his shunts, and finally, I feel his cockhead swell. Hot spurts of cum pulse down my throat in wave after endless wave, shooting straight into my stomach.

The minute Gage is done, he disengages from my mouth and slides his back down the wall, taking my face in his hands and wiping the spit from my lips. "Are you okay? Did I hurt you?" he asks.

"I'm okay," I assure him, leaning into the palm caressing my cheek. We're both exhausted, nothing but the combined sound of uneven breaths to be heard over the silence of the apartment.

"Good, because I think I'd have a heart attack if I killed the love of my life with my cock."

Ignoring the absurdity of his comment, the tail end of it manages to lure my attention, and it feels like a goddamn kill shot to my heart.

"What?"

"What?" Gage echoes, staring at me like he didn't just drop the L-bomb and decimate my entire world.

"You just...you just said the L-word," I sputter, blinking about fifteen times in thirty seconds, trying to keep a cool head when everything in my body is on fire and my emotions are running haywire.

"I did?"

"Yeah, you did. Literally a second ago."

"Oh."

Oh? OH? What in the hell does that mean?

I'm losing it. Like, Chuck Noland in *Castaway* losing it. Did he make a mistake? Was he only saying that because I gave him head? Why did he say it so casually? Am I missing something here? Am I overthinking? Isn't it too soon for him to be saying that? Oh my God, we're not even actually together.

"What the fuck, Gage?" I exclaim, anger broiling in my gut, confusion the only thing holding me back from whacking some sense into his fat head.

It takes a second for Gage to catch up to me, and I'm not sure how he understood my freakout—because I didn't myself—but his eyes widen, and he imposes immediate damage control.

"Shit. I didn't—I didn't mean for it to come out that way. I mean, I did mean for it to come out eventually, but I was picturing like a thousand roses and candles and a yacht. I think I've gotten so used to saying it in my head that it kind of just slipped out."

I freeze, feeling a tsunami of suppressed emotions finally sneak up on me, rising too fast for me to scramble to higher ground. "You say that in your head...about me?" I whisper, trying to negotiate with the tears to subside.

Gage blushes, and I feel heat sear the back of my own neck.

"Yeah, I say it all the time," he answers, characteristically clueless to the internal *Mayday, Mayday!* distress happening inside me right now.

I don't have time for an internal monologue. I don't have time to even catch my breath. This is—AHHH!

"I didn't know you felt that way about me."

He cracks his trademark smile—the one well-fitted to his perfect lips, the one that could stop traffic and probably the hearts of half the teenage girls across America. "Of course I do. I love you, Calista Cadwell. I'm *in* love with you. I'll always *be* in love with you."

The tears have revisited me in gradual drops, waiting for the next to fall before chasing after them in thin rivulets. I don't bother to wipe them away. I don't bother to quiet the volume of the sobs trying to make themselves known.

This is all so much. I know I feel the same way about him, but I can't bring myself to say it. Why can't I bring myself to say it?

"I—"

"Hey, I didn't say it to hear you say it back. I said it because I wanted to."

Gage takes my second of uncertainty to lean in and kiss me, sponging up the salty tears on my lips, cradling my face in his hands as if he doesn't know when he'll be able to hold me again. In this moment, nothing else exists except for him. No fears for my mother, no tireless duties of my daily life, no yawning hole of self-deprecation telling me I've failed or I'll never be good enough. I give him my fears and he swallows them, locks them away so I'm able to breathe through the lifted smog that I've been used to all these years.

I scoot closer to him, not caring that we're on the cold ground or that the sky's splitting into a dark storm right outside the window. He readjusts his legs to make room for me, and when I'm close enough to squeeze between his thighs, I feel something hard poking me in the belly.

I look down at his already-swelling erection. "Already? I thought these things have, like, a cool-off period or something."

He grimaces. "Kind of a permanent state when you're around."

"Oh, uh, I'm sorry for constantly making you hard?"

Gage pulls me onto his lap, his large hands clamping around my sides as his lips graze mine. "Never something you have to apologize for."

I'm about to say something before he reroutes his attention to the tender spot on my neck, diving in and lavishing butterfly kisses over my still-aching throat, tickling me with the slight stubble sprouting on his jaw. I giggle and squirm in his grip as he attacks me with more playful nips, letting my laughter drown out the growls of thunder cruising overhead.

"Speaking of"—kiss—"life-changing declarations"—kiss—"will"—kiss—"you"—kiss—"be"—kiss—"my"—kiss—"girlfriend?"

The smile that's become a permanent fixture on my face sags. "What?" I somehow flub over the single syllable, my stomach simmering with nervous acid instead of fluttering wings.

"I mean, I wanted to ask you with pants on, but here we are." Gage's expression is completely unafflicted by hesitancy, meaning that he's probably thought long and hard about this and rehearsed what he wanted to say.

I gulp. "You want me to be your girlfriend?"

"Of course," he says confidently. "You don't have to say yes, but it'd be great if you said yes. Really fucking great."

"Are you sure?"

"I've been chasing after you since the moment we met. I've never been surer of anything."

"What if I don't say yes?" I ask quietly, tenderizing my bottom lip with my teeth, knowing in my heart what my answer is but needing to seek confirmation all the same.

He sits back slightly, his eyes glinting in the snippets of lightning flashing through the agglomeration of storm clouds. "Then I would wait for you. Forever. I'd fucking wait for you, Cali. Until the day I die. When will you understand that it's always going to be you?"

It's always going to be me.

I close the ravine of space between us, kissing away one last fear that's wriggled free—the fear of being alone. I may not have been ready to say those three big words, but this is a step I'm ready to take that doesn't seem as scary.

"Of course I'll be your girlfriend."

Gage lights up like the city of Las Vegas at night, a gigantic, gum-showing smile pushing back his cheeks, dotting dimples, and forming complementary eye crinkles.

He pumps his fist into the air. "You said yes! Oh my God. I can't believe…"

He stops himself after he notices the absolute bewilderment on my face, and then he clears his throat and lowers his arm. "I mean, I knew you were going to say yes."

"You're an idiot," I laugh, but the excitement in his voice is like a soothing balm on the scars of my heart. He's the one shining halo of sunlight breaking through an everlasting tempest, allowing me a circle of dryness amongst an unrelenting downpour.

"Yeah, but I'm *your* idiot now," he emphasizes. "Hear that, everyone? Gage Arlington is officially off the market! And he's in love with Calista Cadwell!"

I have no idea who he's talking to, but I don't want to ruin the moment. I've never seen Gage so happy before, and I've never *felt* this happy before.

I trusted my heart in his hands—even knowing how malleable it is—and he's cradled it the entire time I've known him, keeping it safe. Not only protecting it but strengthening it with his own love. A simple thank-you won't suffice. He made me fall back in love with life—with myself. And for that, I owe Gage everything I have. Everything I am.

He leans forward on his hands and knees, just a breath away from my face—an unpredictable breath that's taunting me with a tango of his tongue. "And as my first duty as your designated boyfriend, I'm going to have my fill of you right here on the kitchen floor."

A surprised noise gets caged in my throat, and I feel my greedy cunt resume its throbbing, so damn insistent to the point where all the pressure localizes in my belly.

"Now lean back, Spitfire," he orders, one hand pressed to my back to help lower me to the tiles. "It's time for me to take care of you."

31

DILF STATUS: LOADING
GAGE

I've always been afraid of growing old. Well, realistically, I'll probably die in some freak accident before that seventy-year cutoff, but still. I'm afraid of getting wrinkly and not having my penis work and having to take TUMS after I eat anything mildly spicy. Bottom line, I view growing old as something negative.

But this nursing home is great. Not *great*. Great, as in, a new outlook on aging that I never would have discovered otherwise. These old people are thriving here. Is it insensitive to refer to them like that? Would they prefer "elderly" people?

Teague runs ahead of us, circling some poor man in a wheelchair like the Tasmanian Devil from Looney Tunes, and he continues to giggle while he pops in and out of my peripheral.

"Little Man, stay close!" I shout, but I'm pretty sure my warning's already fallen on deaf ears.

Cali clings to my arm as I wheel her mother to her room under the guidance of a nurse in bright yellow scrubs. The whole place is doused in vibrant colors and floor-to-ceiling windows, overlooking a flora-rich cliffside that's home to the most perfect view of Riverside's autumnal sunsets.

Cali's mom was quiet the entire ride over from the hospital, and I didn't try to make conversation with her because I didn't know what to say. Cali hasn't really told me much about her. It's crazy how similar they look, except her head of red—I'm assuming—hair has darkened over the years. She's as beautiful as Cali, and all I can think about is how stunning Cali will be when she grows older.

Speaking of Cali, did I think she'd say yes to my proposal? Not at all. But she did, and it feels like everything's changed between us. I feel like I'm winning at life right now, like there's nothing in this world that could bring me down. She's mine. Even after all the depressing rejections and the "we're just friends" speeches she gave me, she's finally mine. I can call her mine in public without her elbowing me in the ribs. I can scream that I'm hers from the rooftop and she won't threaten to taser me!

When we round a corner and arrive at our destination, a spacious bedroom awaits the four of us, complete with a four-poster bed, a nightstand, a comfy chair in the corner, a flat-screen television, a large dresser, and a triple-paneled window that looks out over the adjoining garden. Red satin curtains hang from the bed as a matching plush bedspread accompanies floral-printed pillows with maroon accents. There's a single lamp that illuminates the room, empty picture frames waiting for new photos to house, and a blooming orchid on the nightstand. The chair in the corner looks to be a recliner that I'd give anything to throw my aching feet up on.

"This is where Ms. Cadwell will be staying," the nurse says in a cheery demeanor. "We'll have her things moved in shortly while you get settled."

She gives us the room while Cali and I help her mother into bed, Teague stomping his tiny feet in his usual giddy fashion, occasionally commenting on how cool his mom's new place is and how boring their current apartment is.

When Ms. Cadwell settles into bed, we make way for a few of the nurses to haul in her luggage, and I snag Cali aside to check in with her.

"How are you doing?" I ask, surfing my hands up and down her arms.

She wedges her bottom lip between her teeth, nursing the tender spot there. "This place will be perfect for her," she answers.

Her gaze flicks to her mother like a skipping stone, and there's just the slightest bit of moisture warping her eyes.

I turn her chin back to face me, wishing she could use me as some magical conduit that transfers all her unwanted emotions to me. "No tears, remember?"

"No tears," she parrots back, sporting a brave visage for her brother. I smooth out those creases on her forehead with a kiss, and the invisible pressure around my heart relents, ushering fresh breath into my lungs.

She looks up at me, long lashes flittering against her brow ridge. "Thank you. I don't know where I'd be without you."

"Probably exactly where you are now but with a lot less orgasms," I jest, elbowing her and wiggling my eyebrows, to which she surprisingly refrains from violence and settles for an eye roll.

The clanking of boxes and the crackle of chatter is the only reason I say what I say next, otherwise there might be a double death in Cali's bloodline if I'm throwing filth around like I'm six beers in and half-naked at a Mardi Gras festival.

Warmth snares in my belly. "You keep rolling your eyes and I'll give you a real reason for them to roll back."

Still got it.

This time, Cali slaps me on the arm. "We're *not* getting it on in the old folks' home!" she hisses under her breath, offering a polite smile to the clueless caretakers as they begin to box-cut through packing tape.

"You seriously don't think these guys are getting freaky under the sheets when the lights turn off?"

"Ugh! Oh, God. I don't want to picture that. *Ever*." Cali shudders in disgust, rubbing her eyes with balled fists like it'll magically erase the image I've implanted in her head. "I need to find the nearest spoon and scoop my eyes out with it."

I cock my head. "Are you saying that you won't hide the salami with me when I'm old and have a shrunken, three-inch peen?"

She sticks her tongue out at me, and if there weren't impressionable minds in the room, I'd go ahead and bite it. "You already have a three-inch peen."

"I'd be offended if I didn't walk straight into that one."

"Just keeping you humble."

"Yep, I'm aware. It's what I both love and fear about you."

Teague, who I'm assuming is already tuckered out from bouncing off the walls, tugs on Cali's shirt with his perpetually sticky hands, doing that weird thing where kids just open mouth cough all the time.

"What are you guys taaalkiiing about?" he pesters.

Cali and I answer him at the same time.

"Taxes," I say.

"Where to eat lunch," she says.

He jumps up and down excitedly, nearly throwing her off-kilter with the force of his yanks, hope and the promise of something cheesy glimmering in deep sea eyes. "Ooh! Ooh! Ooh! Can we pleeeaaaseee go to that Mexican restaurant where they deep-fry quesadillas?"

Dear God. I can feel it clogging my arteries as we speak. What happened to kids eating whatever food you accidentally dropped on the ground?

Cali licks the pad of her thumb and tries to tame Teague's

mess of flyaways, slicking some of his hair and pushing it out of his face. "What about something less...deep-fried?" she proposes, draping the ends of his long bangs behind his ear. "Like a regular quesadilla?"

Teague ponders her counteroffer, swishes it around in his mouth, then stubbornly spits it back out with exaggerated revulsion. "But I like when they deep-fry it! It's so crunchy."

Cali frowns, and I know that she's going to continue arguing with Teague to ensure a stomachache-free afternoon, so I decide to throw my hat in the ring because Uncle Gage has great ideas. (I've taken the creative liberty of referring to myself as Uncle instead of Coach, since that seems more fitting, you know?)

"You know, Little Man. I've heard there's this Hibachi restaurant downtown that cooks your food in front of you. Lots of fire. And the chefs do all sorts of food tricks while you wait."

Teague immediately gives me his full attention, eyes doubling in size, so hilariously spellbound by the idea of chefs cooking *outside* of the kitchen. "That is so cool! I want to go there, Cali! Can we go there instead? Please? Please? Please?"

Cali's whole body jostles sideways as Teague continues his tugging onslaught, and the corners of her lips flex into a half-relieved and half-exhausted smile. "Sure, Squirt. Why don't you go over and thank Gage for offering to take us."

"That's *Uncle* Gage," I clarify.

Cali huffs out a snort, but deep down, I know I'm defrosting that cold, black, shriveled heart in the hollow chamber of her chest. I have a way of growing on people. Like barnacles. I get really deep in there until no amount of prying can uproot me.

"*Uncle* Gage," she corrects, humoring me with a hand on her hip.

Teague skips over to me, a too-big smile on his face, but he doesn't chant my new name.

He stares at me in a strange way, then his eyebrows lower

with a squint of his eyes. "Shouldn't I call you *Daddy* Gage?" he asks innocently.

Globs of saliva cluster in my trachea, pretty much choking me as I slam my fist against my chest a few times to loosen the impediment, all while Teague watches obliviously and Cali watches in high alert in case she needs to give me the Heimlich or some shit.

"Uh, Gage isn't your dad, Squirt," Cali amends quickly, whacking her hand against my back to help me eject Teague's goddamn audacity out of my wheezing body.

"I know that, but he acts like my dad."

Both Cali and I kind of just stare at Teague, not knowing what to say next, and still not knowing how to remedy the chokes and splutters. Eventually—humiliatingly—one of the caretakers brings me a glass of water to ameliorate the irritation in my windpipe, and I thank them before greedily gulping down the entire drink.

"Come on, Cali. Try it! Call him Daddy Gage!" Teague giggles, blissfully spinning around himself.

"Teague, I'm not going to call Gage that."

I set my glass down, leaning on the nearest flat surface for my signature cool-guy pose, my lips jerked into a disarming grin. "Yeah, Cali. Call me *Daddy*."

"I should've let you choke," she whispers threateningly to me.

I open my mouth to hit her with another Gage-specialized innuendo, but she doesn't let me get a word in—which is probably for the best.

Although my brain's definitely not used to the idea, I can't believe I was so afraid of Teague looking up to me. No, I'm not the kid's dad, but I'm the only male role model in his life. That's a title I don't take lightly. It's a privilege to know a kid as extraordinary as Teague, and even more of a privilege to be a part of his family.

"Come on, T. Say goodbye to Mom. We need to let her get some rest."

The caretakers hurry out of the room to allow us some privacy, and I stand by the doorway—just out of earshot—while Cali strokes her mother's dark hair, whispering something to her with Teague smushed to the side of her leg.

I respectfully avert my eyes to the glistening, clean floor beneath me, so polished that I can just faintly see my reflection in the pristine surface. It only takes a few minutes for Cali to come out of the room with Teague tailing behind her, and to my utter joy, there are no tears in her eyes.

"You hungry?" Cali asks, giving my arm a soft squeeze.

My heart sprints under her touch, and still, after all this time, I'm unable to vanquish those Cali-specific nerves that love to worm into the most inconvenient of places, soaking me in sauna temperatures and pulling pigment to the forefront of my cheeks.

"I could eat," I reply, afraid that if I elaborate, she'll tie my tongue too.

Teague's already five strides ahead of us, and Cali rushes to catch up with him before he causes a three-way car crash. I'm right behind them when a hoarse voice deluges my ears.

Cali's mother's bony hand hangs over the side of her bed, clawing for the warmth of another living, breathing human, and her rheumy eyes pin me down, unblinking as she waits for me to connect our palms.

I've never talked to Cali's mother before. I only met her today when we picked her up from the hospital. I slip back into the room without alerting Cali or her brother to my current whereabouts. When I rest my hand in hers, careful not to squeeze too tightly, she musters all her energy to give me a watery smile, emaciated fingers littered with varicose veins clinging to me. She's as cold as a walk-in freezer, and I feel my stomach violently collapse inwards, reeling the rest of my organs in with it.

"You're good for her," she breathes, tears already flecking her sallow cheeks, bloodshot eyes burdened with an equal measure of physical and emotional pain. Her voice is brittle, fluctuating unpredictably, and there's a smoker-like rasp that ties off the ends of her words.

"I'm in love with your daughter, Ms. Cadwell," I whisper, dropping to my knees beside her so she doesn't have to crane her neck to look up at me. My joints orchestrate a cracking crescendo, but the soreness pales in comparison to the ticking time bomb of my heart. "She's my whole world."

"I can see the love in your eyes," she confirms, surprising me when she consolidates enough strength to crush my hand in hers. "Please make me a promise."

Goose bumps respond to her weight-carrying words. "Anything."

"I know my time is limited, but I need to know that she'll be okay when I'm gone. Promise me you'll take care of her," she begs, more tears trickling past the curve of her jawline, disappearing and reappearing in an infinite cycle.

Moisture condenses in my eyes, and I figuratively tuck her words against my chest for safekeeping, love filling every nook of my body. "I will. I promise."

32

ROMANCING THE GIRL
CALISTA

"Gage, where are you taking me?" I ask, only able to see slivers of light through the hands currently over my eyes.

He's been suspicious all day—giggling to himself, curt responses, darting eye syndrome. And now he tells me he has a surprise for me, which could mean one of two things. One: it's the greatest surprise of all time that doesn't pose a risk to my already-high blood pressure. Two: it's the scary equivalent of going bungee jumping while we're naked and stuck together. And knowing Gage, I wouldn't be surprised if this ends up with us getting naked.

"You worry too much," he says, leading me over unfamiliar terrain, hypercautious of navigating me past invisible obstacles. "You'll love it, I promise."

"I love very few things in this world," I grumble, feeling blindly through the air with my hands like an idiot, all while Gage indulges in my ridiculousness with some not-so-discreet snickers.

He guides me through a door, and since it's night, I can't gauge where we are through the gaps in his fingers covering my eyes. A whirlpool of nerves starts in my belly, and my heart clunks rather haphazardly against the scaffolding of my ribs. I don't like surprises. Never have. And although I trust Gage enough not to murder me in the woods, my body doesn't have the capacity to chill the fuck out if it doesn't know what the hell is going on. I feel like I'm walking blindly into artillery fire.

I'm about to open my mouth and bargain for the truth when my eyesight is restored, and I'm met with the dazzling image of a romantic dinner laid out on the floor of my dance studio. Flaming candles border the red, satin blanket draped over the wooden floorboards, and a rose centerpiece sits in between piles of overflowing dishes. There's pasta, grilled chicken, salad, champagne, breadsticks, some kind of rich, chocolate dessert—pretty much an entire restaurant's worth of delicious-looking food. My jaw falls open.

"You did this?" My expression fractures into one of shock, and the anxiety spidering throughout my bloodstream like some black miasma of death slowly burns out into a fuzzy warmth that coats my insides in liquid honey.

A shit-eating grin tips up the corners of Gage's lips, the lowlight from the candles reflecting asterisms in his dark eyes. "Seeing as we're officially boyfriend and girlfriend now, I thought it was time I treated you to that first date."

I don't know what to say, which is ironic considering I'm always equipped with a quick and witty response. I can't even use my extended vocabulary to maim or insult. I have to—*shudder*—dig in my archives and find something nice to say. Gage is a giver. He always has been. So to walk in on something as thoughtful as this…it's hardly a surprise. The real surprise is him keeping this a secret for the entire day.

Still behind me, he wraps his arms around my midsection, resting his chin on my shoulder. He christens my bare skin with silky kisses, and I let myself fall into his touch like an imaginary drop off an infinity pool. That pine scent of his must imbalance some chemical reaction in my brain to make me froth at the mouth for him—it's all working together to test my self-restraint, gambling away my dignity with each deliberately placed pucker of his lips.

My breath cinches tighter than a drawstring, breaking off the moan stirring in my throat. "Gage, you didn't have to do all of this."

"For you? Of course I did," he rumbles against my flesh, slowly directing us over to the center of the room while we're still entangled in each other. And then he lifts his head up, turning to whisper against my neck, his voice steadier than the chugging of my heart.

"Italian food. I was going to cook for you, but uh, I sort of guessed that you'd want something edible."

I quickly turn around to face him, so wrangled in an adrenaline-fueled undertow that I don't bother with talking. I slam my lips onto his, linking my arms around his neck and pulling him into me. My tongue chases after his, colliding with an urgency that has the bottom half of me squeezing in anticipation, and we take turns hungrily devouring one another as if there isn't food just feet away from us.

"I would've eaten whatever you made," I gasp against his mouth, nearly crumbling to ash when he grips my waist tightly, curling his fingers into the curve of my sides.

He chuckles, and the glorious vibration tings through my bones, way too hot and husky to be legally safe. Especially at this dosage. That irresistible, lower-than-low tone of his conspires with the pulse between my legs like they're two partners in crime.

"Didn't want to take any chances and accidentally poison you. I wanted this date to be perfect."

Perfect. I'd grown to accept that perfection doesn't exist. And I would know, seeing as my life is far from it. But Gage...he's...

well, he might be the only person to be able to change my mind.

My cheeks sizzle with a blush probably as vibrant as the heavily seasoned cherry tomatoes scattered on white porcelain. "When did you even have the time to do this?"

We both take a seat on the ground, and Gage gets busy with popping the champagne, doing it as carefully as he can over the ice bucket so none of it splatters the floor. There's a fizzy stream that glugs out of the opening, and he quickly grabs my flute to fill it with a bubbly, light pink mixture.

"Earlier today. When you took Teague to practice."

"And how did you get in?" I question, my eyebrow going full arch mode.

He shrugs bashfully, handing me my glass and moving on to fill his own. "A little birdy might've helped me."

Right. A little birdy whose name starts with *A* and ends in *eris*.

I can't believe he took time out of his day to set this up for me. The "first date" he promised months ago in a desperate attempt to upstage Dilbert.

I take a swig from my drink, hoping that a little liquid courage will keep my confidence from fraying at the edges. I'm still like a schoolgirl with a hopeless crush, losing all sense of cool when Gage fucking Arlington sneaks loving stares my way, just as smitten with me as I am with him—but a lot more obvious about it.

My mind lags, so overfilled with emotion that I forget we're even having a conversation. I'm too self-conscious of the way my heart's bruising itself against my sternum, pounding so loud that it could blow out a silent stadium.

Gage uncharacteristically chews the bottom of his lip, the surrounding flesh reddening with irritation. "Do you like it? Oh, God. Did I overdo it? Is it too much?" He panics, probably seconds away from sweeping this whole spread up and asking me exactly what I want.

"Huh? No! Oh, no. Gage, it's perfect," I reassure him, reaching over to grab his hand. We're not seated that far away from each other, but it feels like my skin's burning with fire ant bites whenever I'm not touching him. "I'm just...I can't believe you went out of your way to do this."

"I think you underestimate the things I'd do for you. I'd move mountains if you asked me to, Cali."

Tears begin to ball behind my eyes—*stupid tears!*—and his words pack so much punch that they would've knocked me on my ass if I wasn't sitting on it. If my head didn't already get the memo, my body's definitely made it its life goal to yell at me, *Hey, stupid lady! You're in love with this boy!*

I mean, I am, aren't I? And it's not just because he treats me like a princess and spends his hard-earned money on impromptu dates. It's because of who he is. It's because Gage is always there for me, even when I don't want him to be. It's because Gage always puts me first, even when I put myself last. It's because Gage believes in me and supports me, even when I don't think I deserve it.

God, he's just...this man means everything to me.

Love tugs at my guts, turns my tongue loose, and feeds gasoline to a fire that wants nothing more than to burn for all eternity in his presence, keeping him warm even on the coldest of days. "Thank you. This is the best date I could've possibly asked for."

He smiles in relief, brushing his thumb over the back of my knuckles like he always does, and I never expected that this sweet, timid side of Gage would make me so insanely giddy. He's singlehandedly drop-kicked my heart all the way to Timbuktu.

Gage got me a *very cheesy* lasagna, one with gooey cheese stringing down the sides, seeping into layers of perfectly cooked, soft noodle beds. They ooze with little globs of tomato sauce, ultimately topped off with a mouthwatering crust of burnt cheese, flecks of parsley, and a hearty powdering of parmesan. Two halves of garlic bread steam on the rim of my plate, glistening with a fine coat of butter.

I drop his hand to pick up my fork, cutting the hunk of lasagna into smaller squares, but Gage interrupts me. "Wait."

"What?"

"Let me feed you."

I almost burst out laughing. "Gage, that's ridiculous."

Though it seems I've suffered another foot-in-mouth incident because my response misses its mark by (apparently) a wide margin. Gage has this little valley right between his brows, and his mouth is weighed down with a particularly heavy-looking frown.

"You're serious?" I choke out.

"Do I look like I'm joking?"

He doesn't. He really doesn't. I don't want to poke the bear, but he can't be mad at me for being a little confused. "Why—"

"I don't do romantic date nights, Cali. I don't do romance. Period. I'm trying something here, with every belief that it's bound to go sideways. Humor me, please. Let me romance the fuck out of you tonight," he implores, giving me the most irresistible puppy dog eyes, meaning every word of it with the fiber of his being.

Normally I'd refuse him with some very clever wordplay, but goddammit, Cupid's taken my eye out with his fucking arrow. Still reeling in disbelief, I surrender my fork to him.

But he doesn't take it.

The carved lines of his face fall to candle-made shadows, and something unidentifiable lurks underneath the depths of his darkening green irises. "Want you on my lap, Spitfire. Then I can feed you."

There's really no room for disagreement. It's a demand—a soft one—but still a demand.

I glance down at the thick thighs beckoning me, and my mouth salivates for an entirely different reason. Gage has officially made me powerless excuse for a woman. I'm gonna fold like a poker player with a bad hand whenever it comes to him.

Having swallowed any chance at a comeback, I crawl over to him and plant myself in his lap, feeling more than secured with the width of his legs cushioning my ass. And it's then that I wish I'd worn something cuter than my boring outfit of a plain shirt and jeans.

Gage doesn't care at all, though. He still looks at me like I'm wearing the most gorgeous, one-of-a-kind, cost-a-whole-month's-rent dress. I'm sitting on the meat of his thigh, so I don't sit directly on his, um, *gearshift*, and he loops one arm around my waist to hold me in place. He then picks up a sizable piece of lasagna on the tines of my fork, eases it between my lips, and watches with hooded eyes at the way my mouth closes around it.

I don't know what I love more—the food or the lust smoldering in his eyes. Jesus. No wonder this Italian restaurant was so expensive. I thought Gage was lying about the inconceivably high prices. The lasagna tastes like something that my poor tastebuds have never even fathomed. It's so rich that everything disintegrates into melted mush beneath my teeth, and the flavors blend together in an equally intoxicating fusion of tangy tomato and creamy cheese. I moan involuntarily, too blissed out to feel Gage's legs shift beneath me.

The fork clatters to the plate and Gage grinds his teeth together, making a strangled noise that sounds like some kind of inhuman hiss. "Baby, you can't be making those noises when you're sitting on my lap."

I have to blink a few times to understand what he's trying to say, and then embarrassment drips down my nape, combining with the cold sweat now clamming up my forehead. "Sorry."

Oh, God. Who moans when they eat?

"No, it's...fuck. Don't apologize."

He doesn't say much apart from some weakly strung together sentences, squeezing his eyes shut like he'll magically dissipate the sexual tension between us—impossible, by the way. I'm halfway to sliding off his lap when he grabs my arm and keeps me from getting any further.

His eyes open, freezing me over. "Did I say you could move?"

His tone skirts along growly, forcibly taking the last of my words and muddling them beyond a coherent response. Everything in my body is craving him, that low simmer of arousal flaring into a high flame of uninhibited desire. It doesn't take a detective to deduce that the hardness pressing into my left leg isn't a set of inconveniently placed car keys.

I shake my head.

"Then sit back down," he orders.

I do as he says, trying my best to keep my hands to myself by plopping them pathetically in my lap, and I glance at his untouched meal growing colder by the minute. It's a delectable chicken dish, crisped to perfection and slathered in a golden glaze.

"What about your meal?" I ask, unsure if he's expecting me to feed it to him too, surprisingly not fully against the idea, either.

He doesn't hesitate. "You're more important. You're always more important."

My initial gratitude transmutes into concern. Concern strong enough to start an argument if I'm not careful. "I can say the same thing about you. So if you're feeding me, then I'm feeding you too," I insist, picking up his fork and slicing right into that juicy chicken breast.

He goes to (unwisely) protest, but I fill his piehole with a healthy serving of Italian food, smiling triumphantly when he gives in and starts to chew. I don't know why I don't look away. I stare straight at him, intimately tracking the movement of his throat as he swallows. Eating food shouldn't be sexy, okay? But anything Gage does is sexy, and right now, I'm failing to fight off these godforsaken hormones.

He nods to the dessert. "The chocolate budino."

I mirror his line of sight to find a mound of chocolate drizzled in caramel sauce, garnished with two mint leaves and a lilac-colored flower. I wipe residual chicken off the fork onto a napkin, then carve out a scoop of this magical-looking dessert that's the consistency of custard.

I gather a silky and luscious heaping, stick it into his mouth, and then yelp when he pulls me into a kiss, his tongue swiping a heaping of chocolate over my own. I can still taste him even through the thick veil of cocoa, but fuck, do I feel like I'm levitating as he feeds me every last morsel. Saliva mixes with sweetness, thickens between us, clings against the inside of my cheeks. Once I've swallowed everything, he continues to kiss me, unsatiated, using his free hand to caress the back of my head. I change my position and swing my right leg over his hip so I'm straddling him, grinding my center over the unmistakable bulge that's grown in his pants.

"This was supposed to be romantic," he breathes against my lips, doing his fucking all to try and maintain some strand of control. I applaud him for that, I truly do.

"It is," I whisper. "Because I'm with you. I don't need some fancy candlelit dinner, Gage. I love it, but I don't need it."

He pulls back, and I cradle his cheeks in my hands. "I just want to do this boyfriend thing right."

"You are. It's annoying, but you're actually doing *everything* right."

There's a glimpse of that cocky attitude I fell for in the first place, and the one that I think I secretly love. "You make it easy, Cali. I might not be good at a lot of shit in life, but I'll be damned if I'm not the best boyfriend you're ever going to have."

You already are, I think to myself. *And you'll be the last boyfriend I ever have.*

33

HISTORY REPEATS ITSELF
CALISTA

I haven't seen Gage at all today since he's been practicing at the rink for the big game. I've been trying to keep up with the Reapers this season, but I underestimated how much information I'd actually retain with an eight-year-old teaching me the ropes of a very complicated, very elaborate sport.

I'm nervous for Gage. I know how hard he's worked to get his strength back, but I can't stop second-guessing if it's too soon or if I should've pushed him harder. What if something goes wrong? What if he's not a hundred percent better and hurts himself again? I don't think I could recover from something like that. I don't think I could *forgive* myself for something like that.

The rink is awash with blue-and-black jerseys, large signs and Styrofoam fingers waving about, Reapers' memorabilia converting eager fans into one united mass of rowdy scream-shouts. The cold chill torpedoes through the thickness of Gage's jersey and settles bone deep, prompting me to burrow even further into my personal polyester safe haven. Unlike Gage's *real* jersey, this one smells of fresh pine and lacks that lingering body odor that could make a flower wither upon exposure.

We haven't really told anyone we're official. The fans definitely don't know. I'm not sure if any of his teammates know. But walking around with his name splayed on my back in giant letters, walking around with his *mark* on me—it armors me with impenetrable pride, the kind unaffected by public insight.

I can't believe I'm in public right now as Gage's official number one fan. The last time I wore his jersey was when I was still convincing myself that I hated his guts. This time, the only thing I hate is that he's not rearranging my guts. That's some damn good character development if I do say so myself.

I'm headed to wish him luck before the game, and I'm just hoping that I won't mess up any of his pregame rituals. When I round the corner into the main tunnel, I find Gage in his giant, padded gear standing next to a decked-out Fulton.

They're turned half-toward each other and half-toward the rink, mumbling about God knows what, and I awkwardly try to get Gage's attention without crashing full speed into their conversation.

But thankfully, it doesn't take long for my boyfriend to notice me and for his whole face to light up brighter than a polar sunrise. He walks over to me and embraces me, which basically feels like the equivalent of hugging a cloud.

"I'm so happy you're here," he says, giving me a slight squeeze before letting go.

My nerves keep backflipping all over the place, and now that Gage has effortlessly captured my heart's attention, the chaos continues as it swoons and tries to jump into his arms. "You are?"

"Of course I am, Spitfire. You're my lucky charm."

"How do you know I'm lucky? I've never seen you play before."

He takes his helmet off and sets it on the ground. "You're my lucky charm when it comes to life, not just hockey."

Oh.

Oh.

Judging by the incendiary heat that's just risen to my head, my cheeks have probably gained a new pink tone to them. I thought all these nerves were supposed to disappear when you become a couple! And these butterflies feel like a swarm of wasps terrorizing my stomach.

I really don't know what to say. At this point, I'm more anxious than Gage is, and he has a game to play in front of the entire world after being off the ice for three months.

"I—"

Completely oblivious to my miniature freakout—or maybe not—he leans forward and captures my lips in a kiss that seems to silence every nonvital activity in my body, and I mentally thank myself for wearing platform boots today so I can link my arms comfortably around his neck. There's just the right amount of sparks. Not too little to be overlooked, but not too much to set both of our libidos on fire. It's a kiss of reassurance and stability. I melt against him, in the safety of his arms, and both of us slowly pull away at the same time.

"And you're wearing my jersey," he notes, taking his gloves off so he can rub the material between the pads of his fingers, as if he needs to be convinced that this is all real.

"I thought you might like it," I offer coyly.

"You have no fucking idea."

Something dark traipses through his eyes, turning green into gunmetal, and his gaze lowers to my lips, which only exacerbates the second heartbeat in my nether regions that was perfectly content with being out of service.

His voice is low, lecherous, promising things that I can't in good conscience resist. "Shit, Cali. As much as I love seeing you in my jersey, I can't wait to see you out of it—"

"Hey, guys! Hey! Still here. Right here. Literally right next to you," Fulton half-shrieks, waving his arms at us like a frenzied traffic cop.

I cringe. "Sorry, Fulton."

"It's okay! No, I'm totally all for you guys getting freaky-deeky. I just don't want a front row seat. I tend to be forgotten a lot. Not in a bad way, though! I kind of don't understand social cues and when to leave."

Laughter furls out of me, shaking my shoulders gently. "Do you also overshare?"

Fulton has to pause and think for a second. "That is what I've been told before."

Oh, Fulton. You sweet, sweet thing.

The truth is, I might've come down here with an ulterior motive in mind. And because this is the best thing my twisted little head has ever come up with, I can't keep hiding this secret any longer.

"You remember when we made that stupid bet over Teague's goal?" I ask, flirtatiously dragging my finger up and down his arm, getting a sick kind of satisfaction when he still shivers under my innocent little touch.

"Uh-huh," he drawls, the corner of his lips tugging up into an arrogant half-grin.

"Well, I went to that tattoo session you booked for me and followed through."

"Oh, really?" Gage brushes his lips over the shell of my ear, his breath warming the stretch of neck located right below. "Where is it, Spitfire?"

I lift the hem of his baggy jersey up just a little and turn around, revealing the inked set of numbers on my lower back, sandwiched right between the crescents of my back dimples. A small, fine-lined tramp stamp.

Gage goes quiet—probably taking in the beauty of it all—

before all hell breaks loose and he screams at the top of his lungs. "What the fuck, Cali?"

The rest of his teammates look over at us, half-concerned, and I shoo them back to their own personal conversations.

I look over my shoulder. "What?"

I've only seen Gage truly mad three different times. Scary mad. Like, mad to the point where his blood pressure was aneurysm inducing. One, when I teased him about Dilbert before he ended up ripping my clothes off. Two, when I teased him about my secret lap dance...and then he ended up ripping my clothes off. And three, when I just showed him the tattoo I got to honor our agreement.

"Calista," he growls in a low, demonic-sounding voice, a guttural warning that starts in the pit of his stomach and vibrates outwards.

I feign confusion. "What?"

"That's not my fucking number."

My fingers instinctively touch the seemingly permanent brand, and I pout, putting to use that one semester of high school when I was obsessed with theater. "Yes, it is," I argue.

Gage runs his hands through his hair and grips the strands, a lick of lunacy raging in his eyes and highlighting that one forked vein throbbing in his forehead. "No, that's *Fulton's* number," he tries in what I think is supposed to be a "calm" tone.

Fulton looks at my back to inspect the tattoo for himself, and all I can hear from behind me is a storm of subsequent laughter.

"Oh my God. Cali, that's awesome!" Fulton enthuses.

I keep the hem scrunched at my navel as I give a half-hearted shrug. "Oops. I must've gotten them mixed up."

Gage's last-ditch effort to remain calm gets thrown down the goddamn drainage pipe. "Mixed up? MIXED UP?" he shouts, somehow louder than the surround sound of a thousand plus voices in the skyscraper arena. "He wears a twenty-one. I wear an eight. AN EIGHT."

He's losing it. He's all sweaty and red and huffing like he's just snorted a line of cocaine or blown down a pig's stick house. If he wasn't swathed in layers, I'm assuming his muscles would be all hard too. Hard and coiling and maybe even glistening with perspiration.

That shouldn't turn me on as much as it does. I'm a cruel, cruel person.

He drags his hand down his face. "Please...please tell me that it's fucking fake."

I stick my finger in my mouth—which he watches *very* intently despite being furious with me—and then pop it from my lips, wiping the wet pad over the dark numbers, even rubbing a bit to show him that they don't smear.

"You're getting it lasered off. I don't care how much it costs. That shit isn't staying on you."

"Come on, Gage. It's small. You'll barely even notice it's there," I insist, knowing full well that he *will* know it's there when he takes me from behind, fucking a girl who's marked with another man's jersey number. God, this is giving me such an adrenaline rush. The tattoo's obviously not real. Henna. Should come off within a few days, but the kill-all expression on Gage's face right now was worth every penny.

His fingers crumple into a fist. "No. Nope. You're not saying anything."

Then he whips around to deal with Fulton, gunning him down with a blood-red haze clouding both his eyes and sensibility. "I'm going to fucking kill you," he mutters under his breath, which is a thousand times more terrifying than if he were to yell it.

All the color drains from Fulton's face. "I had nothing to do with this!"

"I don't care. I'm going to shove my fist down your throat

and rip your spine out, then wear your bloody jersey number as a prize."

Both Fulton and I are speechless.

Dear God. I've created a monster.

The starting anthem for the Reapers blares over the speakers, and the guys file into a single line, ready to make their grand entrance. This is fine. Everything's fine, right? Hockey's an aggressive game. This will make him play better. *Right?*

Before Gage joins the rest of his teammates, he looks me dead in the eyes and smiles like a sick bastard. "I'll deal with *you* later."

REMEMBER when I thought Gage would be nervous to be back? He's not. In fact, I think I gave him enough rage to fuel an islandic village. He's only missed one shot of the entire game, and we're already on to the second period. His blocking is so precise that the other team is getting antsy and making poorly judged shots. He's killing it out there. It doesn't even look like his hip flexor was torn at all with the way he's moving.

"What did you say to him?" Hadley asks, eyes bolted on me while she stuffs a handful of popcorn and M&M's into her mouth.

I deviate from the game. "Huh?"

"Did you flash him a titty? Promise to suck him off if he won?"

I gasp and slap my hands over Teague's ears—who's thankfully too mesmerized by the grown men on skates to pay much mind to the very inappropriate conversation happening.

"Hadley! There are children present!" I scold, but in the same breath, a mischievous smile materializes on my lips. "I just gave him a little something to motivate him."

Am I worried about whatever punishment is awaiting me

after the game? Yes. There's really nothing else for me to say. I don't know how, but Gage will probably find some way to edge me for an hour until I regret ever pulling this prank on him. Or he'll kill me. Both are equally bad.

I remove my hands from Teague's ears, and he presses his grubby face against the plexiglass, looking the most focused I think I've ever seen him. His eyes follow the puck's every move, leaping meticulously from player to player. He looks so proud of Gage, admiration emanating off his little body like a second skin.

Hadley nudges my leg with the toe of her boot. "You dirty little slut. I love that for you. Ugh! Going off and having crazy, passionate sex with a hockey star."

She sniffles and pretends to wipe an invisible tear from her eye. "They grow up so fast."

The arena comes alive with a collective cheer that rumbles underfoot, and judging by Teague's springy celebration, Gage must've blocked another potential goal. The atmosphere, the people, the fanfare—it's such a step up from Teague's minor league games. Hell, the Reapers have a full theme song and a giant Grim Reaper cutout that descends from the ceiling at the start of every game. *And* they have a Jumbotron for kiss cams and capturing celebrity lookalikes.

I'm dating an NHL player. I'm dating a *famous* NHL player. Not just that, but Gage worships me. I'm pretty sure he'd lay his body on the ground so I could walk over a puddle and not get my shoes dirty. I don't know if my life will ever feel real again. Everything's perfect.

I've finally allowed myself to be happy with the man of my dreams, I've come to accept my mother's new living situation, Teague's admitted that the teasing from his teammates has stopped, and I only *sometimes* get existential crises during my three a.m. showers. The studio isn't doing too bad either. With Gage helping finance my mother's stay at the nursing home, extra money from her would-be medication cost is going toward bills and groceries. And with Teague and me not scraping by every week, I'll be able to give him a normal childhood.

Of course, if it was up to Gage, he'd take care of everything with his yearly eight-figure salary. He still supports me teaching, but he doesn't want it to be a source of financial stress. God, he's just...*perfect*.

But as perfect as things may seem, life can't always be stuck on this continuous, upward path. Eventually, the bad weighs it down again, and life has to come back to the middle. A regression to the mean.

And instead of a moderate period following my high one, a low one comes in place of it instead, in the form of a repeated trauma that I'd never wanted to live through ever again.

Out of my peripheral, an offensive player crashes into a defensive player at an abnormal speed, creating a buildup of bodies that tumble across the ice, heading straight for the Reapers' goal. Heading straight for *Gage*.

Everything happens so fast. They're halfway across the ice, and then there's a pile of bodies crushed against the boards. The entire crowd goes silent—nothing but the onrush of frantic shouts from refs in the echo chamber of the stadium. I choke on the breath refusing to budge from my throat. My heart...my heart just stops. It doesn't drop to my stomach or skip a beat. It stops entirely, and time freezes around me like the rest of the world is moving in slow-motion while I'm stuck helplessly in the middle. I can't feel any part of my body. Everything is numb, cold, a flame of life that's been stubbed out like the butt of a cigarette.

I don't know how long I stand there, but he's not moving. Medics start to roll out with stretchers in tow, and the shrill wail of an ambulance pierces my eardrums, which is the only noise to rip me from my paralyzing bubble. The rest of his teammates stay stranded out on the ice, waist-deep in shared confusion and concern.

It's like I'm standing in the middle of the rink with a single spotlight shining down on me, blacking out the empty rows and the bloodstained corners of prior mistakes. Everything is crumbling around me, my world falling to chunks of debris and pulverized masses of a place I used to call home, leaving broken terrain that's impassable when I know Gage is on the other side counting on me to reach him. But I can't. *I can't reach him.*

I shove through the panicked mob of people, ignoring the shrieks of my name by a little, high-pitched voice, bruising myself on the brunt of bodies that all flood toward the nearest exit. Tears ribbon down my face, blurring my vision in ink blots, and the moment my heart restarts with a barely there hum, it cries out to be reunited with him. Cries out above the screeching sirens and the traumatized screams and the culmination of pain swallowing every inch of my body in white-hot flashes of fire.

His lifeless figure is getting farther away from me. Pleas fire off my tongue in quick succession, begging the world to stop for a single fucking second, begging my legs to move faster when they're fighting against the hold of quicksand.

I let the tears impair my vision, I let the ache in my thighs burgeon, I let the breath flee from my lungs. I rub every nerve ending raw because being *forced* to feel is better than being catatonic. I don't know how, but I traverse the eighty-foot-long rink without stumbling or slowing one bit. My hands clamp down on the side of his stretcher, my waterlogged eyes fixed on the beaten and battered state of his body where padding wasn't enough to protect him. Where *I* wasn't enough to protect him.

"Please don't leave me," I cry, holding his gloved hand, letting my body be dragged out of the arena and to the double doors of the ambulance. My fingers don't slip—they don't leave him, even if he can't feel me here.

Hiccups and sobs are slurred beyond comprehension, tear-ravaged eyes burning despite the water that steadily flows down my wind-bitten cheeks. "Please don't go, Gage. I can't do this without you. I need you."

You promised you wouldn't leave me.

34

AN ODE TO MY BROKEN HEART
CALISTA

I'm back in the one place I never thought I'd be again—among the barely living and the graves where once-beating hearts now rest in an eternal sleep. Fluorescents and disinfectants greet me with welcoming arms, the buffering beep of heart rates on expensive machines tailing me down bland, alabaster halls that form unsolvable labyrinths. Snapshots of the game flip through my mind like jaundiced camera film in a projector, and I can still hear Teague's screams ringing in my ears, steeped in an unbridled fear that no child should ever have to experience.

I haven't left Gage's side. It's only been a day, but he hasn't woken up yet. The doctor deduced that he must've suffered major head trauma when he was thrown up against the boards, and that while the damage isn't lasting, it might take him a while to come to. There's a contusion on his head that's swelling, underscored by a plum-colored bruise, but thankfully no bleeding occurred from the injury.

I know he's going to be okay. I know he's going to wake up. But there's a small part of me that's hyper focused on the what-ifs of this scenario. What if he doesn't wake up? What if the injury worsens? I can't...I won't be able to deal with that alternative reality. I need Gage to be okay. *I need him to come back to me.*

His heartbeat is steady, but instead of trumpeting out a life anthem, it sounds more like a funeral ballad. His chest rises and falls rather peacefully, and I rub my thumb over the back of his knuckles, repeating the fruitless ministration as if my touch will somehow bring him back to consciousness. His hand is cold, as pale as the sheets of frost that've started to settle on trimmed lawns in the early morning. The sun's already begun to rise, bleeding warm tones of yellow over the sky like the running yolk from a split poached egg.

Every time my bloodshot eyes trace over his rigid form, it feels like my heart begins to hemorrhage, guilty nerves tossing my stomach into a permanent upset. The tears have receded for the time being, but my cheeks are still overwiped, and my ichor-mottled bottom lip is still overbitten.

Gage is my everything. He's my whole world. If I lost him... I'd lose myself too. If he wasn't on this planet anymore, I'd follow him wherever he went, even if that meant leaving behind the people I care about most. I can't do this without him. I can't breathe without him. I know we only just made things official, but I can't imagine my future without him. He was the one person to give my life purpose again after I found myself stuck in a tireless, repetitive cycle. He saved me from myself—from my fears, from my self-doubt, from my self-hatred. He saved me, and there's nothing I'll ever be able to do to repay him. What he's given me is priceless. What he's given me is a second chance at life. What he's given me is a first chance at love.

I don't know if you know this, but humans are a lot like elephants. And Gage is my elephant. They mourn just like we do, and when their partner dies, their grief can become so detrimental that it results in their death as well. They stop eating and drinking. They even stay close to the deceased and sometimes carry their bodies around as if they're still alive.

Gage is a part of me. He's the best part of me. I've always lived my life with a heart half full—a heart so consumed by responsibilities that it never sought love anywhere else. I was so consumed with caring for others that I'd given up on caring for myself. Gage cares for me on the days when I can't, and that's something that only happens when you've found your soulmate.

Instead of him being the anchor mooring me to the dock, now *I'm* the one stretching *myself* to keep him from drifting off to sea. I'm the one who has to be his rock—who has to be strong for the both of us. And I'll never let go. Not even in death.

"I'm here, Gage," I whisper, squeezing his palm in the idiotic belief that he'll return the gesture. "I'm not leaving until you wake up."

There's a knock at the door that curtails the start of another crying session, and I'm not sure who I was expecting, but all of Gage's teammates are standing in the doorway, holding various get-well gifts for him. Flowers, overpriced chocolates, cards, and even a teddy bear bring a pop of color to this desolate prison.

I don't even know whether I should be glad they're here or not. I feel terrible. I feel like I'm the one to blame, and maybe they feel the same way too. An irrational part of me tells me that this accident wouldn't have happened if his hip had been ready. And yeah, both his physical therapist and team doctor cleared him to get back on the ice, but I could've spoken up and prevented him from playing.

I stand up hesitantly, watching as Fulton strides over to me, and instead of voicing his disappointment, he immediately wraps me in a hug. It's not so strong to knock me off balance, but it's just firm enough to provide me with the support I hadn't realized I needed.

"Cali, we came as soon as we could," Fulton says when we pull apart, a consolatory grimace darkening his naturally peppy demeanor.

The rest of the guys all share the same tortured expressions as they slowly filter into the room, loading their gifts onto the table beside Gage's bed.

So many words are thrust upon my tongue, waiting to charge their way out of my mouth once I open it, but I begin to feel the fear creep back—a new species of fear that's a thousand times stronger than what I've dealt with in the past, one that feasts on the guilt concentrated in my chest. "I'm so sorry this happened," I blurt out. "I should've known he wasn't ready. I should've paid closer attention to his hip. He wouldn't be in this situation if I'd—"

Suddenly, Kit's hulking frame enters my personal bubble, and he brings my face smack-dab into the middle of his chest, where my apology gets muffled beneath his heaping muscle mass and a layer of cotton.

"This wasn't on you, Cali. I was watching Gage the entire time. What happened was a freak accident. There's not a single person at fault," Kit gruffs.

I can't really see anything past Kit's body, but I hear Hayes speak up from somewhere to my right.

"Stuff like this happens all the time out there on the ice. It comes with the territory. I'm pretty sure I've been concussed more times than anyone else on the team, and I've recovered every single time."

When I break away for air, I suck in gasps like a guppy out of water, feeling those goddamn tears straddle my waterline, teasing me with every intention to pave a pathway down my spotty foundation. "I know he'll be okay. This is just...this is so scary."

Hayes takes one of the chairs in the room as Casen takes the other, Bristol leans against the doorway, Kit gives me some space, and Fulton lingers by Gage's bedside.

"Gage is tough. He's been in this position before, and he was conscious within the hour. They just have him on drugs that sedate him," Kit reassures me. "He's resilient. He'll spring back just like he always has. Dude's like one of those STDs that keeps coming back even though you've taken every precaution there is."

Everyone in the room gives a half-hearted chuckle, and I unexpectedly erupt into laughter for the first time since the incident. It feels so good to laugh. It feels so good to feel something other than complete hopelessness.

Bristol crosses his arms over his chest. "The first time Gage went to dinner with you, you should've seen what a mess he was when he came home. I'd never seen him so stressed before."

"Yeah. He had this crazed look in his eyes and couldn't stop blushing when we confronted him about everything," Casen inputs. "He was fully losing his mind, and he barely even knew you."

Surprise tethers me in place. "Really?"

"Really," Fulton chuckles. "Gage has loved you from the very beginning, and Gage doesn't fall in love with anyone. He'll come back to you. You just have to give it some time. But he'd never leave you. Not without a fight."

My heart, for once, is not a floundering set of rhythmless beats. It's still. So petrified by the unbelievable amount of love in the room that it doesn't even know how to function. The fear that once waded through my bloodstream is nowhere to be found, having been deluged with warmth and hope.

"Thank you, guys. Thank you for saying all those things even though you didn't have to," I murmur quietly.

Fulton's mouth matures into a beaming smile. "Of course we had to say all those things. We love you, Cali. You make Gage the happiest he's ever been. We should be the ones thanking *you*."

"He wouldn't have been able to play this game if it wasn't for your help," Hayes adds.

"Get used to us," Kit chirps. "You're a part of the family now, and knowing Gage, you'll be a part of the family forever."

Oh, God. I feel like I'm going to cry again, but for a different reason. Before I can make a fool of myself with more blubbers and whines, all the guys dogpile me, bringing me into one gigantic team hug that I disappear into.

You're not alone anymore, Cali. And you never will be again.

IT'S BEEN hours since the guys left, and I've made a permanent home for myself right next to Gage's side. Thankfully, Hadley's been kind enough to watch Teague while I stay with Gage, wanting to be the first person he sees when he wakes up.

I'm beyond thankful that Gage has such supportive teammates that love and believe in him. After my talk with them, I thought long and hard about the role I played in all of this, and I've come to accept that what happened was out of anyone's control.

I feel myself dozing off, opting to use Gage's arm as my impromptu pillow, when a small voice cries my name from the doorway, the patter of tiny feet rising in volume. I stand up, bleary-eyed, feeling arms wrap around me and a nose bury itself in the notch of my neck.

Teague.

I hug my brother back without regulating my strength,

squeezing him so tightly that I'm afraid I'm hurting him, but he never lets go of me. My pulse trips over itself as my heart scampers against the cage of my ribs. I've missed him so much.

When we pull away from each other, I check his face for residual tears, on a mission to erase the pain from the stress lines etched into his features.

"Are you okay?" I ask, tucking a curl of his hair behind his ear.

"I want Gage to be okay," he says, a wet sniffle whistling through his nostrils, the slightest wobble to his chin. His eyes are large, glistening with a splash of moisture, and they look at me like I have all the answers in the world.

"Me too, Squirt. Gage is strong. He'll be okay."

"What if...h-he...d-doesn't...wake u-up?"

Teague's words rot on my tongue, his worry like a body-deteriorating sickness that I want to cut out and burn alive. I swallow down the sand drying my throat, trying my best to keep my emotions in check. When the first tear starts to fall on my brother's red face, I catch it immediately, wiping it on Gage's jersey—which is stained with my own tears.

"He will." It's a truth forged from hope so bright that it defeats the shadows of grief preying on young, undeserving hearts.

Teague's mouth knots into a frown, and this time, I'm not fast enough to stop the river rapids from flowing freely. "I don't want him to go, Cali. I want him to stay here with us," he sobs, balling his fists and banging them against my chest.

I pull my brother back into an embrace, bearing the hits that rattle my breastbone, doing everything in my power to take his pain. I hate seeing him cry. I hate it even more when I can't be the one to fix things. All I can do now is be here for him. All I can do is love him and tell him that everything's going to be okay.

I'm not running into my mother's arms anymore, crying and

screaming and losing it. Now I'm the one who gets all the tears and heart-wrenching howls of pain. I'm the one who gets to keep everyone afloat. Not *has* to but *gets* to. This is my purpose in life—being my brother's protector. I just wished I'd gotten better at it a lot sooner.

"He's my best friend," Teague bawls, blowing snot bubbles against my front.

He's mine too.

"Shh, shh. I know it hurts, Teague. But we have to be strong for Gage. He'd want us to be strong."

"I-I...don't think...I c-can."

I crouch down in front of Teague and rub my hands down his arms. "You can. I know you can. You're the strongest person I know, which is one of the endless reasons why Gage loves you. And when you love a person, you always find your way back to them. Remember that time you got hurt on the ice?" I ask.

Teague nods, trying his best to fight the quiver of his bottom lip.

"Remember how strong you were? How you got back up right away and didn't cry? Gage needs you to be that strong for him."

My brother rams straight into me with another hug, letting me pet his back like my mother used to pet mine when I was upset, and I siphon each negative worry from his body, determined to carry the weight of his crumbling world and reinforce it. A wail of my own almost leaps up my esophagus, but it's smothered when Hadley voices her presence.

She opens her arms up as Teague runs to her and disappears in her oversized sweater. "Come on, Teague. Let's give Cali and Gage some privacy," Hadley coos, tucking him close to her leg.

We'll be outside, she mouths to me before they desert the room, leaving Gage and me alone once again, the future of our relationship hanging heavy in the distilled air.

I grab Gage's hand—as if the five minutes I wasn't holding it has somehow hurt him—and I bring his knuckles to my lips, trying to warm the frozen flesh with a shaky kiss.

I foolishly thought I had cried all the moisture out of my body, but more tears toe the shoreline of my eyes, and the beginning of my words launch from my mouth in a rocky, fumbling start. "Gage, I don't know if you can hear me, but I'm sorry this happened. I'd switch places with you in a heartbeat if I could. Seeing you in pain...it fucking *kills* me. I feel like I'm losing my mind without you here. Like, you're here, but you're not really here. I just need you to come back to me. I need you to make stupid jokes and pay me cheesy compliments and annoy the living hell out of me. I need you to wrap your arms around me when things get hard because it's the only place in this entire world that I feel safe."

I force a breath as my tears splatter the hospital sheets, permeating the thin material in shapeless blobs.

"I need you to kiss me when I get trapped in my head. I just need you, okay? I can't do this without you. I can't do *life* without you. You've shown me what it means to sacrifice for the people you love. You've shown me how to be strong for myself so that I can be strong for others. You've shown me kindness and understanding in times when I was a complete asshole to you. You've waited for me even when I wasn't ready because you never wanted to leave me alone—because you knew how lost I would be without you."

No spike in his heart rate. No twitch of his fingers. No nothing. Just stillness. Just silence.

"I was devastated when my mom got sicker. I'd never been at such a low point in my life. But with you, it's not just devastation. It's something so exceptionally worse that I can't put into words what it does to me. I'd rather be dead than live with this feeling—this grief that never seems to run out, this impending fear of losing the best thing that's ever happened to me. I was so focused on protecting my family that I hadn't even realized *you're* my family now.

"I was so scared to give you all the pieces of me because I've never surrendered myself wholly to anyone before. I used to be full, unbroken, until the world chipped away at me. Nobody in their right mind wants a bunch of broken pieces. But you have every piece of me. You made them into something beautiful, just like you did with the scars on my palms. You never once saw anything wrong with me, and I love you so, so much for it."

I love him. So much that it doesn't seem remotely possible for this amount of love to fit into a human body. I knew it all along, but I was too scared to say it out loud. This whole incident reminded me that tomorrow isn't promised. You need to say the scary things out loud in the unfortunate chance that you may never get to.

I've lost all composure, sobbing and crying like a child while I rest my head over Gage's lethargic heart. It doesn't bring me the same solace as it usually does. It feels like an unspoken goodbye. A goodbye that I'll never be ready to utter for as long as I live.

"Oh, God. And I lied about the tattoo," I weep, printing my face of makeup onto his shirtfront. "I'm a terrible person. It's fake, okay? I didn't think telling you would put you in the hospital. Not that it's, like, a direct result or anything. Or maybe it is. Maybe you were so riled up that you didn't notice the players coming for you, and now your head is traumatized and it's all because I pulled a stupid prank on you—"

"I knew it."

What? Oh my God. Am I hallucinating? Where did that voice come from?

I suck in a large sniffle and peel myself up to locate the source of the sound, certain that it's just my delirium conjuring up Gage's voice, until my gaze lands on the poorly veiled, crooked half-smile painting his lips.

"Gage? Is that...really you?"

He squints open one eye. "I'm not dead, Cali."

"Oh my God." I immediately wedge my arms under his body and embrace him, holding him so close to my chest that his back comes off the hospital bed, and a couple of groans escape him.

"Sorry!" I apologize, setting him back down on the firm mattress.

He winces. "'S okay. Grandpa's just not as springy as he used to be."

"Oh. Ew."

"Glad to see you aren't treating me any differently. Even though I'm hospitalized. And in pain."

"Do you need me to kiss it better?"

His eyes fully open, but then they lower to half-mast, and he gets that devious grin on his face again. "That depends. Where are you kissing me?"

Aaand I'm starting to feel less sorry for him. "Seriously?"

"Just come here, Spitfire," he demands impatiently—which is bold given his state right now.

I lean in, wary of keeping my weight off his body, and marry our lips, tasting him for what feels like the first time. Even shrouded in the pungent scent of chemicals, he still smells like petrichor and pine, and my heart comes alive in technicolor starbursts. His mouth is chapped, his spit is tasteless, and he doesn't lift his hand to cup the back of my neck, but he's warm with renewed life.

He's okay. My person is okay.

Although I want to bask in this kiss forever, I pull away when I feel tears prick the backs of my eyes and the saliva in my mouth proliferate. "Are you okay? Is there anything I can do?"

Gage grunts as he hauls himself to a sitting position, the tube of his IV moving in tandem with the arm he lays over his lap. "You're here, aren't you? That's all I need. That's all I'll ever need," he replies, taking my hand in his to calm the shaking I hadn't realized was occurring. "Plus, I've dealt with head trauma before, and I turned out fine."

"You know, that does explain a lot," I say.

He angles his head. "Explains what?"

"Explains all the weird shit you do. Maybe a piece of your skull chipped off and imbedded itself into your brain matter."

"I happen to think that I'm perfectly normal, thank you very much."

Of course I can count on Gage to make me laugh after practically coming back from the dead. The resonance of a hearty chuckle successfully cannons into the depressing atmosphere, heralding life like the rosy warmth of a new dawn on the horizon.

Gage leans back, his Adam's apple fluttering in the expanse of his throat. "Fuck, I've missed that," he admits.

"Missed what?" I question.

"Missed your laugh. Your smile. *You.*"

Oh.

My fingers clutch his tighter, and the bluish offshoots of his veins begin to fade as color returns to his skin. "I've been here the whole time."

"I know. I heard everything. And I'd get hurt a million times over just to keep hearing it. There was never once a doubt in my mind you didn't feel the same way about me. It just took you longer to realize it, and that's okay. Waiting doesn't seem nearly as long when you're the one I'm waiting for."

He heard everything. Every secret that I released from the vault. Every soft and squishy feeling that I've hidden behind saccharine sarcasm.

"Thank you." I cry, this time not bothering to wipe the unbidden emotion spilling down my cheeks. "Thank you for coming back to me."

Gage lifts his unoccupied hand to my face, swabbing the

first of many tears while he flashes me eyeteeth. "You'll have to try a lot harder than that to get rid of me."

I know it's a joke, and that good-natured tone of his confirms it, but I can't stop myself from falling into every sob-garbled noise under the sun, smearing the splotches of makeup I left on his shirt with salt-tinged moisture.

I squash my nose over his heart, needing the reminder that this isn't some false reality I've made up in my head, and he holds me as my whole body rocks painfully. I unload every ounce of strength I've clung to, letting his arms heal me in the way they've always been made to do. I know he should be the one coming to me for comfort, but I can't pretend to act like this whole ordeal hasn't wrecked me completely.

"Shh, Calista. It's okay. I'm right here."

"You've ruined me, Gage," I snivel, my heart concaving along with the fortress that's kept me protected this entire time. My reinforced defenses are finally cracking to expose me to the harsh elements. I give in to the vulnerability, no longer afraid of getting hurt because I now know what the worst pain in the world feels like. "You ruined me the moment I met you."

Gage cauterizes my bleeding wounds with his love, scars them over with his heated touch. "You ruined me first, Spitfire. All I'm doing is returning the favor," he whispers.

Just like the first time we met, eyes from two different worlds merge into one, mixing blue and green to create an aurora borealis of color unachieved even by nature itself. But this time, there's no hatred or calculated plan for revenge in them.

Gage never breaks eye contact for a second. "Loving you fucking hurts. It hurts in the best way. Every time I look at you, it feels like my heart's going to burst out of my chest. And fuck, I'd die without a single complaint if it meant that the last thing I ever saw was you."

When I pitch forward to kiss him again, I don't even think about pulling away. "How do you imagine seeing me?"

He smirks against my mouth. "Preferably with my head between your legs. Or riding my face. I'm not picky."

"You know, for a *big, strong* hockey player, I can't wait to tell your teammates how bad you've got it for me."

"Go ahead, baby. They already know I'm pussy-whipped. Might as well throw in how I love to whimper for you too."

35

THERE'S NO PLACE LIKE HOME
GAGE

A few days later and everything's still a blur. After my doctor performed some CT scans on my brain to make sure there wasn't any internal bleeding, I had a very peaceful recovery period of low mental concentration. He told me that as long as I got some rest and monitored my symptoms, I'd be fine to go home.

And after I got wheeled off the ice, the Reapers secured another win under their belt. So thankfully, it was all worth it. Kind of. Okay, it was bad, but it could've been a lot worse. The headaches have ebbed for the time being, which is good news for me because I wasn't really a fan of the whole alien life pulsating shit going on in my whack-ass brain.

The minute I got kebabbed by those players, all I could think about was Cali. Granted, I wasn't allotted a lot of time to think much of anything before my life flashed before my eyes, but still. I followed her voice back to the present—a sliver of light at the end of a tunnel, guiding me to safety past uneven terrain and rain-filled potholes.

There's no way in hell I'd ever leave her or Teague. Not without a fight. And to know that she stayed by my side the entire time...I'm going to hold that over her head for the rest of her life.

Calista Cadwell *loooves* me. She also likes my cheesy compliments. And my jokes. And my kisses. Getting head trauma was so worth it to hear her admit that.

She opens the passenger door for me and helps me out, making sure to handle me with care as we make our way to the house's entrance. Now that winter's well on its way, the brown of the surrounding foliage has been overtaken by the first vestiges of snowfall, dusting powdered sugar over barren lands.

I overestimate one of the steps on the porch and knock into a pillar, feeling pain niggle at my shoulder. "I'm really gonna miss that hospital morphine," I groan.

Cali grimaces. "Sorry. Should've told you there was a step there. Though I didn't think I'd need to since you've lived here for a few years."

I successfully climb the last step standing between me and my glorious, non-chemical-smelling bed. "You're really mean, you know that?" I grumble.

She makes a face. "I'm not mean; you're just dumb."

The silence ironically speaks for itself.

"Ohhh. I hear it now," she says.

"As my primary caretaker now, you have to be nice to me. That includes no name calling or insults to my intelligence."

"How can I insult something you don't have?"

A roguish grin quirks up the corners of my lips. "Every time you make a hurtful comment about me, I'll be keeping track of how many orgasms you owe me."

Cali snorts, rolling her eyes in the way that makes my dick pitch a family-sized tent in my pants. "Please. You're seriously going to keep track of how much head I'm *indebted* to give you?"

I trace my finger along the coast of her jawline, ending my expedition at her bottom lip, where I gently part it from the top with a *flap*. She stares at me the entire time, lust torching her eyes like a gasoline-fed fire.

"No, Spitfire. I'm keeping track of how many orgasms *I'm* going to give *you*," I clarify. "As of right now, we're at two."

Her mouth stays open in shock, goading a shiver to bullet down her spine, and a blush now backdrops those cinnamon freckles of hers. "Care to make it three?" she purrs, threading her arms behind my neck.

I pull her flush against my chest with more strength than I've probably used in the last few days. My hands skate down the curve of her spine, saying a quick hello to her adorable dimples before making their way over her perfect, perky ass and squeezing. "I can make it however many my girl wants."

She arches the slightest bit into my palms. "I was hoping you'd say that."

Cali takes one of my hands and redirects it to the small of her back, slipping it under her shirt and over what feels like a scar on raised skin. It takes me a second to realize what it is, and I run the pad of my finger over an infinity-like symbol.

"Did you...?"

She nods before turning her back toward me and showing me the very *permanent* tattoo she's gotten in place of Fulton's number. A small eight is inked into her skin, and I'm both relieved and overjoyed that I won't have to kill my best friend or live the rest of my life as my future wife's torture victim.

And yes, I said future wife. Because that's what Cali is. Maybe five years out or so—for her sake rather than mine since I could make this decision right now—I'm going to rent out the rink and propose to her. She's the only person in this world who I want to give my forever to...well, aside from the adorable child she's eventually going to pop out. I'm hoping they'll have her fiery head of hair. And maybe her ocean-blue eyes. And maybe her constellation of freckles. And I mean I wouldn't be opposed if we had a few more kids, because that just means there'll be more tiny versions of her for me to love.

Oh, God. Am I crying again? I feel like I'm crying. Come on, man! Get it together.

She turns back around to face me, reclaiming her previous position with her fingers on my nape and my fingers flirting with the possibility of a cheeky display.

"I think your *allergies* are acting up again," she comments, a humorous half-smirk rounding her lips.

"It's actually just eyeball sweat this time," I joke, feeling tar coagulate in my throat the longer she graces me with those big, blue beauties of hers.

Cali laughs, and the dulcet sound is a solar flare in my veins, shaking the foundation of my bones and hurtling warmth toward the center of my heart. And then, this foreign shyness alters the firm set of her shoulders.

"So you like it then?" she asks in a small voice.

Do I like it? DO I LIKE IT?

"Cali, I fucking love it," I respond, picking her up in my arms and swinging her around, pulling more of those heavenly giggles from her. She clings to me like she'll go flying if she doesn't, nose pressed against the slope of my neck, hands grabbing fistfuls of my shirt. The motion should hurt the bruised state of my body, but it doesn't. Nothing hurts when Cali's with me.

When I set her back down, curls of her hair straggle around her slightly pink face, and there's a permanent smile bringing out the divots of her dimples. She looks breathtaking in the low light of the afternoon, visible puffs of breath twisting from her mouth in smoke-like tendrils. The tip of her nose is reddening by the second, and I have to get her in the house before she freezes.

"You know you didn't *actually* have to get my number tattooed on you, right?"

"I know. I wanted to."

I test the weight of her words against my tongue and love the taste they leave behind. *She wanted to.* If my heart wasn't already bloated to twice its size from her love, it would probably blow out of my chest.

Cali's eyebrows go skywards, digging little furrows in her forehead. "You're not going to say something like"—she lowers her voice, which I'm assuming is supposed to be a hilariously inaccurate imitation of me—"why would you do that if we might break up one day?"

"First off, I'm flattered you think my voice is that deep. And second off, that's never going to happen."

I can tell her thoughts are going absolutely batshit in her head, so I cut through that tumultuous sea like the propeller of a boat chopping through waves. "Get out of your head, baby," I coax, brushing the back of my hand over her cheek.

She grabs my hand, the tremor in her fingers matching the one in her voice. "How do you know that?"

"Because I just know these things," I assure her, winking. "When things are meant to be, they always work out. And we're meant to be, Spitfire. There's no doubt in my mind about that."

She opens her mouth, but I shut down her rebuttal with another kiss, swallowing those little buds of self-doubt before they're given the chance to sow their seeds. While I lose myself in the swipe of her tongue and the mintiness of her breath, I fish for my keys and blindly unlock the front door—my movements accelerating the moment Cali's nails pierce the skin on my back and her hips press into my now-awake cock.

When the partition finally clicks open, I'm expecting a dark and uninhabited house, but I'm greeted with the exact opposite when there's a flashbang of light and a synchrony of excited voices.

"Welcome home!" they all shout, causing my stomach to

freefall to my ass and sweat to break out in places people shouldn't sweat.

I scream at a decibel level that only dogs can hear, very *officially* losing my manliness card—though if you ask Cali, she'll tell you I never had it.

I did. I did have it.

I grab the ever-living life out of Cali to shield her from whatever masked intruder's been waiting for us to get home, but once my vision adjusts, the only "intruders" we see are the guys.

There's a large banner hanging from the second-story railing that says, CONGRATULATIONS ON NOT DYING, and balloons occupy the ground, poorly taped streamers sagging from the ceiling. Fulton, as always, misses his mark with a confetti popper, and there's a sad little noise that fires into the ensuing silence.

Once I'm certain my heart won't make the same sputtering sound, I turn to Cali. "Did you know about this?"

A hint of devilry in her eyes. "Maaaybeee."

Fulton drops the cheap cylinder and comes careering into me, nearly knocking me back into the wall as his arms squeeze the last of the breath from my overworked lungs. "I'm so glad you're alive. I thought you were going to die," he cries into my shoulder as I pat his back.

"This has happened like two times before. And I've survived every single time."

"Yeah, but your bones are so brittle now after your hip!" he exclaims way too loudly.

There are some sniggers from the guys, and I stare them down with dead, mirthless eyes, negating their laughter. Dicks. All of them.

"I didn't want to lose my best friend," Fulton whispers, and my brief dance with irritation is replaced with a love so strong that it could topple cities—a love that's been amplified by Cali.

A love that I can now share with the rest of my team. A love that strengthens this family bond even more.

"You're never gonna lose me, Ful."

I feel a tiny set of arms attack my leg, and I look down to find Teague attached to me like Velcro, his cheek squished against my thigh. "I missed you so much, Gage!"

Fulton lets me go so I can pick the little guy up and properly embrace him, my heart pounding out a stampede in my chest that can probably be heard over the residing sniffles. "I missed you too, Little Man."

"You didn't leave us," Teague sobs, the pain in his tone leaden like the weight of a hundred sandbags, and it kills me to think that he's been carrying the burden of all these suppressed emotions on his fragile shoulders.

I'm never going to let him carry that kind of pain ever again. Not like Cali.

"I'd never leave you guys," I coo, rubbing circles and easing the tension between his shoulder blades. "Never."

After Teague snotifies my shirt and refuses to let go for a full five minutes, he eventually peels himself off me so I can hug the rest of the guys, exchanging murmurs of gratitude with them for staying by my side and planning something so unnecessary, yet so heartening at the same time. I missed being home. Yeah, I was only gone for a few days, but mysterious hospital Jello-O and old reruns could never compete with the camaraderie that's been home-grown in these walls for the two years I've been with this team.

After doling out hugs and thank-you's, I bring Cali into the side of my body, loving how she fits perfectly like the last missing piece to my puzzle.

And dare I say it, my *tears* are acting up again. "Thank you, guys. Again. For doing all of this and being here for me."

"There's nowhere else we'd rather be," Hayes says.

"We haven't even gotten to the best part yet!" Kit squeals

—yes, *squeals*—and drags me over to the couch, making me plop my ass down as the rest of the guys join me. There's a sudden burst of light illuminating the vacant space in front of us like that of a high-powered spotlight, and it takes me a second to notice that the coffee table's been moved to the side.

Confusion spumes inside me. "Uh."

A grin lays claim to Kit's face—a grin I don't trust. "Shh. Just watch. You'll love it."

Oh, God. As I walk the thin tightrope stretched precariously over a net of panic, I search for the one person who constantly keeps my blood pressure in check, but she's missing from the couch. Where's my emotional support Cali?

Then, as if I'd willed her into existence, she comes trotting out with two other girls and Aeris, and her little entourage are all wearing *my* jersey.

I'm officially on board with whatever I'm about to witness. They all take their positions with Cali being front and center, and then the starting notes of Gwen Stefani's "Hollaback Girl" start playing.

Oh my God. She's going to dance. For me. I'm finally going to see her perform a full, choreographed dance. I'm finally going to see the last vulnerable side of her that I've tried so hard to catch a glimpse of.

She starts to sway her hips along to the catchy beats—her choreography dulled down to a kid-friendly version for the youngest member of the audience—and I'm having a hard time even focusing on her moves because I'm too in love with watching the pure joy on her expression.

She steps forward and swings her right arm in front of her head, whipping back around to step together before taking a wider stance. Then she pops her hip to the side and throws her head back at the same time, that slender body of hers undulating to the music. When she comes back to standing, the rest of her posse goes low as she extends her leg perfectly straight in some crazy side tilt.

While the other girls perform some floorwork, Cali's owning that fucking stage with every enthusiastic facial expression and clean, hard-hitting movement. Her solo is art in motion. It's everything I could've ever dreamed of. She flicks her hands above her head and twirls around, stopping seamlessly in a half-bent pose before rolling back up again. She flings her hair behind her like a trail of fire, and her next move consists of two bent arms pumping in front of her chest.

The rest of her crew joins her in the sequence and mirrors her, and when they come to a halt, all of them do three consecutive turns on one leg. None of them fall out of sync. They're perfect.

Cali's perfect.

She resumes the upbeat dance by lowering her center of gravity into a half-crouch, keeping her left knee bent and arching her spine to the same side. And when the chorus rises again in the song, the girls give her some space as Cali does a crazy cartwheel type thing without using her arms. She flips into the air with her perfectly pointed feet, body vertical to the ground, and my tongue practically lolls out of my mouth like a rolled-out red carpet.

I knew she was an incredible dancer, but holy shit. I can't believe she did all of this for me. She went out of her way to put on this huge production for *me*. Nobody's ever done anything so thoughtful for me before. Then again, nobody's been *Cali*.

Fuck. I grow more in love with her every passing day, which is goddamn impossible because my love for her has exceeded all metaphysical bounds of reality. It's immeasurable. And at this rate, I'll be a goner when that five-year mark comes around. I'll be surprised if I even last five years to wait to propose to her.

If I thought she was beautiful just simply existing, she's

even more beautiful when she dances. There's no sight of the tortured girl I met three months ago. She's not overthinking or trying to contort herself to please everyone's expectations. She's not punishing herself for things out of her control. She's free. And I helped make that possible for her.

I haven't done a lot of things in my twenty-two years of life, but what I have done is shown the best person on this fucking planet how incredible she is. And that's an accomplishment greater than a Stanley Cup.

When Cali ends the jaw-dropping routine with a pose on the ground, applause explodes from the couch, and I rush to her as fast as my legs will carry me. She rises up to meet me, shock giving leeway to cashmere-soft vulnerability.

"I can't believe this is what you've been hiding from me all this time," I exclaim, feeling my cheeks pinch with a Cheshire grin. "I always knew you were a beautiful dancer, but fuck. That was—I want to watch you dance for the rest of my life."

Maybe it's because she's still catching her breath, but she fails to produce any words, the wideness of her eyes speaking volumes more than the aborted response on her tongue. So I bridge the silence and take her in my arms, dip her, then kiss her with raw abandon. I shatter into unimaginable colors, blends of dusk and dawn sinking their teeth into the juicy flesh of my body. Dark and light play in a chiaroscuro over my eyelids. Unconditional love and undying reverence merge together to fuel the bass-like cadence of my heart.

And when I grant her a second to breathe, she eschews it and pulls me in closer, rejoining our lips as if the sun's never promised to set.

I think I could get used to this.

36

ONE WEEK LATER
CALISTA

"Taking me so well this time, Spitfire. You missed this giant cock, didn't you? Sucking me in real tight with that obedient little pussy of yours," Gage coos, clamping his hands on the curves of my sides, thrusting his cockhead into my cervix and holding me captive with his hypnotizing strokes.

When one of my moans pitches into the air, no longer bayed by the grit of my teeth, a hand comes down on my ass cheek, smacking it so hard that the skin's probably turned red. With each snap of Gage's hips against my ass, he stokes the onslaught of pleasure in my belly.

"God, I love it when you're loud. Letting everyone know I own this cunt."

I bore my nails into the sheets of his bed, clinging to the mattress as my body rocks forward and my cunt squeezes back in retaliation. "And all this talking is making me dry," I growl.

Another slap to my ass—one that ripples my flesh and issues a loud noise into the lust-laced atmosphere.

"You call this dry?" Gage slots himself rather sloppily into my pussy, the evidence of our arousal slicking together in a squelch that confuses my jab at him, and I hate to admit it, but the sound of us together makes me even wetter.

My thighs tremble even as they're supported by the edge of the bed, and my heart rebels in the cavern of my chest with an equally loud echo—one that I'm sure he can hear among the viscous sloshes and the slapping of skin.

Ceasing his onslaught on my ass, he sets his attention on my hair, weaving his fingers through the strands and yanking harshly. "Don't lie to me, Calista. Especially not when I'm inside you."

God, I hate him sometimes. I really do. I hate him with the burning passion of a thousand suns—oh!

Gage speeds up with his punishing ruts, delving somehow deeper, the balls of his piercings bumping inside me. They don't fully set me off, but they're like tickles of cold against my sweltering heat, teasing me with the choreographed roll of his pelvis. My brain's so addled with delirium that my smart-ass reply fuzzes on my tongue, and I'm stripped of the ability to thread together a full sentence.

I can feel his cock dancing just on the peripheral of my G-spot, refraining from giving me that instant gratification, and at the same time whimpers warble out of me, satisfaction rumbles to life in his chest. "Not going to lie to me again, are you?" he taunts.

My tone assumes an acrid bitterness that I unashamedly love the taste of. "Are you going to stop being a pretentious ass?" I hiss, bearing back down on his dick and causing him to falter in his sequence of pumps, his hand sliding out of my hair and slamming against the mattress to steady himself.

I know I should be shaking in my metaphorical boots, seizing up in stomach-turning anticipation for the punishment he's about to give me, but I love playing with him, testing the limits he's willing to stretch and obliterating them completely. That sought-after victory is just outside my reach, and no way in hell am I going to submit that easily.

Gage's breath shudders out of him, but his tongue still curls around a note of irritation. "Wouldn't have to be if you weren't such a brat."

"I'm not a brat. I'm just not some cock-dumb girl drooling over you," I counter, all while getting split on Gage's engorged length, his leisurely pace graduating to a rough set of bottoming thrusts that pinch tears from the corners of my eyes.

It feels so fucking good. The pressure in my lower stomach is almost painful, but it's the kind of painful I chase in increments—and the kind of painful that leaks from my stuffed cunt in milky-white emissions.

He leans forward enough to brush his lips over the shell of my ear, the heft of his ball sack hanging heavy against the backs of my thighs. "I think we both know that's not true."

I wish I could rebound with another witty remark, but my words are on a collision course with the mewls that tumble from my raw throat. My cunt flutters around the plug of his dick, lubricating enough of his shaft to suck him in deeper than he already is, and my walls ripple over the foreign metal of his piercings. They satisfy a recurring itch I can't scratch, and the way Gage weaponizes them makes bliss froth in my belly.

He removes his steeling arm and drags his hand down the arch of my spine, resting his fingers on my healing tattoo, and a shiver folds like an accordion through my body.

"Why'd you get my number here, Spitfire?" he asks, though I know the question is rhetorical.

And considering I'm the putty in his hands for a change, I don't have it in me to engage in flirtatious banter. I need to come. I need it so badly that I'm at the point of praising Gage just so I can feel that liquefying release. *Praising* him. Every time I grow that ego of his, a little part of me dies inside. I'll be eviscerated by the time he pulls out of me.

"Did you really think I'd wear your jersey every time we had sex?"

Gage's cock stirs—whether it's from my bite or the image, I have no clue. "Considering how many times we have sex, that would be ridiculous."

Even though we're having a full-on conversation for God knows why in the middle of fucking, his plows never plateau to a sloppy mess, and that hockey player stamina of his doesn't even jeopardize a single breath. He's all hard muscle against me, the grill of his abs pressing into my ass, and every nerve pathway inside of me is lighting up in preparation for a sensory overload.

"You could've gotten it anywhere else—"

A warning halfway to a growl. "Gage..."

A whimper lurches out of his quivering frame, and he gently forceps the skin of my back between two fingers. "You got it so I would see it every time I took you from behind, didn't you?"

I hydrate my esophagus with a swallow, white-knuckling the covers beneath me, trying to redirect my focus on anything but the hungry kickback of his cock or the shamefully abundant gush now coating his length.

"I got it so I'd turn you on every time I reached for something on the top shelf," I snip.

"Baby, you turn me on by simply fucking breathing," he groans, snaking his other hand to my swaying tit, where he circles the tapered point of my nipple with his thumb before pressing down. Sensitive—as is every part of my body under Gage's Midas touch—I rear my ass back into his torso, blighted by the need to squirm.

He tweaks my bud once more in that torturous seesaw motion, and gooseflesh ignites over my clammy skin, unearthing all kinds of embarrassing noises to grate from my mouth.

"Gage, please..."

He switches his attention from my nipple to the mound of my breast, kneading it with his large hand, rough enough to make my belly contract but soft enough to abstain from leaving a bruise. "You gonna be a good girl now, Cali? You gonna be a good girl and let me fuck your sopping wet cunt? You gonna let me come all over that slutty little tramp stamp?"

I nod weakly, mentally trying to bargain with my hormones to chill the fuck out before I lose the last bit of my dignity, but they toxify the lust-thinned blood running through my system and suck my sensible thoughts into a black hole.

"Use your words," he orders. "Tell me how badly you want to come."

The slightly wet smack of his balls against my legs reverberates in the room as he speeds up, knowing just how much control I surrender when he quickens his pace, and it feels like my innards are mutilating themselves with each pull of his dick. He nicks my G-spot, and the tears now snail down my cheeks.

"I want to come," I whine. "Please. Please let me come. I can't—"

Through my body's convulsions and my water-obscured vision, it's surprising I feel Gage's lips play on the wing of my shoulder blade at all. He peppers tender kisses there, trilling out praise under his breath, and his hand falls away from my tit to offer me respite.

"I know. You're doing so well, though. Taking me without any trouble, using me just like you should. Love everything about you and this God-gifted pussy."

I bow my spine like a cat stretching on a sunlit windowsill, throwing my saffron hair back to waterfall down the small of my back, and I inadvertently pluck a lengthy moan from Gage's vocal cords.

"Christ, Cali. You can't be moving like that," he says through clenched teeth, his hands reclaiming their brutal grip on my hips, the smallest, blink-and-you'll-miss-it blip in his unforgiving pace. "Gonna come in three seconds if you do that."

I milk his hard erection in angry pulses, soaking him to the hilt with my slick, and failing to regulate my breathing through my trembling lips. My whole body is on fire with sweat and tears sullying my face, that tingly sensation in my stomach radiating outwards. "Then stop fucking me like that," I hiss.

I can practically *hear* him grinning.

"Fucking"—thrust—"you"—thrust—"like"—thrust—"this?"

I'm going to kill him. Right after I come. Or maybe I'll kill him with my pussy in a two-birds-one-stone situation. A scream nearly wrenches itself from my throat, and pressure is building in everything south, causing my legs to shake and my grip on the bed to slip. It's almost too much. I almost need a breather, but I'm so close.

"I'm going to—oh, God. I don't know how much longer—" I'm not sure if what I said even made any sense. My underdeveloped thoughts are a bunch of fine-point needles in my pin cushion head, and my impending orgasm—the one he's been drawing out for a good thirty minutes—begins to bubble up from behind my navel. With the position he has me in, it would be a miracle for me to get my cum solely on his sheets.

That bullying motion of his cock ratchets in severity, and now we're shaking the bed's headboard against the wall every time he sends me forward. Dear God, I'm pretty sure all his teammates are still downstairs. Actually, it doesn't matter where they are in the house. These walls are as thin as wafers.

"Since I'm feeling *so* generous today, I'll let you come now," he drawls with all the arrogance in the world, and I'm so glad I can't see his smug smirk.

He's luring me to the edge, sweet-talking me into blindly falling off it, and I'm following him like a pea-brained lemming. "Fuck..."

That ending insult is supposed to end with "you," but I never get it out.

"Come, Calista. Don't hold back. Squirt all over my dick until we're both fucking drenched."

A protest crosses my tongue, albeit a weak one. My eyes momentarily dip down toward the floor, where I curse the carpet that's ironically made this whole session very comfortable for my feet. "Your...carpet..."

"It's a carpet," Gage bites back. "Make a mess everywhere."

I'd prefer to have a relatively easy cleanup, so when I go to debate with him, all he does is growl at me like some barbaric caveman and slip his hand underneath my torso, hovering his fingers right over my lower abdomen.

"Ga—"

"Make. A. Mess. Everywhere."

And then, upon the command of his fingers, he presses down on my stomach, persuading everything to rocket out of me in a geyser—one that still manages to splash onto the carpet even with the obstruction of his cock. I cry out through my orgasm, feeling all that accumulation knock down a dam and flow out of me, a jet of arousal branching off from another one and trickling down the backs of my legs.

Gage groans the loudest he has yet, rumbling the entire room, and those consistent strokes start to turn sloppy. "Fuck. Can I soak that gorgeous back, Spitfire?" His words are wrestled into one long string that barely sounds human, and I give him a matching muffle that poorly imitates a yes.

I feel him slip out of me, feel him swoop my hair to the side, hear the smack of his palm on the root of his dick, then feel him shower my back in an abundance of cum, where warmth permeates along the length of my spine. The splattering of his arousal marries with the syncing of our labored pants, and I wait to move until he gets everything out of him, my appetite slowly becoming more satiated as I step out of my post-orgasm haze.

I never forgot how incredible our sex was the first time, but now it's just dawned on me that I have access to his dick for the —I'm assuming—rest of my life. And Gage Arlington, you may be giant pain in my ass, but that monster cock of yours is heaven-sent.

"Are you okay?" he breathes, one hand stabilized on my hip and the other holding my hair out of the splash zone. His tone is shades softer, so soft in fact that his concern is as clear as day.

"I'm okay. Are you okay?"

Gage swipes his fingers over the small of my back, right over my tattoo, sponging up the thin glaze on his pads. "Fucking fantastic," he replies.

My heart pretty much explodes every time Gage gives me praise, and this time's no different. If I could move without getting cum everywhere, then I'd maul him in kisses.

He gently rests my sex-tousled locks over my shoulder before planting one of his post-sex kisses on me. "Let me clean you up," he says.

He comes back with a towel right away and begins to clean my back, all while dishing out that praise I chase like a fiend, and I wouldn't be surprised if he had a dopey, lovestruck smile smacked right on his face.

"So I'm guessing there'll be an increase in doggy for, like, now until ever?" I joke.

"Of course not. I'm here to please you, remember? You're the one who calls the shots."

"I am?" I mean, I am. But I didn't think he'd ever admit it.

Gage tends to my spine, being extra gentle with me like he

always is during aftercare. "Duh. You wear the pants in this relationship."

I make a little noise of pride and bob my head in confirmation. "I do wear the pants in this relationship."

I still can't see what Gage is doing, but I feel his body displace some of the air around me, and his lips are by my ear as the towel is rerouted to my upper back. "And if I'm lucky, you won't be wearing any at all," he whispers right before he grabs me and flips me onto my back, making me squeal and squirm.

He's leaning over me with a twinkle of adoration in his eyes, and just as I suspected—that dopey, lovestruck smile is stretching his mouth so wide that he's all gums and teeth. But he's not staring at me in hopes that we go for round two. He's staring at me just to stare at me, refamiliarizing his gaze with every stripped inch of my body, keeping record of this memory so he can watch it, rewind it, and repeat it for who knows how long.

I never thought love was real. Or, I did, but I never thought it was for me. I'd come to believe that I'd be one of those rare people who never experienced it, and who was destined to be alone for the rest of their life. But Gage—this stupid, bigmouthed hockey player—barged his way into my life, and now love's the *only* thing I'll ever know. He's given me enough love to last me a lifetime.

"Gage, I love you," I tell him before the tears start to repopulate on my waterline.

"I love you so fucking much, Cali. More than you'll ever know."

It's never just a "you too" out of convenience with Gage. It's never anything less than him hand-wrapping and gifting me the stars, the sun, and the moon. He didn't take my broken pieces and cover up the cracks to magically fix me. He saw them, glued them back together, then let the light shine through those incredible fissures.

He turned scars into stars.

His lips are over mine in the blink of an eye, tasting and feeling like *home*. And when he pulls back just slightly, only allowing space to whisper to me, I know I'm going to crash right back into him.

"And I can't wait to spend the rest of my life with you."

KEEP IN TOUCH

If you'd like to stay in contact for updates on new releases, or just to talk, look down below! Subscribe to my newsletter for more details regarding the Reapers series! ♡

Instagram: @celestebriarsauthor
TikTok: @celestebriarsauthor
Website: http://celestebriars.com/

Keep reading for a sneak peek of *The Flip Side of Fate (Reapers #4)*, Bristol and Lila's story! Stay tuned for the release date! ♡

THE FLIP SIDE OF FATE

1

EX-FLAME COMING IN HOT
LILA

"I can't believe this is really happening," I exclaim, pacing back and forth in front of Kitty's Catwalk, the modeling studio that currently holds the success of my career in the palm of its flawless, manicured hand.

The *clop* of my heels ricochets against the sidewalk, and the barely there coverage of my dress fails to stave off the late winter afternoon chill. Though the constant pacing of my legs and the anxious heat circulating through my body seems to keep me from freezing into a well-dressed popsicle.

Aeris, my best friend, squeals through the staticky receiver of my phone, and I can practically picture her jumping up and down. "Li, I'm so happy for you. You've been working so hard for this moment. I don't know anyone more deserving of this big break than you."

And suddenly, the spine-crushing weight of this meeting settles deep in my bones, kicking my nerves into high-gear and churning my stomach like a rather violent rinse cycle. "Oh, God. What if I blow it? What if they realize there's a better model suited for this campaign?"

Kitty's Catwalk is known for turning girl-next-door types into world-famous models on the front covers of *Vogue* and *Sports Illustrated*. They're known for creating overnight sensations and signing girls who go on to rake in an astounding eight-figure salary each year. Every model they've ever signed has climbed the social ladder and gone on to star in projects beyond their modeling contract—whether it's a supporting role in a blockbuster hit or becoming a self-made billionaire with an empire of clothing and makeup products. These are the kinds of A-list celebrities who get invited to red carpet events, who get swarmed by paparazzi if they simply make a grocery run, who start yearlong trends, and who cause mass hysteria on every social media site because of their tumultuous dating history.

I've worked my ass off to get here today. For the past five years, I've been modeling for swimsuit ads, and I've made the occasional appearance on the little-known catwalk. This could be the start of the rest of my life. And I wouldn't have gotten this opportunity if it wasn't for the massive spike in engagement I've gotten on Instagram.

Since modeling was hardly paying the bills, I decided to take a stab at influencing, pretty much expecting next to nothing on the fame side. It's hard to grow a following—and even harder to maintain interest long enough to be socially relevant. But after one of my swimsuit photos went viral, people started discovering my account, and the likes skyrocketed before I could even comprehend what was happening. Being financially comfortable isn't just a future I'm seeking out for myself; it's a future I've wanted to pave for my parents since the minute they loaned me money to pursue my modeling career.

They supported me throughout the devastating ups and downs, through the nasty, unsolicited feedback of the public about the way I'm not pretty enough to be on front covers, through the projected insecurities of guys and girls alike on the state of my body—how I look too skinny in one picture but have a belly in the next. They never once told me to stop chasing my dream, and for that, I owe them everything in this world.

"There's *no one* better suited for this job. You're the perfect fit. And if they can't see that, then they're stupid, airhead idiots who wouldn't know talent and beauty if it bit them in the ass," Aeris says, and if it wasn't for the hundred-dollar foundation on my face, I probably would've blinked a few tears from my eyes.

While my feet haven't stopped trying to dig a trench in the concrete, my heart's no longer trying to slam itself against the bracket of my ribs. I suck in a breath long enough to stilt the frenetic hammering of my pulse, and for the first time in the past five minutes, my heels come to a clacking halt.

"It just...everything has to go perfect, Aer-Bear. This is my one chance. If I don't land this gig, I'm back to cursing the Instagram algorithm for shadow banning my posts."

Sure, I've gone through endless casting calls before, but the twin, glass doors beckoning me to the equivalent of hell have never looked quite as foreboding as they do now. Either I'll get burned alive in there, or I'll claw my way out of that death pit with my champagne-pink acrylics.

This is the last step in the audition process for me. One meeting stands between me and never having to go back to a normal life ever again. Kitty's Catwalk reached out to me months before for an initial audition, and they liked me so much that I'm one of the few finalists out of thousands of girls who auditioned. It's surreal. I never thought I'd get this far.

Aeris' tone melts into a softer inflection, one that overflows with admiration and lights up my insides in a ray of golden hues. "It will go perfect. You've got this, Li. I believe in you. I'm proud of you. You just have to push the nerves aside for an hour and let fate do the rest for you."

There's that cursed *F*-word. I think I start to see red every time someone mentions it, which is surprisingly a lot.

A lot of people talk about fate, but they dress it up in unbelievable soul ties and Christmas miracles that simply don't exist. I get the appeal, I do. Fate gives people hope, but is it really worth it when that hope is about as fake as a knockoff Louis Vuitton bag?

Fate doesn't exist. Just like soulmates don't exist. Nothing happens because the world deems you lucky enough or the stars align or whatever the hell psychics are saying nowadays. If you want something to happen, you have to make it happen.

"Right. You're right," I ramble, cocking my neck and holding my phone against my ear with my shoulder while I iron out the creases in my skin-tight dress. "I've just got to play it cool. I've got this. I've done this a hundred times before."

"See! Atta girl. And you *have* to call me the minute you hear back from them, okay? I'm thinking we do a girls' night with some champagne and a charcuterie board to celebrate."

A swallow glugs down my throat, and nausea surges right up to my tongue before receding back into the tight knot of my belly. "I promise I'll call you. My call time is now. Oh, God. Okay. I'm going in."

Either the connection's starting to break up, or Aeris is sniffling quietly. "I love you."

"I love you too," I tell her, ending the call and shoving my phone into the purse dangling from my arm. I don't have time to do some meditative breathing or psych myself up. My six-inch red bottoms carry me past the threshold and into the endless hallway that precedes the large, empty, whitewashed room that I know is waiting for me.

The studio is silent. I can't hear anything aside from the staccato rhythm of my heels against the cement floor. I can't feel anything aside from the increasingly urgent need to puke up the Caesar salad I had for lunch. When I get to boardroom 102, my clammy palm nudges the freezing-cold handle, and I open the reinforced door to find a barren landscape of plain backdrops and high-powered fluorescent lights.

A row of casting directors has been set up toward the front of the room, ranging from friendly-looking faces to stony, unimpressed expressions igniting over stress-induced wrinkles. Half-empty water bottles scatter the cloth tabletop, a daunting, inch-thick stack of notes inhabits the lead director's space, and laminated headshots lay strewn about like windblown leaves.

I slowly make my way to the center of the room, hyperaware of instructing my legs to walk straight without twisting an ankle and embarrassing myself in front of my possible future employers.

"Ms. Perkins, so lovely of you to meet us," the lead director, Rebecca, greets, lowering her diamond-encrusted glasses before poring over my file.

"Thank you for making the time to meet with me," I reply, half-surprised that I didn't stumble over my words.

Luxury emanates from Rebecca's slender frame, coupled with the obvious fine taste of the black, sculpted blazer hugging her shoulders. Her bob of hair is slicked back to utter perfection with no tress out of place, and even though the gauntness of her cheekbones alludes to her being older, her makeup makes her look in her late twenties. A cherry tint fades over defined lips, thick brushstrokes of mascara line feathery lashes, and full-coverage foundation conceals every blemish on her otherwise textured skin.

"As you know, we've been looking at you to be the face of the newest Menoulé fragrance. You're exactly the kind of model needed to sell this. You're hot, you've got a fresh look, and you've got an astronomical social media following. Honestly, this job is yours to lose," Rebecca says, flicking her eyes up to me in a nearly knee-buckling look. Dark pools of obsidian sear a hole right into my own eyes, and the air-conditioning does nothing to combat the flush of my skin or the film of sweat over it.

It's mine to lose. All I have to do is convince them I'm the right choice. But I can't seem desperate. I have to come off confident, but not arrogant. Shit. If I say the wrong thing, I can probably kiss this opportunity goodbye.

I straighten my spine as a smile gradually crawls across my lips. "I assure you, I'm the right person for this job."

Rebecca mirrors my smile with one of her own, clasping her long, elegant fingers together on the table in front of her. "That's what we like to hear. However, before we make our final decision, Ms. Perkins, we need one more thing from you."

Anything! I scream internally, trying to quell the desperation slowly overtaking my features. I can taste this victory. It's just within reach. I'm so close, and there truly isn't anything I wouldn't do. Do they want me to fight the other contending models to the death in a *Hunger Games*-style arena? I'll do it. Oh, I'll so do it.

Thankfully, my sensibility catches up to me before I blurt out the insistence that's, well, *insistent* about airing out the fame-hungry demon inside me and the one ashwagandha gummy I'm still running on.

"Of course. I'm up for anything," I assert confidently.

One of the casting directors on the more unamused side of things scoffs under his breath, but Rebecca remains poised and professional, keeping a disturbing amount of eye contact with me. "As you know, you'll be starring with another model for the perfume ad and on the subsequent magazine covers, yes?"

Another model. Right. Totally normal expectation.

"I am aware, yes."

"We want to do a chemistry read with you and the male

model. As soon as possible so we can go ahead with shooting," she explains.

I've done plenty of chemistry reads in the past with costars. And I don't like to toot my own horn, but I think I'm a fairly likeable person. Playing up romance for the public is all show, anyways. It rarely ever turns into something substantial. It's hard to date when you're in this kind of industry—chaotic work schedules and public insight and all. I tried it a few times, and I'm definitely not doing it again. Men make me...*ugh*. They make me want to strangle them most of the time.

Luckily for me, though, sex appeal is something I've never struggled with. This will be a piece of cake. All I have to do is bat my eyelashes, touch his arm a little bit, inflate his ego so he thinks he's the shit, and then *wham, bam, thank you, ma'am*, the job is mine.

"Of course. When would you need me to come back down for the chemistry read?" I ask, scrambling for my phone to set a calendar reminder.

The casting director who's done nothing but stare at me with blistering disdain curls his lips inwards. "We were hoping you'd be up for doing the read right now," he discloses, turning his aquiline nose up and still eyeing me like I'm a piece of half-melted gum stuck to the bottoms of his hideous Ferragamo loafers.

I'm calling him Gangrene Dick in my head. I said that in my head, right? Yeah, I think I did.

Right now? Uh. Right. Okay. Minor setback. I wasn't mentally prepared for a chemistry read today, but I can do this. I think. I just need to focus on what's at stake here—which is only the future of my career as a successful model.

I'm not sure how long I've waited to answer them, but all five pairs of eyes blink expectantly at me. I have to clear my throat because all my saliva's dried up in the time it took for the inner panic to set in. "Of course. I'd be happy to do a read right now."

My voice cracks toward the tail end, and I try to keep a mask of professionalism plastered to my face, but my God, the nerves are starting to gnaw away at my stomach lining.

"Excellent," Rebecca says, pleased. "For the male model, we've decided to go with a rising athlete in the sports world. With the traction he's getting from games, he's the perfect candidate to bridge the gap between high luxury consumers and sports fans. And we think you two would look great together."

An athlete? I've never done a shoot or commercial with an athlete before. But hey, there's a first time for everything. As long as he's not a hockey player. That would be—that would be a fucking disaster.

I've been down that slippery road. Been there, done that. But the worst part of it all? I was really starting to fall for him… until he went and broke up with me out of the blue, insisting that he was "just not ready for a relationship," even though he'd been stringing me along for months.

I set my purse by my feet. "Sounds perfect."

"Great, we're gonna have him come on in, and you two can introduce yourselves."

With bated breath and a concerningly fast heartrate, I lock my gaze on the door, starting to feel more than antsy as I drum my fingers against the sides of my legs. I don't know what to do with my arms. Do I fold them? Do I just let them hang? If I don't move, I'm going to explode.

I'm being ridiculous, right? I have nothing to worry about, so I should just chill. Yeah, Lila. *Chill.* Casting directors can smell fear from a mile away.

A few seconds of silence hang thick in the air before the *snick* of the door echoes throughout the room, and I can hear my future costar laughing about something that someone must've said outside. His body is turned away from me, but from the back, it looks like he has a muscular physique, he's been gifted with some God-given height, and his luscious hair curls down his nape in a way that tells me this man's hair probably won't recede until he's seventy.

But as he turns around—which is some kind of weird slow-motion sequence in my brain—realization hits me with the force of a speeding Mack truck. My first reaction is to freeze. My second reaction is to bubble with molten-hot rage. Because the model they've hired—the one they could've picked from hundreds of teams from any sport in the world—just so happens to be the very person I never wanted to see again.

Bristol Brenner. Captain of the Riverside Reapers hockey team. And the not-ex ex that ripped my heart in half, then shoved it into a shredder, then used those sad, sad pieces of me as cushion for his shoes as he walked out of my life.

A.K.A. the man who's incited so much anger in me that he's become a main talking point between me and my therapist.

So much for fate.

As soon as Bristol sees me, that annoyingly handsome face of his lights up, and his lips crook into a lopsided grin. "Hi, Lils," he drawls with that stupid, honeyed lilt of his—the one sprinkled with just the right amount of gravel to make the lower half of me want to wham into his fucking dick like he's some kind of sex magnet.

He's acting like things are good between us. Lils? Seriously? I can't believe this. I feel like I can't breathe. And it's not because I'm stunned in shock; it's because this douche nozzle is hogging all the oxygen in the room with that big head of his.

Rebecca raises an eyebrow. "Oh, do you two know each other?"

We speak at the same time. Granted, my tone has more of

an *I'll-never-forgive-you-for-as-long-as-I-live-and-I-hope-your-future-wife-cuts-your-dick-off* kick to it.

I shut it down immediately. "No."

"Yes," Bristol says with an ungodly amount of charm. He's got charisma oozing out of every orifice. Hell, I think I saw his eyes sparkle like they do in cartoons. Sparkle! That's not physically possible.

The casting director next to Rebecca—who's less ostentatious with her well-loved cardigan and curly, product-free hair—is oblivious to the mistaken sexual tension she thinks is lingering between the two of us. "This is great news. The chemistry read should go smoothly since you already know each other, and then we can start shooting right away."

Great news. Greater news would be if I found out I had a UTI and chlamydia at the same fucking time.

Bristol closes the distance between us, slings his arm over my shoulder, then pulls me into the side of his hard body. "Lila's exactly the girl you want for this campaign."

The casting directors all turn to one another with murmurs of intrigue, allowing me a split second of time to gun Bristol down with a death stare that could put him six feet under...and then some.

"Ass kisser," I hiss under my breath, physically revolting at how close our bodies are touching. It makes my skin tingle, and not in the good way.

He maintains a perfect, toothy smile, squeezing the cap of my shoulder with his hand. "Didn't bother you when it was your ass I was kissing."

If I'm not—*ahem*—the professional I am, I would slap him right in the face. I can't believe my luck. For the dream job I've been wanting ever since I was a child, I have to work with the only man who's ever broken my heart. Are you kidding me right now? What kind of karma bullshit is this? I'm a good person! I recycle. I help old people cross the street. I donate to those kids in need that cashiers ask you about in the grocery checkout line. I don't deserve this.

The best day of my life has quickly turned into the worst day of my life. Remember when I said I'd do anything for this job?

I meant anything but *this*.

If you haven't read Reapers Book Two yet, be sure to check out Kit and Faye's love story! Keep reading for a sneak peek of *The Worst Kind of Promise (Reapers #2)*. ♡

THE WORST KIND OF PROMISE

1

THE NIGHT OF NO RETURN
FAYE

I look up at the ominous storm clouds as they inch across the desolate sky, draping the night in everlasting darkness. The promise of rain is poised on the horizon, waiting to fall in tandem with my tears. The streetlamp beside me flickers precariously, a large beacon that shines down on me like I'm a moth caught in a filth-covered flame. Cold air spills over my naked arms and legs, raising goose bumps on flesh, and the cement patch I've claimed as home for the time being has made my core temperature drop.

My dress—once a thing of happy memories—has been forever tainted. I can't feel my body. It's like it doesn't belong to me.

See, that already broken part of me has lost another crucial piece tonight, and I don't know if I'll ever get it back.

I look at my phone and check the time. Ten minutes have passed since I called the only person I could trust—the one I knew wouldn't ask questions and who just so happened to be in Pennsylvania visiting a friend.

I called Kit Langley.

Star left defenseman for the NHL's Riverside Reapers. One

of my brother's best friends. The guy I'm secretly in love with—the guy who looks at me like I'm his kid sister.

I'm sitting on the cold, hard gas station curb, wondering why I can't feel the rain penetrate my clothes when a Jeep Wrangler pulls haphazardly into one of the parking spaces, parking diagonally across two white-painted lines. The door swings open with enough force to jar me from my thoughts, and Kit's behemoth frame lumbers out of the vehicle. The minute I meet his dark eyes, I feel mine surge with water, and despite my efforts to keep my emotions at bay, all of my tears flood out of me like a fast-rising tsunami.

Kit races over to me and yanks me up by the arms, pulling me into his large chest. His grip suffocates me, but I don't try to pull away. He's mumbling something into my hair, his hand cradling the back of my head, the rapid thundering of his heart a steady medium in my ears.

When his embrace loosens and he backpedals to look at me, his eyes are alight with worry, a muscle in his jaw flickering. "What happened?" he asks.

I'm not alert enough to form a coherent sentence, but my voice box is vibrating before I have the chance to clamp my lips shut.

"I..." My chest feels tight, like there's a thorn twisting in my sternum. Pair that with the tears wanting to make a quick getaway, and I'm pretty much as useful as a push sign on a pull door.

"Faye, breathe. You're okay. I've got you," Kit says, the softness in his tone wrapping around me like a gentle caress. His hands are still on my arms, and he's craning his neck down to look at me.

A few sobs slip unbidden from my mouth as I inhale shakily, forcing my bloodshot gaze to focus. My vision is peppered with all sorts of ink blots, and my tongue feels like it's swollen to twice its size.

Anger tears across his expression. "Faye, who hurt you?"

"He's...I..."

Come on, Faye. You're safe. You're with Kit. You're not in danger anymore.

But was I ever in danger, or was it my past playing tricks on me?

The minute I stop trembling from nerves, I break down into a gigantic, blubbering mess, clinging to the back of Kit's shirt. He hugs me with the same bone-crushing desperation, absorbing the weight of my pain, wringing every tear from me until I'm nothing but a hollow shell.

He uses his thumb to brush away the moisture glistening on my cheek.

My stomach rolls with nausea. "My date. H-he—I said no..." I choke, the sweat on my brow now covering every bare inch of skin.

Kit's eyes heat with understanding, and every muscle in his upper body ripples with iron-hot rage. The cords in his neck are taut, the veins in his forearms like individual rivers of power snaking up to bulging biceps.

"Did he—"

"No," I whisper. "It wasn't his fault. I sent mixed signals."

I'd gone back to his place, we'd started kissing, and then he'd rolled on top of me, and that long ago night came rushing back with such ferocity that I froze. I couldn't speak, I couldn't move, and he took that as a sign to start undoing my dress. It felt like he was peeling off the tattered walls that protected my soul.

"There's no such thing as mixed signals. Either you're into it or you're not. And it's pretty fucking clear when a chick isn't."

"But I was," I whisper. "Until I wasn't."

Kit reaches out to, I don't know, maybe cup my cheek, and I flinch. He stops and lets out a litany of swears so harsh they feel like sandpaper grating against my skin.

"Where. Is. He."

It's not a question.

I trap the plumpness of my bottom lip between my teeth. "Kit, stop."

A guttural rumble stirs deep within his chest. "I'm going to kill that son of a bitch."

"Kit..." I reach out to lightly touch his arm, and he seems to melt a little, but not much.

With a bracing breath, he rakes his hand through the front of his hair, looking about a second away from hitting whatever poor, helpless object is in the vicinity.

"I'm taking you to file a report."

"No," I say, panicked. The last thing I want to do is explain this whole horrid, confusing story to another person.

"I'm not doing this with you right now, do you understand?" he snaps, gritting his teeth. "You're going to get in the car and go to the police station."

I flinch at the bite in his tone, wrapping my arms around my midsection. "Nothing happened."

"Well, clearly something happened."

Unable to maintain eye contact, I drop my watery gaze to stare at the middle of his chest. "Not tonight."

"Then when?"

"A long time ago."

"Does Hayes know?"

At the idea of telling my brother the truth, panic whirls through me like a Category 5 hurricane, determined to bring me to my knees. "No. And he can't know."

In hindsight, I probably shouldn't have said that, because the lid that Kit's already struggling to keep on his anger has completely blown off into the stratosphere.

"You're calling him." He firmly grabs my wrist, urging me toward his car.

I plant my heels into the ground and pull back, managing to

break free from his steel vise. Granted, it takes all my strength and a good amount of my breath.

"If I go with you, we can't tell Hayes."

"Faye..."

I'm thrown by his gentle protectiveness, the uncharacteristic softness I didn't think Kit was capable of, much less willing to show me. Kit's callous. He isn't compassionate or particularly thoughtful, but it's not because he actively chooses to be an asshole. He just isn't perceptive when it comes to others' emotions. But I've never seen him so distraught before.

"Please, Kit. I can't bring Hayes into this. You know how reckless he can be. If he finds out, he'll lose it."

Humorless laughter dances out of him. "Oh, and you think I'm super calm, cool, and collected right now?"

Even with my skittering pulse, there's enough fire inside of me to light a match. It scalds my insides, wanting to burn every weak part of me, wanting to turn that meek little girl still crying out for her mother into flakes of ash. "I don't need you to play hero! I just need you to be here for me. I called you because..."

His eyebrows jerk together expectantly. "Because?"

"Because I trust you," I finish.

Ever since Hayes joined the Riverside Reapers—a National Hockey League team born and bred in Riverside, California—I've had a crush on Kit. He and my brother have been friends for four years, and even though they don't always see eye to eye, they're always there for each other.

As much as I trust *Kit*, I don't think I could trust him with my *heart*.

Kit doesn't believe in strings, whether they're attached or not.

I know liking an unreformable womanizer is a disaster waiting to happen. Kit doesn't date. He never has. He's almost always pictured with a new girl, and each relationship lasts as long as a hockey game. If I wanted to get my heart broken, I'd let Kit manhandle it all he wants. As much as I wish things could work out between us, I'm smart enough to know that Kit can't give me what I need—he can't give me stability or reassurance or unconditional love.

Like any well-adjusted young woman with a burning hatred for romance, my endless search for love is in part thanks to my absent father. When my mother died of cancer, my father abandoned his parental duties, leaving me and my brother to fend for ourselves. The only thing he was good for was the money he sent us.

I knew Kit was going to be in town this week. And a part of me wanted to reach out, to grab lunch with him, to just *see* him. But I knew better. So I was going to let him coast through Pennsylvania without so much as a text.

Not only would keeping my distance benefit me, but it would probably save Hayes from going into cardiac arrest. Hayes is a...protective...older brother. He's never approved of my previous boyfriends. He never thought they were good enough for me. If he found out I liked one of his best friends, his whole world would implode. He'd probably ship me off to a nunnery overseas. After he castrates Kit.

Kit's lips wrench into a frown, and I wish we were meeting under different circumstances. I wish he was disarming me with that million-dollar grin of his, the one that makes paper-thin wings flutter in the pit of my belly.

"I'm sorry for losing my cool." He sighs, letting the knots of his muscles slacken, his voice returning to a lukewarm drawl. "You're scared. Flying off the handle isn't going to help either of us."

Upon seeing me shiver, he glides his hands gingerly over my arms, generating a spark of heat within me.

"Come on. Let's at least sit in the car while we talk things over."

I nod through the debilitating lump in my throat, letting him guide me to the passenger door.

The minute I get into the safety of his Jeep, the roar of the outside world comes to an anticlimactic stop. All I can hear is the mingling of our breaths and the jittery whirring of the heater coming to life.

"What happened?" he asks, his hands white-knuckling the steering wheel.

I shift uncomfortably against the leather seat, a yawning hole of dread opening inside of me, threatening to drag me under and fill my lungs until they forget what crisp air feels like.

"I was on a date with a guy. Everything was going well. We went out to eat, then he invited me back to his place. It-it all happened so fast. We were in the living room, laughing about something stupid, indulging in glass after glass of wine...and then he was on top of me. He was on top of me, and I couldn't scream, no matter how hard I tried. I tried saying no. I was frozen." A string of words, almost all obstructed by the thickening saliva and errant tears in my mouth.

My head sloshes with the insuppressible memories, and my gut does a nosedive all the way to my toes.

"When I finally got the courage to move, I pushed him off me. He had no idea what was happening. I just freaked out. I was so embarrassed. I grabbed my things and ran like hell," I supply, my hands shaking despite being planted safely in my lap.

This night has brought up a past trauma I've tried so hard to bury. Trauma that's haunted me for five years now. It's teleported me back to the night of my senior prom—when I was raped by a man who claimed to be my friend. Ever since then, I've been wary to go on dates, to trust men. And yet, I went on this date voluntarily, thinking I could gain control over my trauma.

I was wrong.

Kit doesn't say anything for at least two minutes.

And then he loses it.

He curses so loudly that it echoes in my ears, and he punches the steering wheel, rocking the entire car in the process. I'm surprised he doesn't break anything. His ivory-colored fists are strained, and his arms twitch with an ungodly amount of tension. I think he's going to lash out again, but all he does is inhale deeply.

Kit rests his hands on the steering wheel, the surface of his knuckles throbbing with a crimson hue. "What do you want to do?"

The last thing I want to do is go home. Or be by myself. But I don't really have another option.

I want to stay with you.

"Take me home," I finally decide, the weight of my solitude bearing down on my shoulders.

Kit's leg bounces against the underside of the steering wheel. He's so large that he takes up the whole space, even with his seat pushed all the way back. His head is flush with the ceiling, his elbow eating up the entirety of the console between us.

He ponders me for a moment, swishing my weak words around in his mouth, then grimacing like he hates the taste of them.

He sticks the key in the ignition. "I'm not taking you home."

I buckle my seat belt even as uncertainty courses through my veins. "Then where are you taking me?"

"To my hotel room," he says, looking over his shoulder as he backs out of his makeshift parking space.

With his arm right by my head, I get an intoxicating whiff of the bergamot cologne he always wears, which only lightly masks the heady musk of him. I covertly breathe him in, losing myself in his scent, the proximity, the safety of it all.

When I open my eyes, we're barreling down an empty ribbon of road, vegetation flashing past my peripheral.

"I don't know if that's a good idea," I tell him, worrying at the hem of my dress.

Kit slams down hard on the brakes, nearly making me face-plant into the glove compartment. My seat belt strains against my chest, squishing my boobs, and I recoil from the momentum.

He fully twists toward me, glaring. "What are you talking about?"

"Us. Being alone. In a hotel room together."

The truth is the only place I'd feel comfortable right now is in that goddamn hotel room.

"Are you afraid of me?" Kit asks, pained.

"No. I know you'd never do anything to hurt me. It's just—"

I've never been in a room alone with you.

Seeing that this is apparently argument-worthy, Kit pulls to the side of the road, puts the car in park, and flips his hazards on. "You're out of school, right?"

"My finals ended a month ago," I admit, turtling in on myself.

"I just want to get you somewhere safe, okay? If you're worried about missing work, tell them something came up—which it did—and that you need time off to be with family."

I'm not worried about my job as a teaching assistant. I'm worried about having to confront my very real, very terrifying feelings for Kit. The good thing about Kit living all the way on the other side of the country is that I don't feel inclined to give in to my temptations. But right here, right now, I want to give in so badly, even after the night I've had. All I can think about is lying in bed with him and having him hold me until I fall asleep.

The look on Kit's distractingly chiseled face would be

butterfly inducing if it weren't for the hard lines marring his features. "I promised your brother I'd look after you."

I cross my arms over my chest, doing my best to look sure of myself. "I can look after myself."

"Clearly, you can't."

I wince like he'd just physically burned me. Honestly, that would probably be less painful than whatever heart-squeezing sensation is erupting behind the cage of my ribs.

Kit registers what he said a second too late, regret immediately shadowing his eyes. "Fuck, Faye. I didn't mean that."

Tears sear the backs of my eyes, and I swallow down the vomit threatening to spray the floor of Kit's car. "No, you did. You're right. I need to handle this. I'm not your problem." I unbuckle my seat belt and reach for the door handle, but the little lock above it clicks down.

Kit knocks his head back against the headrest. "I didn't... there's...this is all a lot to process," he confesses. "I can't imagine how hard this is for you."

All I do is nod, because now my mind is channel-surfing back to three hours ago when I thought I'd end the night with a kiss goodbye. The buzz from both the alcohol and adrenaline are starting to wear off, meaning I'll have to consciously try to weather this torrential storm.

I don't know what to say. I'm paralyzed again.

I suddenly feel Kit's hand squeeze my palm, and it jolts me back to the present. The warmth of the gesture brings a comfort I haven't known until now, not even when I've searched for it in other people.

"Look, Faye, when you called me...I've never been so afraid in my entire life. I was worried something bad had happened to you, and I was right. I need to know I'm keeping you safe, otherwise I'm going to lose my mind." There's a brokenness to his words that impales that failing organ in my chest.

Lose his mind? Does he really feel that way?

His fingers tighten around mine, almost painful enough for me to acknowledge it.

"If I go with you, you have to promise not to tell Hayes," I murmur ashamedly, and I know I'm in no position to negotiate, but I refuse to burden my brother with all this drama.

"You're seriously asking me to keep this big of a secret from your brother, who's one of my best friends, and who I also happen to live with?" His barb, sharp and stinging, clings to my side and burrows into flesh and muscle.

He's right: keeping a secret this catastrophic from my hotheaded brother isn't going to end well. But the alternative is possibly seeing my brother in handcuffs as he's being taken away for aggravated battery.

I'll get on my knees and beg this man if I have to. "Please, Kit. He never has to find out about this. He'll kill that guy on some crazy vengeance trip."

"You're lucky *I'm* not going to kill that guy," Kit growls.

Oh, I am. Hayes might have enough rage to fuel a small village, but Kit beats his already impressive strength with a six-foot-five body of pure muscle.

"I appreciate it, I do. And now I'm just asking you to keep a teensy, tiny secret."

Kit sucks his teeth. "I'll contemplate it if you at least let me get you under a roof. You're half-soaked. The hotel is only ten minutes away."

I have a feeling that's the closest to an agreement I'm going to get from Kit, and considering he has the resolve and patience of a grizzly bear, I'm not looking to argue with him for the rest of the night.

"Okay," I acquiesce. "But you have to *promise* to think about it."

Kit holds his pinky out to me. "I promise."

I hesitantly hook my pinky with his, letting myself get lost in the wilderness of his umber eyes. There's warmth nestled in the inner rings, but with it comes a dash of concern.

Fuck, Faye! This could've all been avoided if you just focused on yourself, your career. If you stopped chasing after guys to fill that hole in your heart.

I pull back, severing our arrangement. "I should've *done* something."

"Stop," Kit snarls, the intensity behind the command alone shaking me to the core. "This is *not* your fault. You need to understand that."

Kit leans over the center console and hooks his forefinger under my chin, his thumb tracing the edge of my jawline. "This is *his* fault, okay? This is all on *him. He* took advantage of you. This small-dicked asshole took your freedom, your choice, and he'll be paying for every second of it for the rest of his miserable life."

"Why do you care so much?" I blurt out before I can stop myself.

The first smile of the night surfaces over his extremely kissable lips. Extremely kissable, and extremely dangerous.

"Because we're friends."

Friends? I've never hated one word so much in my entire life.

If you haven't read Reapers Book One yet, be sure to check out Hayes and Aeris' love story! Keep reading for a sneak peek of *The Best Kind of Forever (Reapers #1)*. ♡

THE BEST KIND OF FOREVER

1

THICK THIGHS RUIN LIVES
HAYES

Tits or ass: that's the eternal question. That's the question I've been asked my entire life, by friends, flings, teammates, my ex-girlfriend. I'm not going to lie. For a long time, I was a tits man. But tonight, I think my answer is gonna change.

And that's thanks to the girl's thighs currently straddling me. They're lean with muscle, and it's clear she sticks to a rigorous workout regimen. I'm a thigh guy. Definitely. Is it wrong that I want her to crush my head with them? I really shouldn't be thinking about this when I should be wining and dining sponsors, but she's wearing such a short dress, so short that from this angle I can see practically everything.

Her lips ghost the shell of my ear, and her tongue tickles the column of my throat, doing wonders for my hard-on. I understand that I'm fully making out with a girl at a sponsor party. I understand that there's media around every corner covering the new merger between the Reapers team and Voltage Sports Drinks. I should be mingling instead of acquainting myself with the inside of some girl's mouth.

I don't care, though. I need the distraction. After seeing my ex with one of my hockey rivals—after she cheated on me during the biggest game of my career—I lost my mind.

It's my fourth season playing for the Riverside Reapers. I entered the NHL draft when I was nineteen, and I was fourth overall-pick in 2019. My quick puck handling is what put me on the map, but at the time, I was racking up eighty penalty points in my collegiate midseason, which made me the most penalized player in NCAA hockey at one point. Not something scouts are necessarily looking for. I'm a hothead when I get on the ice. If somebody bodychecks me or gets between me and the puck, I'm not afraid to hit them back—whether those hits are illegal or not.

It's been my dream to go pro since I was little. My parents signed me up for minor ice hockey when I was eight, and I've been playing ever since.

Despite me getting lucky enough to enter the NHL, my life hasn't been a walk in the park. My father's a shitty excuse for a parent, and my mom is dead. I'm honestly not sure which is worse.

Sherry passed away of cancer when I was eight, and it broke my dad. He became distant, closed off, a shell of the man I remember from my childhood. I didn't realize I'd lost two parents that day.

I don't think my mom was even planning on telling us she had breast cancer. The only reason I found out was because my dad got a call from the hospital after she was admitted for fainting. We all knew she had been acting a little off more than usual—curt answers, lapses in memory and judgment, distancing herself from us. I chalked it up to her being stressed with work.

I was wrong.

After she died, my father abandoned me and my sister. I had to take care of my younger sister, Faye, while I juggled school and hockey. We still had a roof to live under because of the monthly paychecks our dad sent us, but besides that, he wasn't in our lives. He disappeared to some faraway, forest-grown part of the Michigan mountains where he made sure his tracks weren't traceable. He wasn't there for any of Faye's milestones. He wasn't there to see me off to college. He wasn't even there to cheer me on at my first NHL game. The only contact he's maintained is the occasional text whenever he needs something.

I want to forget this whole week. I want to stop feeling. The alcohol's already helped a bit with both, but if I can rely on one thing in this damned world, it's good sex.

In my defense, I haven't slept with anyone in sixty days. And that's a deliberate abstinence, okay? I haven't really been able to trust anyone after my ex-girlfriend, Macy, broke up with me.

While I was ruminating over what went wrong, incriminating pictures of her tongue down Quentin Cadieux's throat surfaced in the media. Quentin Cadieux, center for the Atlanta Avocets, and the bane of my fucking existence. Both me and Cadieux were top prospects for the Riverside Reapers, with me being chosen out of the two of us. And ever since then, he's made it his life's goal to make mine a living hell.

When I confronted Macy about the photos, she admitted to only using me for my money, my name, and my fame. She dumped me before I could break up with her.

The girl in front of me is shaking the bed with how much she's bouncing on top of me. We went from a fifteen-minute make out sesh to her riding me like rent was fucking due.

I'm not sure I even asked what her name was. She knew my name, though. Sponsor parties are always crawling with puck bunnies.

I can't stop staring in awe at the way her perfectly proportioned tits recoil as she fully clenches around me, her head lolling back, dark hair spilling down her shoulders like ink.

My hands are gripping her thighs so tightly that red marks are rising in their wake. I love when girls are loud, but fuck, is she *loud*. I bet the whole party downstairs can hear us, despite the outdated EDM music playing. Her moans are heaven-sent, and they unravel the knot of desire in my stomach. She's rolling her hips and playing with the curve of her breast, two images that rev the static inside of my brain. The warmth in my groin intensifies, erupting into a fire that sears every inch of me. Her perky ass slaps against the tops of my thighs.

I'm close to coming. My dick is practically begging me to release inside of her, and it's a good thing I snagged a few condoms before leaving the house because no matter what dude you talk to, pulling out rarely works.

The minute I saw her across the room, I think a part of me knew how the night was going to end. Before I even got the chance to talk with my teammates, her hand was stroking me. Yeah, self-control has never been my strong suit.

"Fuck..." I groan, though I think it comes out more like a frustrated growl.

We move together in a synchronized pattern of movements, and I watch her pick up the pace. Her pussy squeezes up and down my length as she nears her climax, and when she comes down hard on the hilt of my pubic bone, an avalanche of arousal suffocates me. The tip of my dick tingles, and it feels like a supernova is exploding in my veins, coloring my vision with constellations. Before I know it, I'm spilling myself into the latex in hot, wet bursts.

When I get up to dispose of the condom, she has the bedsheets pulled up to her chest.

"Are you coming back to bed?" she asks, hope playing in her umber eyes.

"I should probably head back to the party. You know, rub shoulders with some sponsors, maybe a few geriatric sugar daddies," I joke, but her lack of laughter hits me in the face like a wicked slapshot.

"Oh, right. Will I see you again?"

My cock loves the idea of seeing her again, but I really shouldn't be entertaining a relationship when I have my career to focus on. This was a one-time thing.

A wrecking ball of anxiety swings to the center of my chest, making the air in my lungs diminish. "Sure, I can get you tickets to an upcoming game."

I take my time getting dressed, because I'm definitely not in a rush to get back to the party.

My response must've been convincing enough because she perks up, tucking a strand of hair behind her ear. "That would be great. Uh, can I see your phone?"

I hand my phone over to her, slowly slipping one pant leg on at a time so I don't look like I'm in a hurry to get out of here.

Look, I don't want to hurt her feelings, alright? I know she's gonna put her number in there, and I'm not going to stop her. I'll just let her down nice and easy over text. That way I don't have to deal with the tears and the yelling.

She hands me back the device, exposing her tits as she reaches down to pick up her shirt. "I put my number in there. I hope you use it."

I'm only able to nod because I'm currently contemplating how moral it would be if I proposed we go for a second round.

Verdict: not moral.

I shake the thought from my addled brain, say a quick goodbye, and give her a half-hearted hug. Then I slip out of the bedroom, ready to sprint for the exit to evade any prying eyes. And I foolishly think I'm in the clear before I come face to face with the last person I wanted to run into.

The top buttons of my shirt are undone, my hair's a mess from the girl gouging her fingers through it, and I'm pretty sure I saw at least three hickeys decorating my neck in the mirror.

"Coach?" I sputter, the air around me seeming strangely distilled.

"Hollings, I—"

Coach takes in my disheveled state, and then his eyes turn as round as frisbees.

"Please tell me that's not Sienna Talavera's bedroom," he bellows, that one vein on his forehead pulsing with a mind of its own.

Who?

My back goes as stiff as a board when I hear that drill sergeant voice of his, like it's a conditioned response. "I...I don't know, sir."

I've never heard that name in my entire life.

"Sienna. Talavera," he reiterates slowly. Those behemoth arms of his are barred over his chest, reminding me how easy it'd be for him to squash me like a cartoon mouse.

I wait for him to elaborate, and judging by the death glare he's giving me, I know I just fucked up. My hands are so clammy that I keep wiping them on my pant legs, my heart is galloping like a racehorse in my chest, and my stomach is seconds away from revolting the hors d'oeuvres I polished off an hour ago.

Coach expels what I think is supposed to be a cleansing breath, but his nostrils are still flared. "Son, Raymond Talavera owns the sports drink company sponsoring our team," he explains.

Fuck me.

"Coach, I swear, I had no idea," I blurt, desperate to temper the anxiety racing through me at warp speed.

"Hollings, this cannot get out, do you understand? If Raymond hears that you slept with his daughter, he'll pull, and we need his sponsorship."

"I promise I won't say anything, Coach."

"If it comes down to it, the team owner will have no

problem picking Talavera over you. Every player is tradeable, expendable."

"Understood."

Shit. I can't get traded. I can't imagine the rest of my NHL career—if I even have one—without my teammates. Not only would I have to move, but I'd have to somehow seamlessly weave my way into already-lasting relationships.

"And Sienna? Do you think she'll talk?" he asks.

"I took care of it." Right? Sure, I'd offered to get her tickets to the next game, which she clearly doesn't need, but we parted with a hug. We both knew the deal going into the night.

"I—it won't happen again," I swear.

How have I fucked up...fucking? I'm great at fucking. If I wasn't a professional hockey player, I could probably make it as a porn star.

"It better not. And I better see you working your ass off at practice tomorrow."

I nod, trying to keep my nerves from catapulting themselves up my throat.

"Look, Hollings. I want to give you a piece of advice. And I'm only saying this because I truly want you to succeed, okay?"

That doesn't sound good.

The redness in his face has started to fade. "Mistakes like this can make or break a career. I know how much hockey means to you. But with the way you've been playing recently, you're treating this privilege like it means jackshit. And now you go and complicate things with our biggest sponsor. You're lucky I'm the one who caught you and not some news-hungry paparazzi. You need to start thinking before you act, otherwise a warning will be the least of your worries."

"Yes, sir," I say, my voice hiking a pitch louder than intended. Anxiety batters at my chest like exploding shrapnel, and I fear that my knees are going to give out despite my back being against the wall.

Coach knits his furry eyebrows together, deepening that wrinkle on his forehead. "I expect you to fix this," he demands, and just like that, my world full of carefree living has just been turned on its axis.

"And *do not*, under any circumstances, repeat what happened here tonight."

ACKNOWLEDGMENTS

I'd like to say a huge thank you to my incredible agent, Jill Marsal, and my hardworking editor, Deborah Dove. I'd also like to thank my father. Dad, you've been so patient and understanding through my entire journey as an author, and I'm so grateful. Thank you for being my rock. Thank you for always being a proud parent and bragging about me (even though I don't deserve it). I don't know where I'd be without you. Whenever I feel down, you lift me up. Whenever I don't believe I can do it, you remind me I can. That's something I'll hang on to forever. I love you.

ABOUT THE AUTHOR

Celeste Briars is an indie author who specializes in spicy, hockey romances. She's a UC Davis alumnus with a bachelor's in psychology. She loves creating memorable meet-cutes and happily ever afters. When she's not writing, you can find her binge-watching horror movies, playing with her cats, or dancing the night away with her friends. If you're looking for books with spice hot enough to question your religious values and feel-good moments that make your heart sing, please cuddle up with a Reapers novel and stay a while!

Printed by Amazon Italia Logistica S.r.l.
Torrazza Piemonte (TO), Italy